The
Godmother

SCEPTRE

Also by Amanda Brookfield

Alice Alone
A Cast of Smiles
Walls of Glass
A Summer Affair

The Godmother

Amanda Brookfield

SCEPTRE

First published in 1997 by Hodder and Stoughton
A division of Hodder Headline PLC
A Sceptre Book

10 9 8 7 6 5 4 3 2 1

British Library Cataloguing in Publication Data

A CIP catalogue record for this title is
available from the British Library.

ISBN 0 340 67149 1

Typeset by Palimpsest Book Production Limited,
Polmont, Stirlingshire
Printed and bound in Great Britain by
Mackays of Chatham PLC, Chatham, Kent

Hodder and Stoughton
A division of Hodder Headline PLC
338 Euston Road
London NW1 3BH

For Edward

With special thanks to Kevin Duncan, Gyll Foster, Sara Westcott and Edward Brookfield for their patient and generous responses to all my questions.

1

'Give him to Rachel,' said Joy, pointing with the christening candle across the room.

'Yes, give him to Rachel,' echoed Tony, her husband, emerging from the kitchen with a fresh pitcher of wine. 'Let the godmother have a go.'

The wriggling bundle of yellowing silk, trimmed with cob-webbed lace, was passed from hand to hand along the line of guests, like a parcel at a children's party, thought Rachel, regarding its approach with all the wariness of a native being invited to speak a foreign language.

'He's bound to cry,' she declared, smiling through her fear, feeling all eyes upon her as she laid her white suede handbag on the arm of the sofa and rubbed her hands together in a show of eagerness for the challenge ahead.

But Leo, who was six months old and who had been placed in the woefully haphazard care of his eleven-year-old sister, Isobel, for the last twenty minutes, did not cry upon being delivered to his godmother. He frowned at her instead, twisting his fist into his mouth and kicking out at the restrictions of the long christening robe, now entwined round his stocky legs like clingfilm.

'I'm not sure he approves of his costume very much,' Rachel ventured, cradling the baby in stiff arms, wary of projectile milk-dribble staining the front of her white linen jacket, or, worse still, her chest being mistakenly identified as a source of nutrition. A frisson of repulsion and curiosity had zigzagged through her the day before upon finding Joy with her T-shirt hoicked up unceremoniously over one ripe and veiny bosom, so that Leo could feed while she guided Sam, her dyslexic nine year old, through a French reading book about farms.

'But they all wore that gown,' remarked a brisk, mousy-haired woman with Tony's nose, 'it's family tradition.'

'Oh, I see.' Her arms were aching now. The woman turned away, giving Rachel the chance to step out of the social throng, none of whom she knew anyway, and sit down beside her handbag. Gingerly, she propped the baby up on her lap, straightening the copious folds of the gown as tidily as she could and doing her best to contain the wriggling limbs. For a moment she thought wistfully of her other three godchildren, all of whom had long since acquired mouthfuls of teeth and a taste for beautifully undemanding, postable activities like video games and Barbie dolls. 'Bad luck Leo,' she whispered, giving the voluminous family heirloom another tug, 'I should hate it too.' The baby offered a feisty kick by way of concurrence and then promptly put his head in the crook of her arm and closed his eyes. Hardly daring to move for fear of interrupting this astonishingly rapid – and most welcome – submission to the pull of sleep, Rachel lifted her eyes for a few moments in order to study the room.

It was still only a few months since Joy and Tony had made their daring exit from the London rat race, transplanting the family from a four-bedroomed semi in Wimbledon to a charming but dilapidated farmhouse a few miles outside Turon, a medieval town that nestled in the upper regions of the Loire valley. A daring move indeed. Something to be admired as an attempt to make a dream come true, one of those life moves about which most mortals end up doing nothing more than talking. Upon studying the undisguisable chaos of the Daltons' new sitting room, however, the peeling wallpaper, the bunches of wires sticking out of the walls like skeletal fingers, the scores of boxes stacked along every spare inch of wall, Rachel could not resist a shiver of relief that the experience was being endured by Joy and not herself. Leo hadn't been part of their plan either, she remembered, casting a wary eye at her lap, her godson's conception apparently having occurred quite by accident during the chaotic and unforseeably long business of trying to sell the house and settle all their affairs in England. Joy, while professing to be appalled at the discovery of this unscheduled pregnancy, had seemed to revel in it too, perhaps, thought Rachel wickedly, because she was secretly thrilled to have proved that a fifteen-year marriage could still muster enough passion to overlook the use of sexual prophylactics.

'Well, if it is such a disaster, why not consider your options?' Rachel had asked, trying to be blunt but kind, when Joy first broke the news, weeping into a glass of wine which she said she really shouldn't have, but from which she nevertheless gulped with unabashed need.

'Christ, Rachel,' she had gasped, hugging the small hump still easily disguised by a generous sweatshirt, 'there's a child in there. At twelve weeks it's got all its bits. I know it may be hard for you to understand, not having children and so on, but to have its life terminated, even now, would be tantamount to murder.'

'OK, OK – sorry I spoke.' Rachel held both hands up. 'Though I do remember,' she couldn't resist muttering, 'there was a time when you waved a banner for abortion rights . . .'

'That was years ago, for God's sake. It's different when you've had children, believe me. The very thought that . . . Oh, it's impossible to explain.'

Rachel had nodded in a show of empathy, hating the familiar, unspoken criticism for the fact that she herself had not borne any children, that she had committed the unmentionable sin of choosing to remain single, to nurture a career instead of a family. Once, friends like Joy had challenged her openly about such things, expressing either pity or fascination with her single status, teasing her with suggestions for life partners and having late babies. Now they no longer did so. An omission which Rachel suspected was connected directly to the fact that, at thirty-nine, she was now perilously close to the category of spinster as opposed to unmarried woman, an age well past the point where acquaintances expected or even wanted her to change her ways.

Leo yawned, absently pushed a thumb into his eye socket, scowled at the unexpected pain, and then settled back to sleep, the dimpled fingers of one hand closing round the third button of Rachel's suit jacket.

The trouble was, thought Rachel, watching the button being tugged by its cotton roots and not minding, the trouble was, something did feel different these days. Some new, unclassifiable emotion was pushing its way into the perfect bubble of her world, something which she did her best to ignore, but which felt disturbingly like a growing sense of pointlessness behind all that she had created, all that she had achieved. The ebb and flow of such thoughts, apart from being unpredictable and distressing, was also highly inconvenient. As board director of an international advertising agency, earning in excess of a hundred thousand pounds per annum, with a luxurious flat in Chelsea, a soft-topped Audi Cabriolet and her own named parking slot in the underground cubby hole of a directors' car park, Rachel Elliot was not in the habit of entertaining doubts of any kind. As well as being a formidable businesswoman with a string of happy clients and successful campaigns to her credit, she had lovers, she had hobbies, she had friends, she had good health. Dissatisfaction – or whatever it was – had no business creeping up on her like that. How dare it? she thought now, looping her little finger into the cup of Leo's free hand and being surprised at the hungry clench offered in reply.

'Rachel, you are sweet. Thank you so much. I know babies aren't exactly your thing.' Joy held out her arms for her son. 'Both Tony and I are absolutely thrilled that you agreed to be his godmother – and of course that you could come all this way. Really, it means a lot to us . . . friends like you . . .' She sucked in her lower lip and then blew out hard. 'Well, we go back a long way you and I, don't we?'

As Joy took the child Rachel felt the pull on the button increase until, with a yank, the little fingers were forced to let go. 'We certainly do.' She studied Joy's face for a moment, trying to judge whether the veins standing out round her eyes and the straggly limp hair spoke of something more than the exhaustion of moving countries and taking care of children. Though their friendship dated back to the shared horror of an old-fashioned boarding school, testimony to the mutual problem of having fathers in the armed forces, Rachel no longer felt that she really knew Joy very well. In recent years, their meetings had slumped to one or two a year, over the occasional dinner-party table, or a snatched evening at the theatre. Wimbledon was a long way from Chelsea and, as Rachel found with nearly all her girlfriends, marriages to men whom she barely knew and whom she struggled to find obviously endearing, inevitably took their toll on the degree of intimacy which she was able to maintain. 'No second thoughts, I hope?'

'Second thoughts?' Joy rocked Leo gently in her arms, her hips swaying with a practised, unselfconscious ease that made Rachel almost ashamed of her aching arms, ashamed of her timidity over something so small and peaceful.

'About France. About living here.'

Joy's expression tightened into a concentration of brightness. 'But how could I? This is what we've always wanted, what we've both worked towards for years. Tony had absolutely had it with the whole architectural scene in London. Here he's his own boss – converting barns and all that kind of thing. He loves it. And after holidaying round here for so long he's built up scores of useful connections. He's already got more work than he knows what to do with. And oh, Rachel, you should see Tony's plans for this house. It's going to be positively dreamy. We'll have to force relatives and friends like you to join the queue to come and stay. And the school is fine,' she swept on, 'even though the classes are bigger than the children are used to. Isobel is already jabbering like a local, though poor Sammy is obviously going to take a little longer to find his feet. And as for this one . . .' she nuzzled Leo's yellow fuzz of hair, 'he could be on Mars for all he cares, so long as he's got a steady supply of food and a dry bottom . . .'

'Oh, good,' murmured Rachel, wondering if Joy was aware that she had accounted for everyone's state of happiness but her own.

2 ∫

The best thing about being alone was the freedom, mused Rachel, as she glibly fibbed about having an airplane to catch and levered herself out of the squash of the Daltons' cement-floored sitting room in order to escape back to her hotel. Although a light rain was still falling it felt warmer outside, more welcoming. She shivered again at the recollection of the stone walls of the house, the plastic flapping in place of window panes, the way the loo door had refused to close, forcing her to sit awkwardly with one leg outstretched in case any other unsuspecting guest had chosen that moment to barge in. Apart from Joy and Tony she had known no one at all, only close family having been able to make the journey and none of their new local friends being familiar to her.

With a satisfying click the doors of her hired Mercedes obediently unlocked themselves. As she slipped into the driver's seat, Rachel threw a wistful glance at the peachy straw hat in the back. Joy should have warned her. Smart outfits but not a hat in sight. And it had suited her, too, especially with its wide brim pulled ever so slightly down over one temple, so that she could peer out imperiously from underneath, feeling grand and pretty all at the same time. She didn't often get a chance to wear hats these days, weddings and christenings being somewhat a thing of the past.

Although September had barely begun, the imprint of autumn had already touched the landscape bordering the narrow tarmac road on which Rachel sped away: armies of drooping sunflowers smothered the fields to her right and left, their blackened heads nodding in the damp breeze like old men despairing at the ways of the world. Sensing that her good mood was in danger of slipping away, Rachel turned on the radio, tuning into a light, fizzy pop tune that sounded vaguely familiar. She tapped her fingers on the steering wheel and hummed quietly, squinting at the signposts because she had left her spectacles in the hotel. Some ten minutes into her journey an avalanche of grey clouds scudded past like shifting scenery, allowing a new assemblage of fluffy white tufts and a beaming sun to take their place. The sunflowers were replaced by acres of harvested corn, rolled into golden cylinders, their wet surfaces glistening on this new and brilliant stage like giant polished tins.

Turning away from the fields, towards the less dramatic pastures that lined the sides of the Loire itself, Rachel braced herself for the first glimpse of the château in whose environs she was fortunate enough to be staying. It perched on a piece of high ground beside the river like a fairytale castle, complete with Rapunzel-style pointed turrets and vertical slits in its towering walls. The hotel itself was in a converted side-section, where French lords were said to have once stabled their horses. Set further into the extensive grounds, carefully masked behind several rows of tall trees, lay a kidney-shaped swimming pool; flecks of its shimmering azure could just be glimpsed from the four windows of Rachel's second-floor room.

A team of maids had come to close the shutters and turn down the sheets on her bed the evening before, bustling in when she was only just out of the bath, smiling approvingly at the vast white towelling dressing gown in which she emerged, their eyes saying they had seen it all before and much more besides, that such states of undress were entirely expected of such patrons at such times of day.

When she arrived back after the christening the shutters were still open, allowing the rain-washed air to drift in and lighten the oppressively regal atmosphere of the room, of which the four-poster bed formed the centrepiece, its sides decked with sweeping brocaded curtains of the kind that Rachel associated with honeymooning couples in old films.

Settling herself against the wall of embroidered cushions arranged along the tapestried headboard, she took a desultory nibble of the mint chocolate which had been left on her pillow, willing herself to sink into the stupour of self-indulgence which her surroundings demanded. She reached for the telephone beside her bed to dial room service, but changed her mind. There was nothing she wanted after all. Nothing at all.

Beside her lay most of the contents of her small suitcase, rummaged through earlier that day in her hurry not to be late for the church. In her absence, invisible hands had folded and arranged every item into tidy shapes across the bed, the line between assistance and intervention clearly dictating that the repacking of the suitcase itself was not permitted. Rachel picked up a neatly folded pair of white silk stockings and threw them in the direction of the open suitcase. They flew badly, too light to reach their destination, fluttering down instead, like tired wings, on a black leather book near the far edge of the bed. On noticing the book, Rachel rolled over and picked it up. Still lying on her stomach, she extracted a gold ball point pen from its broad spine and began to write, her hand sweeping fluently across and down the lined page.

September 12th

Turon is beautiful. I arrived midday Saturday – such a relief to be out of London – and at this palace of a hotel. Tony and Joy's house is in the most magnificent setting, complete with its very own mini-tributary of the Loire running through the back garden. The children all look suntanned and healthy – even little Leo – far more so than they would after a summer in London. Joy was too busy with arrangements for the christening to talk properly, but she seems very pleased with the move down here.

Rachel paused and sucked the end of her pen. Over her shoulder, slats of afternoon sunshine streamed in through the open windows, illuminating the page to such a degree that the whiteness of it hurt her eyes. Absently, she rubbed one temple, where the edge of a dull pain was surfacing. She should have eaten properly. Instead, she had picked at Joy's home-made pizza squares and triangles of liver pâté, eating enough to be polite, presenting an appearance of sociability while inside she had held herself in check.

Such a forceful entrance of the sun brought with it an irritating sense of obligation to swim. There was no excuse not to. Especially now that the masterful sweep of her hair, so artfully streaked and styled by the formidable Petrona at the hairdresser's, had successfully sailed through the occasion for which it had been designed. It didn't matter what she looked like now. It didn't matter what she looked like until Tuesday, in fact, when she was due back in the office.

But Rachel did not want to go swimming. An apathy that had nothing to do with the late heat of the day was pressing upon her, bringing with it a melancholic longing to be home. The thought of the evening ahead of her, the business of dining alone, of having to sleep amidst the suffocating grandeur of the room, was suddenly deadening.

The mood swing left Rachel exasperated. Like so many of her feelings these days, it was all the more unsettling for being so totally unforeseen. She had deliberately made this weekend a long one. She had been looking forward to bedroom mints and kidney-shaped swimming pools and elegant meals alone. As in the more immediate past of leaving the Daltons' ruin of a farmhouse, she had been looking forward to the prospect of time for herself. And yet now that it had actually arrived, the satisfaction of that prospect seemed to dissolve like a mirage, as if it had been an image of purely false allure. For here she was, right inside the brochure, so to speak, lying in one of the very stately rooms she had found so enticing in its photographic form, only to find it empty. Rachel could hear the seconds ticking by on her gold bracelet of a wristwatch, each one reinforcing the unpleasant notion that the time for which she had yearned as a reward now felt little better than a refined form of punishment.

With a fresh burst of energy, she returned her attention to her diary.

The christening went off beautifully. Hearing it all in French was somehow more romantic and all the godparents spoke together so there was no problem over embarrassment about my accent. Joy and Tony had gone to great trouble over the reception afterwards – very brave of them given the constraints of the house, so many of the rooms still being completely uninhabitable. I did my godmotherly bit, shook hands with the relatives and so on, though, her writing slowed and she gripped the pen harder; *though for some reason I wasn't really in the mood. I held Leo for a while.* She paused again, for longer this time. Then she put a full stop, a large globule of a punctuation mark that took some time.

She closed the book abruptly and cast it to one side. Raising her bottom off the bed she unzipped her skirt and slithered out of it, intending to pull on her bathing costume at once. But she got sidetracked by the sight of her skinny white thighs and the marble slab of her stomach. She ran her hands down the sides of her waist and over the sharp mounds of her hip bones, marking the edges of her like pearly stones. She had always been proud of her slimness, had worn it like a badge of achievement, if she was honest, strutting it in tight suits and tailored shirts at work, as if a sylph-like silhouette spoke volumes for the worth of the person inside. As if it said, 'Trust me, I know how to take care of myself, I am in control.'

But lately Rachel was not so sure. Upon recent examinations of the carved whiteness of her limbs, it was the word 'skinny' which sprang most readily to mind. A word redolent of deprivation and pity; a word suggestive of nothing more glamorous than undernourishment. Between her hips the skin sank in a gentle curve, a blank space that pressed inwards, away from the world. She stroked this space now, trying to imagine it filled. Over the years she had regarded the ballooning bodies of pregnant friends with incredulous curiosity, fascinated and even slightly sickened at their vast waistlines, at the obvious uncontrollability of it all. But now something about the concave ski slope of her belly made her sad. She remembered again the weight of Leo in her lap, the sheer density of him.

Swinging her legs quickly over the side, Rachel got off the bed. Small points of light danced in front of her eyes. She stood still for a moment, trying to collect herself. A swim will clear my head she told herself, starting to undo the mother-of-pearl buttons on her sleeveless cotton blouse. But her movements were arrested once again by the sight of herself in the full-length, gilt-framed mirror beside the bed. Two tubby cherubs eyed her skittishly from its top corners. Beneath their gaze stood a skinny woman of nearly forty. A woman with smart, expensive, fairish hair framing a pale, bony face, saved from mediocrity by the dark brows and lashes which drew attention to the clarity of her grey-blue eyes. Rachel stood quite still, examining the reflection as she might a portrait of a stranger, scouring the map of the body for evidence of happiness.

When the telephone rang she threw herself across the length of the bed, lunging for the receiver like a lifeline. It was probably work, she thought excitedly, some unforeseen crisis, some pre-production muddle which only she could sort out. Frank Alder had probably asked for her personally, said that only Rachel Elliot would do, said that she was the only director in the agency who really understood the skincare market . . .

'Rachel, is that you? Christ, this is a lousy line.'

'Nathan?'

'Can you hear me all right? You're faint as hell.'

'Where are you?'

'Heathrow. Flew in today. Paris on Tuesday. Have we time to meet up?'

The crackles on the line suddenly dissolved. 'Wow, that's better. What the hell are you doing over there? I had to call all over to get your number. Lucky some of your team work weekends or you wouldn't have got me at all.'

'Oh Nathan,' Rachel felt quite breathless, 'it's good to hear you. I'm here for a christening – I'm the unwise choice of godmother – it's an old schoolfriend—'

'Well that's great, Rachel. We'll take a rain-check then . . .'

'Oh no need. We could meet tomorrow.'

'Now you're talking. It will be good to see you.'

'Me too.'

'I'm at The Grosvenor. I'll call you in the morning.'

'Perfect.' Rachel lay on her stomach on the bed, her legs bent up behind her, crossed at the ankle. She rubbed the arches of her feet together as she talked, soothed by the demand to make arrangements, to do something other than think about herself. 'How are things, anyway? How's the world of high finance?'

'Just great, Rachel,' he replied with an easy laugh, 'markets crazy as usual. Hitting the big time in Eastern Europe. I'll tell you all about it tomorrow.'

Her spirits edged down half a notch. Nathan liked to talk about his work. 'Until tomorrow then. Bye now.' After replacing the receiver Rachel pulled her skirt back on, hastily did up the buttons of her shirt and hurried down the cushioned quietness of the corridors to reception with her plane ticket. She would ask them to phone the airline on her behalf. It was pointless staying the night after all. It had been a simple mistake to make, thinking she needed time away when she didn't. It was another joy of being on one's own that altering plans could be indulged in at whim, without the hassle of disappointing or pleasing other people. She could do with a day at home anyway, she told herself a few minutes later, as she made her way back to her room and began packing. She spent too little time there as it was.

3

Nathan Kramer and Rachel Elliot had first met five years earlier at the home of Rachel's elder brother, a paediatrician who had married an American dental nurse and settled in Washington DC. Rachel was on a visit for the christening of her then four-month-old nephew, Craig, while Nathan was an economist at the World Bank, an institution which he deserted soon afterwards for the more verdant financial pastures of an investment bank in New York. Duncan Elliot's wife, Mary Beth, an eager apprentice in the game of networking dinner parties that defined the slow slither up the Washington social ladder, had arranged a supper party supposedly in Rachel's honour, but which in truth had more to do with showing off her new roomy Bethesda home than wanting to make her sister-in-law feel welcome. Rachel, in Mary Beth's eyes, needed very little help in being made to feel welcome or anything else. Those crystal grey eyes of hers – so unlike dear Duncan's hound-dog brown ones – faced all comers with such unnerving directness that Mary Beth found herself sucking in her stomach and making false announcements about post-maternal career plans just from the sheer pressure of it.

Although the idea of a sit-down dinner for sixteen filled Mary Beth's head with dizzy images of the kind she most treasured in her glossy upmarket magazines, a combination of good sense and cowardice prompted her to opt for a buffet format instead. On the morning of the dinner she made Duncan shift chairs and tables around the ground floor of the house before he left for work, issuing instructions like a novice stage manager anxious about a first night. Carmen, their recently acquired Hispanic maid-cum-child minder, had been treated to a frilly black and

white outfit in honour of the occasion, together with several
torturous sessions on how to receive coats and flowers.

After observing all these shenanigans from behind copious
sections of the *Washington Post* (which Mary Beth retrieved from a
plastic bag hurled into the front garden every morning but never
actually seemed to read), Rachel decided to make a tactical withdrawal downtown on the pretext of some sightseeing. Though
Craig's elder brother had soared in her estimation by his dogged
five-year-old attempts to shift all the rearranged furniture into
more interesting positions, she still found the strain of being
a bystander to family life quite draining. So much noise. So
much sudden escalation of mood. So many demands. That
Mary Beth was the kind of mother who shrieked at the antics
of her offspring and then buried her head in their tiny chests
for forgiveness did not make the observation of their habits any
easier. She was all extremes, all insecurity herself; quite unfit, in
Rachel's eyes, to assist other humans in the business of adapting
to the world.

Studying the understated bleakness of the Vietnam War
Memorial steadied if not exactly cheered her nerves. More
envigorating were the avenues of pastel blossoms lining the
parks and roads of Washington's central square mile, like
cheerleaders with fistfuls of bright pom-poms. After peering
through the railings skirting the sloping lawn of the White
House, Rachel wandered back along the glass rectangle of the
reflecting pool and up towards the Lincoln Memorial. At the top
of the steps she sat down a few feet from the pensive marbled
president and gloomily contemplated the prospect of her last
evening's entertainment. Her sister-in-law's bejewelled guest
list of aspiring politicians and lobbyists had already been the
focus of enough dissection and celebration for Rachel to want
no part of it. As her eye was caught by an airplane following the
busy flight path into the city airport, she toyed enviously with
the idea of escaping in the same direction herself that afternoon.
Craig's christening had, after all, been dutifully attended. The
delights of catching up with a brother to whom she had never
felt particularly close and who seemed to be fattening himself
on a highly dubious system of medical care, had quickly palled.
She longed to go home, back to her lovely new Chelsea flat, then

gleaming under fresh coats of paint, and containing no tensions other than those she chose to introduce herself.

Nathan Kramer came as something of an unexpected treat. He had the kind of hairstyle which Rachel associated with American film stars of the eighties, spruce blond spikes that stood effortlessly to attention. Contributing to this impression was something of a rugged jaw line, complete with a faint silvery scar which ran from the lobe of one ear to a point directly below the dimple in his chin. Attracted, against her better judgement, Rachel moved cautiously. While quite within her powers, an eclectic sexual life was not something she had ever managed. She was too busy at work, for one thing. For another, there was always the tedium of self-recrimination afterwards, a silly irrational female reflex which, however hard she tried to quell it, usually got the better of her in the end. Although there had been various sexual liaisons over the years, there had been nothing long term in the relationship department for a good while. Not since Robbie, in fact, from whom Rachel had finally shaken free a decade previously, at the tender age of twenty-five. The pitiable or traumatic state of most of the relationships with which she had grown acquainted in the meantime had hardly been an enticement to join the fray.

Having recently emerged bloodied but undaunted from a highly charged marriage to a fellow economist, Nathan Kramer advertised his availability in the first flash of his blue eyes, the faint swagger of his hips as he strolled nonchalantly across Mary Beth's sherbet-lemon carpet and introduced himself to the most attractive woman at the party. Rachel greeted him with a slight tilt of the head and a faint smile which acknowledged some degree of flattery as well as interest. His kind of woman, Nathan decided at once, helping himself from a tray of drinks and taking on the stare of the intense blue-grey eyes with all the excitement of a hunter embarking on an attainable – but by no means certain – chase.

'I'm in advertising,' Rachel declared by way of an introduction, 'on the board of McKenzie Cartwright. You might have heard of them.'

'You bet I have. Been there long?'

'Five years. Before that I was with Burton, May and Saunders.

A much smaller outfit. Interesting creative work, but no big budgets. I always wanted to try my hand at the international scene.' She spoke with deliberate incisiveness, judging correctly that this would impress him, make him feel safe enough to confirm that the attraction was mutual. It was men's talk really, of the kind at which she had come to be most adept, having quickly discovered during the early stages of her career that the easiest way to beat men at their own game was to talk their language. It was like wearing camouflage.

'McKenzie Cartwright . . . what do they bill these days?'

'Two hundred.'

'I take it that's in millions?' The dimple in his chin changed shape when he smiled.

'What about you?' went on Rachel, deliberately ignoring all knowledge acquired through Mary Beth's weighty pre-dinner briefings. It was his turn to talk; his turn – in this pre-mating ritual – to be allowed to show a few colours.

They slept together just once before she returned to England, between midnight and two o'clock that morning, after leaving the tail end of Mary Beth's party on the pretext of going to a club. Rachel had enjoyed her sister-in-law's expression of undisguised shock when she asked for a house key, though Duncan's surly nod brought back less pleasant memories of censorial elder brothers and parents, of running the gamut of family distrust and old-fashioned judgements about rebellious females forging on alone.

Not wanting to discredit herself entirely, Rachel had insisted on getting back by half past two, a time scale which dictated a certain amount of haste but no mean degree of pleasure. They went straight to Nathan's flat, a smart, if rather clinical two-bedroomed affair just off Dupont Circle. Rachel observed the picture of his wedding day, on a high, undusted shelf in his bedroom, without comment. She knew there had been a wife, just as she knew there had been no children. There seemed little point in probing further. For his part, Nathan displayed an equally forthright lack of curiosity. While a small subterranean part of Rachel might, if it had been allowed to, have found this insulting, it was reassuring too. No questions meant no threat, no possibility of having to surrender control, except in the act of love itself, into which she threw herself with sensual abandon. Love, the emotional counterpart of such pleasure, played not even the shadow of a role in the two hours they spent together. And if it had, Rachel would almost certainly not have handed Nathan Kramer her telephone number, placing it on top of one sculpted pectoral muscle as he lay in bed trying not to fall asleep, before she slipped out of the door and scurried down the curling stairwell to the yellow cab waiting in the street below.

4 ∫

Rachel decoded the alarm, slammed the door shut with her heel and flung her coat across the hall chair. After the fussy grandeur of the Hotel Turon the sight of her own flat was instantly soothing. Kicking off her shoes, she made an almost reverential tour of the rooms, flicking on lights and pulling curtains, savouring the taste of being home. The sitting room was two steps down at the end of the hallway, a long, elegant rectangle that ran the full length of the apartment, all the windows of its furthest wall overlooking the pretty lawn and shrubbery which, theoretically, she shared with other residents, but which always felt like her own. She had used the garden more than ever that summer, sitting out in a reclining seat on her square patio, sipping wine and breathing in the musky smells drifting on the breeze of late evening, glad that her co-residents were either too idle or too shy to do the same.

Her previous residence had been a small but handy one-bedroomed flat between Knightsbridge and Kensington, slightly lacking in character but slick and serviceable – ideal for a resident whose average homecoming was around ten o'clock at night and whose weekends were either spent in a blur of indolence or out visiting friends. While Rachel's work patterns showed no sign of change, her early thirties had seen a burgeoning need for a more comforting domestic backdrop to her hectic life, somewhere that felt less like a living unit and more like a home. The move to McKenzie Cartwright, whose offices took up several floors of a shimmering blue edifice between Covent Garden and The Strand, had presented the obvious moment for change. With the help of Anita, visibly bending under the weight of a then hefty ten-month-old Charlotte, slotted into a contraption the size of a large rucksack, she had flat-hunted her way southwards, finally settling on a street within walking distance of both the King's Road and the Embankment. Though the street contained several rather seedy-looking hotels, it was a part of London that she had always loved, and a mere fifteen-minute drive away from her new employers.

And location was everything, Anita reminded her, as they had surveyed the empty flat together on a wet Saturday shortly after completion, both women equally dismayed at the unsightly pockmarks and stains revealed by the removal of the previous owner's furniture and pictures. On the ceiling above their heads two bare lightbulbs swung gently on a draught cutting in through the crusted window frames overlooking the garden, a detail of dilapidation which on all of Rachel's previous visits had been masked by several pairs of handsome green velvet curtains.

'And I thought I could live here,' she muttered, tearing off a loose section of faded William Morris wallpaper flapping near at hand. 'It's a fucking pigsty.' She offered an apologetic scowl at her goddaughter, who, too young even to mimic the more ill-advised phrases of her seniors, was at that moment enjoying the unmatchable solace of a pink lollipop. 'And he never said anything about taking the carpets,' she added, digging the toe of her shoe into one of the gaping crevasses separating the floorboards.

'It's only cosmetic.' Anita waved her arms at the room. 'The survey was fine, remember?'

'I'm not sure I believe it any longer.'

'What you need is Priscilla Pargiter,' declared Anita, retrieving her daughter's sweet from the floor and licking off the dust before handing it back over her shoulder. 'Don't be put off by the name. Everyone says she's marvellous. When Giles and I win the pools and move to a twelve-roomed mansion on Highgate Hill, she'll be the one I call.' She scribbled a phone number on the back of an old shopping list and pressed it into Rachel's reluctant hand. 'And don't tell me you can't afford it with that spanking new job of yours, because I shan't listen to a word.'

Five years on Rachel had no regrets about taking Anita's advice. Priscilla Pargiter, clad in a tank-sized kaftan dress and tinkling like a wind charm, had breezed into the flat with gushing visions about upholstery and wallpaper that made Rachel secretly afraid. She sketched pictures with her arms as she talked, enthusing about colours and materials whose names sounded like the roll-call of an exotic menu. Rachel, who had been both too desperate and too busy at work to resist, watched from the sidelines as her bomb site of a home was transformed into effortlessly stunning schemes of colour and design. Too pleased with the results to mind that the realisation of such an achievement had required the intervention of an imagination other than her own, she found herself entering a new phase of satisfaction with life in general; a plateau of contentment that bordered on the smug.

Her circle of female friends meanwhile, all of whom had by then entered the long and in some cases bewildering tunnel of motherhood, latched onto Rachel's new surroundings with equal relish. All sparks of envy were quickly defused by gratitude at having access to such a refuge from the domestic hubbub of their own homes, somewhere they could uncoil from family tensions, soaking up the decor and Rachel's wine stocks with equal relish. Any sense on Rachel's part of being invaded rather than complimented by such attentions, was purely momentary. She had seen quite enough of the clutter in the lives of such friends – the way that family rubble had to be cleared and stacked to make room for basic necessities like eating and sitting down – to sympathise deeply with their need to escape. After a spell at the homes of Anita or Joy, she herself would return to her flat like a monk in retreat, welcoming the cool silence of its empty space, the knowledge that all imprints upon its surfaces were hers and hers alone.

Rachel dropped the brochure hailing the attractions of the Hotel Turon into the kitchen bin and pressed the play button on her answering machine. While the tape was rewinding she poured herself a glass of white wine and leant back against the fridge, closing her eyes.

Two clicks.

'Hey Rachel, it's Nathan. Just to say I'm in town for a couple of days and would like to see you. I guess you're at work. I'll call you there. Ciao till later . . .'

Typical Nathan: succinct and unstumbling. Rachel sipped her wine, which had seen better days, but which was at least cold.

'Rachel, Anita here . . . just calling for a chat really. Actually no, what I'd really like is to invite myself round – if that's OK – I mean I know you're frantically busy and all that. It's just that things are looking a bit bleak at the moment . . . could do with a break to be honest. After playing the hero amongst all those Russian rebels Giles seems to expect the entire family to go into worship-mode – he bellows at the children for not being perfect and at me for . . . oh anything that takes his fancy. And I've been trying to do that piece on leisure centres I told you about – OK so it's not as glamorous as covering wars but someone has to fill the cereal bowls in the morning . . . Charlotte's been waking and coming into our bed at all hours of the night and the twins are in this chronic phase of thinking their day starts at five o'clock . . .'

There was a short pause and a sigh. *'You're going to run out of tape. Sorry. Feeling low and all that. Could I come round some time? Giles is on early shifts soon and could field the kids. Let me know. Thanks so much . . .'*

Rachel put down her glass of wine and returned her attentions to the fridge. There was a pot of taramasalata, whose sell-by date had recently passed but which smelt all right, and a packet of mini wholemeal pitta bread which might be revived by a few seconds in the microwave. Behind her, the answering machine continued to play.

'Ah, so you're not there,' said the quiet, but subtly accusatory voice of her mother. *'Just ringing to see how you were, dear. We had your big brother to stay over the bank holiday – they all came down by train – they've got one of these family rail cards, Ian said – so much cheaper and easier than using the car. They seemed very well, even little Malcolm, who as you know suffers terribly with his ears. Ian seems to be running several Scottish hospitals single-handed and Clare is back doing something part-time in a library which she says she enjoys. I can't think how she manages it with the children to look after. They asked after you of course . . . I said you were fine as far as we knew. It's high time you came to see us, dear, it's been ever such a long time. Do you think you could manage a Sunday lunch? I do know how terribly busy you are. I'll call you later in the week . . . Oh and your father sends his love.'*

Rachel dipped her index finger deep into the soft pink paste and scooped an unseemly clod into her mouth, savouring the garlic-fishy flavours as she swallowed. The circles of pitta bread had only responded in part to the reinvigorating effects of intense heat, their centres going soft while their edges had turned testingly brittle. With the determination born of real hunger, Rachel ate steadily, using the stale bread as a spoon and sucking the taramasalata off the bits that were too impossibly hard to bother with.

When her answering machine stopped she became aware of rain drumming on the patio outside. Licking her fingers, she went back into her sitting room, her stockinged feet slipping on the sections of parquet floor between the rugs. There the noise was louder than ever, thanks to a whisking wind driving directly against the windows. As she listened, she began to distinguish another sound too, a high-pitched whining that sent shivers across her scalp. An animal of some kind. A fox maybe. Something suffering. She frowned, curious but reluctant to be drawn to any drama being enacted in the sodden darkness outside. Foxes could get painfully locked in the act of copulation, she remembered, this compelling fact flitting into her head from nowhere, sliding unexpectedly out of the dark recesses of her memory reserved for such trivia.

Still resisting the mounting urge to peer outside, Rachel crossed over to the mahogany shelves that housed her music centre and began trailing a finger along the library of CDs. Behind her the whining stopped briefly and then started up again, more loudly this time. Apprehensive, her imagination grappling with unappealing images of interlocking foxes, Rachel strode across the room and lifted the bottom corner of one of the long blue curtains covering the glass-panelled door leading into the garden.

Either because it was intelligent enough to know – even from its limited vantage point in the dank darkness – that this was the entrance to the room, or because it had glimpsed Rachel approaching and darted into a position from which it would be seen, the cat was sitting waiting for her right beside the door. On seeing Rachel, it reduced its yowl to a pitiful mew. Her first instinct was to drop the curtain. She did not like animals particularly. Though they were all right in other people's houses – even quite pleasant sometimes – she had always shied away from adopting a similar burden for herself, her mind associating such things with unwanted smells and coatings of hoover-resistant fur.

Upon finding the snapshot of a warm dry sanctuary blacked out, the cat immediately reverted to its high-pitched wail.

The curtain was lifted again, more brusquely this time.

'Go away.' She mouthed the words with exaggerated care, glaring hard through the rain-smeared glass.

The cat, which was black, with white patches circling its eyes and white tips to its ears, cocked its head and opened its mouth very wide in return, making no sound now, as if it too was merely framing words rather than audibly expressing any views.

'Buggeration.' Rachel wrenched back the curtain and unlocked the door. 'I don't want you, puss,' she said, as he darted in between her legs and trotted, tail high, over towards the hand-woven Peruvian rug which Anita had helped her choose from an intimidatingly chic and cramped carpet shop in the Brompton Road. The cat sat down and began licking its stomach in a businesslike way, its pink tongue pushing the fur into manicured tufts.

'Just for tonight then,' said Rachel, returning her attentions to her CD player and opting for a Fauré piano quartet. 'And that's it. So don't go getting any ideas.'

Determined to ignore her intruder, Rachel settled herself on her sofa with her briefcase on her lap and a full wine glass at her side. As one of the more senior board directors at the agency, she had overall responsibility for two accounts, Mallarmé Skincare Products plc, which billed a mighty eighty million worldwide and of which she was inordinately proud and fond, and a national chain of DIY shops called Blackers, which was in the throes of financial crisis and from which she had been hoping to extricate herself – and the agency – for several months. The papers she removed from her briefcase related not to client business however, but to a general presentation on the staffing and recruiting policies of the agency. While the presentation itself contained many ideas of which she was justly proud, its creation related directly to the plum and soon-to-be vacant post of Head of Account Management. The extra work would be daunting, but it was time her career took another pace forward. To become a departmental head was the obvious step. Alan Jarvis had all but said as much himself many times in the past.

She held up the sheaf of papers, squinted at the print and then threw them to one side in annoyance.

'Glasses, bloody glasses – where the hell are you?' Quite used to talking to herself when the occasion demanded, Rachel did not notice the cat casting her a wary eye from its cosy corner of the rug, while she rummaged ineffectually in her briefcase before extending her search to the hall. Having located the glasses in the side pocket of her handbag, still parked on the hall floor beside her suitcase, she sank back onto the sofa and closed her eyes. She was tired. Flying, however short the distance, always wore her out. It dried her skin too, she reflected, touching one cheek morosely with the tips of her fingers. The presentation could wait. Perhaps it wasn't even necessary. It was her turn for promotion, and Jarvis knew it.

Stealthy, on velvet, freshly prinked paws, the cat hopped up onto the sofa and crept towards the vacant lap. Half-asleep, Rachel felt the warm cushion of its body arrive. It turned just once, before settling itself across her stomach and thighs. Her dreaming self welcomed the heat and weight of it, slipping easily from sensations of the present moment to recollections of a similar pleasantness earlier in the day; until the cat had become a baby, pushing up from the deep heart of her like a blossoming flower.

5

Clothes have to work harder these days, thought Rachel, grimacing at her reflection in the mirrored walls of the lift before striding out onto the fourth floor. She was wearing one of her favourite suits, of soft creamy wool with a pencil-shaped, knee-length skirt and a flatteringly tailored jacket, trimmed with triangular black velvet lapels.

'Morning, Rachel,' trilled Kath, McKenzie Cartwright's main receptionist, flicking her pretty brown eyes up from the gossip page of the *Daily Mail*.

'Morning, Kath, hard at work I see,' observed Rachel dryly, but smiling to show she meant no harm.

She strode off down the maze of corridors, exchanging brief pleasantries with several colleagues, before arriving at the open-plan square of four desks that housed a gaggle of secretaries, two rubber plants and a photocopying machine. Melissa, Rachel's own secretary, smiled at once and then frowned.

'What are you doing here? You're supposed to be in France.'

'Too much to do.'

Melissa, who had a plump but pretty face, with smudged freckles and glossy dark hair, followed Rachel into her office. 'And there's me thinking I'm going to get an easy day for once. Coffee?'

She began fiddling with the cappuccino machine that lived on a table in the corner of the room, a prized possession of Rachel's whose services were much sought after by the rest of the department.

'And have one yourself,' Rachel murmured, flicking through the pile of post on her desk with one hand, while the other moved deftly over the keys of her computer.

'Put a call through to Frank Alder at Mallarmé, could you? Tell him I'm around if he needs me. Then tell Felicity downstairs I'll want a progress report on pre-production for the Allday Sunlotion launch – the shoot's going to be in Bermuda not Florida now and we've only a few weeks to go. And could you retype this little lot,' she held out the file containing her presentation on account management policy, 'by eleven o'clock, if possible, so I can talk it through with Alan before lunch. Which means I'll need a ten-minute slot with him. If Julie gives you a hard time, let me know.' Julie Stern, the managing director's tiger of a PA, had been known to reduce some of the humbler secretaries to tears for daring to make demands upon her boss's precious allocations of time.

Melissa placed a cup of frothy coffee on Rachel's desk and turned to retrieve her own.

'Any messages?'

'No, apart from a . . .' Melissa studied some writing on the palm of her left hand, '. . . Mr Will Raphael. Something about photography lessons. Said you had his number.' She looked up. 'Thinking of a new career?'

'Bloody hell, I forgot – I was supposed to call ages ago – back in August when things looked quiet enough for me to take up a hobby.' She gave a wry smile. 'Steve Betts, the Allday director, recommended him. Damn.'

'I'll call him back if you like,' Melissa offered, remembering the friendly and deferential voice of Mr Raphael with some warmth.

'That's very sweet of you, Mel, but I really feel I ought to do it myself, seeing as I've already left it embarrassingly late. I can't remember where the hell I put his number . . .' Rachel began rifling through the drawer on her right, where she kept receipts and other personal odds and ends.

'Anything else?' Melissa stood in the doorway, coffee in hand, trying not to look disappointed that her quiet Monday had fallen to pieces, while a part of her felt sorry for a woman who had nothing better to do on a day off than come into the office. Not everybody liked Rachel Elliot. She was too smart in every sense, too self-contained for most people's tastes. In the two years that Melissa had worked for her, however, she had developed something of a protective fondness for the woman, based on a recognition that behind the cool and brisk exterior lay a scrupulous sense of fair play and an appealingly dry sense of humour. There were no tricks up her sleeve, no hidden agendas. Unlike some of her fellow directors, who seemed to relish dodging deadlines and dicing with uncertainty, Rachel had a reputation for down-the-line directness and reliability. She fought for creative ideas that she believed in and rejected others out of hand. She made no secret of her ambitions either, a fact which clearly intimidated her male colleagues and which earned her few friends amongst those of her own sex. That she was easily the most senior – and among the most attractive – of the female executives did not exactly help. Nor, in Melissa's view, did it count in her boss's favour that she was so irrefutably single. Unfair though it was, getting as far as Rachel had without publicly shackling herself to a member of the opposite sex seemed to be regarded by her less independent sisters in the business as a form of cheating. The more vitriolic amongst them even liked to rumour, during hair-combing and lipstick sessions in the ladies' lavatory, that the ambitious Ms Elliot had slept her way to the top, via Jarvis and a string of others. Melissa, who knew better than most quite how hard her boss drove herself, and who suspected the existence of a man in New York, doubted this very much indeed. In addition to which, she retained a particularly vivid and poignant image of Rachel alone in her office late one Friday night, crumpled and heaving over a box of tissues. Melissa, who had popped back upstairs from a party in the bar in order to retrieve her make-up bag from the bottom drawer of a filing cabinet, had crept away empty handed, her heart pounding with the guilty sense of having stumbled upon a secret. It wasn't right for anyone to look so alone and sad, especially not on a Friday night. The thought of offering comfort herself flickered and died. Rachel Elliot was not the cry-on-your-shoulder type, not at all. It would have felt like cruelty to intervene.

Jimmy Chartsworth appeared behind Melissa, looking unkempt but somehow dashing, as was his wont, the ashen colour of his face suggesting a weekend of intense social activity, but the sparkle in his eyes telling the world that such habits were to be envied rather than give cause for concern. His office, from where he directed operations on a number of small but flourishing accounts, was opposite Rachel's, on the other side of the quadrille of secretaries, a geographical fact which meant that he was regularly to be found batting his handsome eyelashes shamelessly between the trailing fronds of the pot plants. Melissa, who suffered irritating heart palpitations when it came to Jimmy, sauntered with careful nonchalance across to her desk.

'Good morning, Melissa, my darling.'

'Good morning, Jimmy.'

'Do you really want that delicious cup of foaming caffeine, or are you prepared to donate it to a worthier cause?' He placed both hands on either side of her computer screen and leant right over the desk.

'Stop harassing my secretary, Chartsworth,' called Rachel cheerfully from her office, 'she's got work to do. Come and help yourself if you want.'

Jimmy straightened himself, shoved both hands deep into the pockets of his jacket and offered Rachel a brief bow. 'I might just do that, thank you.' He winked at Melissa before going off in search of a clean mug.

Rachel doodled in the margin of her pad while Frank Alder, European Managing Director of Mallarmé Skincare Products plc, talked at considerable length about the spectrum of marketing and advertising issues facing the company, his gravelly voice reiterating points from presentations she herself had made.

Rachel was beginning to wonder why she had bothered to come into work, why, instead of lounging in bed with tea and papers, she had woken with a start at 6 o'clock, fizzing with energy and impatience. She felt inclined to blame the cat, guileless though it looked, curled up on the end of her bed, its handsome bush of a tail tucked round one broad cheek like a feather pillow. Rachel had wiggled her toes to awaken it and then shooed it out into the dripping brilliance of the garden. Clearly having imagined that hospitality might include breakfast, the cat exited with haughty reluctance, taking up a stiff-backed position just a few feet from the sitting-room door, its glassy green eyes brimming with reproach. Rachel, who feared that feeding itinerant pets might only discourage them from returning to their rightful owners, had observed these reactions with stony resolution, roughly pulling the curtains shut and marching back to her bedroom, where she pretended to enjoy tossing amongst the pillows until the boredom and discomfort grew too much and she got up to run herself a bath.

There was something mildy upsetting about the fact that no one but Melissa seemed to have remembered that she wasn't supposed to be at work at all. Instead of having one of those catch-up days that she had intended, usually only possible on a weekend or bank holiday, she had found herself sucked into the hubbub of account management life. Managers on all the products for which she was responsible buzzed in and out of her office with questions and problems. Ever wary of losing touch with the real business for which she was employed (she had seen colleagues stumble from divorcing themselves too much from the nitty-gritty of account handling) and also being of a nature that found it wrenchingly hard to surrender control of anything, Rachel went with the flow, skipping lunch in the process.

Alan Jarvis was apparently out of bounds until after six o'clock. Waiting to see him was going to make her late for Nathan, whom she had agreed to meet at six-thirty in the foyer of his hotel. She probably wouldn't have bothered – would have asked Melissa to fix something for later in the week – if she hadn't observed for herself that 'out of bounds' meant engrossed in a one-to-one with Cliff Weybourne, the agency's new board director, imported at some considerable expense – transferred like a footballer for an obscene fee – from one of the hotshop agencies that had sprung up on the heels of the recession. What was more, he had been recruited for the specific purpose of leading new business pitches, the agency's record for winning fresh accounts having fallen somewhat over the last year. Rachel, who knew that leading the bid for the Mallarmé account had been the making of her and who believed that going after new business was a treat that should be shared fairly amongst directors suffering the daily grind of servicing difficult accounts, had been sceptical about this appointment from the first. Further acquaintance with the new arrival had done nothing to allay her fears.

Frank Alder had moved onto a meandering analysis of the

imminent launch of Allday Sunlotion. Rachel, while making suitable noises of concurrence, found her thoughts drifting in not altogether professional directions. Bermuda in November. Even after fifteen years in the business it was impossible not to be excited. In these days of tight budgets, shoots in anything beyond converted warehouses were a rare treat. Abandoning her doodle, which had begun as a spider's web but turned into a fat animal face with pointed ears, she cleared her throat in preparation to interrupt. Frank, dear man though he was, could ramble for hours if not taken in hand; he liked to end on a point of impressive gravitas, but sometimes seemed to have trouble finding it.

Rachel seized upon a pause. 'The pre-production meeting is set for the third week in October Frank, just as we agreed. The final draft of the media plan is being drawn up as we speak – a few spots in January to catch the winter sun-seekers and then a real blitz in May and June. It's looking good Frank. All of us on this side of the fence are very excited.'

Nathan Kramer did not like to be kept waiting, especially not when he was jet-lagged and hungry and trying not to drink because he wanted to enjoy wine with dinner and have a clear head for Paris the next day. Though Rachel had rung to explain, very sweetly, that she was running late, he still felt annoyed. They should have skipped meeting up this time after all, he thought, his eyes aimlessly perusing the by now very familiar front page of the *New York Times*, while his stomach whined for food.

But the moment he caught sight of her, emerging head high and eyes alert through the grand swing doors, he changed his mind. Nathan liked powerful women, women whose body language reflected their inner confidence, their soaring levels of self-esteem. His wife had been of a similar mould, too much so, in fact, for the marriage ever to have had a hope of success. Their egos had clashed like Titans. He still saw Melanie sometimes, when business took her to New York; they would lunch in civilised fashion, while he tried to quell the abdominal flutters that the sight of her long, stilettoed legs still provoked, calming them with recollections of how domestic stress had once intervened to turn things sour.

'Hello, Nathan. You look well.' Rachel kissed him on the cheek with cool, unhurried lips that made him instantly want more of the same. 'Sorry about the delay. Office politics, I'm afraid.' She slipped off her jacket and slung it over the arm that was carrying her briefcase. 'Shall we go for a drink somewhere first?'

'Sure, if you like.' He touched her shoulder to bring her attention back to his face. Her eyes looked tired, he thought, noting the faint pouches of fatigue with a little twist of dismay. 'We could go upstairs,' he said quietly, 'you know, do the room service thing. Would you like that?' Rachel, who was struggling with the by now discomfortingly familiar sensation of having arrived at something to which she was looking forward enormously, only to find that it tasted of nothing once she got there, smiled briefly. She was not in the mood for the 'room service thing' at all. Nor was she in the mood for Nathan's all-American-boy grin, telling her he wanted to have sex before dinner. As at the office, she began to wonder what she was doing there, what strange motives had impelled her to come at all.

'I'd like a drink and a sit-down meal, if you don't mind, Nathan. Sorry to be dull. I've had a bit of a day.'

'That's fine, just fine.' His smile tightened into a mask of disappointment. 'Got anywhere in mind?'

'The new Logan place is supposed to be very good. I've been wanting to try it for months,' she lied. 'We could walk it easily from here.'

'Great. Let's go.' He clapped his hands with a heartiness that told her his ego was still bruised and followed her out into the street.

She linked her arm through his for the walk, taking extra care to match her pace to his long strides, wanting to do every-thing she could to re-establish harmony. While she asked him about work, her mind motored down sliproads of its own. The artificiality of their relationship – the safe containability which had so attracted her five years before – was at last beginning to get her down, she realised, gripping his arm harder as if to hide the thought. She knew herself too well to worry that this might be a sign that she was falling in love with Nathan Kramer or that she wished him to grow emotionally more passionate with her. She associated it instead with the general malaise with which she had been affected in recent weeks, the distinct sense that wherever she longed to be, once she got there, there was nothing but emptiness to hold her hand.

They ate quite quickly, taking up and pursuing lines of communication with professional determination, each wrapped up in preoccupations that felt impossible to share. The restaurant was furnished in the convenient but elegant style that characterised all of Logan's eating haunts, with a menu that was short and expensive enough to make patrons feel they were getting something special. Rachel ate a colourful heap of goat's cheese, chicken and pasta which sat in her stomach afterwards with mystifying obstinacy, dissuading her from joining Nathan with a dessert and thereby contributing to the shadow of a pout that lurked beneath the polite expressions on his handsome face. To make up for it, she invited him back to her flat afterwards, suddenly unable to face the sterile prospect of his hotel room, with the usual clinical brightness of the bathroom and the uncomfortable awareness that other couples, many many other couples, had heaved their way towards sexual climax on its gently creaking bed.

As Rachel led the way into her flat she found herself looking out for the cat. She drew the sitting room curtains more tentatively than usual, her eyes scanning the darkness for any signs of movement. But all was still and quiet. She poured two whiskies, flicked Fauré back into action and went to sit beside Nathan on the sofa.

Nathan felt he had been made to wait a long time, long enough not to be reticent about turning his attentions, after only one sip of whisky, to the pink buttons down the front of Rachel's shirt, each one as enticing as the sugared topping of an iced gem. He used his teeth as well as his hands, licking the skin of her cleavage in a way that Rachel – unless she had fought the emotion hard – might even have found ridiculous.

'I'd better go to the bathroom,' she whispered after a few moments, this being her customary euphemism for inserting her cap.

'Sure, baby, sure.' He lifted his tousled head from her chest, his eyes glazed with a drugged look of arousal. 'I'll wait for you in there, shall I?' He motioned towards her bedroom with his head, his fingers fumbling with the buttons on his own shirt whose badly creased untucked ends reached almost to his knees.

'Yes, if you like.' Rachel picked up her handbag and walked quickly from the room. Once inside the bathroom she closed and bolted the door before leaning back against it, taking deep breaths in through her nose and inwardly cursing the fact that this voluntarily adopted system of irregular sexual encounters offered no guarantee for being in the mood when the possibilities presented themselves. It did not help that her period was due. Her stomach felt unpleasantly bloated and tight; her skin, shining in the bright mirror-light, looked – to Rachel's habitually self-critical eyes – as greasy and blotched as that of a ripening teenager. She got out her powder compact and dabbed hastily across her cheeks, frowning at the realisation that without a sense of her own desirability she could feel little desire. The sight of her cap, with its saggy rubber middle, did little to fast-forward her libido. She sank down onto the bathroom stool for a moment, regarding the contraceptive with distaste, overcome by a sense of absurdity that such an ugly, flimsy thing could mean the difference between conception and sterility, between life and nothing at all.

'You were a long time,' drawled Nathan, trying to keep a sense of injustice from his tone.

'Was I? Sorry.' She slipped into bed beside him and pressed her face to his chest, wanting to stifle the images playing leap-frog inside her head. A faint smell of rubber lingered on her fingertips, reminding her that there was sex and there was procreation, the same act, but worlds apart. While Nathan's mind zigzagged in colourful streaks of its own, unburdened by intellectual preoccupations of any kind, Rachel fought and lost the battle between sensation and thought, her mind homing in instead on an almost palpable sense of the slim rubber barrier planted deep inside. And when, a little later, she cried out, a strange guttural sound flying from the back of her throat, her lover could not have known that this was no prompt for the celebratory, pumping finale that he offered in response, but rather a cry of protest that the barrier was there at all.

Nathan fell asleep almost at once. Rachel quietly left the bed and returned to the bathroom, feeling strangely tranquil and alert. Her period had come. Usually it was a nuisance; but this time it reassured her. She sat at her kitchen table, both hands rubbing the slight curve of her stomach as the cramps came and went. She could have a child if she wanted to. She was not yet forty. There was still time. She had money. She even had a partner . . . but here the steady march of her thoughts faltered. It was somewhat ironic, she mused ruefully, getting up to fill the kettle, that just as she was facing up to the fact that she had little in common with Nathan Kramer beyond a preference for chocolate-chip ice cream, her heart should take it upon itself to have a volte-face about motherhood. But Nathan was all she had.

Sitting back at the kitchen table, Rachel reached for her shopping list pad and began to draft something of a time-plan. Bermuda in November. Pregnant by December. Baby the following autumn. Three months' maternity leave . . . She stopped abruptly, faintly appalled by her own eagerness to make such crude calculations and by the audacity with which she was banking on Nathan's cooperation. But then Nathan had made no secret of the fact that he did not want children. Which did rather simplify things. She would just have to ask him straight out. Invite him to be an honorary parent – no strings attached. Just how he liked it. She couldn't help smiling. He might even be flattered.

She returned her attentions to her pad. Back to work by the following January at the latest. Aged forty-one. She would be sixty-one when her child was twenty. A young sixty-one, she reassured herself. Not like her own mother, who though a much younger parent, had clearly burnt all bridges with her younger self. Rachel shivered and got up to squeeze out her teabag over the sink. Tiny droplets of brown splashed up its white sides, before starting to dribble down again, like muddy tears. Rachel watched them absently, assailed by familiar, ineradicable childhood memories of not fitting in, of repeatedly disappointing those whose love one needed most.

The spare bedroom could accommodate a nanny. It was large enough for one corner to be sequestered for a shower cubicle. If she moved her computer and desk into the sitting room – there was plenty of unused space down the far end – the study could be transformed into a nursery. The memory of Priscilla Pargiter loomed large. With her help, anything would be possible. But not yet. One step at a time.

Still restless, Rachel padded through into the sitting room and curled up at one end of the sofa, bringing her knees up to her chin and tucking her hands into her armpits. The sense of emptiness, the dissatisfactions of recent weeks, all suddenly seemed to make sense. She had been in denial, as Nathan would have put it, stifling a longing that had at last burst through. She took these last thoughts back to bed with her, where the most vital component of her speculations lay spreadeagled on top of the duvet, small buzzing sounds coming from his nose. He cooperated with the sweetness of a sleeping infant as she gently pushed him over to one side and pulled the duvet up around her shoulders. After one final snort the snoring stopped altogether. Although he had curled up a couple of feet away from her, Rachel could feel the heat of his body spreading through the bed. Having sat for so long in the relative chill of her sitting room, this warmth was welcome indeed, though it triggered no impulses in her to nestle any closer. But it would be nice to want to, she thought sleepily, bringing her knees up to her chest and closing her eyes; it would be nice to want the man as well as the child.

6

Rachel was awakened by faint grunting sounds coming from the floor. Nathan was doing his exercises, a daily programme of fifty press-ups, fifty sit-ups and some curious hip-swivels done at breakneck speed with his elbows cartwheeling around his ears. Wanting to tease, but warier than usual of bruising her lover's highly sensitised male pride, Rachel sidled past in order to retrieve her dressing gown from the peg on the back of the bedroom door.

'Coffee?'

'Uh.'

'I'll take that as a yes. I can stretch to toast as well, if you like?'

Nathan, at that moment having completed the last of a series of fifty, jumped to his feet and clapped his hands. 'Toast would be great, Rachel.' Sweat was running freely down his nose and temples. A small dark wet patch at the top of his briefs bore testimony to the exertions suffered by the admirable scrubbing board muscles of his torso. Catching sight of himself in Rachel's full-length mirror, he took up a body-building pose. 'Not bad, huh, for a guy who's kissed goodbye to forty?'

'Marvellous,' she replied, smiling as she was meant to, while inwardly she wondered whether it was just nerves, lack of sleep or plain sod's law that was making Nathan suddenly appear so childish and unappealing. 'You're just a little boy at heart, aren't you,' she accused gently, planting a kiss on a dry section of his shoulder.

'They say that's my greatest asset.' He grinned at her before burying his head in a towel and rubbing vigorously.

As she made to leave the room he caught her hand. 'Have we got time . . . ?'

'No, we haven't,' she whispered, putting her mouth to his ear to explain that her period had arrived in the small hours.

Nathan let go at once. He wasn't good with the monthly business; it didn't fit in with any part of the aspect of women that turned him on. It wasn't just the thought of all the blood, it was deeper than that, something to do with the notion that deliciously cool and powerful creatures like Rachel Elliot weren't ultimately in control after all, that in this one aspect they were victims like any ordinary female.

'I'll take a shower.'

Rachel hummed quietly to herself as she moved round the kitchen in bare feet, absently rummaging for breakfast things, while her thoughts floated along in a bubble of their own. Thousands of women had babies without partners. It would be easy. It would be perfect. Problems – as she had learnt from countless husband-related confidences over the years – came from fathers. Even Anita had been known to say it was easier to be a mother when Giles was abroad. When he was around she nagged him to do things, she explained. Whereas, when he was away she was quite happy to cope alone. Husbands who cared more about football results than their families, husbands who preferred pubs to helping with bath-time, husbands who got jealous of their children – Rachel had heard it all. A thousand times.

Of all the relationships with which she was acquainted, the only one which seemed to have arrived at a plateau of mutual satisfaction was between a couple called Naomi and Graham Fullerton, whom Rachel had met in her twenties. Naomi had been a highly respected media buyer at Rachel's first agency, but threw it all in to marry Graham, a premature grandfather of a man with a bushy beard and an infectious throaty laugh. Shortly afterwards they had moved to a small town in Suffolk, where Graham joined a practice of country solicitors while Naomi concentrated on producing a family. They had four girls, the second one of whom, Jessica, was another of Rachel's godchildren. The Fullertons' marital contentment seemed to Rachel, from two decades of biannual weekend visits, to reside with a clear definition of roles. While Graham paid the bills,

Naomi applied all the energy which had once so impressed her bosses into running her home and family. The children emerged from their bedrooms each morning as immaculate as handcrafted dolls, wearing colour-coordinated embroidered smocks and with pretty ribbons neatly securing their glossy plaits and curls. The house itself had been extended, remoulded and improved several times over, while the garden boasted toy-town grids of paths and flowers and climbing frames – not covered in rust and mud like the toppling structure stuffed into one corner of Anita's garden, but each edge and line gleaming with vibrance and colour.

That Naomi Fullerton had made a career out of her family was a fact which had dawned on Rachel many years back. While admiring her friend for the sheer feat of such an achievement, Rachel had never been foolish enough to imagine that she could be happy with such a scenario herself. Somehow, Naomi had learnt to live for the pleasure of other people; for the clockwork precision of domestic routine; for the reward of an appreciative bear hug from her husband at the end of the day. Such selflessness, as Rachel well knew, was simply not within her power. She would have been more like the Anitas of the world, kicking and screaming to the bitter end. Which was probably why she liked Anita better, she thought with a sigh, absently scraping a charred corner of a piece of toast into the pedal bin and making a mental note to call her back that day. Dear, desperate, career-juggling Anita, compromising on all fronts and winning on none. What would she say when Rachel told her of her plans to have a child? The thought was not exactly appealing. Telling people was going to be the hardest part, she realised. Especially at work. Rachel shuddered, for a moment daunted by the prospect of seeing it through.

'Is that for me?' Nathan took the piece of toast from her hand and put it on his plate. 'Sleep OK?'

'Fine, thanks.' She put the butter in front of him and busied herself with chasing truant coffee grains round her mug with a teaspoon.

'Paris should be good.' Nathan spoke energetically through a mouthful of buttered toast. 'We'll be talking about new budgets for old countries. Emerging markets is most definitely where it's at. The opportunities for investment there are fantastic.' His Adam's apple jigged as he swallowed.

'It sounds brilliant,' Rachel enthused, mustering a herculean effort of will to clamber somewhere in the region of his wavelength. 'It's the same with advertising. All our big clients are opening factories over there – Prague, Budapest, Moscow – you name it. We're looking at how to adapt campaigns for those markets all the time. There are millions to be made.'

'You said it. Billions, even.' His eyes twinkled with reassurance. Nathan liked to talk about money. It was something one could latch on to, something to be measured by and feel sure of. 'So when can we do this again?' He licked away a fleck of butter from the corner of his lips and winked at her. 'Not so rushed next time, uh?' He glanced at his watch. 'Shoot, I've got to go. Any chance of a taxi, babe?'

'I'm due for a trip to the States in November,' Rachel offered casually, reaching for the telephone. 'A stop-over on the way to Bermuda. We're shooting a suncream film there. I was planning to see my brother, but if you could make it down from New York . . . save me from my thuggish godson . . .'

'Sounds good to me. Call me soon so we can talk dates. I'll fix something up. Something special, perhaps.'

'Oh, I don't need anything special,' she said quietly, putting down the phone and cupping her hands round the back of his neck. 'Just bring yourself.' At the thought of her deviousness her mouth creased into a small, guilty smile. It would be such a relief to tell him of her plan. When the time was right.

Nathan, who interpreted the wickedness of the smile along quite different lines, increased the pressure of his arms around her back.

'You be a good girl now, you hear?' he said huskily, holding her close. 'You're very special to me, Rachel, very special indeed.'

7

Anita Cavanagh, aware that the twins were applying paint not only to the paper she had pinned on each side of their easel but also to all reachable sections of the kitchen wall, told herself that it did not matter, that a writer of her experience and calibre could rise above such distractions in order to finish composing a witty feature on the range of facilities offered by London leisure centres.

The background green of her laptop screen shimmered unhelpfully. Outside, the rain danced off the windowsill; beyond, she could see the thinning grass of their meagre lawn, rapidly being converted to a sea of mud. The twins would love it, she thought glumly, recalling their recent clamour to be let out of the house, how their breath had steamed up the glass panels of the back door as they scrabbled to be released, like puppies wanting a walk. Only four more months, she told herself, before the blissful release of nursery school and the unimaginably wonderful prospect of five mornings to herself.

Bored of flat surfaces, the twins had begun painting each other, beginning with their faces and hands and then moving on to their clothes. Anita glanced up at the clock. Almost twelve, thank God. Almost the witching hour. Two minutes early wouldn't harm. It had been a hellish morning after all. The wine box sat on a shelf above the washing machine in the utility room. Taking a tumbler from the dishwasher she slipped out of the kitchen, willing the twins not to follow. Resisting the urge to swig, she took several sips in quick succession, standing alone with only the whirr of spinning sheets beside her and the sound of rain on the roof overhead. A few seconds' peace. Exquisite.

'Me and Eddie are tigers,' roared Laura when their mother reappeared a few minutes later. They growled and leapt under the skirts of the kitchen tablecloth while she managed to pretend to be scared and to tap out a few quite incisive sentences all at the same time.

'You tigers are going to need a bath,' she said, laughing in spite of herself at the sight of their round smeary faces and matted hair and shooing them upstairs.

Leaving her offspring splashing noisily amongst a fleet of plastic vehicles, Anita slipped back down to the kitchen and gave herself a refill before settling down to call Rachel. Supremely cool, terrifyingly successful and wonderfully kind Rachel, whom she couldn't help liking enormously, even if being near her was inclined to make one feel like a rough pebble beside a polished stone. Rachel was her oasis of sanity, a tireless fount of objectivity and strength, someone to help crisis-lurching part-time mothers get everything back in perspective again.

They had met back in the late seventies, in the days when Rachel was still buying space in magazines and Anita was writing articles for *Campaign*, the magazine which agencies loved to slander, but to which they all pandered shamelessly none the less. Having come to interview Rachel for a tiny and uninspired piece on the escalating costs of media space, she ended up taking her out for a long and very enjoyable lunch. They talked with that ease peculiar to women who sense interests in common; Anita made no secret of her long-term hopes, how she was using *Campaign* as a ladder rung towards much dizzier heights of journalistic achievement. Rachel, though more guarded about her own ambitions, had been wonderfully receptive and encouraging, quite unafraid to speak her mind.

But Anita's career plans had not counted on the knee-knocking charms of one Giles Cavanagh, a keen young political journalist with an ambitious agenda of his own. From almost the moment they met, Anita somehow found herself subjugating the needs of her career to that of her lover's, initially because she was besotted, and then later because a pattern had been set and she was terrified of being deserted. Even before they eventually got married, given the choice of regular work in London or accompanying Giles on a spell abroad, Anita would invariably choose the latter, thereby securing the continuance of the relationship but at an immeasurable cost to herself. Gradually the demand for her work dwindled. Hardly surprising for a freelance without a speciality who was seldom there.

The Cavanaghs' first child, Charlotte, to whom Rachel was godmother, was born when Anita was thirty-three and desperate for something to fill the disappointment left by the failings of her career. Although motherhood certainly provided consolation of a kind, it came as quite a shock too; not just because Charlotte's three-hour colic-screaming sessions lasted for four solid months, but also because of the unutterable enslavement of it all. That Giles could continue flying out to hot spots at a moment's notice, while his wife was tied to a treadmill of on-tap feeding and broken nights, only served to heighten this sense of entrapment. Given such a context, the decision to have a second child was hard. But Anita, having suffered as an only child herself, was adamant that Charlotte should not have to do the same. The news that she was pregnant with twins was a shock of almost catastrophic proportions, the sole redeeming feature being that Giles, deeply affected himself, came up trumps by engineering an admirable phase of home-based work that lasted well into Eddie and Laura's second year. While doing a lot in terms of acquainting their father with the delights of caring for small infants, it was not so helpful where the marriage itself was concerned. It often seemed to Anita that the two of them now sat on opposite ends of an unstoppable see-saw of resentment and envy, typically characterised by spiralling arguments-cum-discussions as to whose suffering was the greatest. A large mortgage taken out on a dilapidated Camden maisonette during the late eighties meant there was little prospect of alleviating the mundane miseries of their situation with extravagances like nannies and second cars. It was all they could do to manage two weeks a year on an English beach.

'If it wasn't for you,' Anita reminded Rachel on the phone on the morning of the twins' spectacularly creative painting session, 'I think I would go barmy.' Guilt at having left the children unattended in the bath for too long was making her gabble. 'The twins between them have just about repainted the kitchen walls – limey green and orange – it's quite ghastly.' The thought of Rachel sitting in a broad-backed swivel-chair before a vast, orderly desk prompted a fresh gulp of wine.

'Poor Anita,' murmured Rachel, unable to resist the thought that alternative and more acceptable forms of entertainment could have been found for bored three year olds and that it was typical of Anita to have let a situation slip beyond her control. She began to flick through the pages of her diary in order to settle upon a suitable evening on which to meet. It was not easy. A reputation for working late led inevitably to the arrangement of early-evening meetings, which could run on until all hours. Saturday night was free, but she had promised to drive to her parents for lunch on the Sunday and did not want to be up till all hours the night before. 'How about next Thursday?' she suggested, making a mental note to tell Melissa not to book anything for after six that afternoon.

'Next Thursday. Wonderful. Perfect. I'll stay the night, if that's OK.'

'Would you like to check it with Giles . . . ?'

'Absolutely not.' There was something faintly reckless in Anita's tone which triggered the jangle of old alarm bells.

'We could make it sooner if you like . . . I could do Saturday . . .'

'Nope. Thursday's great. Better fish the kids out of the bath. 'Spect it will be dyed yellow like the walls. Bye for now.' There was a giggle before the line went dead.

'Shit,' said Rachel, loud enough for Melissa, who sat closest to her open door, to turn and raise an eyebrow at a colleague. 'Stupid, stupid girl.' Rachel gathered up the papers she needed for Jarvis's bi-weekly board meeting and left her office still muttering under her breath. Should she phone Giles, she wondered, or pretend she hadn't noticed? It was so hard to know how far to interfere or leave well alone. Besides which, Anita would deny it, like she always did, before shame or common sense or God knows what prompted her to dry herself out again.

As Rachel strode down the stretch of lush, cornflower carpeting that led towards the most salubrious of the agency's conference rooms, the one that Alan Jarvis rather pompously insisted on using for any meeting that required his presence, she caught herself wishing for someone in whom she could confide. Friends like Anita were so needy, so brimming over with intimate revelations of their own, that it was hard to reverse the process, especially for one more inclined to cope with emotional dramas on her own. It was so much easier to be depended on, she thought with a sigh, taking her seat at the middle of the long, polished mahogany table, so much easier being the one to listen instead of the one to speak. The only person with whom anything like the reverse had been true was Robbie Dexter, the boyfriend of two decades ago whom she had finally jettisoned during a damp camping holiday in Wales. Dear Robbie, so dogged and unjudgemental, so eager – even at the tender age of twenty-five – to dig in and settle down. As the first grand passion of both their lives and with a history of courtship that stretched back to their teens, breaking up had been hard. The reassurance of such unquestioning love, which had so eased the passage from late teens to adulthood, from school to work, from home to living in a bed-sit in London, was something for which Rachel would always be grateful. The crunch had come with Robbie's decision to start his own landscape gardening business in Cornwall and an invitation for her to accompany him. After a few weeks of cowardly prevarication, Rachel finally settled matters in a leaky two-man tent at the bottom of a verdant Welsh valley. Hurt, but pitiably forgiving, Robbie had sloped off into his new life like a beaten dog. A trickle of cryptic postcards featuring geographical highlights of the Lizard Peninsula followed for a while; but after a few months even these brief connections had faltered and died.

Rachel smiled absently at the other senior members of the agency drifting in to take their seats, her thoughts meandering from peculiarly tender recollections of Robbie to her forth-coming trip. She twisted the pencil in her fingers. As far as her cycle was concerned, the dates were unbelievably per-fect. One encounter with Nathan might even be enough. If luck was on her side. She sipped some water, suppressing a smile.

'Are you with us, Rachel?'

She glanced up, blinking the dreaminess from her eyes. 'Not remotely, Alan, but do go ahead. I'll join you when I'm ready.'

Alan Jarvis chortled, appreciating as always the cool self-possession of the one female in the agency senior enough to attend his board meetings. He rapped his knuckles on the table and cleared his throat, before rattling through the agenda with characteristic haste.

When it came to the matter of problem accounts Rachel spoke up unhesitatingly about Blackers, using the direct approach which she knew was the one most likely to be respected.

'Alan, we've been too generous for too long. Blackers is nothing but trouble and a time-consuming one at that. It's time to resign the business. They have no budget for next year. They do nothing but phone up with absurd requests for data and analyses which their own marketing people should be perfectly capable of producing. There's still the question of Quantum's research – which they commissioned and now say we should pay for. I say we cut our losses and get out.'

Alan Jarvis eyed her over the top of his half-moon spectacles. 'Not like you to turn from a fight, Rachel.'

She swallowed hard. 'It's not a fight worth winning. They've got nothing in the pipeline. They're in deep financial trouble. They'll be out of business by Christmas and in the meantime we are just wasting our time.'

'The word is they're about to be taken over. Could be a very good prospect indeed a few months from now.' It was Cliff Weybourne, the new recruit, who spoke. His head was angled towards the top end of the table so that Rachel could only see the side of his face and not its full expression. There was a puffiness to his cheeks and neck, bearing out the rumours of too much good living. Though cleverly tailored to disguise the curving bulge of his torso, it was clear that he was considerably overweight. As if sensitive of these physical imperfections, he had a habit of constantly adjusting his wide power-ties as he talked, tweaking them down over the buttons of his shirt, as if hoping to conceal some of the expanse that heaved behind.

'You're welcome to take them on, Cliff,' Rachel said sweetly, fixing her eyes on his face until he was forced to turn and acknowledge her presence. She held out both hands. 'Blackers are all yours. With my love.'

'That's very kind, Rachel, but I've got a lot on my plate.'

'Ah . . . yes of course. New business. Silly me.' She returned her attention to the head of the table, aware that the chill in the atmosphere was now obvious to everyone else in the room. It made her afraid, but she pressed on. 'I want out, Alan. Mallarmé is launching new products all over the place – you've seen Alder's five-year plan – I really think my time would be better spent concentrating on servicing them. Their advertising spend could literally double in the next couple of years.'

'Yes, yes. I was coming to Mallarmé.' Alan Jarvis placed both hands on the table and leant forward. 'We seem to have finished apart from that. If there's no other business,' he removed his glasses and began polishing them with one of the paper napkins stacked beside the plate of biscuits in the middle of the table, 'perhaps the rest of you would be happy to leave. I know you're all busy. If Rachel and Cliff could give me just a few moments longer. Thank you all so much.' He slotted his glasses back into the dent on his nose and examined the end of his pencil while the other directors trooped out.

'The Mallarmé Christmas weekend thing. I'd like Cliff to be involved.'

'Whatever for?' For the last five years Rachel had organised what she jokingly called her annual 'bonding session' with Frank Alder, when sixteen representatives from the client and agency were invited to spend two days billeted in a country hotel, getting to know each other over pleasant food and hearty, fashionable activities like go-cart racing and clay pigeon shooting. It had been Rachel's idea in the first place, after a dicey year in which client–agency relations had grown dangerously strained over a botched launch of a product that turned out to cause allergic rashes if used too generously on dry skins. The first weekend had been such a success that it was now a regular feature in the hectic December schedule.

Cliff Weybourne, blinking expressionless eyes at the print of Impressionist waterlilies above Rachel's head, remained silent. His eyelashes were very short, Rachel noticed, hardly visible at all.

Alan Jarvis was firm. 'You're right, they are expanding rapidly. I don't want them giving business to other agencies. Cliff has a lot of experience launching new products in this market. I think it would be useful for him to get to know some of the Mallarmé team.'

'They can have lunch, then. I'll arrange it.'

'Rachel, Rachel,' Alan Jarvis's tone was growing weary. He had been in the business long enough to know that women were more prone to displays of emotion than men, but he was not in the mood for pussyfooting around feelings, especially not Rachel Elliot's, a lady with enough experience to know better. 'Rachel, I forbid you to take this personally. It's pure business sense. By all means introduce them beforehand if you want to, my dear. But that weekend is in Cliff's diary and I want it to stay there.'

She hated it when he called her 'my dear', the element of patronage in his tone redolent not just of his ultimate, inarguable seniority, but also of his maleness. There was no equivalent to a 'my dear' for any of the men who sat round that table, she thought furiously, stacking her papers to hide the tremble in her hands.

'And there's to be no ill-feeling about this, Rachel. You know as well as I do that any whiff of dissension in the home ranks can be the cause of the most terrible trouble.'

'No ill-feeling at all, Alan.' Her eyes glittered. 'I'll tell Frank Alder immediately. He'll be thrilled.'

'As indeed am I, Rachel.' Cliff Weybourne extended his hand across the table, reaching so far that the swell of his belly rested on its polished surface. Rachel accepted the hand without meeting the triumphant gaze of the small black eyes. Her dislike of the man intensified in those moments, extending beyond professional distrust of his motives and methods, to something infinitely more personal and instinctive. She squeezed the fat fingers only briefly, before slipping free and leaving the room.

Stuck to her desk was a yellow post-it note in Melissa's writing.

'*Will Raphael called again. No message.*'

'Damn,' Rachel murmured, screwing the piece of paper up into a tiny ball and then flicking it towards an ashtray full of paper-clips. She still hadn't called back. How unforgivably rude. With fresh determination, she dug around the drawers of her desk for his number, before spotting it pinned under the pot in which she kept her pens and pencils. Photography lessons indeed, she thought, pressing the digits; who had she been trying to fool?

Impatient now to get the call over with, she took two deep breaths while waiting for the receiver to be picked up. But the rings were abruptly interrupted by a recorded message.

'This is Will. Please talk to me.' There followed a short beep, so short that Rachel found herself hesitating.

'Er . . . Rachel Elliot speaking – Steve Betts' colleague at McKenzie Cartwright. Returning your call – sorry for not having got back to you sooner – thank you so much for offering to help, but actually I've changed my mind – I mean I simply do not have time to learn about photography or anything else outside work at the moment. Sorry to have bothered you unnecessarily and . . . um . . . thanks again – very much.'

She replaced the receiver, slightly disappointed at her own incoherence, but relieved that the whole matter had at last been resolved without the potentially awkward necessity of personal contact.

She took several more deep breaths before picking up the phone again. Calling Frank Alder was going to be much harder. The man knew her well. If she was not to give away any hint of dissatisfaction with regard to Cliff Weybourne's involvement in the account, she was going to have to deliver a very tight performance indeed. Alan Jarvis was right if only in that respect alone; one hint of agency discord was enough to send clients scurrying for cover; and before you knew it all sorts of destructive rot could set in.

8

Margaret Elliot flicked the kettle switch on, waited ten seconds and then fed two slices of thick white bread into the toaster. She had been married to Henry Elliot too long to think it inconvenient or odd that it gave her husband pleasure to see the kettle boil and the toast pop at the same time. Wanting to grant her spouse the prospect of the simultaneous enjoyment of warm toast and slurpable tea was one of innumerable small rituals which had become embedded in the routine of the Elliots' daily life; using the flowered crockery at breakfast was another, the striped cups having, at some indefinable juncture in their lives, been consigned to the demands of tea-time, together with the restorative powers of two digestive biscuits, balanced on the left-hand side of the saucer, opposite the teaspoon. Cake, like church and apple crumble, was for Sundays. Deep down, Margaret Elliot acknowledged the comfort of such rituals, the way they precluded the necessity of choice-making and self-doubt. Time had to be managed very carefully, she found, especially after a certain age. The awful business of Henry's early retirement had taught her that, if nothing else. All those dreadful days of door-slamming and angry silences, underlined by the shouting but unmentioned feeling that she, Margaret Bowling, was not enough, that without the British Army to sustain him, Henry believed his life to be worthless. Echoes of such feelings, the sense of time dragging till it hurt, still reverberated at the back of her mind, reminders, if she ever needed them, that the present system, regimented and inflexible though it was, was infinitely preferable in every respect.

She gave the teabags one good stir before placing both the pot and the toast rack on the table. Though she was looking forward to seeing her daughter, she felt apprehensive too. Rachel was always so fiery and unpredictable, so prone to speak her mind. It drove Henry mad. Visits from her brothers, even now, with wives and children in tow, always seemed to pass off so much more smoothly. But then, as Margaret had said and thought many times in her life, boys were easier than girls right from the start: big appetites and big hearts. None of those impenetrable, cunning sulks which had so punctuated Rachel's girlhood; none of that baffling unhappiness, the selfish obstinacy to go her own way no matter what.

'Jam or marmalade, dear?' she asked, pouring tea into the large, bone china cup beside her husband and substituting a plate for the cereal bowl which had contained the spoonful of prunes which Henry consumed in the interests of keeping himself regular. Margaret herself had recently developed a bold preference for cod liver oil capsules to achieve the same purpose. Though it was a question she had posed most mornings of the forty-seven years of their married life, the answer was one that she had never mastered the art of anticipating.

'Jam, I think.' Henry Elliot patted his moustache with his napkin and folded the paper for a better view of the columns on the lower half. 'Blackberry.'

'Blackberry? Ah yes, there's a little left, just enough. I'll put it on the list for tomorrow.'

'Very good.'

Margaret wanted to talk about lunch, about which she was feeling increasingly nervous. In the days when Henry had been a lieutenant-colonel she had prepared meals on a grand scale as a matter of course. She had kept a red leather notebook in which she wrote the names of the guests and details of what she had served, so as to preclude the possibility of lumbering any second-time visitor with the burden of having to consume the same dish. There had been another book, too, a gift from Henry's dear mother, all about place settings and how to make napkins look like doves, and which side to serve and take away. Coming from very humble origins herself, Margaret had been quite overwhelmed by the glamour of it all, painfully aware of the importance of not letting Henry down, of not getting in the way – as bad wives were rumoured to do – of promotion. Such books were now stowed away in a plastic box on one of the spotless shelves in their spacious attic, in between Duncan's train set and Henry's camera equipment, dating back to the now unmentionable difficult patch, when cameras had been one of the many instruments taken up and abandoned during that first shocking emptiness of retirement.

Margaret spread a thin layer of marmalade across the swathe of butter she had applied to her own toast and began eating, all the while watching for a break in Henry's concentration on the headlines, a chink that would allow her in, allow her to say that she was nervous about the day. It wasn't just the thought of Rachel that made her so, for there were to be other guests too. The new vicar was coming, together with his son, whom she had heard was a delight, but whom she had only ever eyed from a distance. It was the notion of the son which now troubled her, since the invitation had been extended to him with Rachel in mind, a fact of which she feared Rachel could not fail to be aware and about which she was now having severe second thoughts. But it was so hard to stop trying, so hard to give up on hopes of happiness where one's closest family was concerned.

At the petrol station Rachel bought some flowers and a box of assorted chocolates. Though there was a distinctly autumnal chill in the air she had decided to drive with the roof down, so as to make the most of the sunshine. While waiting to sign for her purchases she fiddled with the loose corners of the green silk scarf which she had wrapped around her head to protect her hair from the wind, tucking it into the polo neck of her bottle-green jumper – a favourite old cashmere that went well with the dark caramel of her corduroy trousers. That her parents made a habit of dressing up on Sundays had always induced in her the wicked urge to do the opposite.

The man at the cash till winked when he handed Rachel her credit card and receipt. Rachel offered a weak smile in return, uncertain whether the facial gesture was friendly or lascivious. At thirty-nine it was no longer possible to be sure of one's judgement about such things. Upon reaching her car, she glanced back in his direction to see if the look had been followed up by a more sustained show of appreciation; but the man's attention was focused on his next customer. Chiding herself for caring even a little, Rachel carefully laid the freesias and chocolates on the passenger seat and continued on her way.

As she sped through the bedraggled suburbs of west London she could not help wishing that she was driving somewhere other than Gerrard's Cross, somewhere altogether more suited to the inspiring crispness of the day, the sense that life, after all, might be full of new beginnings. The thought of seeing her parents again engendered the usual mesh of complicated feelings, not the least of these being a tireless hope that this time it would go well, that this time there would be no disappointment, no sense that, deep down, they cared for nothing but themselves.

'Hello, Mother. How are you?'

'Not so bad, thank you dear.' There followed a fractional pause, a pause that seemed to embrace the whole flawed history of their relationship, as Margaret took in her daughter's appearance before holding out both arms for an embrace. 'But darling, how lovely to see you, and looking so ... so ... *fashionable* too. Flowers *and* chocolates – how sweet. Come in. Your father's in the drawing room.'

As Rachel stepped inside she was assailed by the familiar, uncategorisable scents of her childhood, together with the usual discomforting sense of not being at home. The Gerrard's Cross house, to which her parents had moved shortly after her father's retirement, had always struck her as the most soulless of resting places, not just because the house itself was of unattractive grey brick, with big, unimaginative square rooms, but also because it was surrounded by expensive, spacious residences equally lacking in interest or originality. A roost for the disappointed middle-class, Robbie had called it once, encapsulating her thoughts with that knack he sometimes had.

'Rachel, my dear.' Henry Elliot put down his pipe and levered himself out of his armchair. 'Good to see you, good to see you.' The thatch of his moustache prickled her cheek in exactly the spot it always did. The sweet smell of his tobacco hung not only in the air but also in the tweed of his jacket, in the folds of skin visible over the top of his shirt collar. He wore a dark blue and green striped tie with some military emblem stitched into the middle of it. 'Shall we have sherry now, Margaret, or wait for the others?'

'The others?'

Margaret Elliot wrung her hands under the crisp white front of her apron. 'Just the vicar. And his son.'

'I didn't know Reverend Timms had a son.'

'No, he doesn't. This is a new one. Reverend Berenson. Your father and I like him very much, don't we, Henry? Not so lively as Reverend Timms, but terribly clever. His wife passed away several years ago. Stomach cancer.'

'How sad,' Rachel murmured.

'His faith helped him through,' added her mother soulfully. She extracted her hands from their hiding place and pressed them together in a movement suggestive of prayer.

'I'll get the sherry, then,' put in Henry, using brisk tones reserved for any occasion threatened by the intrusion of sentimentality.

'Could I have wine instead? Would you mind, Dad?' Rachel shuddered at the thought of the sweet sherry which constituted her parents' favourite pre-prandial tipple. 'Only if you've a bottle going, of course. I'm really not bothered.'

'We've got the one for lunch . . .' began Margaret, casting a questioning look at her husband.

'No matter, no matter. I'll fetch another from the cellar.'

'No honestly, I'll leave it. Please, don't go to any trouble, Dad.'

But her father was already on his way to examine his precious wine stocks, under the guise of wanting to please, but the set of his body telling Rachel that, only minutes after her arrival in the house, old rhythms were re-establishing themselves, that no matter how she hoped and tried, there would never be any escape from the repressive cycles which had spun through the phases of her youth. She had her role and she was stuck with it: difficult Rachel, aged thirty-nine, going on twelve.

Reverend Berenson worked so hard at giving the impression of erudition that Rachel found herself suspecting a history of frustrated scholarliness, a shadow of a sense that deep down the vicar believed himself more suited to ministering to the needs of an Oxford college than the cultural wasteland of a suburban metropolis. While giving the impression of conversing, he in fact dominated the lunch table to an almost offensive degree, steering each subject and sentence towards his own aims, using every attempt of Rachel's to expand the dialogue as a platform for further anecdotes or expostulations of his own. Her parents clucked and swooned appreciatively, clearly happy to labour under the illusion that they were basking in the presence of an intellect far superior to their own. Their daughter, however, found herself chewing unnecessarily hard on her thin slices of roast beef, forcing herself not to step out of line and pondering bitterly on the pitiable lack of conversational energy being shown by the wordless, bespectacled, thirty-something son, so thoughtfully positioned opposite her.

There were enough established channels of contention on the subject of her single status for Rachel to perceive at once that Luke Berenson had been invited with her own interests very much in mind, and for her at the same time to manage to rise above the appalling implications behind this fact in order to defy her mother with indifference. Lack of skill or success in this particular branch of social engineering had never deterred Mrs Elliot's persistence: there had been other sons in the past, other brothers or cousins, invited along under the pretext of being granted the privilege of sampling Mrs Elliot's home cooking, but in reality to be viewed as prospective husbands for her daughter. Rachel was far too inured to these clumsy Mrs Bennet-style tactics to care. What she did not, and could not forgive her parents for, was their unshakeable belief that it was some failing in her that had resulted in the kind of life she led, that it was because no man had felt able to take her on, that caused her to remain single. On occasions they still referred regretfully to the departure of Robbie, all subsequent evidence of their daughter's love life being so paltry as to convince them that she had thrown away her best chance at twenty-five.

'Do you stay with your father often, Luke?' Rachel asked now, handing over the cream jug and using a sugary voice which she reserved for those she despised most.

He raised his eyes from an intimidatingly full bowl of stodgy raisin and apple crumble and smiled for the first time since they had all sat down. It was a nice smile too, broad enough to cause the large wire frames of his spectacles to shift position where they rested on his cheeks.

'Now and then, like any dutiful child.' His voice was flat and dry. Doing justice to the dessert presented a new pretext for absorbing all his energies. She wondered exactly how old he was. In spite of a fresh, almost cherubic face, there were wires of grey running through the sweep of sandy hair pushed back off his forehead and in the more closely shaven section just above his ears.

'Luke works in the Inner Temple,' put in Margaret, her eyes bright with admiration.

'How nice for him.' Rachel, reckless with disappointment and irritation, could feel herself in danger of being rude. 'The Inner Temple. Wow.'

'Both our boys are doctors,' put in Henry quickly, 'one in Scotland and the other in Washington DC.'

'Marvellous,' exclaimed the reverend. 'And what do you do, Rachel, to keep the wolf from the door?'

'There are no wolves at my door, reverend,' she replied, thinking for some reason of the cat. 'I work in advertising. I'm a board dir—'

'Advertising, eh?' He put down his spoon, his beady brown eyes twinkling in an unbecomingly adversarial way which put Rachel on her guard. 'That must be very . . . stimulating for you.'

'Stimulating? It's hard work, certainly.' Keep calm, she told herself, keep calm. There was no point in minding whether she impressed this man or not. It did not matter what he thought of her or her profession. She knew all the arguments backwards, having defended herself round countless tables, where people with less interesting, less well paid but traditionally more revered professions began by discussing their favourite adverts, asked her if she was responsible for any of them and then concluded with a jolly round of – invariably ill-informed – slating of the industry as a whole.

'A lot of wasted talent in advertising, so they say.'

'Do they?'

'Well, it's no secret that we've always felt Rachel could have done a lot better for herself. But there you are,' Henry folded his napkin into a neat square which he lined up exactly parallel to his place mat, 'that's children for you.'

'They will go their own way, won't they?' chimed Margaret, nodding her head at Rachel in a show of fond maternal despair.

'Thoughtless of us, isn't it,' agreed Rachel, her eyes ablaze.

'Now Rachel,' warned her father, detecting the same spirit of confrontation which had prompted defiant nocturnal cot-clambering some thirty-eight years before.

'I'd love to be in advertising,' said Luke Berenson, quietly, but with great determination. 'Those beer ones are my favourite, the ones with the eskimo and the talking polar bear. Brilliant. Have me in stitches every time. I don't care whether it sells more of the stuff, it's like comedy in its own right.'

'Thank you,' breathed Rachel, sinking back into her chair, forcing herself to remain calm.

At which point their spiritual elder, clearly unimpressed by the turn the conversation was taking, embarked upon a short account of his passion for the writings of Matthew Arnold, concluding with a recitation of the final stanza from 'Dover Beach'. Throughout this discourse Rachel noticed how Luke concentrated on arranging his spoon and fork over the top of a wedge of uneaten pudding, pushing down hard, as if hoping to compress the remains out of sight entirely.

Margaret Elliot, apparently not having witnessed anything to discourage the prospect of a relationship between her daughter and the vicar's son, suggested that the 'young ones' take themselves on a walk, while the less advantaged supped a glass of port. It reminded Rachel of being commandeered to play as a child, usually with a strange and unfriendly-looking counterpart, as if having fun was something that could be taken up and dispensed with at will, without effort or cost or inspiration.

But it was wonderful to get out of the house. Luke led the way down the narrow gravel path to the front gate, his hands thrust deep into the pockets of his blue chino trousers, his shoulders and neck hunched, as if in preparation for a low-beamed door. When he reached the pavement he stopped and waited for her to catch up. Behind them Margaret waved before closing the door.

'Christ, I'm sorry.' He shook his head miserably. 'Insufferable. I should never have agreed to come. Sorry.'

Rachel, delighted by the revelation of emotions that matched her own, burst out laughing. 'Oh sod them all. Let's walk.'

'And he got poor old Matthew Arnold all wrong,' he added, as they set off down the street, scuffling through the shallow trail of curling brown leaves. 'He always says "vast edges blear" instead of "drear" – it drives me nuts every time. But there's no point in saying anything. He won't listen. He never does. Never has. Too many sermons perhaps,' he muttered, kicking a stone. 'Too much time telling other people how to live their lives.'

They walked on in silence for a bit. The air was thick with the sweet smell of rotting leaves. Rachel concentrated on her breathing, matching each exhalation to every stride, restraining herself from an eager concurrence with these opinions. In her experience criticising parents was the prerogative of their children. Outsiders had to be very careful indeed.

'I suppose I was invited for you, sort of thing,' he said at length.

She grinned, in spite of herself. 'Yes, I think that just about sums it up.'

'Sorry.'

'I wish you'd stop apologising. It's hardly your fault. Although I'm nearly forty my mother has retained the flattering habit of regarding me as a reluctant wallflower who needs help filling her dance card. Dad's not much better. I should apologise to you. Parents like mine are a rare treat.'

Having crossed several tree-lined roads, they arrived at some railings guarding a large rectangle of green, the near corner of which housed a metal climbing frame in the shape of a pirate ship. A wet start to October had allowed the grass to recover some lushness after the ravages of a peculiarly tropical summer, while the foliage of the trees skirting its edges blinked prettily with spots of red and burnished gold.

'There's just one snag,' remarked Luke, holding open the gate for her and standing to one side to let her through, 'of which I suspect your mother is unaware.'

'One snag to what?'

'To any joyful coupling that she may have in mind.'

'And what's that?'

It was his turn to laugh, all the strains of lunch clearly far from his mind. 'I'm gay.'

Rachel slapped her thigh and let out a whoop of mirth. 'Oh great – oh I love it – that has absolutely made my day – I'd give anything to tell her.'

His face crumpled with dismay. 'I'd rather you didn't . . .'

'Don't worry.' She swallowed the laugh at once, reading genuine alarm in his sombre brown eyes. 'Of course I won't. I wouldn't dream of breathing a word.'

As they strolled round the perimeter of the playing field, half under the verdant awning of trees, a quieter mood settled upon them, bringing with it a quite unexpected sense of intimacy.

'My mother would have understood, but I hadn't come to terms with it myself when she was alive. As for my father . . . well you saw for yourself. I've done my best for him – I don't really like the law, but it earns me a good living and it keeps him of my back. I'd really like to be a nurse – something more caring – though I know it sounds corny and you're probably creasing up inside.'

'No, no I'm not at all. There are heaps of things I could never say to my parents, things they could never understand . . .'

'Like?'

'Like I'm nearly forty and I want a child but not a husband.'

'Brilliant. Go for it.'

She stopped and turned. 'I'm going to.' She laughed, brushing the hair back from her eyes and shaking her face at the wintry blue sky. 'I'm really going to.'

They arrived at the pirate ship just as a cluster of whining children were being herded back out into the street. Luke climbed to the top of the metal ladder-cum-mast and swung himself out to one side, holding on with only one arm. 'You can buy brochures on genetically suitable partners these days, can't you?'

Rachel, who was leaning up against the rungs beneath him, secretly marvelling at the looseness of her tongue before a virtual stranger, caught herself grappling with the impulse to say even more. But at the same time she distrusted it.

'I have a suitable partner in mind, actually . . .' she ventured.

'That's lucky.' He began to clamber down.

The sun seemed to be pulling back from the world, not so much lowering itself as withdrawing, taking with it what was left of the warmth of the afternoon. Rachel shivered and burrowed her hands into the sleeves of her jumper, the fingers of each hand gripping the wrists of the other for warmth. 'I could not do it the clinical way,' she began. 'I . . . I don't know why, I just . . . couldn't.' She shuddered. 'Not my style.'

'I suppose you are sure, are you? I mean, there might be other reasons why—'

'Absolutely sure,' she cut in at once, riled by this odd combination of timidity and presumption. 'I've always been one to know my own mind.'

'Yes, I can believe that all right,' he murmured, his eyes twinkling behind the large circles of his glasses.

'And I have every reason to believe that I shall succeed. We Elliot women are very fertile, you know,' she declared stoutly, shaking her hands free of her jumper sleeves and blowing on her fingers. 'My mother,' she added with a scowl, 'has been known to take pleasure in reminding me of the fact.'

'Your mother . . . there's an intriguing thought. How will she take it, do you suppose?'

'My mother will be appalled. So will my father.'

'You're braver than me,' he said quietly, linking his arm through hers as they walked back to the park gate. 'I've got friends who have told their parents they're homosexual and, with a few beautiful exceptions, it's been very hard for all concerned. My . . . my partner was one of the lucky ones. His parents are wonderful.'

'Does he work in the Inner Temple too?' she asked, mimicking the hallowed tones adopted earlier on by her mother, in the hope of erasing some of the seriousness from his face.

'He died.'

'Oh dear, I'm so sorry.' She looked at her feet, cursing herself for being inept, for not reading the signs with more care.

'Yeah, so am I. Not yet ready to talk about it, I'm afraid. Not cross or anything. Just can't talk.'

She saw that he was swallowing and looked away.

'Better get back.'

'Yeah.'

'I'll tell my parents we fell in love and want a spring wedding.'

He chuckled at that, but did not look at her again.

By the time they arrived back at the dejected remains of a fuschia that tumbled along the low wall bordering her parents' front garden, Luke had recovered his composure. Rachel plucked off one of the drooping crimson flowers and squeezed it between her fingers. 'Er . . . thank you,' she muttered, flicking the crushed petals to the ground, 'usually my role is something akin to the Marj Proops of middle-class England. I don't tell people things.'

Behind him the sun was just sinking below the roofs of the houses on the opposite side of the street, illuminating their edges with a fiery orange glow. The effect was to make Luke look paler than ever, and much younger suddenly. Clearly embarrassed by the compliment, he took off his glasses and began polishing them on the baggy hem of his jumper. His eyes were a pretty almond shape, she noticed, trimmed with absurdly long sandy lashes.

'Well, we made friends, didn't we?' he remarked, slipping his glasses back on and leading the way up the path. 'Just like we were supposed to. And no hanky panky at all,' he added with a chuckle.

'There's still time,' she said, the sight of her mother's pale face bobbing behind a curtain, stirring her, as always, towards mischief.

9

I have decided to have a child.

Rachel had been avoiding her diary for days, deterred by some deep reflexive fear of committing such an enormous decision to the concrete whiteness of the page. Even now she had deliberately picked a moment that was hurried, a snatched slot of time before the door bell went, heralding the appearance of Anita with that striking swathe of grey ripping through the middle of her short black hair – the twins' calling card, she liked to call it – and that worryingly hysterical enthusiasm at having escaped her family.

Rachel paused, aware, as always, that she wrote for an invisible audience, one that heard and judged. It was important to sound lucid.

I have decided to ask Nathan to do the honours (!) when we meet in a few weeks' time on my way to Bermuda. The timing of the Mallarmé shoot really couldn't be more convenient . . . I can't help feeling confident – utterly sure – that I am doing the right thing. This flat will accommodate a baby very easily, and a nanny too. It will be nice to have . . . but there she stopped and put a line through the last six words. She had written enough. What mattered was the decision itself, not the labyrinthine, ineluctable emotions that had prompted it. She thrust the book to one side and let out a great sigh. It would be so much easier when she was pregnant, when everything was to be done rather than thought about. Waiting for things to happen was always hateful.

Thanks to a double dose of chickenpox visited upon the poor twins, the rendezvous with Anita had been postponed to a Friday evening in late October. Rachel had been writing her diary in the sitting room, having had a quick shower and changed into black leggings and an electric-blue polo neck jumper that hung almost to her knees. The colour brought out the shimmers of blue in her irises, the softness engrained in the steely grey. Her hair, she noted wistfully, while trying to comb some sense into it in front of the bathroom mirror, was in need of attention again: the streaks of blonde were growing out already and the swept-back shape was now too heavy to stay in place for long. A similar exasperation earlier in the week had prompted the unprecedented purchase of some aerosol hairspray, an expensive gold-canned product promising 'natural body and hold', which had since between consigned to the bin. Its fragrant mist had settled upon her hair with quite unnatural efficacy, bestowing the kind of lifeless sheen which Rachel had always disparagingly associated with wigs. To make up for her hair she had spent longer than usual on her eyes, drawing a careful line of blue across the top of her lids and then painstakingly teasing out her long fine lashes with some black mascara. It was not for Anita's benefit that she took such trouble, but for her own. If she couldn't face herself in the mirror, she certainly couldn't face anyone else.

On the low table at one end of the sofa was a glass of water from which Rachel sipped absently, doing little more than wetting her lips. She had wanted a proper drink, but had somehow found herself deterred from the idea of indulging alone by suspicions about the possibility of Anita's renewed acquaintance with the bottle. While fearing the worst, she none the less hoped for the best. Over the last five years or so Anita's behaviour towards drink had displayed the spasms of absolute love or hate that are the preserve of the true addict. It was impossible to know what to expect, which part of the downward or upward curve she would be riding on any particular day.

Supper had been selected from the extensive freezer section of an expensive supermarket during her lunch hour. The chore of shopping had been exacerbated by particularly rebellious trolley wheels and an inability to focus. Segments of time whizzed by while Rachel found herself standing dazed and confounded before chests of microwaveable feasts and aisles of bread and vegetables. Colours and prices swarmed in a blur of nonsense, while her hands hovered over items and then lost their nerve. Never having taken much pleasure over the purchase of food, the realisation that she was dawdling ineffectually, that an activity which normally took her fifteen minutes was taking five times that long, was disturbing. As a result she bought much more than she needed to, coping with the inability to choose by selecting several things where one would have done as well. In the queue at the checkout Rachel eyed her full trolley with something like incredulity, examining the contents as she sometimes did a stranger's, as if a perusal of the packets and tins on which individuals chose to sustain themselves might offer up a glimpse of their personalities, a taste of the private domestic dramas being enacted in their homes. Anyone studying her own groceries, she thought ruefully, would assume she was feeding a large family with expensive tastes, a lack of interest in cooking and a collective penchant for unusual bread-types.

In front of her a chinless barrel of an infant was seizing each thing as it was placed on the conveyor belt and hurling it back into the trolley, while its mother smiled, shaking her head at the checkout girl, clearly too overcome by love to muster the energy for reprimand.

'He loves shopping,' she murmured, catching Rachel's eye.

Rachel offered a generous smile in return, inwardly marvelling at the separation of emotions in her own heart, at the way she could feel such determination to produce a child herself and at the same time experience nothing but guarded revulsion for the toddler wedged into the trolley in front of her.

She was truly astonished at quite how many babies and pregnant mothers now seemed to populate the world. Having until recently passed prams and pushchairs with unseeing or, at best, impatient eyes, it now felt as if they were everywhere, as if some shadowy force was bent upon reminding her at every possible moment of every day, of the new avenue down which her instincts were being drawn.

Common sense had prompted Rachel that afternoon – albeit reluctantly – to take the precaution of booking herself an appointment with a Harley Street gynaecologist, deliberately taking her custom to a doctor completely unacquainted with the history of her life or her body. She wanted a straightforward analysis, without the burden of chit-chat or judgements of any kind. She would get enough of that from other sources, she thought dryly, bending to retrieve a large bag of fresh spinach which the porky-faced child had slung at her feet. Imagining her parents' mutual horror at their daughter managing to produce a baby but not a husband, made Rachel smile with fear and then hate herself the instant after. She had never pleased them in anything; how puerile to think she could change the habit of a lifetime now; how belittling even to care.

A selection of boxes and one loaf of red-pepper bread now sat beside the sleek, black-faced microwave in Rachel's kitchen. Seven minutes to produce four exotic dishes. Not bad at all. She checked the cooking instructions for the third time and then pressed the replay button on her answering machine. There were a series of promising clicks but only one short message.

'Will Raphael speaking. What do you mean, you've changed your mind?'

His voice was low, and teasingly indignant. Almost as if he'd sensed the relief behind the delivery of her message and was deliberately making complications.

'Bloody cheek,' she exclaimed out loud, before pulling out the bottle of Chablis she had wedged into the freezer half an hour before and filling up one of the two empty glasses that sat beside a bread basket full of coral-coloured poppadums. 'I mean I've changed my mind,' she declared to the machine. 'I'm too busy. Period.'

These one-sided expostulations were interrupted by the door buzzer.

When Rachel leant forward to greet her, Anita took a dramatic leap backwards, making a big show of trumpeting into a handkerchief and waving her hands across her face. 'Horrible head cold,' she sniffed, flapping the hanky and shaking her head. 'Only thing keeping me going is whisky and Disprin. Been like it all week. Think it's connected to the chickenpox but can't prove a thing.'

Rachel, who lived with the firm conviction that people with horrible head colds or any similar afflictions should not be so generous as to consider stepping beyond the quarantined confines of their own homes, instinctively shuffled backwards.

Then she remembered that Anita was almost certainly drinking again and that alcoholics, especially lapsed ones with a history of broken resolutions to their credit, could be fantastically cunning. She found herself studying her friend's nose for signs of handkerchief abuse and listening out for a telltale nasal twang. But Anita's nostrils looked markedly untroubled, as did the rest of her face – her eyes black and clear, her skin its usual alabaster, a fashionable pallor which she liked to heighten by the application of garish lipstick. The handkerchief, meanwhile, looked decidedly unglued and fresh.

'Whisky and Disprin, eh?' she remarked, her heart softening as it always did when she actually saw Anita instead of just thought about her.

'I hope you're not going to be a bully, because I don't think I could bear it.'

Rachel opened the door wider and stood to one side. 'No, I'm not in the mood. How does Chablis and Disprin sound?'

'Just to be here is bliss,' sighed Anita, stuffing the handkerchief into the side pocket of her red woollen jacket and stepping into the hall with a look of grateful awe across her face. Rachel, pleased to see her pleased, as always, led the way through into the sitting room, where Anita promptly flung herself into one end of the sofa with a theatrical sigh, throwing one arm along its smooth leather back. 'You look so well, Rachel – I always say blue is your best colour – so sickeningly unstressed, so unlike the rest of us cronies. I'm in need of a *very* long moan by the way, I hope you don't mind. Giles has plummeted new depths of irascibility and uncooperativeness – is that a word? – and the twins have picked every scab they can reach and are bound to be scarred for life. I don't mind about Eddie so much – scars can be quite becoming on a man, don't you think? – but Laura, with that version of Giles's nose for a plonker, is going to need every bit of help she can get. And, just to cap it all, your goddaughter is being monstrous. Firstly,' she held up her fingers to count off the points, 'she has declared herself to be jealous of the twins' spots – of all things. Secondly, she wants hair as long as a poisonous child called Nigella, whose mother clearly has nothing better to do in the mornings than weave horribly impeccable French plaits, and thirdly, she flew into a tantrum about my coming to see you. I'd have slit my wrists days ago if I'd thought Giles could cope with the mess. Can you believe little Charlotte thinking, at the ripe old age of six, that she's every right to join me for dinner with her godmother? After an early Christmas present I expect, the little vixen.'

Anita's habit of putting down her own children, a form of self-deprecation once removed which Rachel associated with the more keenly disappointed of her friends, could at times be quite entertaining. She smiled, as she was meant to, at the same time handing over a glass of wine and sitting down next to her. 'Dinner's just an electromagnetic wave or two away from being edible. Tell me when you're hungry and I'll press the necessary buttons. It's good to see you,' she said with genuine warmth, 'it's been far too long as usual. Sounds as though things have been rather tough.'

'Pure hell,' agreed Anita, with a cheerful grin. 'I even suffered the humiliation of having my latest piece sent back . . .' She pressed her lips together hard, faintly smudging the neat outline of her lipstick. 'Fucking embarrassing actually.' She glowered at her drink. 'What a boring subject, though. I mean, leisure centres, I ask you – no wonder I came up with a load of crap.' She let out a loose throaty laugh for which she had once been famous, and raised her glass. 'Sod them all.'

Rachel laughed too, refreshed and comforted as always by Anita's frank admission that life was hard and full of disappointment. It made a welcome change from the usual human predilection – of which Rachel knew herself to be guilty – for exaggerating one's state of happiness. Why was it, she wondered, taking a sip of wine, that humans so often felt the need to present a bold front to each other, as if happiness was not an emotion but a measure of success?

'And how are you Rachel, how are things?'

'Not bad.' She beamed, tucking her legs up to one side of her and resting her glass on her knees. Anita, she noticed, had not yet touched her own drink, but was fiddling with the stem and running her index finger round the rim.

'Oh God, what the—' Anita jerked forwards, spilling a few drops of wine on her lap, as the cat, appearing from nowhere, landed beside her arm. Unperturbed by Anita's shriek, it began massaging the soft leather with its paws, clearly sizing up the possibilities of claiming a seat on the sofa itself. 'I didn't know you had acquired a pet,' she gasped, putting one hand to her chest as if to steady her breathing. 'Gave me such a fright.' She swigged from her glass. 'Sorry. Phew! That's better. Nice puss. What's your name? Mind my bloody drink.' The cat was now making its way towards Rachel, picking its way daintily through an obstacle course of bags and cushions.

Not having seen the animal since its one night stay several weeks before, Rachel was quite as surprised as Anita. 'The little devil. It must have slipped in when I opened the front door just now.' She stroked the soft fur, feeling its back arch in appreciation. 'It's not mine at all. It must belong to a neighbour. I'll put it out.'

'Oh no, don't. He's rather fine.' Anita reached out to rub the cat under one ear. It leant towards her, its wide face set in an inviting grin. 'I'd say he's got some Persian in him – look at the shape of his face and that wonderfully fluffy tail.'

'How do you know it's a him?'

Anita pursed her lips and made a squeaky noise aimed at reclaiming the attention of their intruder, who had straightened itself and was now walking round in small circles on Rachel's lap. 'Of course he's a he – all butch and pleased with himself, like any normal male.' She chuckled. 'Though if you think I'm going to check you've got another think coming – have you seen the size of those claws?'

'Ow, yes.' Rachel stood up, tipping the animal to the floor, where it recovered its composure huffily, before stalking over to the rug on which it had curled up on its previous visit. 'I'll catch him. You open the door.'

'Oh, let's leave him for a bit. He's not doing any harm.' Anita bent down and began crooning again, holding out her hand while the cat cocked its head in a show of playing hard to get. 'Cats are fine, so long as you're not pregnant of course. There's this disease you can get,' she went on, warming to her subject, 'I did an article on it once – toxoplasmosis – symptoms like flu and nothing to worry about so long as you don't happen to be carrying a foetus inside you. Hardly something which is likely to worry you.' She returned her attentions to the cat which was now lying on its back with a dreamy look in its eyes. 'What a flirt,' she laughed, 'just look at him—'

'Why, what happens if you're pregnant?'

'Oh, everything. Blindness, encephalitis, brain damage – a real picnic. Comes from the faeces apparently,' she concluded cheerfully, leaving the cat and picking up her glass before going over to study an impressive black-and-white photograph of a suspension bridge, which hung above the mantelpiece. Behind her, Rachel sneaked a wary look at her uninvited guest, who closed one eye.

'I've always loved this – all those luxuriant shadows and elegant lines – so simple and yet so refined. Hey,' she spun round, 'weren't you going to do a photography course or something? Have you started yet?'

'Oh, I changed my mind,' replied Rachel airily, her thoughts still on brain-damaged foetuses and whether Anita might be doing her thing of exaggerating a story for effect. 'Work is ridiculously hectic at the moment. Everybody always uses Christmas as the deadline by which they want everything and then of course I've got my trip to America and Bermuda for that shoot I told you about—'

'It's a hard life eh, Rachel?'

'You know as well as I do it's not as glamorous as it sounds . . .'

'Oh, do I?' Anita raised her dark eyebrows and then dangled her empty glass. 'Any more of this?'

'Heaps. Let's eat, too.'

The two women retreated into the kitchen, leaving the cat curled in a ball before the authentically darting flames of Rachel's coal-gas fire, watched over by a photograph on the mantelpiece – a much darker-haired, rounder-faced version of Rachel which Robbie had immortalised with an instamatic and which had somehow established itself as one of the immovable archives with which she lived.

Not long afterwards, without exactly intending to, Rachel found herself crossing the invisible border into that alluring territory where not even the prospect of a hangover is enough to deter the refilling of a glass. It had been a long time since she got drunk. A very long time. And Anita was the best of drinking partners, since, regardless of her problems, she had a famous capacity for arriving at a point of happy intoxication and staying there for a long time before toppling less happily down the other side. It was, as always, unwise and certainly – given Anita's history – irresponsible. But it felt that night as if it was the only way in which she was truly going to relax herself; so much was bottled up inside, none of it was going to be uncorked without a bit of help.

As it turned out, things were uncorked on every front, spurred on by a second bottle of Chablis – less chilled than the first but consumed even more quickly – and Rachel's eventual impatience with the subject of Anita's unsatisfactory home life. Timid of confessing outright to her recent decisions about her own future, Rachel did her best to steer the conversation in the right direction, hoping Anita might work things out for herself.

But Anita was in no mood for working out anything. 'Christ, I need a cigarette,' she declared, ignoring Rachel's second throwaway remark about late motherhood and sighing deeply at the desire – invariably experienced some way through the second bottle – for nicotine. She began rummaging furiously through her handbag.

'You just say children are awful because you've got some.'

'They are awful.' She punched her bag with both fists. 'Shit.'

'Well, perhaps I'm not prepared to take your word for it.'

'Is there an off-licence round here?' Anita seized her purse and then put it down again, very slowly. 'What did you say?'

'I said,' Rachel repeated, 'perhaps I am no longer prepared to take your word for it.'

Anita folded her arms and frowned, sticking out her jaw like Giles sometimes did when defending one of his lefty political viewpoints. 'I hope that doesn't mean what I think it means.'

'And what do you think it means?'

'That you might, possibly, be considering, at some stage, having a child.'

'Of course I bloody well might. And I think it's bloody arrogant of you to assume otherwise.'

Anita let out a laugh of undisguised incredulity. 'You can hardly blame me for that, Rachel my dearest.' She pushed her handbag to one side and leant across the table. 'All that matters,' she went on more tenderly, 'is that you don't make a mistake.'

Her lipstick was still vibrantly red, Rachel noticed, an observation which deflected her outrage for a moment, making her wonder, tipsily, what component made it so resistant to napkins and food, and whether it came off on the rare occasion that she embraced her husband. They hadn't made love for three months, she had confided earlier on, a typical Anita-style revelation which had left Rachel secretly marvelling at the fact that she probably had sex more often than many women with partners resident in the same bed.

'You would be mad, quite mad, to have a child, Rachel,' Anita was declaring now. 'Children are parasites from the word go. You would go grey overnight, you would lose that sylph-like figure, you would lose – most important of all – your independence. You may have sufficient funds to employ the best nanny that money can buy, but it's not that simple, believe me. You would feel torn in two. You would long to get away, to work, to anywhere – for peace, for sanity and all the elements of life that you now take for granted. And yet you would feel the compulsion to stay at home too, not just because your breasts have swollen to the size of ripe watermelons, but also thanks to that mysterious, damnable bond which ensures that every reproductive female on this planet drags a millstone of guilt round her neck every time she absents herself from the little darlings for more than a nanosecond. Nannies do not solve this problem. You have a perfect life Rachel. Do not, I repeat, do not, fuck it up now.'

'Well, thank you for your support, Anita.' Rachel's voice was breathy with indignation. 'I'll bear all that in mind, of course. How could I not, since you are such an unarguably fine representative of motherhood, so intimately acquainted with its challenges, so admirably on top of things.' She picked up the second empty wine bottle and marched with it to the bin, knowing that Anita would know what she meant by the gesture, knowing that it would cut deep. 'I'll keep my ideas to myself in future,' she muttered, thinking suddenly of Luke Berenson and the absurd fact that she had received more emotional encouragement from a total stranger than from one of her oldest friends.

'We can't change what we are,' said Anita fiercely, fighting her corner with a last flutter of energy which even Rachel, through her fury, recognised as bordering on the courageous.

'Oh yes we can.' Her voice was all determination and hope, very quiet. 'We can. We can be what we want to be, every one of us. Otherwise . . . otherwise there's no point.'

'Maybe.' Anita hung her head in defeat. She longed for one more drink, but did not dare to ask. 'I'm going to buy some cigarettes,' she mumbled, thinking that at the same time she could treat herself to a little something, just a couple of swigs to see her through till bedtime. 'Shall I take a taxi home afterwards?'

'No, no.' Rachel shook her head wearily. 'Of course not, you twit. I'll leave the door on the latch. And Anita,' she looked at the floor. 'Sorry if I've been mean. I'm all uptight at the moment . . .'

'Me too. It's just that . . . you know I love the children, you know I'd die for them, but at times . . . at times they've almost destroyed me too. I would hate to see you crushed by anything, Rachel, you're so strong, it wouldn't be right.'

'Go and get your fags, before you have me in tears. I'll put on the coffee. Oh, Anita, just cigarettes, eh, there's a good girl. We're drunk enough already.'

. 'Sure,' she replied, thinking that one of those airplane-style mini-bottles could be despatched on the way back, and that, for by no means the first time in her life, the famous undetectability of vodka was a blessing indeed.

10

While Rachel knew that some of the best gynaecologists in the world were reputed to be male, she had always preferred any scrutiny of the more private areas of her body to be undertaken by women. Anita, who raved about the swarthy Latin looks of the doctor at her local family planning clinic, took a rather different view. 'People make judgements about each other all the time, whatever they do,' she claimed. 'Doctors of either sex will secretly be deciding whether someone is fat or pretty, just like the rest of us do. Wear your best frock and enjoy it, that's my attitude.'

'But it's not mine,' murmured Rachel to herself as she slipped out of the office in the middle of the morning in order to keep her appointment in Harley Street. Once safely settled inside the cab, she pulled out her mobile from the side pocket of her handbag and dialled her own number at work.

'Melissa, it's me. I had to pop out for something – decided I'd better tell you in case you thought I'd got locked in a lavatory or a lift. It's some family business. Nothing terrible or urgent.'

'Fine,' replied her secretary, secretly wondering what kind of business could crop up so unexpectedly without being either of those things. 'Will you be back in time for your three o'clock?'

'Oh goodness, yes. And remember, tea as well as coffee, and see if you can rustle up some of those biscuits we had last week, the ones with the raisins in – Frank Alder ate nearly the entire plateful.' It was the final pre-production meeting before the shoot in Bermuda and her client was showing typical last-minute nerves about details which had been agreed for weeks. The film required the services of two models, one black and one white, lying side by side on their stomachs in the shallows of a beach. They were to be topless, but not exuberantly so. While the question of degrees of nudity seemed at last to have been settled, there were fresh worries about the chosen colours for the bikini bottoms. Rachel had promised to try a couple more options, but was fearful that too great a choice would only lead to greater indecision.

Though tedious, the inevitable bustle of sorting out such last-minute issues was providing a welcome distraction from other, less controllable aspects of office life. Ever since her minor showdown with Cliff Weybourne, Rachel had been suffering the disquieting sense that she was being edged out of the sphere of influence to which she had grown accustomed. That there was no tangible evidence for these suspicions, nothing she could quite put her finger on, only made it worse. Meanwhile, the matter of the new departmental head was still unresolved, an unnecessary prevarication which Rachel felt was bad for the agency as a whole, but about which – given her overtly personal interest in the matter – she felt it would be inappropriate to complain.

'And check my plane tickets are on the way, could you Melissa? I'd prefer to get my hands on them days as opposed to hours before take-off.'

'Will do. See you later.'

Rachel slipped her phone into her bag and leant her head back against the weathered upholstery of the cab. The prospect of getting away was growing increasingly attractive. America. Nathan. Her stomach tightened. Bermuda. Lots of work, but sunshine and luxury too. The hotel looked spectacular. It could be brilliant.

Thinking again of her appointment, she crossed her legs. Anything to do with gleaming metal instruments and smells of disinfectant made Rachel sicker at heart than most. While her mother liked to blame it on a prolonged stay in hospital for a life-threatening bout of double pneumonia at the age of five, Rachel herself believed that it went much deeper than that, that a fear of medical practices was something she had been born with, like grey eyes and having a second toe longer than a first. If anything, her phobia had grown worse over the years: doctors, with all their intimate knowledge of corporeal failings and functions, made her feel ignorant, and therefore vulnerable. Nothing, in Rachel's experience, was quite so disempowering as ignorance: it removed the possibility of judgement and choice; it made people pliant and afraid.

'So, Miss Elliot, you want to have a baby.' The leathery round face of the doctor, with its androgenous clumps of thick grey hair, was not what Rachel had been expecting at all. She's not my kind of woman, she thought at once, her heart sinking as she extended her hand to meet the hearty grip. She waited for instructions to remove her clothes, eyeing with distaste the white pallet of a bed poking out from behind the half open door of an adjoining room.

'Cup of tea? I'm having one.'

'Tea? Well – oh yes – thank you.'

A tray of cups and a small teapot was brought in by a young girl in a tartan skirt and red jumper.

'And no calls, thank you, Jennifer,' instructed Doctor Abbot, proceeding to pour tea and offer sugar, behaving for all the world as if they were two cosy members of a WI group, meeting for a chat about church flowers and the takings on the last bring-and-buy sale.

'I'm quite pushed for time . . .' Rachel began.

'And so am I, Miss Elliot, I assure you. But when it comes to discussing babies I have all the time in the world. Congratulations, by the way. It is a wonderfully exciting thing to want a child. You must be very pleased with yourself.'

Rachel, caught off guard by such kind enthusiasm, found a lump blocking her throat. 'Thank you,' she managed, blinking hard.

Dr Abbot pushed the tea closer and selected a pen from a small ceramic pot beside her telephone. 'Now, as you probably expected, there are certain questions I need to ask in order to carry out the check-up that you have requested. Lots of women don't bother, you know, which does make things difficult if they run into problems. This way we can bash anything on the head before it gets out of hand. You look quite splendidly fit, so I'm sure we'll whizz through most of this.' She tapped her pen on the pile of papers in front of her. 'But let's get the basics out of the way first.'

Rachel began undoing the buttons of her shirt.

'That won't be necessary, Miss Elliot. If you could just roll up your sleeve. That's it. Perfect. There we are. This might get to feel a little tight, that's all.' She studied her watch for a few moments before and after pumping. 'Blood pressure fine. Now let's get you on the scales. Slip your shoes off. Lovely. Could do with a few more pounds on you, but not to worry. Off you get now. Thank you. And now I'll need a sample of your urine. I don't ask people while they're in the waiting room; I always think it can be embarrassing – disappearing into the loo with a plastic jar and having to come out again.' She handed Rachel a plastic bag containing a conical see-through pot with a lid and showed her to a toilet adjoining the consulting room. 'Take your time,' she called cheerily, as Rachel closed the door. 'I know it doesn't always happen the moment you want it to.'

When Rachel reappeared the doctor was back behind her desk, spectacles on the top of her broad nose, bat-wing handwriting flying across a page.

'Splendid. Good girl. I'll give that to my nurse while we finish our chat.'

The questions were mostly quite straightforward, as indeed were Rachel's answers. Yes, her periods had always been regular; yes she did notice vaginal discharge about halfway through her cycle; no she was not taking any kind of drugs; no she didn't smoke; yes she kept to a sensible diet. The warm tea and Dr Abbot's cosy approach made it very easy, so easy that even when the difficult questions came they were not nearly as hard to answer as she had feared.

'Do you have any children?'

'No.' The pen scurried as they talked.

'Have you been pregnant before?'

Rachel cleared her throat before answering. 'Yes. When I was twenty-two. I had an abortion at nine weeks.'

'Any pain or bleeding afterwards?'

'A little . . . not much pain, a bit of blood.'

'Anything that required antibiotics to sort out?'

Rachel shook her head, reliving for a second the brilliant relief of stepping out of the sterile whiteness of the clinic into the afternoon sunshine, how beautifully unencumbered she had felt, how free.

'Nearly there.' Dr Abbot peered over the top of her glasses and delivered the most heartwarming of smiles. 'Experience has taught me that every question, even the most obvious, has to be asked. I have had women begging to be referred to infertility clinics when the only thing wrong was their technique. The human body is blessed with several orifices; some people get quite confused as to quite what to do with them all.'

Rachel couldn't help laughing out loud, though the doctor restricted herself to a broad smile.

'Right. Where were we? . . . Ah yes. Do you have a partner?'

'Yes.' Rachel felt the blood ebb from her cheeks. Suddenly the room didn't seem quite so warm after all. Lying to this woman did not come naturally. But the idea of the truth scared her too; it would sound too calculated, too weird. And she did have a partner. Nathan. And yes, he was healthy, non-smoking and all those other things that mattered as far as the doctor was concerned.

'Has he fathered a child before?'

'No.'

'Does he ejaculate inside you?'

It was hard not to squirm. 'Yes.'

'Common problem,' the doctor murmured, 'you'd be surprised.'

Suddenly it was over. Dr Abbot pushed her pad of paper to one side and came round to perch on the side of her desk.

'It all sounds marvellous.'

'The . . . the abortion doesn't matter, then?'

She made a clucking noise. 'No, no. If you'd had a post-operative infection of some kind then maybe. Infections and scarring can result in blocked tubes. But in your case there was nothing of the kind. You've no history of family problems. You're clearly ovulating beautifully. Time intercourse for twelve to eighteen days after the start of your period and keep your fingers crossed. Lady Luck, I'm afraid, will always play a large part in the proceedings. None of us can do anything about that. But then that's what makes the whole business such fun, I always think.' She rubbed her hands together gleefully. 'Gives us all an excuse to practise hard.'

Rachel, who found it difficult to imagine this friendly barrel of a woman in the embrace of anything more erotic than an armchair, caught herself scanning the room for signs of a family. There was only one picture on the desk, of a smiling, bald-headed man with spectacles and gaps between his teeth.

'Is that your husband?' she asked, the question slipping out before a sense of impropriety could get the better of her.

'Yes, that's my Geoffrey. We tried for years and years.' Her beaming face showed no signs of strain at the admission. 'That's the way it is sometimes. He died a few years back. Heart condition. Smoked like a chimney, the silly love, though we're not sure that's what finally shut everything down. Now then,' she had sat back down behind her desk and begun scribbling on a pad, 'by no means compulsory, but I do recommend them.' She tore off the prescription and handed it to Rachel, who was struggling with the impulse to express sympathy, coupled with the sense that the moment for doing so might already have passed. She frowned at the handwriting on the page before her, which resembled a series of Impressionist seagulls.

'Folate supplements,' explained Doctor Abbot. 'One tablet a day reduces the incidences of neural tube defects.'

'Neural tube defects?'

'Spina bifida and so on. Don't look so worried, Miss Elliot. Healthy babies are born to women of all ages every day of the week. The most important thing is that you want to have a child and that you give yourself the very best possible chance of doing so. You can buy these tablets in any chemist actually, you don't even need a prescription. I should see which works out cheaper and go for that.' She stood up and held out her hand. Her own cup of tea, Rachel noticed, had barely been touched.

Rachel took the hand with considerably more enthusiasm than she had at the beginning of the interview. 'Thank you. You've been very kind.'

'Not at all. And the very best of luck. Come back and see me when you strike lucky.'

In Rachel's experience, no method for crossing the Atlantic was entirely satisfactory. Though she had colleagues who swore by double whiskies and knock-out pills, in her view the time allowed for sleeping was too short, too readily interrupted by unwanted sing-song announcements about landing cards and duty free perfumes, to be restorative in any sense. She opted on this occasion for an early evening flight, resigning herself to the dazed exhaustion that lay ahead, followed by the frustration of waking with a racing pulse five hours before the next day was supposed to have started.

Rachel sighed and took another sip of her complimentary champagne. It was foolish to drink, she knew, but on the other hand she felt she owed it to herself – both as a small, anticipatory celebration for what lay ahead, and as a reward for having successfully survived all sorts of last-minute complications without losing her temper or missing the plane. Not only had Steve Betts, the director, been struck down with shingles, but one of the models had twisted her ankle in a nightclub. While lying in the ebb-tide of a pearly pink beach required little from an ankle, the question of a replacement director at such short notice had been taxing almost to the point of impossible. A substitute had at last been found – someone highly recommended and expensive, whom Rachel had taken care to sell to Frank Alder in the most glowing and confident of terms. But inside she worried still. Bringing a storyboard to life could be a complicated business. A little magic was invariably required, even on a Bermudan beach.

That the flight was delayed one hour by the last-minute

discovery of an electrical fault did little to allay a hovering sense of doom. As the airplane taxied back from the runway, Rachel reminded herself that such inconvenience was infinitely preferable to an unscheduled landing in the middle of the Atlantic Ocean. But the reality of such a prospect shimmered hopelessly out of reach. As did the good humour which had been beaten out of her by the whirlwind rush in which she eventually left the flat earlier that afternoon. Having popped home intending only to shower and change, she had been assailed by a series of unwanted calls, the more unexpected among them coming from Naomi Fullerton.

'What a treat. I was expecting your voice box. How are you, Rachel? It's been ages.'

An unhelpful picture sprang to mind, of Naomi curled up in the broad creaky arms of the straw rocking chair beside her beloved black beast of an Aga, cup of tea in hand, open magazine on her lap, her various children despatched to tea parties or settled round her in prettily coordinated outfits and hair bobbles. Anita would have been easier to reject. But Naomi was different. Partly because she rang so seldom (invariably making Rachel feel guilty for not having got there first) and partly because of the determined ostentation with which she played her role as mother. As a female still very much on the opposite end of such a spectrum, Rachel had learnt to be very careful about not saying anything that might suggest she considered herself superior, or busier, or more fulfilled in any way.

'Naomi – lovely to hear you, but I'm afraid this is a bit of a bad time. I'm in danger of being late for an airplane.'

'Oh, that sounds exciting. Where are you going?'

'America – Washington then Bermuda.'

'Really?' The word, though innocent enough, seemed to Rachel to contain accusatory overtones, as if Naomi believed that, as an old friend, she had every right to be informed of such large-scale manoeuvres before they occurred. 'Any chance of getting you over here before Christmas? Graham and I would love to see you. And so would Jessica, of course. She's taking her grade II piano this term.'

'Is she?' Rachel felt herself growing faintly hysterical. 'That's fantastic. Tell her best of luck and everything.'

Jessica, the third of Graham and Naomi's four girls, was by far the most precocious and accomplished of her various godchildren, having, at the tender age of seven, already taken up two instruments, elocution lessons and ballet. She wanted to have her own television show when she grew up, she said, one that had dancing and news. Rachel could be quite enchanted by such revelations when in the mood. But standing in a bath towel with wet hair trickling unpleasantly down her neck and the hands of the kitchen clock racing at twice their usual speed, made her less receptive to such disclosures. 'And I'd love to see you all – terribly soon. Let's talk when I get back. Tell Jessica I'll get her something special for Christmas from America.'

'So you'll call me, will you?' Naomi sounded sceptical.

'Yes. Absolutely. Soon as I get back.'

As Rachel scurried back towards the bathroom her fax machine whirred into life. Grabbing a towel and rubbing at her wet hair – she had tried and failed to get to the hairdresser's that afternoon – she returned to the study, her bare feet squeaking faintly on the polished wood floor. A single page had emerged from the machine, with just one line written across the top of it.

I said, why have you changed your mind? W.R. Fax: 01813687551

Rachel screwed the message up into a ball which she lobbed, with satisfying accuracy, into the wastepaper basket beside her desk. By the time she had finished getting dressed yet another message had arrived. This time from Melissa.

Just signing off and wishing you luck. No more last-minute panics unless you count an urgent-sounding call from your favourite client of Blackers Inc . . . I put him through to AJ. Julie says they fixed a lunch. Send us a p-c. Yrs enviously, Mel. PS Jo says to tell you the ankle hardly looks swollen at all so DON'T WORRY.

Rachel, smiling to herself, crumpled this missive in her fist and hurled it in the direction of the last one. This time she missed. On going over to retrieve it, she caught sight of Will Raphael's note, now half-unfurled in the bottom of the bin. His fax number was just visible on the top right-hand corner of the page. With a feeling akin to the irritation with which one bats a persistent fly, she tore off the corner and marched over to her fax machine.

Because I am busy. Because I am entitled to. Because I'd make a lousy photographer. RE.

From the retrospective vantage point of the airplane, Rachel felt rather pleased with this reply. It contained a certain curt cleverness, she decided, sipping the last of her champagne, of the kind that invariably eluded her in the cut and thrust of real conversation.

After a bad spell of turbulence that left Rachel with the unsettling sensation that bubbles were forming in the innermost recesses of her ears, she remembered the morning's post, stuffed at the last minute into the zip pocket of her overnight bag. There had been something that looked interesting, she recalled, eagerly pulling out the wadge of envelopes and sifting through it. A bank statement, a Christmas appeal from Save The Children, a catalogue from a warehouse clothes company and – here it was – a letter from France. Rachel smiled at Joy's self-consciously spaced and tidy handwriting, a hangover from her days as primary school teacher, when she liked to swear that handling classfuls of rowdy children quite put her off ever having any of her own.

As she ran her thumb under the gummed seal of the envelope, it occurred to Rachel that the Daltons may already have responded to exactly the same kind of teasing urgency with which she herself now wrestled, the overpowering sense that now was the time to effect a life-change, that soon it would be too late. Having a child was going to be her volte-face, she decided, pressing out the creases in the letter, her version of running from London and working to make a dream come true.

Dear Rachel,

I hope you are well and not too busy at work. How's that lovely flat? It was fantastic of you to come over for Leo's christening – both Tony and I really appreciated it – and so will Leo when he's a bit older! I can't believe it was so many weeks ago already and that Christmas is just around the corner.

We'd never spent time down here during the winter before and I have to say it has been a bit of an eye-opener! We've had so much rain all the Brits keep saying how much it reminds them of home. There's an amazingly large group of English people in the area, we've discovered, and even though we have by no means given up on our resolution of integrating ourselves with our French neighbours, I have to admit that there is nothing to beat having a jolly good moan with someone who misses the same things you do and who has the wherewithal to make a decent cup of tea. You wouldn't believe how tasteless French teabags are – everyone agrees – and the milk is mostly that longlife stuff, which the children can't bear and use as an excuse to dollop ten spoonfuls of sugar on their cornflakes! Talking of the children, your godson continues to go from strength to strength (literally). You would not believe how enormous he is – and how demanding. He makes the other two – or at least my recollections of them at this age – seem placid beyond belief. I'm still up at least three times every night. I've tried him on formula milk but he's just not interested, so I'm still wandering round with my buttons undone all the time. It is beginning to get me down just a bit. Especially now we're heading into winter. Apparently it's very common that late children are more of a handful. They are more likely to be geniuses too, apparently – we shall see!

The good news is that Tony continues to have more work than he knows what to do with – mostly, as I say, from English people doing up places of their own. This means, of course, that our own house is still very much in the condition that you saw it at the end of the summer. Tony keeps meaning to get to it at weekends, but he is usually so bushed I don't like to bully him too much. The only real problem is that now that it's so cold and damp, we really are beginning to feel all those unfilled cracks and crannies. A hell of a wind can blow in these parts, we've discovered, and of course since the house is exposed on all sides, we do rather get the brunt of it.

Isobel's French is practically fluent and even Sam is beginning to get the gist of things, which is a great relief. Tony, as you know, was always pretty good anyway, so it's just yours truly who is still struggling to make herself understood by the natives. I've bought a few grammar books and do try and do an hour or so every day, but it is hard to concentrate with Leo around and so much to do about the place. Je veux parler très bien mais je ne peux pas! How's that? Only took me ten minutes with a dictionary (just joking).

I wonder if you could do me a favour, Rachel. I know you're busy and it's a cheek of me to ask, but would you mind awfully finding out if I could subscribe to Good Housekeeping *over here – how much it would cost to have it sent over and so on. I would ask my family, but they are already providing a steady supply of all those things – like teabags! – that I miss so dreadfully from Tesco's. I know it sounds silly, but it would be such a treat – it's such an attractive magazine and full of so much – and besides which it might help me with some ideas for this building site we call home!*

How many exclamation marks would it take, Rachel wondered angrily, scanning the last lines of the letter, before Joy dared to admit that she was unhappy.

I keep telling myself that with Tony's business going so well one day we'll be able to afford to retire somewhere really tropical and easy, where leaky roofs won't matter and I'll have servants to sweep away the cobwebs. But then we all have to dream.

Yes, we do, thought Rachel, puzzling over the depressing possibility that dreams were not designed to come true, and that when they did they invariably needed replacing with something new. Would having a child bring with it a similar sense of disappointment for her? She tried to imagine what it would feel like to cherish her own baby, to embark on that juggling act she had heard so much about, flying between hearth and office, effortlessly producing nappies and documents like some fairy godmother with a wand. But all that came was a fuzzy warm feeling in the pit of her stomach, a gush of irrational conviction that in her case all would work out for the best.

As Rachel gingerly pressed the tip of her spoon into a small square of lemon-coloured dessert, she experienced, not for the first time, a pang of guilt at having omitted to notify Duncan and Mary Beth of her impending stay in their territory. She was booked instead into the Omnivera Hotel in Georgetown, a white-fluffy-bathrobe type of place, just a few miles from Duncan and Mary Beth's handsome oak front door. After careful consideration she had decided to devote all of her spare time in Washington to Nathan, who was flying down from New York specially and who – almost as if he had picked up on some of the momentous significance for her in this particular visit – had promised a surprise that would 'blow her mind'. If they wrapped up early in Bermuda she would call in on Duncan on the way back, she told herself, blinking heavy eyelids at the lemon pudding, which wobbled disconcertingly, and which had begun to leak a suspiciously colourless tributary of fluid from underneath its edges. On the screen in front of her the opening credits were rolling for a submarine thriller which she had seen with Nathan earlier in the year. She started to put on her headphones but changed her mind, closing her eyes instead and starting to count, for the hundredth time, the number of days since the beginning of her last period. Thirteen; unlucky for some, she thought, smiling to herself as the blank weightlessness of sleep intervened.

12

Nathan's surprise took the form of a wood and concrete enclave, nestling amongst the high, fir-lined niches of the Virginia mountains. Swiss-style chalets clustered around a massive, sprawling central complex containing every amenity currently in fashionable demand for individuals fortunate enough to reside in a certain income bracket. Ethnic restaurants, two heated swimming pools, a fitness centre, a massage parlour, beauty salons, a bowling alley and a cinema were among the more prominent attractions advertised on the billboard in reception. Nathan was effusively impressed, a reaction which triggered in Rachel an unforgivable desire to appear perversely British and nonchalant, a desire which she put down to the grouchiness of intense fatigue and mounting nervousness about revealing the real ulterior motive behind her stop-over on the East Coast.

The chalets contained none of the rustic accoutrements suggested by their carefully rugged exteriors. Instead, Rachel found herself wading through the lush pile of absurdly silky carpets, strewn with heavy reproduction furniture and framed by yards of velveteen curtains with elaborate pelmet and side cord arrangements. The kitchen, crammed with every device imaginable for the preparation, storage and disposal of food and crockery, had Rachel cowering in the doorway, her jet-lagged brain flicking unhelpfully to thoughts of airplane cockpits and the unpleasant bumpiness with which they had finally made contact with the tarmac of Dulles airport. Some of the more hysterical passengers had actually clapped.

'Not bad, huh?' Nathan came up behind her and placed one proprietorial hand on each breast, while performing a gentle pelvic tilt in the region of her lower back. Rachel prised herself free with a nervous laugh, feeling suddenly like an imposter. The fact that her mental clock was still ticking several hours out of step was doing nothing to help her composure. She had awoken at four o'clock that morning, rolling from one side of her beautiful five-star bed to the other, trying every variation on the sheep-counting theme she had ever heard of, and much more besides. Breakfast and a head-drilling shower had helped. But after a perky patch during which she had walked several blocks to find an English newspaper, her limbs suddenly seemed to quadruple in weight and a thumping headache started. Retiring to her room with the intention of grabbing a nap before Nathan arrived, she had found herself hooked onto the phone instead. The crew, due to fly out the next day, were now showing more signs of nerves than the clients themselves. The sprained ankle was causing particular anxiety for the new director. What about artistic freedom? he complained, many times. What if he chose to do a close-up of the girls' feet? How could he be expected to work with constraints like damaged joints? It wasn't professional.

It was with some weariness, therefore, that Rachel pulled on her shoes and hastily touched up the fading lines of her make-up before venturing down to reception to greet the man whom she hoped would father her child. Nathan, oblivious both to the extent of her exhaustion and the nervous preoccupation burning in her mind, welcomed her with his usual bracing cheeriness. They were headed for the mountains, he told her proudly, in a monster of a four-wheeler that he had hired specially for the occasion. They were to set off at once. Used to an automatic, Nathan ground the gears so frequently during their laborious stop-start progress through the dense traffic of downtown Washington, that Rachel's whole body was clenched with tension by the time they finally hit the clear open road that took them north. They cruised pleasantly enough after that, past white-gated fields of vast properties, and colonial-style mansions with names like The Homestead painted in handsome letters on their roadside mail boxes. The drive took well over three hours, the last part involving a torturous zigzag up through the Virginian mountains. Nathan, tired himself by this stage, talked in a desultory way about the grip of superior rubber on tarmac, while Rachel sleepily eyed the dense squadrons of towering trunks, wondering where all the famous blue ridges were and who had thought up such a description in the first place.

'It's super, Nathan, really super,' she exclaimed, after they had been left alone with a set of keys and several colourful booklets on facilities and mealtimes. 'A super surprise. You clever thing.' She turned and kissed him, registering a pleasant hint of a new aftershave. 'Does your cleverness extend to mastering any of these machines? Could you, for example, rustle up a cup of strong black coffee for a girl who's been awake since the early hours and who doesn't want to ruin the evening by falling asleep at the wrong moment?'

'Poor baby. Is she tired?' He stroked her hair gently, using the movement to draw her face closer still. For a few moments Rachel allowed herself to drift on the pull of his arms, before reality awoke her with a jerk. It would be wrong not to tell him first. She needed to tell him before they made love. 'Coffee,' she whispered, giving him a little push. 'Please.'

Nathan, it had to be said, excelled himself amongst the hi-tech gadgetry of the kitchen, emerging not only with a jug of coffee, but a trayful of food as well, together with a bottle of champagne which had been left in an ice-bucket as a welcome gift. He was wearing a dressing gown, Rachel noticed with a start, not until that moment aware that he had slipped off to change. In view of this attire, it was with some surprise that she found herself being led not upstairs to the bedroom, but out onto a wooden porch at the back of the chalet.

'Nathan, really, it's cold and dark,' she began, pulling her cardigan about her more tightly.

But Nathan, humming a fanfare, put down the tray and pulled off a tarpaulin covering something in the far corner of the balcony. Steam billowed into the chilly night air.

'A hot tub.'

'A what?'

'Bubbling hot water. We sit in it and look at the stars. What do you think?' He was already undoing his dressing gown. 'It's what sold the place to me. My folks used to have one of these when I was a kid. The whole family would pile in it sometimes after dinner, tell ghost stories and that kind of thing. I tell you, they're great for atmosphere.' His body looked faintly luminous in the dim light as he slipped into the water. In an instant he was submerged up to his neck. His teeth gleamed through his smile. 'Hey, could you push the tray a little closer do you think? Now get in for Christ's sake – you're shivering to death.'

Hurriedly Rachel slipped off her clothes. Her bare flesh tingled to attention at the shock of the mountain air. Tiptoeing to minimise contact with the icy wooden boards, she scurried over to join him, hugging herself from a combination of cold and modesty. She felt skeleton-thin, transparent through to the bone. For a moment the heat of the water took her breath away. Then her body began to ease into the deep embrace of the wet warmth. Overhead the sky was a bed of black velvet, bejewelled with light.

'It's beautiful, Nathan,' she gasped, craning her neck upwards and stretching her limbs out in slow swimming motions, gaining confidence as the blanket of water drew her in. 'Oh God, it's beautiful.' She thought of what she had to say, of how easy it would be.

Nathan was eating crab sticks, dipping them into a tub of mayonnaise and popping them into his mouth like sweets. He had ordered the food in advance, he explained, chewing hungrily, pointing out zuccini wedges and onion rings and other delicacies piled high on the plates. 'Quite a feast,' he added, licking away an errant blob of mayonnaise near the dimple in his chin. 'Get stuck in Rachel, it's all getting cold. I only gave these things a couple of minutes in the micro and it's kind of arctic out here. Wow, this is so good.' An exploratory foot felt its way under the water over to her side of the tub. She seized it playfully, making as if to pull him under the water.

'Eat,' he said, laughing, keeping his balance sufficiently to hold out a plate of food. Rachel, who believed that vegetables of any kind tasted better without generous coatings of deep-fried breadcrumbs, opted for one of the fleshy tubes of crab-meat, secretly sure that its chewy texture – though greatly enhanced by the addition of mayonnaise – had never enjoyed a close acquaintance with shellfish of any kind.

'Nathan, there's something I need to ask you.' She licked her fingers, resisting the temptation to rinse her hands in the water lapping round her chin.

'Ask away.' He had placed one foot on each of her bent legs and was absently kneading her kneecaps with his toes while he ate.

'I know this might come as something of a shock but . . . the thing is I have a favour to ask you. Rather a big favour, I suppose. I hope you'll try to understand . . .'

'Anything within my power, baby, you know that.' He reached out to pour the champagne. A mini tidal wave washed over the edges of the tub and slapped onto the wooden floor.

'It's just that,' Rachel clasped her hands under the surface. She was hot now, almost feverish. It was odd to feel sweaty, with cold so close at hand. Her hair was sticking to the sides of her cheeks and temples. She brushed it back with wet hands, feeling a shiver of relief as a breeze drifted across the balcony, cooling her head. 'I would be most honoured – flattered – pleased—' this was hard after all – 'if you would consider fathering my child.'

'Your what?' Nathan pulled his feet away and sat up. 'You're pregnant?'

'No, no.' It was a relief to laugh. Of course such a sudden mention of babies was bound to make a man like Nathan nervous. 'I'm not expecting anything more than the act itself,' she explained eagerly, leaning towards him, the water slopping up around her shoulders. 'I have decided that I would like to have a child. I *want* to do it on my own. There would be no recriminations afterwards, no crawling back for money or commitment from you. You'd be quite free, I promise.'

To her immense surprise, Nathan responded to these reassurances by hurling his glass at the balustrades a few feet to their right. There was a chiming explosion as the glass shattered, spraying invisible shards into darkness. 'How dare you, Rachel Elliot.' He heaved his torso out of the water and sat on the very edge of the tub. Steam rose from every pore of his skin, giving the impression that he was about to burst into flame.

'I'm only asking . . .'

He shook his wet fringe from his eyes. 'You are only asking me to screw you – deposit my stuff – and ciao. Auf wiedersehen. And I'm not supposed to mind? Like I can plant babies all over the place and it doesn't matter? Like I'm some kind of stud? Like I've got no heart?'

'I thought you weren't interested in children . . .' she faltered.

'I'm not,' he snapped. 'But that does not give you the right to ask me such a thing.'

'I'm sorry.' She felt trapped in the water. Though her body was too hot, the air was too cold. There were no towels. 'I'm sorry, I had no idea . . .'

'You know what? You're crazy. What do you want to wreck yourself with a kid for anyway?'

'That's my business.'

'You're telling me. Leave me out of it Rachel.' He gave a bitter laugh. 'Though don't imagine that you getting pregnant wouldn't affect things between us. I mean, Christ – do you think we could just carry on as before with a kid crying all over the goddam place? Give me a break.'

In spite of the cold Nathan was still sitting on the edge of the hot tub, heedless both of his nudity and the cold. Steam was rising only from his legs now, the rest of his body having cooled to meet the chill temperatures of the mountain air. 'Hell, I'm going inside.' He slung on his dressing gown and stooped to pick up the tray of food. The pot of coffee she had requested sat untouched, cold as stone. 'I am truly sorry you did this, Rachel. Truly sorry.' He shook his head.

After he had gone Rachel turned her face up towards the tapestry of stars and stared hard at the pinpoints of light till their edges blurred. The caress of the wind through the trees sounded like whispered laughter. A faint trace of creamy scum was forming on the surface of the water. The towel landed with a dull thump beside the tub, flung with a mute anger that ruled out negotiation or reconciliation of any kind.

They found their way to different bedrooms, knowing that the next morning they would part company for good. Rachel's request had taken them into emotional terrain from which it would have been impossible to withdraw and in which they could not coexist.

As Rachel lay awake, her mind galloping obstinately on, refusing to let her body rest, a deep sense of failure began to mushroom inside. To have miscalculated so badly was upsetting, deeply shocking in fact. She wanted to go home, to retreat and regroup. The thought of Bermuda, of having to maintain control, perform the usual tightrope act of keeping all parties happy, made her suddenly quite sick with apprehension. It felt like a stage-call for an actress who had lost her nerve. The uncrackable Rachel Elliot would be required. Her teeth chattered at the thought. For, as a grey dawn crept up over the green ridges of the mountains, it seemed to her that the uncrackable Rachel Elliot was full of cracks, deep invisible fissures that made her afraid.

Just before she finally drifted off to sleep the comforting face of Dr Abbot swam into view, bringing with it an echo of a voice that had wished her luck. All the luck in the world was no use to her now, she thought bitterly, considering and rejecting the possibility of slipping into Nathan's room and trying to make it up. He wouldn't trust her now, or ever again. The stormy set of his big square face, the disappointment in his eyes, had told her more plainly than words ever could how badly she had underestimated him, how selfishly naive she had been all along.

13

It rained every day. Sometimes only for twenty minutes, sometimes for two hours. It was impossible, everyone said, unprecedented; it couldn't continue. But continue it did, day after day,
until Rachel stopped bothering to listen to the forecast or to quiz
the hotel staff as to their opinions on the shapes and sizes of
the shifting clouds, forming and merging round the island like
malevolent shades.

Rain itself was a technical problem that could be overcome, as
Rachel knew from previous unhappy clashes with the calami-
tously unreliable moods of the British climate. A bit of post-
production dabbling with the right instruments could work
wonders on grey skies and sodden grass. The hailstorm effect
of torrential rain on coral beaches and turquoise seas, however,
was another matter entirely. Not only was filming impossible in
such conditions, but the aftermath of each heavenly outburst was
not unlike that of a ferocious bombing campaign. The moment
the skies cleared, scores of locals – hired specially for the task –
would leap into action with leaf brushes and rakes, smoothing
over the pockmarked shore and scattering bucketfuls of dry
sand (laboriously collected whenever such a rare opportunity
presented itself) to cover the worst areas.

Meanwhile, the models sulked under umbrellas, chain-smoking
and picking their spots. The one with the bad ankle insisted
on having a footstool as well as a deck chair brought onto
the set, though the joint in question looked to Rachel to be
perfectly shapely and undamaged. The two girls would stroll
nonchalantly to take up their positions in the water whenever
required, too aware of the unarguable splendour of their long

limbs and pretty curves to be modest. The dark-skinned one was particularly beautiful, Rachel thought, noting with more than a trace of wistfulness how smoothly stretched a teenaged skin could be, how invitingly flawless and pert. She restricted any comparable states of undress of her own to the rectangular confines of the hotel swimming pool, wise enough to absent herself from arenas in which she knew she could not compete. The persistent mess of her hair, another calamity of the damp air, the intermittent downpours and life-sapping sun, she kept hidden under a broad-brimmed straw hat, which at least, she felt, granted her some vestige of style, something to hide under if nothing else.

After witnessing the sorry state of play for himself for a couple of days, Frank Alder tactfully jetted out of the proceedings. He left an overwrought product manager in his stead, a young man whose petty concerns over issues largely irrelevant to the hourly challenges being faced by the film crew caused Rachel to resort to the uncharacteristically cowardly tactic of avoiding him altogether. If ever forced into direct conversation she agreed with everything he said and made a point of forgetting it the moment after. Instead, she faxed Frank Alder directly each day, restricting herself to brief but honest progress reports, operating with the detached surface of her mind that she reserved as her last shield against panic. A lot of money had been invested by Mallarmé in these two weeks. Five hundred thousand pounds to be exact. Not to mention the media budget of five million, most of which had already been committed to airtime over the coming year. Too much money for mistakes. Too much money for a botched job.

As the days wore on, and the business of huddling under umbrellas and staring at the leaden skies with the crazed intensity of madmen began to feel almost normal, Rachel found herself longing for the cool pragmatism of Steve Betts. His substitute, a much younger man with a tight blond perm and a twitchy mouth, continued to go through the verbal motions of his job, but with a dazed expression and flailing hands that seemed to communicate an inexpressible terror going on inside.

At the beginning of each day the most senior members of the shoot would gather to examine the rushes and decide which, if any, could be used. Dark clouds were as much of a concern as the rain itself, since they badly affected the light and the atmosphere, and could take a torturously long time to disperse afterwards – almost, thought Rachel, as if they were lingering to mock the petty goings-on of the poor forked beasts below. As the talk of what could be achieved in the cutting room increased, so did a sense of doomed camaraderie. Alcohol consumption was reaching record levels. And drugs, too, though there was less proof of that.

During the second week a bad atmosphere was worsened by the inevitable flurry of sexual liaisons between inappropriate parties. A member of the lighting crew, who had been married only a few months, was sleeping with a young waitress whose pretty black eyes had also been admired by several unmarried colleagues. Similar problems of camp rivalry were surfacing over the two models, rumoured to have bestowed sexual favours upon various members of the entourage but who seemed to thrive on switching their affections and sitting back to study the reactions.

Only two more days to go, Rachel wrote in her diary, one evening towards the end of the second week, *and the nightmare will end. We had a record four hours of uninterrupted sunshine this morning, though the afternoon squall was as bad as ever. I have decided we should reduce the film from forty to thirty seconds and increase the number of product shots from two to four. Frank Alder is willing, though the creative team are threatening to mutiny. But then they are not going to have to suffer the consequences quite as I am.* On a new line she wrote: *Still no reply from Nathan.*

She had composed a letter to Nathan on the very first day of the shoot, apologising for her misjudgement and inviting reconciliation. Not because she entertained any serious hopes of rekindling their relationship, but because she could not bear the sense of unfinished business that their method of parting had created. A silent, interminable drive back to Washington, followed by not even a handshake of a goodbye. They had known each other – albeit sporadically – for almost five years. It seemed wrong – it felt like even more failure – not to be able to round things off properly, without some form of civilised affection at least.

For once, writing the diary did not help. A sense of order on the page was irrelevant, she realised, quite futile in fact, when it came to the new confusions of her real life. Still holding her pen, she strolled outside and leant her elbows on the railings of the window-box balcony adjoining her room. With perfect grand irony, each night had been cloudless and still, unveiling a seamless canopy of stars that seemed quite unconnected to the elemental tantrums of the day.

With work there always was an answer in the end, she thought, peering into the darkness, down towards the sea, straining her eyes to match shapes to the snatches of laughter. With work there was always some compromise that could eventually be reached, like a longer pack shot or a shorter film; nothing was insoluble. But in this other matter, the matter of a baby, she could think of no answers at all. Worse still, with Nathan gone, a new pulse of urgency had arrived, drumming inside her head like the pendulum of a boxed clock.

A breeze rippled through the palm trees edging the compound of the hotel. Their arched trunks, bent in submission to years of onshore winds, were just visible in the moonlight, like giant limbs thrusting up through the sand. The laughter on the beach, the strains of music drifting up from the open window of the bar below, seemed to come from another world. There will be another month, she told herself, gripping the railings with such passion that the pen slipped from her grasp and disappeared into the foliage below. There will be another cycle, another man. There had to be.

A little later, after she had crawled between the two sheets covering her bed, her mind, as if keen to escape the insoluble conundrums of the present, switched immediately to the past. There she saw a simpler version of herself, a vibrant, confident, blossoming version, who tossed her head dismissively at the world. How easy life had once seemed. How sure she had been. How beautifully unafraid. Rachel smiled to herself as Robbie Dexter plodded into view, a part of that old unwavering self, his hair ruffled, the worn patches on the knees of his interminable jeans.

With a start Rachel blinked open her eyes and sat up in the dark, as the fear throbbed inside her chest. For a few moments she could barely breathe. Adrenalin pumped through her veins, filling her with that crisis energy which is the last resort of human strength. Yet there was nothing for the adrenalin to do, nothing on which to focus. She tried to channel her thoughts towards identifiable problems – towards images of rain and rushes and children – but nothing took hold. The anxiety was without shape or solution, a nameless darkness to do with getting older, more uncertain, more alone. The attack stopped as quickly as it had come, the charge of energy leaving her in a state of near exhaustion as it flooded out of her body. Rachel let her head fall back onto her pillow, gulping in air as if strangling fingers had been released from her throat. 'Stupid woman,' she gasped out loud. 'You stupid old woman.'

With rough, angry movements, she pulled on the clothes that lay across her chair and sketched some colour onto her face. Eat, drink and be merry for tomorrow we die, sang her mind, while her lips pursed themselves for a dash of pink and her eyelids fluttered under dabs of crystal blue. A drink and a bit of company was the thing – the only thing – she told herself, slamming the door behind her and striding down the corridor towards the sounds of merriment emanating from the hotel bar.

14 ∫

'I thought you'd be browner,' remarked Anita when they met for a drink in the agency a week or so after Rachel's return.

'I told you, it was work – I wasn't there for a bloody holiday.'

'Pardon me.' Anita lit a cigarette and blew a tunnel of smoke rings at the ceiling. She had poured her first glass at eleven o'clock that morning and was feeling deliciously mellow in consequence. Such placidity was close to bliss, she thought lazily, eyeing Rachel through a screen of grey smoke and thinking that she was being tediously crotchety and middle-aged.

Rachel, whose heart had sunk upon registering the faintly aromatic scent of Anita's breath and the dreamy smile that accompanied it, felt all her sympathies crushed by a great sense of weariness. Instead of mustering all efforts towards a tactful offering of help – as she had intended – she found herself ignoring the subject altogether.

The noisy and packed environs of the McKenzie Cartwright in-house bar were hardly suitable for a heart-to-heart of any kind. Rachel had managed to secure a small round table in the furthest corner, near the wall of windows that overlooked a granite no man's land strewn with paper litter and mangled plastic bags. But there was no avoiding the strains of Bryan Ferry's 'Jealous Guy', which a young copywriter with floppy bleached hair had played several times in succession, draped over the side of the juke-box in a disconsolate fashion suggestive of personal identification with the song's theme. At the table next to them an art director in dark Buddy Holly spectacles was holding forth to a bored-looking account manager on the subject of creative autonomy. Beside them a new secretary with an engaging smile was enjoying the competitive attentions of three media buyers. 'It's like a real party,' sighed Anita happily, 'and with some scrumptious men too. No wonder you work such long hours, you wicked girl.'

Rachel, who knew her friend was too far down the road towards total inebriation to be taken seriously on any level, merely rolled her eyes. 'You've got a one-track mind, Anita, did you know that?' As she spoke, she caught sight of Cliff Weybourne entering the room amongst a crowd of mostly unfamiliar faces. Hastily, Rachel adjusted her position, using Anita's frame to block the new arrivals from view. 'Drink up,' she urged, swigging from her own glass, 'it's getting late.' Two minutes, she told herself, and they'd be gone.

The Bermuda footage was proving salvageable, thanks to a final twenty-four hours of brilliant sunshine and some extremely advanced – and expensive – post-production work farmed out by the agency's creative team to a company called Filmstyle. It was work which the agency was going to have to pay for, however, and which would take a considerable chunk out of the project's profits. Though it looked as though Frank Alder would get his forty-second commercial after all and not too far below the standard he had been led to expect, it was no secret that the shoot had been dogged by bad luck and problems. Rachel had endured something of a rough ride in consequence, keeping all parties calm, presenting endless versions of the re-cut film and enduring the sympathies of her colleagues. Being pitied was something she had always found insufferable.

'Still keen on the baby business?'

'The baby business?' Rachel, aware not only of Anita's but Cliff's eyes upon her across the room, managed a careless laugh. 'Hardly. Besides, I've got a cat. The two don't mix, if I remember correctly.' The cat had been waiting for her upon her return from the shoot, posing beside the garden door like some kind of fireside ornament, its ears pricked and its tail curled neatly round its front paws. Instead of minding, Rachel had thrown down her bags and scooped it up in her arms, overcome with pleasure at finding something to welcome her home. As if baffled by the erratic behaviour of humans, the cat had held itself stiffly throughout this fond embrace, and then shaken out its fur several times after being deposited back on the ground. When Rachel pushed open the door for it to enter, the animal hesitated for a moment or two, as if such a decision was not to be undertaken lightly.

'You can borrow Giles if you want,' drawled Anita, now seriously drunk. 'He hasn't laid a finger on me for months – might as well put his dick to some use—'

'Excuse me butting in.' It was Cliff Weybourne, bending down towards them, his lizard eyes wide and unsmiling, his jet hair prinked to perfection. 'Rachel.' He held out his hand. 'I wanted to say well done.'

'Well done?' She was caught off guard.

Anita, picking up on the theme, rubbed her hands together gleefully. 'Is it something to celebrate? Oh, goody – I love celebrations.'

'This is Anita Cavanagh, my friend from—'

'Ah yes, how do you do.' He flicked the most cursory of glances across the table before returning his attention to Rachel. 'Well done indeed, for pulling it out of the bag. I've just been talking to one of the directors of Filmstyle. He says the film is looking excellent. The worst November weather in Bermuda since records began and you come home with a sunlotion commercial. Impressive.'

Rachel pressed her lips together, not trusting herself to speak, falling back on the hope that he would get bored and go away. In the background, at last weary of Bryan Ferry, the copywriter had begun wailing his own version of the song: '*I didn't mean to hurt you, I'm sorry that . . .*'

There was a chorus of expletives and groans from those seated nearest to him.

Cliff gestured with his head at the bar. 'The man's here, as it happens. Not involved in the film personally, but says he'd like to meet you.' He tweaked his eyebrows suggestively. 'Will Raphael, he's called. Quite a talented photographer, they say.' He turned and beckoned at someone in the group.

That Cliff Weybourne should know anything at all about the personnel involved in the frenzied damage-limitation exercises being conducted in Soho dark rooms was galling in itself. That

Will Raphael, of all people, should be even remotely involved added another unpleasant twist to the situation.

Rachel cast a longing glance at the door while the tallest of the men grouped at the bar, a slim, dark-haired man in white drainpipe trousers and a black leather jacket, nodded at Cliff and stepped off his bar stool. His hair was long and smooth, brushed straight back off his face, revealing a high forehead and large brown eyes. As he approached, Rachel, determined not to appear put out, eyed him steadily over the rim of her glass. She was on the point of extending a dignified hand when Anita let out a small but piercing shriek. 'I told you there were some gorgeous men in here,' she squeaked, 'I told you.' She got to her feet first, elbowing past Rachel and Cliff in her eagerness to be welcoming.

'Anita Cavanagh – not in this business at all, but a very close member of the family, so to speak.' Her words were noticeably slurred now, running off her tongue in breathless cadences, while her eyes gazed but did not seem to see. 'Delighted to meet you. Delicious jacket, by the way. Positively delicious.' She chewed the last word like a mouthful of food.

Rachel's attention was momentarily diverted by the evident smirk of distaste with which Cliff looked away. A deep reflex of defensive loyalty surged inside. She had to get them out, before poor Anita unwittingly gave any more cause for such disdain.

'Well, thank you very much,' Will replied, ignoring Cliff's look of complicitous horror and patting the leather which had been so exuberantly admired. 'It's an old favourite.' His ears moved when he smiled.

'We were just going, actually,' Rachel blurted.

'What a shame.' He turned to her and bowed his head very slightly. 'Rachel Elliot. How do you do, at last.'

'Mr Raphael. Good to meet you.' Rachel seized Anita's elbow and flashed her most sparkling smile at no one in particular. 'I'm afraid we really must be on our way. Thank you, Mr Raphael, for all your sterling work on my client's behalf – Cliff has just told me—'

'Oh, I've done nothing. My involvement in Filmstyle is purely managerial these days.'

'Oh, I see – well thanks anyway.' She managed to keep

her gaze somewhere in the region of his collar, which wasn't particularly hard since he was so tall. Beside her, Anita had worked her arm free and, with the puzzled look of a hurt child, was massaging the spot where Rachel's fingers had pinched the skin.

'It was my pleasure.' His voice sounded lower than she had remembered it from the telephone and full of a formality which now – she was certain – reflected a strong desire to be allowed to return to his colleagues. A quick glance at his face for verification of this fact, however, found him watching Anita, who had sunk back down into her chair and taken up a head-on-arms position that looked worryingly conducive to sleep. 'I only do my own work these days,' he said slowly, swivelling his gaze back to Rachel. 'Apart from giving a few private lessons. But then you know that.'

Rachel had hoped to avoid discussion of the aborted photography lessons altogether. 'As I tried to explain . . .' she began.

'Oh, you explained all right.' Though his tone was accusatory, his eyes were full of amusement. 'A woman of very few words, clearly.'

Rachel was in no mood to be laughed at. While her mind thrashed around for some appropriately feisty response, in her heart she felt nothing but flat and weak. It did not help that Cliff was shuffling his feet and looking longingly at the bar, clearly bored of the game which he had stage-managed thus far, and that Anita was now tossing her head and moaning.

'If you'll excuse us,' she stammered, tapping Anita on the back and beginning to gather up their bags and coats. 'Come on, Anita, please,' she pleaded, noting out of the corner of her eye that Cliff Weybourne was sloping away and praying that Will Raphael would follow suit. 'Nice to have met you,' she called airily over her shoulder, not looking round. Anita, though upright, was now clinging to the back of her chair and swaying dangerously.

'We must go *now* . . .' Rachel hissed, horrified to find herself almost gagging on the words. With a monumental effort of will she swallowed the tears away. It was the culmination of a tough few weeks, she told herself, still juggling ineffectually with coats and bags, beginning now to feel uncomfortably hot and close to panic. It was just a question of coaxing Anita outside. No one was looking at them. There was no question of a spectacle. Not yet, anyway.

'Can I help?'

Christ, he still hadn't gone. 'No, no, we're fine, honestly. She's just a little . . .'

'Tired?' His brown eyes were not laughing now, but very grave. 'Here, let me.'

Somehow Will Raphael got his arm round Anita in such a way that she could give the appearance of walking whilst having to employ only the minimum of effort herself. Rachel took up the rear, clasping their belongings, keeping her eyes firmly fixed upon the back of his trousers, noting two stray white threads that hung from the left back pocket, dangling below the hem of his jacket.

The sight of two taxis emerging round the corner, yellow lights glaring, at precisely the moment that the agency doors swung shut behind them, lifted Rachel's spirits immeasurably, as did the brilliant chill of the December air. It woke Anita up a bit too, though she had to be prised free from Will's jacket, to which she was clinging with white-knuckled determination.

'Sorry and all that,' she mumbled, as they eased her onto the seat of the cab.

'I'll call home,' said Rachel, tucking Anita's coat round her lap as if she were an old lady and kissing her tenderly on the cheek. 'Let Giles know you're on the way . . .'

'Tell him the bitch is drunk again, you mean . . .'

'Shush now. You'll be better for some sleep. I'll call you tomorrow.'

She backed out onto the pavement to find that Will was holding open the door of the other taxi.

'Where shall I tell him?'

'Chelsea. Near the Embankment.'

'You must live near me, then.' For a minute she thought he was going to ask to share the ride, but instead he put his head inside the window to pass on the directions to the driver.

'Thank you very much,' she said, embarrassment flooding in from nowhere, reddening her cheeks in spite of the cold.

'Would you like me to phone her husband?' He was all businesslike. His breath made little clouds that hid his face.

'No, no, it's quite all right.' She patted her bag. 'I've got a mobile.'

'Ah yes, of course, you would have. A mobile. Good.' He grinned. His teeth were very long, she noticed, and neatly packed. The taxi driver tapped impatiently on the glass window. 'Well, good to have met you,' he called as the door swung shut. 'Good to put a face to a voice.'

He turned away immediately, tugging his jacket collar up round his ears and striding quickly up the street.

Watching from the back of the taxi, Rachel could not help experiencing some paltry relief that he was heading away from the entrance to the agency, that there would be no possibility, that night at least, of Will Raphael sharing any of the juicy tidbits of gossip no doubt being savoured inside. Her face burned again at the very thought. A drunken friend and the Bermuda episode were hardly matters likely to entertain the palates of agency gossip-mongers for long, but still it rankled to have given them any fuel at all.

As the taxi sped through the dark streets, Rachel found herself sliding to the middle of the seat, away from the windows, as if fearful of being recognised by the neon snowmen and Father Christmases winking at her from shop windows and lampposts outside.

15

Not even a five-mile tailback on the M4 could cast a shadow over Rachel's relief to be heading out of London. It confirmed her belief that these days she was only ever happy when on the move, that she had lost touch with the ability to feel settled in the present. Even her flat, her luxury cocoon of a refuge, the place she thought of longingly during every absence, now seemed to lose its allure once she entered it. Quietness, the absence of all thoughts and stimuli but those emanating from her own imagination, were things that these days she seemed only able to cherish in prospect, the reality of acquiring them bringing nothing more than a sort of deep boredom. It was almost as if she had grown too familiar with herself, too familiar with the small library of her own mind.

As she edged along in the heavy Friday night traffic, heading towards the luxury hotel near Bristol that was to play host to the Mallarmé and McKenzie Cartwright Christmas thrash, it occurred to Rachel that she had done something along the lines of falling out of love with herself. There was no self-belief any more, no certainty about anything. Worst of all, there was no desire to be herself, not unless something fundamental changed, something earth-shattering and self-effacing. Like having a baby. The preoccupation with the subject was unbelievably tiring, a relentless wheel of a thought that came round again and again, driven by a mechanism that she could not control. Sometimes her mind ached from being so constantly besieged.

'I must be bored of being selfish,' she murmured, not quite believing it, since the freedom to design the shape of her life was a privilege which she had nurtured very carefully over

the years, treasuring it ever more dearly as friends fell foul
of compromises and commitments that she could never have
imagined for herself. But the luxury of having no limit imposed
on the gratification of personal whims was quite meaningless,
if one hated oneself and there were no whims, Rachel thought
hopelessly, pulling up the handbrake and folding her arms.

Sitting alone in the dark cubicle of her car, she felt a strong
urge for the comfort of interruption. She strained her eyes to
make out the features of the silhouettes in cars on either side
of her. Were they alone too? Were they escaping or returning,
longing for solitude or company? She stared so long at the man
on her right, that his head turned, some sixth sense roused by
her scrutiny. It was too dark to smile, so she nodded instead, a
minute salutation from one human being to another. But the
man returned his attention to his windscreen, without offering
so much as a head-wobble of acknowledgement in return.

Turning to Radio 4 for consolation, Rachel found herself thrust
into a confessional on the emotional implications of infertility.
One participant admitted to a consultation with a witch doctor
while holidaying on the Ivory Coast; another to fantasies about
slaughtering puppies. A third confided in hushed tones that two
decades of childlessness had been broken by the death of her
father. Her firstborn (she had since had three more, all boys) had
been conceived on the very night her father died. Possibly at the
very same moment. As a breathy round of incredulity hit the air-
waves Rachel stabbed the *off* button and reached for her mobile.

She hadn't spoken to Anita since the unhappy fiasco in the
agency bar. The hazardous balancing act of offering support
without getting in the way grew no easier with time. Giles,
when she phoned him that night, had been his usual laconic
self, talking in the clipped manner with which he delivered news
reports to the background thud of bombs; stiff and stoical in his
charcoal flak jacket, firing spurts of information that invited no
questions in response, no possibility of interjection or dissent.
Anita was on a downward swing, he said, nothing that hadn't
been coped with before. His parents had been drafted in to
offer domestic reinforcements. Rachel's concern was, as always,
greatly appreciated. He would keep her posted as regards any
significant developments. Over and out.

Giles' mother, who took the call that Rachel now made from her car, presented a subtler defence based on euphemisms about tiredness and the strain of coping with the arrival of the twins' back molars. It took all Rachel's powers of persuasion before she agreed to fetch Anita herself.

'Rachel?'

'Anita, how are you?'

'Pretty bloody gloomy.' She lowered her voice. 'Giles has called in the green-welly brigade. Can't do a thing.' Rachel was well acquainted with the habits of Anita's in-laws, a pair of hearty seventy year olds who came from a thoroughbred, home-county stock of jolliness and good order. Anita, whose own parents had died a decade before and who, even in her strongest moments, thrived on a much less orthodox lifestyle, had never exactly risen to the challenge of making her in-laws feel at home. The merest sight of their springy grey hair, their crisp no-nonsense smiles, their obvious determination to get a hold of her family life and pummel it into shape, was enough to make her stick a cigarette in her mouth and flick ash into the toilet bowls. It was a subject, given Rachel's differences with her own parents, upon which the two women had enjoyed many years of synchrony.

'Poor you. Hell on earth, I should imagine.'

'Times a million.'

'Your best tack is probably to sort yourself out in that case. Nothing will get rid of them quicker.'

'I know, I know.' Anita sighed. 'God, it's the thought of Christmas that is really getting me down today. I mean, Christmas. All that tinsel and jingle-bloody-bells, playing happy families . . . leaving Santa a pint of beer and a biscuit for fuck's sake. Bloody carrots for the bloody reindeer. It's all just a big lie, isn't it? I mean, what's the good of pretending life is full of tooth fairies and aerodynamic sleighs when actually it's all a pile of shit?'

'Because the children have got plenty of time to discover the shit part for themselves.'

The traffic was at last starting to move. Rachel lodged the telephone between her shoulder and ear in order to get a steadier grip on the wheel.

'Yeah, yeah, yeah. You're right, of course. It'll be turkey and the Queen's speech as usual. The children hate turkey – and mince pies for that matter . . .' She muttered inaudibly for a while, the first real indication that she was not in entire control of her faculties. '. . . Yuletide charades with everyone eyeballing me every time I take a slug of port. My only problem, you know Rachel, is that there's simply too much going on at home.' Her voice had taken on a determined edge, as if she was as intent on persuading herself of the validity of this excuse as Rachel. 'I'm stressed out, that's all. Everything will be fine once the twins start school . . .'

Rachel stopped concentrating for a while, partly because she was in danger of being sucked in amongst the spurting tyres of an articulated lorry, and partly because talk of Christmas was distracting her with images of what she had to look forward to herself on that score. The previous year she had endured the usual family rituals in Gerrard's Cross before catching an airplane to meet Nathan in New York. Looking back on the episode now, it seemed as if it had happened to another person. The city had lain under a pretty sparkle of frozen snow, not enough to produce unseemly black sludge in the streets, but sufficient to outline the bare trees and square rooftops with rims and caps of crystal, like the icing trim on a cake. Nathan's flat was near Times Square, the converted third floor of what had once been a warehouse, with giant windows and ceilings as high as church rafters. For four days they had done nothing but make love, go to movies, sleep late, eat brunch, browse round shops and return to the flat, often to go to bed again. Even the thought of Nathan's electric toothbrush, whirring round the contours of his handsome teeth for five minutes every morning and evening, was not sufficient to cloud the memory. There would be no lox and bagel brunches this year. There wouldn't even be Gerrard's Cross. Her parents were flying out to Washington to be with Duncan and Mary Beth. Rachel had been invited but had declined, unenticed by the prospect of family charades of the kind Anita was so dreading and unwilling to return anywhere near the scene of so much recent personal mess and disappointment. Her eldest brother Ian, no doubt assuming that she had other plans, had not asked her to join them in Scotland. Not that she would have accepted anyway. Clare's side of the family were bound to be there too, with their unignorably large children and all that shrieking Highland mirth.

Instead, for the first time in her life, Rachel faced the possibility of Christmas on her own, a possibility about which she felt faintly incredulous, since, like the rest of the world, she knew herself to be the kind of lady with plans laid in advance for every occasion. There was always Joy or maybe Naomi. But the thought of a draughty French farmhouse was as unappealing as the chocolate-box brand of a family Christmas at which the Fullertons so excelled. Party frocks, mulled wine and kissing the vicar. Rachel shuddered. Besides which, she had recently agreed to visit the Fullertons over Easter. To call back and ask for hospitality at Christmas in the meantime was unthinkable. A woman with plans, a woman envied for her independence and self-possession, does not easily knock on doors and beg to be taken in. Like some kind of latterday Mary, thought Rachel – fighting waves of increasingly hysterical self-deprecation – but without the man at her side or the child in her belly.

'Rachel, are you still there? Don't say you're cross with me too?'

'Cross? No, don't be silly. Just a murderous truck or two. I'd better go. I'm almost at my turn-off. You take care of yourself, you hear.'

'Where are you off to this time?' Anita's voice was sly with envy.

'Somewhere called Great Hampton Lodge. Clay pigeon shoot-ing and go-cart racing with a client. A Christmas treat,' she concluded flatly.

'Christ, you lucky sod.'

'Aren't I just? Lucky is my middle name, Anita, I thought you knew that by now.'

Rachel accelerated past the speed limit, enjoying, in spite of other preoccupations, the way the car surged at the touch of her foot. There was no way but forwards after all, she told herself, her heart filling with fresh resolve to seize all of life's possibilities with both hands and wrestle them under control.

16

A message at reception to the effect that Mr Cliff Weybourne had been forced to postpone his arrival until the following morning, set the seal on Rachel's good spirits. In the privacy of her room, she performed a little celebratory jig. Frank would not like it at all, she thought gleefully, doing a twirl with a hand towel; he hated to be reminded that any business could be more pressing than his own.

Dinner on the first night took the relaxed form of a cold buffet. Frank Alder waited until the assembled party had laden their plates with food before banging a fork against a glass and gracing them all with his customary speech of welcome. Though his references to the Allday Sunlotion film were hardly effusive, his warm praise for McKenzie Cartwright in general and Rachel in particular sounded genuine enough. Not even mentioning Cliff's absence, he went on to conclude with instructions that speeches were banned for the following night, as was the failure of anyone to have a good time. Joining with the smattering of applause, Rachel allowed herself a smile of satisfaction. Frank Alder had taken several years of careful nurturing. To allow him to play such a leading role in an event which was funded entirely by the agency, was one of the innumerable ways in which she had skilfully pandered to a man whose only weakness was his ego. A little flattery and deference applied in the right areas could work wonders, she had discovered, especially if the originator of such compliments was female and not entirely unattractive. Sometimes she even imagined a hint of a father-daughter thing in his attitude towards her, a decidedly dubious subtext for a business relationship, but one which she deliberately chose not to analyse beyond the fact that it was both manageable and greatly to her own advantage. Alder and Elliot certainly constituted a team with which the wily Cliff Weybourne would have difficulty competing, she reassured herself, catching Frank's eye across the room and raising her glass.

At last it felt good to be somewhere. Her eyes trailed appreciatively round the chattering groups, noting the elegant backdrop of handsome oak wall panels, tastefully littered with oil paintings of sea shores and poppy fields. These were her people, after all. This was her world. The ratio of sexes was no accident either; it made for a better party atmosphere she found, to keep the numbers of men and women roughly equal, particularly given Saturday night, when high spirits of varying origins had been known to lead to a step or two of dancing. At Rachel's suggestion a jazz band had been signed up that year, the idea being that they could perform quietly in the background during dinner and liven things up later on if required. Looking at the polite conversations being conducted now it was hard to imagine that such an investment in entertainment would prove justified. But Rachel knew from past experience that a few shared escapades with bullets and go-carts could lead to the most extreme abandonment of inhibitions. Last year the mousiest of marketing directors had caused a sensation by ripping off his dress shirt and performing ten minutes of gyratory aerobics round a dining-room chair.

Having made a point of saying a few words to everyone, working her way round the room with a polished ease that would have made her socially aspiring American sister-in-law seethe with envy, Rachel slipped away for something of an early night. It would be a long day tomorrow and long days had, increasingly, to be prepared for, she found, if they were to be coped with as deftly as she intended, without the debilitating accompaniment of puffy eyes and a weak heart. Feeling the knives of anxiety twist in her stomach at the mere thought of needing to sleep, Rachel decided to treat herself to a pill from a bottle acquired during a particularly stressful patch a couple of years before. *Not to be taken when pregnant*, the label said, which reminded her that she still hadn't done anything about getting the folate supplements recommended by Dr Abbot. Grimacing at her own ineptitude, she scooped out a fingerful of nightcream and deposited three large blobs on her cheeks and the tip of her nose. She rubbed the cream in with both hands, wondering all the while if middle-aged women dependent on moisturiser and sleeping tablets had any right to flatter themselves with images of pushing prams and being loved. Minutes later the tingling heaviness began, together with the not entirely pleasant sensation of having her veins injected with molten lead.

Cliff Weybourne arrived in time for breakfast, his face as smooth as polished chalk, his black hair freshly cut. Even though olive-green corduroys and a brown mohair jumper offered little camouflage for the generous contours of his figure, there was something sickeningly spritely about the man, Rachel decided, eyeing him over the rim of her coffee cup as he sprang from table to table, firing smiles and shaking hands. He spent longest of all talking to Frank Alder, bending his head confidentially near his ear for one comment, before standing up and slapping his newspaper on his thigh as they both laughed out loud. Rachel tensed, hating the notion that there was a man's club after all, that no matter how hard her outer shell, there was a society that she could never join, a society that would always be more assured, more powerful in the end.

Having helped himself from a buffet of hot-plates, Cliff made his way over towards Rachel, who – in keeping with her aversion to breakfast conversations of any kind – had taken the precaution of seating herself in the furthest corner of the dining room, at a table laid for one. Beside her a large window presented a snapshot of their grand surroundings: gravelled paths and evergreen shrubs skirted an elegant carpet of a croquet pitch, this morning covered with a lacy cloth of white frost. On a terrace below that were two tennis courts, where a keen pair in white track suits and headbands were defying the bitter cold with a set of racy pink tennis balls and rackets with giant heads.

'May I?'

Rachel nodded at the empty seat opposite her. 'Of course.'

'Seen the news?' He smacked his newspaper with the back of his hand. 'Blackers have been taken over by The Glastonbury Group. They're going to invite five agencies to pitch for the business. I was up till all hours with Alan last night. We're on the shortlist apparently. We could get Blackers and a lot more besides.' He put down his plate, on which balanced several toppling pyramids of fried food, and helped himself to a place setting from a neighbouring table.

Jets of fat spurted from the sausage at the prick of his fork. 'It's bloody fantastic. Alan is delighted, as you might well imagine. Not the easiest of markets to advertise.' He had a method of rerouting mouthfuls into one cheek in order to facilitate the business of talking with the section of his mouth that remained vacant. 'Homecare products, do-it-yourself weaponry – there's so bloody much of it and so little to tell them all apart. Going to be a hell of a pitch. Money no object, Alan says – *carte blanche*. Hey, *carte blanche* for Blackers. Not bad, eh?'

Rachel delivered the merest shadow of a smile to acknowledge this witticism before casting her eyes over the newsprint in front of her.

'If we win the business I'll see to it that Alan considers you for the account, of course.' He drove a hefty wadge of fried bread through a pool of egg yolk and tomato skin.

'That's very sweet of you, Cliff, but there's no need, really.' She folded the newspaper and handed it back. 'I would much prefer to concentrate my efforts on Mallarmé, as I have explained to Alan many times. You can keep those power drills and lavatory fittings all to yourself. As you say, a hell of a challenge for all concerned.'

'Absolutely.'

Rachel made a big show of folding her napkin and looking at her watch, thinking all the while how dispiriting it was to fire missiles at such a leathery hide.

'Are you any good with a gun then, Rachel?' There was a hint of a leer to the question, which caught her by surprise.

'Oh yes, Cliff,' she replied coolly, pushing back her chair and standing up. The presence of an as yet undetected speck of encrusted egg yolk to the left of his mouth filled her with a perverse and cheerful optimism for the day ahead. 'I've no problem when it comes to guns.'

'I'm delighted to hear it.' He chuckled, clearly amused rather than warned by the steely look in her eye. 'I look forward to a full demonstration.'

In fact Rachel hated guns. After her first experience of shooting, on a similar weekend four years earlier, vivid pink and purple bruises had sprouted over her right shoulder and upper chest, gradually turning yellow and greeny-blue, like flowers fading past their prime. Though her technique had since improved sufficiently to avoid incurring such physical injuries again, firing bullets at flying discs was not a prospect she had learnt to relish for itself. It was the end results that interested her – the relaxing of business barriers, the curious camaraderie that sharing such experiences allowed.

She smiled at Frank Alder as she passed his table. As usual, he was kitted out in full country squire regalia, complete with a monogrammed cartridge bag, a tweed cap and spotless green hunters, all of which remained suspiciously impervious to the ravages of time. This year there was the addition of a handsome brown leather cartridge belt, which he had placed on display across the table, between his side plate and a glass of orange. The knobs of each bullet gleamed with evidence of polishing. Fancy dress, she thought, broadening her smile. The man was hopelessly pompous – quite unteasable – but really rather sweet, she decided, taking care to admire the belt before going back up to her room.

Before they were allowed to select padded vests and guns, a lecture on safety was barked at them by a veiny-faced man with strikingly protuberant ears that trembled with the delivery of each sentence. There was to be one trap firing, two clays at a time and four stands. Four people at each stand. Twelve bores for the men, sixteen bores for the ladies. Ear plugs were recommended but not compulsory. All beginners would receive as much help as they desired.

As Rachel's turn to take the stand approached, apprehension gave way to a customary determination to appear strong, not to conform to a whimpering female stereotype of any kind. She held the stock tightly into her shoulder as she fired, shouting 'pull' in a voice that hit the still cold air without any trace of the hesitancy lurking inside. Two clays flew out, catapulting into the grey sky and hovering for just an instant before they began to fall, plummeting to the earth like stones. Rachel missed the first three, nicked the fourth and missed the fifth and sixth. Her eyes, watery with cold, squinted at the targets. As she missed and missed again, her mind began to feel as if it was spinning too, firing into nothing, focusing on nothing, adrift on the biting air. A sense of absurdity descended from nowhere, threatening to overwhelm her. What was she doing, on this grey, bitter December Saturday – a day for hot drinks and curling on sofas to watch old films – firing a gun at a blank sky? Both feet had grown quite weightless with cold. An obstinate, unseemly dribble was trickling from her nose, sniff-resistant, tepid on her upper lips. Cold air was snaking into her ears and eye sockets, filling her head with icy pain, blurring her vision until even the sky was no more than a grey fuzz.

She was the last to fire in her group. Several people who had either given up or finished were standing chattering and laughing several yards away, the vapour of their breath mingling with the grey swirls rising from the mouths of the smokers. Even before she started Rachel had caught herself longing to join them, longing to be brave enough to behave as if she did not care. Like the petite brand manager with heart-shaped lips who hadn't even had a go. How sweet it would be to act the sissy for once, to admit defeat with a few girly simpers of distaste and fear. How tiring to be the fearless Rachel Elliot – a match for any man, whatever the game. How utterly futile.

The helper from her stand had fallen back to smoke a cigarette with some of the others. Loading her gun for the last time, Rachel found herself focusing on the prettiness of the grass around her feet, where untrodden blades were still sugar-tipped with frost. Not catching anyone's eye was paramount suddenly; not giving the impression of misery being the least she could do, maybe even the only salvageable achievement of the morning.

Shooting at the next stand was a young account manager called Chlöe, who had flaming red hair and startled blue eyes. Though the hair had begun the morning tucked away up under the brim of a big woollen hat, great tresses of it had since broken free and were now cascading impressively down the quilted back of her protective green vest. Exhilaration shone in the blush of her cheeks, in the confident way in which she swung her gun, aiming it skyward with the ease of a finger pointing at a board. At the third stand, Frank Alder painted an altogether more traditional, if less compelling figure; elegant, but slow. One hit in five, maybe four. Beyond him, the most surprising contributor of all: Cliff Weybourne, as poised and alert as an athlete on the starting block, with split-second reactions that ensured the clash of bullet and target every time. There were no nicking of edges for him, no near misses, but mini explosions of erupting clay, orange shards raining, dark with speed, upon the tops of the black trees clumped along the skyline below. He hit all but one. The ginger-haired Chlöe hit twenty. Frank got eight. Rachel three. Three out of twenty-five.

Once the shoot was over everyone gathered round, blowing into cupped hands for warmth, exchanging jokes and congratulations. The dampness in the air seemed to muffle their voices, sucking out the trill, inducing an urge to shout to be heard at all. Rachel, grey and stiff, clung to her gun, nodding her head with the best of them, only the fear of appearing forlorn giving her the strength to mould her frozen face into something resembling a smile.

'Well tried, Rachel. I like your style. Very promising. I like a woman who tries.' Cliff Weybourne heralded his arrival at her heels with a hearty slap between her shoulder blades. The smack of his hand on her back, so shockingly hard and uninvited, wrought a surge of such irritation that she gasped out loud, digging her nails into her palms in order to prevent herself from hitting back.

'I was bloody awful. Never got my eye in.'

She was rescued by Frank Alder, who appeared on the other side of her. 'Tough conditions today. Though it didn't stop you, Cliff, did it? Most impressive, most impressive. Out of our league, eh Rachel?'

'He certainly is.' When she tried to lick some life back into her lips, the saliva dried in an instant, leaving tiny cracks that felt raw and sore. On impulse, she linked her arm through Frank's, needing suddenly to feel aligned with him, even if it was ineptitude that granted her the privilege.

'You'll get him on the racetrack though, won't you Rachel my dear? If I recall correctly, you're something of a tiger behind a wheel.' He roared with laughter. Rachel, sickened by the realisation that rivalry between her and Cliff should be both so obvious and a cause for such mirth, let go of his arm and moved away.

After a hasty lunch they were herded into a minibus and driven to a tarmac oasis passing under the name of Formula 1 West. This time, insurance waivers had to be signed, promising that if limbs, eyes, or lives were mislaid during the course of the afternoon's entertainment, they had only themselves to blame. A young man with cigarettes and pencils slotted behind his ears then delivered the second safety lecture of the day. Helmets were mandatory, as were grey overalls of curious dimensions that bore little relation to the human shapes for which they were supposedly designed. The most ill-fitted of all was Cliff, whose trouser legs terminated two inches above the tops of his white socks and whose brown mohair tangle peeked through the buttons straining across his belly like stomach hair gone wild. Only Chlöe managed to sport her costume with anything like panache, aided considerably by her flaming film-star tresses and a pair of heavy-soled ankle boots which contributed excellently to the overall effect. In a bid to heighten the atmosphere of the occasion, loud speakers blared 'Simply The Best' as each set of cars took up their positions, adding considerably to the din of engines as they roared away. Rachel, during a faltering set of warm-up laps, found herself grappling for the second time that day with an overpowering sense of the absurd. How had she endured these games before? What on earth had she been playing at?

But when her race started, something clicked into place. All her uncertainties and fear dissolved in the few instants it took to raise her left foot from the brake and press her right hard down on the accelerator. Effortlessly, she cruised past Cliff Weybourne, past the others in her heat, and settled into the lead. The noise of the engines filled her head, adding to the intoxicating impression of speed as the ground, so near at hand, rushed past. It was like flying. She felt immortal. When the marshall waved his chequered flag at the finishing line, her pulse and her go-cart slowed with reluctance. Though Rachel was unaware of it herself, the glow of triumph remained with her for many hours afterwards, greatly heightening the effect of the striking blue evening dress she wore to the dinner that night and lending a vibrance to her appearance, which the more astute among the assembled company realised had been absent for many weeks.

17

Frank Alder was a good, if slightly lumbering dancer. His answer to the more challengingly rhythmic numbers was to keep time with his hands while his feet played small shuffling games of their own. When it came to slower tunes he steered Rachel round the room in the frame of his arms with a steady elegance that spoke volumes for the ballroom skills of previous generations. The jazz musicians, having been allowed to strum and croon exactly as they pleased throughout the meal, were now called upon to supply a medley of requests quite unrelated to the brand of expertise for which they had originally been hired.

Rachel was old enough to experience a tingle of gratitude as well as pleasure at the way several heads turned in appreciation when she entered the dining room. Where once such appreciation had been a certainty, she was now learning the wisdom of not expecting it.

When exactly did one become an old lady? she had wondered earlier that night, drawing a pencil line round the edges of her lips and pouting in self-mockery at the result. At what point was one supposed to surrender the eyeliner and confront the world with grey hair and a headscarf? How would she avoid joining the pitiable ranks of those who tried too hard, those for whom the very visibility of their efforts undermined any of the beautifying effects achieved? Once upon a time Rachel had been thrilled that the industry in which she worked thrived on an image of youthful ebullience, on the dynamism of its few elderly members. Now it made her secretly afraid. It was all very well feeling good in shimmering dresses, but the daily grind was there too. Children were supposed to keep you young, she thought slyly, remembering Anita's warning and discarding it in the same instant. But the thought of a child was scary too.

She rammed on the lid of her lipstick. Everything scared her these days; it was intolerable. Since she had forgotten to wind the lipstick back into its tube, the lid succeeded only in crushing the contents it was designed to protect. Instead of a smooth torpedo of red, Rachel was left with a sticky, misshapen crayon, like one of the expensive paint sticks she had given Charlotte after the twins had been at them. She dropped the entire mess into the bin beside the dressing table and tried to wipe her fingers clean with a tissue. Though the worst came off easily, a faint pink stain remained on her fingertips; a reminder of the effort behind the costume, the cost of looking good.

But it was impossible not to enjoy herself that night, especially not after the wheels of her own self-respect – and everybody else's – had been thoroughly oiled by several glasses of good wine and four courses of excellent food. Back on the dance floor, opposite Ted Bealey, an old friend from the Planning Department, Rachel felt her body loosen and her blood flow. Dancing with Frank had been an altogether more reserved business, some part of her kept in check by a deep sense of propriety to do with the age gap and a niggle of a worry about the affection lurking in his old-man smile. But with subsequent partners she began to let herself go a little, moving her hips fluidly in time to the music and floating her arms to the front and sides, stretching her fingers as if to feel each pulse more keenly. Ted, clearly inspired by such synchronised abandonment, began to jig more vigorously himself, jerking his hips to the left and right and beckoning Rachel to do the same. Laughing, Rachel joined in the game, moving closer, until the pair of them were nudging alternate hip bones and waving their arms like mad things.

The song had not quite finished when Cliff stepped between them with a hip-thrust of a request to join in the fun. Beads of perspiration glistened on his chalky face; the thick layers of his black hair, usually brushed tidily off his temples, had fallen forwards and were sticking to damp patches on his forehead. He had so far devoted most of the evening to an unabashed courtship of Chlöe, the red-headed account manager, whom he had sat next to at dinner and whose admiration he had since been trying to secure through some peacock-style rituals on the dance floor. While not wanting to pay him the compliment of appearing impressed, Rachel had none the less observed these curiously elegant antics out of the corner of one eye, amazed to note the poise with which the small tidy feet supported the swaying bulk on top.

Patting the left side of his chest in a mime of exhaustion, Ted bowed out. Rachel continued dancing, though with considerably less vigour, letting her eyes rove around the room in a bid to avoid meeting Cliff's look of smug satisfaction while she waited for the tune to end. Instead of pausing for its customary breather between songs however, the band turned the last chord of one song into the first of the next – a much slower one that placed immediate pressure on remaining couples to regroup into more intimate poses. Rachel began backing away but Cliff was too quick for her, springing forward and throwing his arms around her shoulders, his body already swaying in time to the new, heavier rhythm.

'Cliff . . . I'm really tired . . . dropping in fact. I really don't think—'

'Oh, come now Rachel, don't give me that. We could be friends, you know, you and I. We could work very well together. Very well indeed.' His arms pressed harder; they were lower on her back now, pulling her in.

'Really . . . I'd like a drink . . . I'm so hot.' She could feel the damp palms of his hands sticking to the silk covering her back.

'I'm hot too, believe me . . . but everyone's looking, you know, everyone's wondering if we can work this thing out between us. It would be nice to prove them wrong, wouldn't it? Nice to show we're proper grown-ups. No in-fighting. A tight team.'

It was true, their partnership on the dance floor had definitely been noticed. Frank Alder, now reclining in an arm chair with a cigar and a tumbler of brandy, was studying them particularly hard. Cliff was right: it would be cause for even more gossip if she broke away after just a few bars of music. Far better to see it through, to suffer in silence for appearance's sake.

Feeling her resistance lessen, he pulled her closer. In her high heels she was almost as tall as he. He could see the glass freckles of sweat on her bare chest, count every stone in the glittering clusters dangling from her earlobes. Her arms on his shoulders hung loosely, leaving her hands trailing with an insouciance that excited him. A moment of mistiming and their faces touched, a hot brush of cheek on cheek, before she jerked her head back out of range. Some devious shuffling on Cliff's part ensured that their legs touched too, though she managed to keep her hips firmly to herself – an achievement which necessitated a bend at the waist that was almost comic and certainly unnatural.

'Come on, Rachel, relax now. I'm not going to bite, you know. I'm just a man. A man who admires you very much.'

'Oh, and I admire you Cliff, believe me. You are a person of singular abilities.'

'Thank you, Rachel. How generous of you to say so.'

The music seemed endless. Her back, aching from the effort of staying so stiff and separate, gradually began to relent, until only her head remained free, her chin pointing slightly upward, like a swimmer reaching for air.

'I loved today,' he murmured, 'I loved the way you beat me.'

'You beat me, Cliff, remember.' Her voice sounded high pitched and strange. 'The best score of the lot—'

'Ah, but not on the fast track. Christ, you drove like the devil.' His hands, which had travelled even further down her back, arrived at the upper curve of her bottom and squeezed. Energised by repulsion, Rachel pulled away at once. The music stopped in the same instant.

He held up his hands in a mockery of innocence, grinning at the expression on her face before taking her hand and planting a kiss on the knuckles. 'Thank you so much, Rachel, that was delightful.'

When reception telephoned at seven-thirty the next morning, Rachel experienced a few seconds of blissful, unregistering drowsiness before the full horror of the night's event dawned on her again.

'. . . Sleet and snow are forecast for Wales and the Southwest,' declared the radio above her head, 'with temperatures sinking to below freezing tonight. Motorists are warned that driving conditions will be hazardous and are advised to stay at home unless journeys are unavoidable.' Turning down the volume, Rachel lay back and pulled the sheets up to her eyes. In a picture on the wall opposite, St George was slaying a dragon. A willowy princess looked on, suppliant and doey-eyed, waiting for her rescuer to finish off the job.

Cliff Weybourne had tried to have sex with her. The fact of it felt both solid and impossible. He had knocked on her door in the small hours, said he was making an early start for London; said he had important papers about the Blackers takeover; said he was sorry to wake her, said it was important; said . . . she couldn't remember what else. Enough to make her stumble, sleepy and dry-mouthed, to her door, to stand frowning at the passage light, pushing the hair from her eyes as she held out her hand for whatever he had to deliver, her brain in too much of a dozy whir to wonder at the strangeness of such a request. And he was dressed to go, with his black briefcase on the floor at his side and with a sheaf of papers in his hands. But instead of handing them over he had pushed his way in, pushed her too, so that she half-walked, half-stumbled back onto the bed. Before adrenalin gave her strength, his hands were inside her nightie, one up under the hem, the other in through the undone buttons at the front.

'Jesus, Rachel, Jesus,' he grunted, his tongue licking her face.

It was hard to do anything but gasp at first, the attack was so quick, so utterly unexpected.

'You want it,' he grunted, 'I know you want it.'

She tried to kick with her legs, but the weight of him was too much. 'Get out, get out or I'll scream.'

'Oh yes, scream . . . that's fine . . . scream.'

She tried to. She opened her mouth and pushed, but nothing came out, not even air. In the end she used her teeth, biting into the soft roll of flesh pushing over the top of his starched shirt collar, using an energy and venom inspired by fear. He let out a howl and leapt back at once, clutching his neck. In the same instant she rolled free and ran for the door.

'Get out, you bastard.' Her body trembled so much it was hard even to keep a grip on the smooth metal handle of the door.

Cliff was dabbing at his neck with a clean white handkerchief, staring at two rosy specks in horror. 'You bitch.'

'Just get out, now, please.' She could feel her energy begin to sap away, as the surge of adrenalin receded and shock began to take over.

Cliff, the handkerchief still pressed to his neck, was looking round for his briefcase.

'You're not going to get away with this,' she whispered, edging towards the light in the passageway.

'Get away with what? I made a bad call, that's all.' He began adjusting his tie and hair. The bleeding at his neck had stopped, though the skin looked very bruised. 'You gave me the come-on tonight, you can't deny it. Then you let me into your room. You were hot for it Rachel, any man could see that.'

'How dare you . . .'

'How dare I?' He actually laughed, throwing back his head and closing his eyes for a few moments. 'We are grown-ups, my dear. The fact that you went off the idea is not exactly my problem . . .'

'You wait . . . you'll see.'

'Sure, I'll wait and see.' He raised his hand to pat her shoulder but she ducked out of reach. 'My, my, touchy, aren't we? Funny really, I would never have taken you for the frigid spinster type, but then life is full of surprises. Your copy of the documents is over there on the table, by the way. See you Monday. It's been a good weekend, don't you think?'

She watched him walk away, his footsteps soundless on the lilac hallway carpet. Having locked the door, she looked at her watch. Five o'clock in the morning. Outside it was still pitch black, though she could hear a mounting wind signalling the approach of bad weather in the beat of its huge wings. Suddenly icy with cold, she had slipped back between the sheets, pulling them round her neck for warmth while she rubbed her feet together. The movement was soothing, sending heat not only round her legs but across the bed as well.

The aftermath of shock brought an unbelievable sleepiness. As she closed her eyes it dawned on her that, with courage, she now had the wherewithal to eject Cliff Weybourne from her life completely. It offered comfort of sorts. Less comforting was the irony of other, crueller thought associations which tiptoed with her towards the brink of sleep. Would she have kept a baby fathered by Cliff Weybourne? Would rape have been worth a child?

18 ∫

On Christmas Eve Rachel was ambushed by a throng of school-age carol singers on her doorstep. While the elder ones managed only a self-conscious nonchalance, the under-tens belted out the verses with unabashed energy, nudging and smiling happily at each other as they went along. A small crowd gathered, head-nodding encouragement and appreciation, united for a few moments by this shared pleasure, as a blue sky or a fall of snow unites those who smile about it below.

> *We wish you a merry Christmas,*
> *We wish you a merry Christmas,*
> *We wish you a merry Christmas*
> *And a happy New Year.*
> *Glad tidings we bring to you and your king*
> *We wish you a merry Christmas*
> *And a happy New Year.*

Rachel put her bags down on the pavement and waited for a path to clear to the wide stone steps leading up to the front door of her building. As they launched into the second verse, she caught herself humming and squeezing her toes in time to the music, old echoes of childhood feelings stirring inside. But then it occurred to her that, for adults, Christmas was just a remembered joy, and her toes froze inside her boots.

When they had finished, the smallest child, its sex disguised by a yellow balaclava covering all but two large hazel eyes, stepped forward rattling a blue charity box on the side of which was a handwritten label, saying *Crisis At Christmas*.

'We're collecting for people who are going to have a horrid Christmas,' it said solemnly, jigging the box under Rachel's nose.

'What a worthy cause,' she murmured, slotting a pound coin into the slit.

The leader of the brood, a beaming woman with ruddy cheeks and a floppy-brimmed black velvet hat that bounced over her eyebrows, began herding her protégés away, mouthing 'thank-yous' at the contributions clinking into the box. A few moments later, the strains of 'In The Bleak Mid-Winter', delivered at a cheerfully breakneck speed, started up further down the street.

A wadge of crisp white envelopes sat in her letterbox in the main hall. Thanks to the added burdens of the festive season, the postman had not been arriving at his usual hour. Rachel had caught herself missing their doorstep exchanges, a few pithy comments on the rain or the hazards of British beef having had a mysteriously heartening effect on many a dank morning in the past.

She missed the cat, too. After putting in a brief appearance upon her return from Bermuda, it had vanished, Alice-in-Wonderland-style, apparently for good this time. To miss a cat seemed to Rachel to be quite close to hitting rock bottom. She had never wanted the thing in the first place, had only grown attached to it because of its own impudent persistence. Two tins of gourmet jellied chunks now sat gathering dust on the windowsill. Rabbit and chicken liver. Fifty pence a mouthful. The animal had disappeared the day she bought them, a coincidence that seemed fraught with meanings she did not care to understand.

Having hurled the tins to the back of an empty shelf, she made a cup of tea, turned the central heating dial up several notches and took her post through into the sitting room.

There was a card from Anita. On the front an irate Father Christmas was tugging at a parking ticket wedged into the windscreen of his sleigh. Inside were the usual printed greetings, under which she had scrawled, *In 'Coventry' in the country with G's parents. Being stuffed with food, but at least no cooking which is good. Thanks for Charlotte's parcel (weighs a ton!). Hope Gds Crss is not too gruesome. We're here till Dec 30. See you at the Robsons' New Year thrash as usual?*

Rachel smiled at the expostulating Santa, cheered as always by the faintly anarchic tone of any communication from Anita, and wishing – reluctantly – that she was close at hand. To be in serious need of someone to talk to was a new and highly unenjoyable experience. As was the realisation that isolation and independence were not such poles apart after all.

She also felt a mixture of guilt and alarm at having lied so easily about her whereabouts. Was it entirely normal, she wondered, running her finger under the flap of the next envelope, to find the horror of spending Christmas alone preferable to the admission of any such thing, even to a close friend? Was it so peculiar not to want to give the world permission to feel as sorry for her as she felt herself?

In a last bid to be plucky and make the best of things, she had left work very early that afternoon in order to stop off at an expensive delicatessen on the way home. Without so much as a glance at a price, she had purchased six quails eggs, three strips of smoked eel, two pots of Russian caviar, one bottle of champagne and one of claret, some smoked salmon pâté and two loaves of freshly baked, nutty brown bread, still warm from the oven. At the last minute she threw several jars of delicacies into her basket as well, spurred on by some recommendations from the shop owner and a determination to be as extravagant as possible.

The second card contained the printed message, *Seasonal Greetings from Filmstyle.* Beneath this there were some black loops which, on closer scrutiny, turned out to be an idiosyncratic representation of the name, Will Raphael. The picture on the card was a photograph of a woman, seated at a table alone, head in hands with her eyes closed. The entire scene was black and white, save for a robin, perched on the windowsill behind, and a single red rose, arching out of a slim crystal vase. Rachel studied it for a few moments, disliking the image, yet curious as to how the effect had been achieved. It was halfway between a photograph and a painting. The woman had long straight hair and a peaceful face that somehow made up for the emptiness of the room. In the bottom right hand corner were the initials *WR.*

She sipped her tea and added the new cards to the ones already decorating her mantelpiece before turning to Nathan's. It was something of a surprise, after so many weeks, to hear from him at all. It also made her feel guilty for having drawn a thick red line through his presence on her Christmas card list. A colour photograph, of the mass-produced variety, fell out of the envelope, depicting Nathan and a tall blonde girl in ski outfits of dazzling yellow and pink; their mittened hands were waving with puppet-like symmetry at the camera lens. Printed across a section of blue sky in the top left hand corner were the words: *Happy Holidays from Cindy and Nathan. With love to you all.*

Rachel scowled at the fresh-faced slalem star, with her flawless, gleaming portals of teeth and her vibrant tumble of hair, looking so yellow against the backdrop of blanket snow. Their happiness looked suspiciously manic, she decided, letting the meanness wash through her, instinctively despising and distrusting any brand of love whose proprietors felt the need to advertise it so garishly to the world. She put the card down and then picked it up again. The notion that this Cindy, although more perfectly formed in every respect, might be a younger version of herself, did nothing to fan the embers of her festive spirit. Good teeth, fair hair. They were not so unalike. But what really jarred was the fresh-faced enthusiasm of the girl, the unmistakable glow of a self-conviction which Rachel was beginning to associate with youth and which she had, until so recently, taken for granted herself.

On the other side of the picture there was a faint message, Nathan's biro clearly having had quite a struggle against the laminated surface of the card. *Getting married at New Years. All the best. Nathan.*

So he wasn't just skiing and screwing with the Toothpaste Queen, he was marrying her too. Rachel shook her head in wonder at the exuberant expressions on the tanned faces of the snow-bound pair. True love indeed. She tossed the card to one side and took the cold remains of her tea through into the kitchen.

Images of Anita lurching into the back of a cab assisted greatly in the decision to leave the claret to breathe for a while instead of gulping it down on the spot. Having unpacked her purchases with deliberate briskness, she flicked on the little string of lights entwined round the verdant nylon tree in her hall, ran herself a scalding bath – mountainous with foam – and went to fetch her portable radio from the bedroom. A man with a crooning voice was reading the lesson about the shepherds embarking on the curious challenge of following a star. There followed an inspiring rendition of 'While Shepherds Watched' the unwavering trebles somehow making the old words sound full of fresh meaning, while the notes soared on some impressive acoustics offered by the tiled walls of the bathroom. Just as she was in danger of experiencing a twinge or two of religious fervour, an intermittent buzz started up in the background, as if someone was hoovering a carpet in the choir stalls. The buzz grew louder and nearer until, as the batteries entered their final death throes, the only thing being transmitted was a furious spitting sound. Reaching out a deft, big toe, crested with bubbles, Rachel switched the radio off. This Christmas was going to be one of those times, she told herself, something that had to be lived through, endured, until it stopped, like a bad dream, like getting Cliff Weybourne out of her room.

At the thought of him the water seemed to lose some of its heat. She slipped further down amongst the peaks of foam, seeking more warmth. Nothing was working out these days, absolutely nothing.

All the way back from Bristol, ploughing through horizontal sheets of icy rain, Rachel had exalted at the prospect of turning the horror of recent events to her advantage. The following morning she had marched into Alan Jarvis's spacious office without a moment's hesitation, planting herself in the middle of his creamy sheepskin rug with all the confidence of the truly virtuous.

'Rachel? Is something the matter?'

'You could say that Alan, yes.' She made no attempt to hide her agitation. 'This is not going to be easy . . .'

'Sit down. I'll get Julie on to some coffee—'

'No thank you, not for me.' She inhaled deeply; the room smelt of a mixture of furniture polish and Alan's aftershave, a flowery sweet smell that made her faintly nauseous. 'The simple fact is that . . . that during the course of the weekend I have been . . . I was . . . abused by Cliff.'

'Abused? You mean he was rude to you?'

'I mean,' she hesitated for an instant, 'I mean that he harassed me . . . sexually.'

'You are accusing Cliff Weybourne of sexual harassment?' There was no hiding the incredulity in his tone. 'Well . . . I knew that the two of you had something of a personality clash but really . . .'

'He came into my bedroom, Alan.' The sense that she was losing his sympathy, that she had never even had it to start with, gave her the courage to speak more bluntly. 'He threw himself at me. He assaulted me.'

Alan was rubbing his chin nervously, studying her out of the corner of his eye. 'This is very . . . very difficult indeed.'

Rachel stood up. 'No, Alan, it is not difficult. Cliff Weybourne tried to force me to have sex with him. It is intolerable that he should be allowed to continue working here. He may try again, he may attack other women . . .' Aware that she was in danger of sounding hysterical, she sat back down on the slippery edge of the leather sofa and placed both hands on her knees. After careful consideration of her wardrobe she had opted for a dark blue trouser suit with a white shirt buttoned up to her neck: infallibly chaste, unarguably businesslike.

'Look, Rachel . . .' Alan Jarvis came to sit next to her, lowering his voice to a pitch of tender concern. '. . . I know Cliff is a hard man to work with. Believe me, you are not the only person who has problems with him . . . but he is also a shrewd and imaginative businessman. Clients love him. He has he been doing an excellent job on the new business front.' He put his hands together, interlocking each finger. 'And . . . well, in simple terms, he would be extremely costly to get rid of.' When their eyes met he blinked first. 'So, Rachel, I want you to think very hard for a moment and tell me whether you are absolutely certain that you wish to persist with this allegation. Sometimes . . . misunderstandings arise during occasions like these . . . when everybody is feeling jolly and so on . . .'

'There was no misunderstanding, Alan. I have endured my quota of uninvited gropes, believe me. I know the difference.

This was attempted sexual assault and, I can assure you, it was not very pleasant.' Her voice trembled.

'No, no,' he soothed, touching her hand for a second, before going back to his desk. He picked up the telephone and held it for a few moments before pressing any numbers. 'You are prepared, I take it, to confront Cliff with these accusations yourself?'

'Oh yes,' she replied quietly, 'I am indeed.' A tight elation was gathering in her stomach. She would hold nothing back, absolutely nothing. The truth was unignorable. Alan Jarvis had his weaknesses – he was a bit of a ditherer, he liked an easy life – but he was also a man of integrity. They had known each other a long time. He trusted her. And she him.

Cliff Weybourne entered the room a few minutes later, his pale face composed but unsmiling. Julie materialised with a tray of coffee behind him, the studied neutrality of her face warning Rachel that the mysteriously osmotic process of in-house gossip had started already. The coffee was poured and passed round, while the two main protagonists arranged themselves between the generous cushions of Alan's handsome three-piece suite, as if preparing to discuss nothing more taxing than a Christmas gift for a client, or the noise problems generated by the recent refurbishment of the ladies' lavatory.

Alan Jarvis kicked off the proceedings, while Rachel chewed the inside of her cheek and studied something invisible on the palm of her right hand.

'Cliff, I'm afraid Rachel has come to me this morning with some very serious allegations of inappropriate conduct on your part during the course of the weekend.'

Cliff sipped his coffee and shook his head, casting a sidelong glance of theatrical regret at Rachel before speaking himself.

'She threatened to do this Alan, but I never thought she would. I really didn't.' He put down his cup and turned to face Rachel. 'Let's leave this here, shall we?' he pleaded. 'We can, you know, Rachel. It's not too late to back down.'

She shook her head, her eyes never leaving his. 'I am accusing you of sexual . . . harassment.'

With a curt laugh Cliff returned his attention to Alan. 'What about this then?' He tilted his chin up so as to give their arbiter a better view of his neck. 'Evidence of quite a passion, I'm sure you'll agree. A lovebite, I believe it's called . . . quite a trophy, I'll admit.' Though the mark was bite-sized, there was no evidence of blood; just innocuous swirls of pink and blue. Cliff leant forwards, resting his elbows on his knees, looking earnest, ignoring Rachel's open-mouthed horror at this easy dismissal of proof on which she herself had been relying. 'Look, Alan, of course I would far rather this had not come out – generally I'm not a believer in relationships crossing the work threshold – but the fact of the matter is Rachel and I' – he had the audacity to shoot her a complicitous smile – 'almost had what you might call a fling. At quite a late stage – for which I apologise Rachel – I changed my mind. I'm afraid it dawned on me quite how unwise it would be, from the work point of view and so on. I pulled back. I returned to London.' He clapped his hands together. 'As far as I'm concerned the matter ended there. I'm just sorry that there seem to be all these hard feelings on Rachel's side.'

'How dare you,' she hissed.

'Now Rachel, it's only fair that he should be allowed to give his version of events.' Alan Jarvis's tone was already weary. The steadily increasing number of reports on sexual harassment cases in the papers had given him neither the appetite nor the confidence for dealing with such issues himself. Rachel Elliot was a good soldier, a very good soldier indeed, but recently she had been showing signs of what Alan Jarvis regarded as typically female distress; she had been moody and preoccupied, not her old self at all. He had even consulted his wife, Hilary, about it, who had mentioned the menopause and said not to worry. In his opinion Rachel still looked a bit on the young side for all that sort of thing, but it did make some sense. He was reminded of quite what a gloomy business Hilary's own hormonal crisis had been, crying and hot flushes all over the shop.

'You have been under a lot of stress recently, Rachel,' he began.

'Stress has nothing to do with this, Alan.' Her voice had gone up a pitch. 'This man,' she glanced at Cliff, reposing beside her, one hand flung across the back of his chair, his legs crossed while he studied her with unblinking eyes, 'this man tried to rape me. He entered my room in the middle of the night—'

'She let me in—'

'You said you had some documents for me—'

'And so I did—'

'Whoa there, please, both of you. First it's sexual harassment and now it's rape. Let's hear it from the start, each in turn, get everybody's cards on the table and take it from there. I want this sorted out quickly and properly. We cannot afford this kind of thing.' In an effort to regain control he had assumed the belittling tone of a reproving headmaster.

Rachel spoke first, doing her best to keep to the absolute facts, and managing to hold her voice steady. She mentioned the dancing that preceded the assault, how Cliff had made unwelcome advances even then, how she had opened her door only because of his insistence that the papers could not wait until the following day. How she had been forced to use her teeth in self-defence.

Cliff gave his reply eagerly. 'This is quite frankly ridiculous. It all started long before the dinner or what happened later. There was a kind of tension between us from the start – a sense of competition. It was exciting, I admit, and I played along with it. It didn't go unnoticed either. We had quite a dance together after dinner. You can be sure that got noticed, too. Ask any witnesses you want – there's a whole roomful to choose from.' He paused and softened his voice. 'Alan, I think I've been a man long enough to know when a female is interested—'

'Jesus Christ, this is intolerable.'

Alan's hand silenced her. 'Go on, Cliff.'

'As I was saying, Rachel here was being quite a flirt with everybody – well, with Frank and a couple of others anyway – but then we'd all had a bit to drink and so that was nothing to write home about. But when the evening broke up I was left under the definite impression that there was more there if I wanted it.' There was a glimpse of a collaborative smile, as if to say we men know about such things. 'I did mention some documents, but only so that she had a pretext for opening the door . . . I mean, it was obvious I could have left them for her at reception, wasn't it? She could easily have yelled at me to go away, not got out of bed at all. Anyway,' Cliff rubbed his hands, 'Rachel opened the door at once . . . and . . . well . . . she wasn't wearing much, if you know what I mean.' He cleared his throat.

'So things got a little . . . hot . . . more or less at once, until, like I said, I changed my mind. And I guess she just couldn't take that.' His eyes, as he met her gaze, were unrepentant, faintly mocking, even.

Alan Jarvis stood up and went to stand beside his window, where he ran his thumbs up and down his braces while he considered what to say next. 'It seems to me there has been a simple case of misunderstanding, a desperately unfortunate misunderstanding. And the best thing would be for both sides to acknowledge that openly, shake hands, and put it behind them.' He turned to present them both with an avuncular smile.

'He tried to assault me, Alan,' said Rachel in a small voice.

'He might have got the wrong idea, but then it seems that you did too . . .'

'I am not a flirt. I do not believe in . . . intimacy . . . of any kind with colleagues at work. In all my time . . .'

'Not what I've heard.'

She turned slowly, more incredulous than afraid of what new lies he might come up with. 'And what have you heard, may I ask, Cliff?'

He tweaked at the handkerchief in his breast pocket as he talked, tucking and tugging it into a neater shape, a lemon triangle, to match the colour of his shirt. 'Bermuda . . . quite a few extracurricular activities of one kind or another, I gather . . .'

'Bermuda?' She spun back to face Alan, who had the grace to wave his hand dismissively.

'There are always rumours like that, Cliff. They are irrelevant here, I think.'

They were both discharged after that, told to go away and think about it, like naughty children being given a second chance. As the door closed behind them Cliff had the temerity to shake her hand, saying that as far as he was concerned there were no hard feelings at all.

The next day Alan announced that Rachel was to be new Head of Account Management and about time too. After a sleepless night rehearsing resignation and revenge, Rachel was momentarily caught off guard. Almost worse than being disbelieved, or being offered a promotion in return for silence, was that Alan Jarvis had clearly failed to see the most basic fact in her defence:

that she would not have had sex with Cliff Weybourne if he had been the last man on earth, if copulation between them had meant the survival of the entire human race.

Without the support of Jarvis, taking the matter further would mean giving evidence in a court of law. While bracing herself to take such a route, Cliff's wily retelling of the tale illuminated the weakness of her position with terrible clarity: she had slow-danced with the man; she had opened her bedroom door to him in the small hours. Rachel could see the faces of the jury now: a middle-aged single woman, going one step too far and then regretting it. A woman scorned, wanting her pound of flesh. It was hopeless.

Unwilling to accept a bribe, yet fearful that resignation might look like an admission of defeat, Rachel had stalled for more time, promising to deliver her answer after the Christmas break. Meanwhile, the agency hummed with the unmistakable drone of rumour, infesting the expressions of colleagues with invisible meanings that left Rachel feeling powerless and wary. Even Melissa felt like the enemy, her looks of baffled curiosity revealing none of the sympathy that bubbled beneath, sympathy that she would have expressed but for the fire in Rachel's eyes, a blaze of warning to any who dared to venture too near.

By the week of Christmas Eve a fresh scandal had broken concerning the agency barman and a young motorbike courier called Leonard. A used condom had been found on top of the cistern in one of the ground-floor lavatories. Cleaning ladies were cited as witnesses, together with a copywriter working late on a storyboard for the Glastonbury new business pitch. Rachel's release from the role of victim was marked by invitations to give her own opinions on this new subject, invitations which she despised but to which she made a show of conforming, driven by a new, keener sense of survival. While the barman laughed it off with camp flicks of his drying up cloth, Rachel found herself feeling bitterly sorry for the boy Leonard, whom she sometimes glimpsed skulking by his motorbike in the car park, his angular face pinched and white, his pretty pink mouth drawing greedily on the stub end of a cigarette.

From the safe and comforting cocoon of her bath, Rachel could feel the whole ugly episode slipping from the spotlight of certainty which had at first burned so brightly in her mind. Perhaps Cliff was right, she thought now, perhaps she had been encouraging. What had actually happened, after all? An unwanted embrace. A rough fumble. Nothing more. Nothing she couldn't handle. Was it really worth resigning over? She flicked at a few snowflakes of foam on her arm and sighed. She felt drained suddenly, quite incapable of anger or anything else.

Bubbles clung to the sides of the tub while the water swirled away. Wrapping a large towel around her chest Rachel padded through to the kitchen to check on the progress of the claret. It wasn't so hard to understand Anita's friendship with the bottle, she thought grimly, taking an appreciative sip and wandering over to study the calendar pinned to the wall above the dishwasher. The line separating chaos from control was a fine one indeed; so much easier to topple down on the wrong side than she had ever previously imagined.

She counted the days of the coming holiday. Only six. Under a week and Anita would be back in town. A second opinion was definitely what she needed, Rachel decided, thumbing through the calendar's library of pictures – a series of stills from famous advertising campaigns, which Melissa had given her for Christmas the year before. She paused at April, the month of her birthday. The page was titled with the slogan from a popular bubble-bath commercial. *Claron. The beginning of a perfect evening*, it said. Underneath these words, a semi-naked model peered wistfully through the curtains of her bedroom window, clearly hopeful of having her flimsy robe ripped off by a handsome passer-by.

Hoicking up her towel, Rachel let the picture drop and cast a wary eye at the undrawn curtain of her own window above the kitchen sink. It would take more than a pint of bubble bath to make her dreams come true, she thought wryly, pulling the curtain across with such a yank that she spilt a drop or two of wine on the floor.

At the sight of Robbie Dexter's tousled hair and eager smile in the middle of her television screen, Rachel gripped the sofa cushion to her stomach and leant forward to get a better look. There were wisps of grey in the hair curling over the tops of his ears, but his figure looked much the same. He wore a round-necked Aran sweater and was standing in a pair of dirty black wellingtons, muddied jeans bunched into the tops of them, his fingers hooked casually through the loops in his waistband. The familiarity of the man and the pose, not seen for over fifteen years and coming on a third full day spent entirely alone, with nothing to do but brood over her multifarious troubles, filled Rachel with an irrational, stomach-flipping sensation of relief.

He was talking about sheep. Charollais sheep. Hurriedly she checked the *Radio Times*. An Animal Special, thirty minutes on unusual breeds, slipped in between a Christmas edition of a soap opera about oil riggers and a comedy quiz special involving a dartboard and a tub of green slime. She knew about the green slime from the trailers, of which there had been several the previous evening. Although it was well into the afternoon, Rachel was still in her dressing gown, encamped on her sofa amongst a medley of coldcare medicines and tissue boxes. The television, usually reserved – like alcohol – for solace and time-filling beyond the watershed hour of six o'clock, had been resorted to as a last weapon against boredom and the rack of self-analysis. On the table beside her sat a pile of newspapers, a sachet of Lemsip, a pot of tea and a jar of pickled walnuts. Though opened, the jar remained untouched, a whimsical repellance having induced her feverish mind to observe the brown convolutions of its contents and be reminded suddenly of brains.

Behind Robbie, scores of broad-backed, long-nosed sheep with pasty pink faces could be seen standing in disconsolate clusters under several towering, leafless oaks, whose black boughs were spread like deep cracks on the surface of the smudgy grey sky. It was raining gently, a fact of which Robbie, typically, seemed to be unaware. He was talking animatedly about dietary supplements and the importance of nurturing delicate breeds with extra gentleness. Rachel, spellbound by the sight of the familiar face, found her thoughts surfing waves of fond recollections. He looked good. Positively attractive, in fact. Her mind scrabbled for a clear recollection of the reasons she had left him, reasons which – thanks to her new circumstances and the passage of time – had grown quite opaque.

The camera angle shifted to reveal a red-bricked cottage with a coil of dark grey smoke curling out of its chimney. Garden tools were leaning up against the wall to the left of the front door, beside a boot-scraper and a . . . The withdrawal of the picture left her feeling robbed. A woman with posy-pink lips and staring eyes appeared in its place, a fat snake slung across her shoulders. Rachel narrowed her eyes at the screen, while a shiver crept down the back of her neck; a shiver which began as repulsion at the reptile but ended as something quite different. Robbie Dexter. She turned the television off. After all these years.

The stuffiness in her head, having enjoyed only temporary bouts of eucalyptus-aided relief, cleared in a couple of instants.

'These creatures need baby-sitting,' Robbie had said with a laugh, 'so it's fortunate that I've friends in Drakeshead who are prepared to man the fort from time to time.'

Rachel got down an atlas, dusted the cover with a clean tissue and found a map of the British Isles. Drakeshead was in Devon. So he had hardly moved at all.

'Robert Dexter,' she said to the man at directory enquiries, 'middle name' – she recalled without any effort at all – 'Timothy. Drakeshead in the West Country.'

A robotic voice recited the number twice. Two minutes later Robbie himself was on the other end of the line.

'Dexter Landscaping,' he said, 'how may I help you?'

'Robbie, it's Rachel – Rachel Elliot.'

'Rachel . . . Rachel – you're joking – wow – Rachel. I mean, hello – how the hell are you?'

'I'm fine,' she began, 'well, actually I'm full of cold and have just spent a boring Christmas cooped up in my flat.'

'You poor old thing, that's too bad.'

'I just saw you on the TV—'

'Oh, you were watching it? A friend in the British Charollais Society set it up – quite a laugh really – just a space filler, but never mind. My goodness, Rachel, what a surprise. What are you up to these days?'

'Same old thing. More money, less time – you know.'

'Married with five kids by any chance?' The chuckle of a laugh that followed was one that she recognised instantly, welcoming it in her heart as an old friend.

'Single as ever. What about you?' Her voice, assisted by the slight husk of ill-health, was a careful study of friendly insouciance.

'There was someone . . . for quite a while . . . but not now. Didn't work out, you know . . .' It sounded for a moment as if he was speaking through clenched teeth.

'I'm sorry to hear that.'

The conversation had reached a point where a sense of direction was required for it to be able to continue. Fifteen years could not be summarised in a few enquiries about rare sheep and the potential existence of life-partners. The attempt either had to be abandoned completely or given a more definitive shape.

'I rang on impulse really, because . . . because I thought it might be fun to catch up sometime . . . you know, meet up in the New Year or something.'

'Why not? Good idea.'

Was that reluctance or shyness, she wondered? It was like moves in a chess game, but with no time to think in between.

'It was just seeing you on the box like that – such a coincidence – I just felt I had to act on it.'

'I'm so glad you did. The trouble is, I don't come to London much . . . I mean, well I don't suppose you fancy a trip to the country, do you?'

'I'd love it.' The words were out before she could stop them, charged with a genuine eagerness to see him, an eagerness that was quite beyond disguise.

'How about this week then?' He sounded slightly breathless. 'Oh, but of course you'll be working—'

'No, I've got the whole Christmas break off. I'm due at a New Year's Eve party back here on Friday. But I've no plans to speak of in the meantime.' Am I making things too easy, she wondered, marvelling at this verbal flinging of herself down a telephone line, but at the same time feeling justified and driven by the extraordinary coincidence that had prompted it, the sweet ease with which everything was falling into place. Two minutes later and she would have missed Robbie's section of the programme entirely.

It was also impossible not to relish the pleasure of speaking to someone who still only knew her as she had been fifteen years before. It made her feel young and interesting. Robbie had always been so unjudgemental and affectionate, so exactly the kind of tonic she needed now.

'I've got a very fast car.'

'Yes, you would have.'

She could hear the smile in his voice.

They made plans for Rachel to drive down the very next afternoon, by tacit agreement leaving the trickier question of the exact duration of her visit undefined. The rest of the conversation was taken up with less arduous practicalities, like how long the drive would take and which landmarks to watch out for during the last couple of miles.

'It sounds like the back of beyond,' she said, laughing at the long scrawl of instructions in front of her, which had begun on the back of an envelope and extended into the margins of an open magazine.

'Perhaps you'd better set off now to be sure.'

'Perhaps I'd better.'

'Will I recognise you?'

'Oh God, I hope so.' Her heart gave a little lurch at the recollection of the dispiriting reflection confronting her in the mirror that morning – a face full of cold, dark suitcases under her eyes, white cracks on her lips, a clown nose. 'The shape of me is much the same,' she faltered.

'That's good to hear. I've gone to seed all over the place.'

'It certainly didn't look like it.'

'Wait till you get a closer look.'

A moment of embarrassment followed as the more intimate implications of these exchanges sank in.

'It'll take me at least a day to straighten the house, so I'd better get cracking, get the spare bed made up and all that sort of thing.'

She was grateful for his hearty tone. 'Oh, anything will do for me – please, don't go to any bother.'

After the phone call Rachel collected up her dirty tissues and punched some life back into the sofa cushions, setting them at pretty angles in the seat corners. After that she tidied up the detritus littering her kitchen, loaded her dishwasher and filled several bags and boxes with bottles and newspapers to take to the recycling dump the next morning. It felt like clearing out a lot more than the clutter of a failed Christmas. It felt like a clearing of something inside her head too, the sort of fundamental reorganisation that precedes a fresh start, a chance, after all, to become something else.

20 ∫

Will Raphael saw Rachel several minutes before she caught sight of him. He hesitated for a moment, half turning back towards the park to check on the child, before returning his gaze to the car park. It was almost empty, with only a handful of cars positioned between the deep wide puddles, each littered with soggy clusters of newspaper pages that had not quite managed the journey from car boot to recycling container. She was wearing red trousers and a green padded coat, the collar of which was turned up, encasing the lower section of her hair and pushing it forwards so that it fell round her cheeks. It looked longer and looser than he remembered, as if it had recently broken free of a hat.

She was struggling with the papers, taking too many at a time, so that it was impossible to lift them up into the high letterbox flap without dropping a few on the way. She kept having to bend down and retrieve the ones that escaped, shaking her head with a happy impatience which assured him he remained unseen. When she had finished with the papers, she got back into the car and drove towards him, or rather, towards the bottle banks, which were situated nearer the tarmacked path and patch of grass which signalled the start of the park.

'It's Rachel Elliot, isn't it?' On his head was a black cap, worn backwards so that the peak stuck out over the upturned collar of his jacket. He gestured at the bags of bottles wedged into the passenger seat of her car. 'What's this, an advertising lady with a conscience?'

Though curiously unsurprised to see him, the remark rankled at once, wiping the smile from her face. 'Aren't advertising ladies supposed to have consciences, then?' The two bottles she had been holding clanked into the bottom of the container. He stood watching her in silence. She wondered if he had heard about the Cliff Weybourne débâcle, whether the two of them had yet shared a drink and a laugh at her expense.

'Good Christmas?'

'Perfectly lovely, thank you,' she replied, wondering why he did not excuse himself from a conversation which was clearly giving neither of them any pleasure, why indeed he had intitiated it in the first place. If ever presented with the danger of an unwanted encounter herself, she had no qualms about hiding behind trees or stopping to study imaginary items on the soles of her shoes.

Oh God, perhaps he wants more gratitude, she thought, busying herself with bottles and forcing out a few sentences of appreciation. 'Mallarme are thrilled to bits with the film, by the way – brought the TV blitz forward to January.'

'How's your friend?'

'My drunken friend, you mean?' Her eyes glittered. 'Absolutely fine. It was kind of you to help out. We were both very grateful . . .'

'Good, good.' He looked impatient suddenly, shifting his weight from one foot to the other and casting looks over his shoulder.

'Worried about a dog?'

'A child.'

This unexpected remark was followed by shriek of glee from behind. A young boy, aged about five, came tearing towards them, straggly sandy hair streaking back off his face and his small hands pumping the air for added speed.

'This is Jack,' he said, when the boy had arrived, red cheeked and panting at his side.

'Pleased to meet you, Jack.' She rubbed her palms together briskly. 'Well, I've really got to get on . . . I'm off to Devon for a couple of days . . .'

'Devon? How nice. Whereabouts?'

'Er . . . Drakeshead – to see an old friend . . .'

'He can't be that old.'

'I beg your pardon?'

'Or you wouldn't be blushing.'

'I'm not,' she retorted, pressing her palms to her cheeks, furious both at herself and his impudence.

'Lucky you, is all I can say. It's grimy old London for us, isn't it mate?' He put a hand on the boy's shoulder and pulled him closer. 'Can we help with those?'

'Yes please, please, please,' piped the boy, racing round to the open car door and starting to help himself from the remaining bag of empties.

Rachel nodded, fighting an absurd impulse to explain that the quantity of wine bottles related only to the infrequency with which she got round to recycling them.

'Quite a habit you've got here,' remarked Will, lifting up the child so that he could reach the slot in the recycling container.

'I was about to explain,' she began, but stopped at once when she saw that he was laughing at her, his eyes full of mischief.

'I know you were,' he said quietly.

He placed the child back on the ground and then whispered something in his ear. The boy set off running in the direction from which he had come. 'I've given him a two-minute head start,' he confided, as they both stood aside for a cyclist with bulging pink thighs, who appeared from nowhere, bursting past on a rush of wind. 'Used to be three, but he's getting faster.' He swivelled his cap the right way round and pulled some gloves out of his coat pocket.

'How old is he?' asked Rachel, to be polite.

'Six going on thirty-five.' He chuckled, before adding, almost in a whisper, 'I don't suppose you would let me photograph you, would you?' He made a big to-do of putting on the gloves. They looked home-knitted and had Father Christmas faces on each finger. 'Smart, eh?' He held up both hands and grinned. 'Jack gave them to me.'

She couldn't help laughing.

'His mother got earrings – Christmas trees the size of tennis balls.'

She was still smiling and shaking her head when he said, 'Would you?' and she knew she hadn't misheard after all. It was such a bizarre request that she laughed again, out of nerves this time. Common sense told her to refuse, not only because it felt curiously personal to be asked such a thing, but also because of all the negative associations already resident inside her head where this man was concerned – the fiasco of the photography lessons, the mess over the Bermuda film, the business with Anita, not to mention his association with Cliff Weybourne.

'I don't make a habit of issuing such invitations. Commissions are more my style.' He beat his gloved hands together and turned to check on the boy, whose concentration on running had been interrupted by the attentions of a large but apparently friendly Alsatian. 'A cheek and all that, I know.'

'Why me?'

He sucked in his breath. 'Now that's more difficult.'

'Well try, then.' She crossed her arms, in a show of having all the time in the world, her curiosity overtaking any flutter of urgency about getting on her way. He was right. It was a cheek, and she wanted some justification for it. 'I'm hardly Miss England material.'

He looked genuinely appalled. 'Oh goodness – no – I mean I wouldn't be remotely interested if you were.'

'Well, thanks very much.'

'No – I didn't mean – it's that . . . I feel you have a story to tell – in your face – there's a lot there. I could show it.' He shrugged, almost with irritation, clearly dissatisfied at this description of the impulsion behind his craft. 'Just a couple of hours. Please? You might even learn something about taking photographs,' he added slyly.

She couldn't help smiling. 'Look, I'm terribly flattered and all that, but the answer is still no. I'm just not the right kind of material – can't sit still for two seconds – always blink when the flash goes—'

'You would be fine—'

'No.' She gave him the most aggressively determined stare, thinking as she did so that he was certainly good looking, as Anita had so crudely observed, and that at the same time there was something guarded in his expression which somehow defused the possible inference of anything improper in the request.

'Well, I guess that's that then.' He tugged at his gloves, stretching the Father Christmas heads until they looked gaunt and pop-eyed. 'Better go. Got a race to run.' Then he turned and sprinted away, calling the boy's name, spurts of mud splashing onto the ankles of his trousers.

Rachel stood watching him go, faintly intrigued in spite of herself. She had always hated being photographed. Ever since she was a little girl every snapshot had induced a prickle of disappointment at the sight of herself, at the realisation that any delusions of film-star beauty existed in her head alone. Yet she felt a curious regret as she watched him charge away, waving and calling to the child. She remembered his Christmas card suddenly, the starkness of it, the hope bursting from the puffed chest of the robin, the suggestion of warmth among the shadows.

As she turned back towards her car, Rachel found herself wondering about the wife. Were they separated or was she the stay-at-home bun-baking sort, happy to absent herself from a spot of male bonding in the park? The thought led her inexorably on towards a glimpse of herself in a similar role, not armed with oven gloves, but with a child that needed fresh air. There followed an outrageous image of Robbie Dexter playing the role of father, an image which good sense told her to quash, but which shimmered obstinately none the less, fuelled by an imagination that had been quite stuffed with solitude and was at last taking its revenge. But there would be an alluring symmetry to it, she reasoned, as the last of her empty bottles crashed into the darkness beneath her hands, a sense of life coming full circle, of making good in the end.

21

The cockerel crowed five minutes before the ring of the alarm, a sequence of events which was as integral to Robbie's morning routine as picking the sleep from his eyes while he sat on the loo and applying the blade of the razor to his upper lip before he tackled his cheeks. Throwing back the bedclothes, he swung his legs over the side of the bed and sat for a moment with his head in his hands, curling his toes at the cold draughts snaking out between the gaps in the floorboards and up through the thin carpeting. As he stretched, he groaned with the abandonment of one confident that he is alone, his large bony hands reaching with unconscious elegance towards the bare bulb dangling from the middle of the ceiling.

Having splashed cold water on his face from a chipped basin in the corner of the room, Robbie crossed over to the window and lifted one edge of the material which he had pinned up as a temporary curtain some three years before. The darkness of the new day still crouched warily outside. Errol Flynn, the cockerel, named in recognition of its sometimes over-zealous servicing of its harem of ten hens, switched into full throttle once again, its raucous shrieks cutting through the stillness of the morning. There had once been two cockerels, the ebullient Errol and a distant cousin of his, called George, who was, if anything even more enthusiastic when it came to its manly duties concerning the hens. So much so that the hens themselves eventually revolted by refusing to produce any eggs at all. With some reluctance Robbie had donated George to a large farm on the other side of Drakeshead, transporting him in a cardboard box peppered with breathing holes and filling the van with a stench of chicken shit which had lingered for months afterwards. By the following week egg supply and hen-coop harmony had been fully restored, together with a small income from Phil Giddings, the butcher in Drakeshead, who liked to tuck a few egg boxes between his trays of sausages and prime cuts. This income would have been considerably larger if Robbie hadn't eaten quite so many eggs himself, his appetite and a long-established antipathy towards shopping overcoming any fashionable concerns about the clogging effect such habits might be having on his blood vessels.

When Errol had finished his morning chant, the dawn chorus was taken up in a more desultory fashion by a few plaintive bleatings from the sheep, penned into the small field immediately in front of the house. Of the three fields Robbie used in his two-weekly rota, it was the scrubbiest and least satisfactory. But thanks to the fiendish activity of worms, which built up in the soil and could wreak the most terrible havoc in such delicate ruminants' digestive systems, he was forced to use every scrap of land he had.

Robbie sighed, pulling on the T-shirt and pullover that lay on his chair from the day before, and thinking, as he did most mornings, that the Charollais were far too much hard work for a hobby and that he really ought to get shot of them once and for all.

Surveying the chaos of what he had blithely referred to as his spare room on the way downstairs and feeling as always that the demands of his day would never fit into the time allowed for them, made Robbie feel more aggressive towards the sheep than usual. As did a glimpse of the towers of paperwork crowding round the smeary screen of the Apple Mac on the dining-room table. Though he had been meaning, for several months now, to allocate a day a week for admin alone, the intention kept getting overtaken by events. Today, for instance, it was imperative that he make some move towards cleaning the house, towards getting things looking generally shipshape – for Rachel. Rachel. At the thought of her he stopped and caught his breath. Rachel Elliot, who had apparently volunteered to march back into his life with all the panache with which she had once marched out of it. It was impossible not to feel thrilled; yet Robbie was filled with dread as well, as anyone one might dread the re-emergence of something so closely associated with great pain.

What would she look like after so long? How would he feel? How did she feel? What did she want? As Robbie spooned sugar straight from the open packet that lived beside the kettle onto a steep mountain of cornflakes, before tipping half a pint of milk into a moat round its edges, it was this last thought that preoccupied him the most. Rachel, he recalled with some trepidation, was not a lady who drifted into things. She had made up her mind to see him. She wanted to see him. And he, true to form, had agreed at once, had allowed himself to be swept along in the slipstream of her plans, experiencing – in spite of everything – a welcome echo of times past, when the wants of Rachel Elliot had always taken precedence over any meagre desires of his own. Leaving her had been the hardest thing he had ever done in his life, harder even than telling Polly Drayton, as he had back in October, that after seven years of their misshapen zigzag of an alliance, it was time to part for good. The thought of Polly brought with it the usual *frissons* of guilt which no amount of cornflake crunching could suppress entirely. It was clear to him that he taken the best years of her life and offered nothing in return. She was back living with her parents now, the twenty-eight-year-old daughter of a publican, serving bar snacks and pulling pints with that fixed, cheery look he knew so well, the one that was a mask for disappointment.

As Robbie continued with his morning chores, bestrewing the near corner of the field with fresh hay for the sheep and checking their water trough, the thought of Rachel's imminent arrival – the prospect of being viewed through her eyes – made him see with a new and shocking clarity that he had somehow slipped into becoming something he had never quite intended. Visions of his own future had always contained a wife, a family, a warm, well-ordered home. Staring at his cottage now, noting the missing jigsaw pieces in the roof, the crumbling corners of the chimney stack, he felt the same lurch of affection that had prompted him to bind his soul to a building society some five years before. But he felt a sense of shame as well, since he knew that its shambolic state reflected some deep failing within himself, some inability to grasp the business of living and mould it into the shape he wanted. The fact that Polly lacked it too probably lay at the heart of all their problems. While adept at teasing damp wood into a roaring fire or cajoling sheep through a foot-bath of copper sulphate, Polly had always looked to him to provide any spark of inspiration where their relationship was concerned. She was a follower, not a leader; someone who needed to feed off another's imagination in order to give the appearance of having any herself.

Like me with Rachel, he thought glumly, pulling the hose from the trough and heading back towards the house, his heart curling with fear at the thought of her, of how she might judge him and all that he had become.

Rachel spent the first part of the drive trying, and failing, not to think about babies. Not so much their physical attributes as what they represented, what effect a child would have on her life. Most important of all, becoming a mother would provide some other peg on which to hang her emotions and hopes, something entirely separate from her career. Though she had not yet made up her mind whether it would be courageous or cowardly to resign from McKenzie Cartwright, the idea of a long-term future there had been soured for good. Not just because of Cliff Weybourne, but also because she was now resolved upon the business of changing her life. Getting in touch with Robbie was all part of this new confusion of change, she told herself, deccelerating sharply in order to move across into the exit lane. In the midst of such imponderables the thought of a baby was soothing: it was her secret hope, her hidden jewel of a plan that meant in the long run nothing else mattered at all.

As the West Country drew nearer, so did images of the past: Robbie, shared holidays, favourite films and old jokes, spun through her mind on a carousel of dazzling speed and intensity. Memories from her early working days soon joined the fray – the pleasing terror of delivering her first presentation, the disappointing boredom of attending her first shoot – all those hours spent in a show-case house in Richmond while scores of people debated the best ways of illuminating a can of furniture polish. She recalled one fresh-faced account director in particular, who, on one memorable occasion, had dared to arrive late for a big meeting on the grounds that his seven-week-old daughter had chosen that morning to offer up her first smile. Rachel, then a twenty-something hot-head, hungry to prove herself in a man's world, had experienced a barely disguised impatience at the blatant soppiness of such an excuse. Remembering that impatience now, she felt ashamed. It had taken bravery, she realised, to bring this tale of fatherly ecstasy into the boardroom, to own up to priorities other than those typed on the agenda sheets in front of them. The couple of women account handlers at McKenzie Cartwright who had children would never dream of doing anything similar, she thought sadly. It was more than their jobs were worth.

It was only after she left the motorway and began trying to decipher the scrawled directions on the piece of paper beside her that Rachel allowed herself to focus properly on the potentially awesome business of a reunion with Robbie Dexter. She would have been far more afraid, she realised, if she had not seen him on the television, looking somehow more glamorous than she remembered him, more rugged and more mature. She had forgotten what a nice voice he had too – low and slow – and how all his movements were unhurried and deliberate, as if originating from the most deep-seated self-belief; a quality towards which she felt more urgently drawn for the fact that it was so terribly absent in herself.

As Robbie had promised, there was a dead-end sign ten yards past the Fox and Hounds on the left. Her car crept along the narrow lanes like a sleek black cat, unaware of the eyes observing its progress, eyes belonging to people like Polly Drayton as she stood at the window of her bedroom above the front bar, chewing the dry ends of her hair, smelling the chip fat on her skin and clothes, its oily stench mingling with the debilitating self-hatred of frustrated love.

Rachel made the last turn, noting as she did so the hand-painted sign saying, Station Cottage, half-buried by brambles – as Robbie had warned her it would be – its arrow pointing skywards, as if the residence it described was to be found smothered under pillows of grey cloud. Rachel took several deep breaths to clear the tightness in her chest as she drove the last few yards, steering her car as best she could between the hard mud gullies forged by tractor wheels. As she rounded the first bend, the cottage suddenly came into view, its bricks looking somehow less red, less spruce than they had appeared on screen. A profound sense of unreality threatened to overwhelm her then, an absurd notion that she was about to step onto a film set and play a role for which she had no script. She parked behind Robbie's mud-splattered white van, remembering with a heart thud how they had once made love on the front seats of something similar, how they had laughed at the uncomfortable inconvenience of the gear stick, how triumphantly reckless they had felt afterwards.

Robbie was putting the hoover away when he heard her car pull up. It lived, suspended by an old and noble hook, at the top of the cellar steps, amongst a jungle of brooms, buckets and used dusters. The hook, which Robbie had hammered in himself during a patch of zealous domesticity shortly after moving in, chose that moment to rebel at the considerable weight to which it had been unwisely subjected for far too long. With a resounding crash, the hoover toppled down the cellar steps amidst a billowing cloud of dust punched out of its overstuffed bag, taking in its wake two buckets, three aerosol cans and the only broom without a loose handle.

'Fuck.' Robbie started down the steps after it and then changed his mind. The hoover had done its job. It was impossible to think beyond that moment to the unimaginable point of ever needing it again. There was just time to wash his hands at the kitchen sink before she knocked at the door. In his terror he tripped on the loose flagstone by the dresser as he left the kitchen, lunged sideways and hit his shoulder on the wall, knocking a faded print of an English beach badly askew. He was still adjusting it when the front door swung open to reveal Rachel Elliot framed in its archway. A Rachel of softer lines and wider eyes. A Rachel who was taller than he remembered and slimmer too, but otherwise so exactly the same that for a moment he was too shocked to speak.

'Hello, Robbie.' The apparition came to life, smiling broadly, so broadly that he guessed she was as afraid as he was. With so much fear, it was hard to separate out the pleasure. As to resentment, he found there was none at all.

'Rachel – you made it then.'

She walked towards him, across the brown rectangle of carpet that he had been hoovering just minutes before, playing with the shoulder strap of her handbag, her eyes darting around to cover up the awkwardness of the approach. Robbie stood with one hand still on the picture frame. She looked so fresh and elegant. His usual dirt and disorder wouldn't have suited her at all, he thought, remembering how he had hurled the jumbled contents of the spare room into the attic, where the debris of his life lay in incoherent unattended heaps that grew larger and more bedraggled as the years went by.

She stopped and cocked her head at the picture. 'That's about right I think. No – perhaps a shade to the left. That's better. Do I go in here?' She stopped short of him and stepped through the doorway that led into the kitchen. Robbie followed, ducking automatically under the low beam, cursing himself for having failed to kiss her. There followed a curious wave of sadness, a mixture of nostalgia for what they had lost, and of apprehension for what might lie ahead. It made him wish for a moment that she had not come.

'It's lovely, Robbie, lovely.' Rachel peeled off her gloves as she walked round the room, inspecting pictures and cupboards like a prospective house-buyer, the points of her heels clacking smartly on the cracked, freshly washed tiles. Too timid, now that the moment had come, even to catch his eye, such businesslike curiosity was her only refuge. She felt brusque and unnatural, but quite powerless too. To be so close to Robbie again was far stranger than she could ever have imagined. He was so familiar, yet so unknown.

'Robbie – I—'

'Would you like a tour of the estate, then?' He rubbed his hands together and then eyed her footwear doubtfully. 'But it wouldn't be a good idea in those, I'm afraid.'

She looked down at her brown suede shoes and wiggled her toes, wanting to make light of her silliness for having worn such things, for having allowed herself to be guided by vanity rather than good sense.

'I'm sure I've got a pair somewhere that would fit you – boots, coats, scarves, brollies – you name it – I've got hundreds of the damn things – breed on their own I think.' Relieved to have something practical upon which to exercise his concentration, Robbie began rifling through a large wickerwork basket at the far end of the kitchen, flinging out items of footwear and clothing between sentences. After some to-do and more than a little awkwardness, Rachel settled for a pair of scuffed black boots.

Though they were an obvious choice, it gave Robbie an unexpected jolt to see them on Rachel's feet. They were an old pair of Polly's, abandoned upon receipt of the new fur-lined leather ones he had given her the Christmas before last. Polly had always had a bit of a thing about cold feet; poor circulation, she said, like her mum.

Walking round outside, Rachel took off the glossy, Cossack-style hat which she had retrieved from the back seat of her car and tossed her hair at the sealed grey of the sky, enjoying the prickle of cold on her scalp. A formal introduction to some outhouses and several chickens required a leap across a muddy ditch, about three feet wide. There had once been a footbridge, Robbie explained apologetically, referring to a soggy plank that had finally caved in the winter before. But Rachel laughed away the necessity of such a thing. It suited her mood perfectly to have to jump across. Better still, a slightly awkward landing on the other side provided the perfect pretext for hand to meet hand, for real contact to be made at last. There was no lingering over the moment, but each felt better for it having happened, as if reassured by the solidity of their own bodies in the midst of so much emotional uncertainty.

Rachel couldn't help thinking the Charollais very ugly when seen close-to: they had piggy eyes and Roman noses which gave them an air of what struck her as quite inappropriate haughtiness. But they trotted over to Robbie with an eagerness that was almost endearing, their short stout legs working hard under the tumescent woolly bulk of their bodies. Robbie's assurance too, was curiously impressive, she decided, watching him move amongst the surging animals, rubbing foreheads and patting backs as if they were a pack of friendly dogs. Rachel stood a little to one side, hands thrust into the pockets of her coat, happy to play the spectator.

'It's feeding time at the zoo, I'm afraid,' he called, striding deeper into the jostle of sheep, tugging at ears and tail stumps and bending down to inspect hooves. 'They need supplements at this time of year. Most of them are pregnant, you see, so they need more than this old field can provide – but not too much, mind you, or they'd grow too big and then we'd have a hell of a time at lambing.'

'Lambing?' Rachel's imagination flashed with images of Christopher Timothy elbow-deep in the rear end of something bovine. 'Is that soon, then?'

'Not till mid-April probably. I was late with tupping this year. There's a while to go yet.'

'Why are you looking at their feet?'

'Foot rot. That warm spell before Christmas – all that rain and so on – gave us a hell of a time of it.' He was bending down, talking into the ground, so it was hard for her to catch every word. '. . . Better now it's colder . . .'

Rachel's own feet were beginning to feel icy and more than a little damp, thanks to deep dry cracks in the soles of Polly Drayton's boots. She hopped from one leg to the other, hugging herself, having to work harder now at looking interested.

'Bloody creatures. I'll have to get the clippers out again.' Robbie clumped back across the field towards her, irritation etched across his face. 'If it isn't one damn disease it's another—' he checked himself. 'You poor old thing, you look frozen. Let's go inside. The sheep can wait for once. I'll make a pot of tea and stoke up the fire. We could have toast and jam – if you like,' he added shyly. 'There's not much for supper I'm afraid – just cold meat and so on – I'm still not much of a cook.'

'That makes two of us.' She laughed, and linked her arm through his for the walk back to the house. 'It is *so* good to see you Robbie Dexter.'

He squeezed her arm with the fingers of his spare hand. 'And it's good to see *you*, Rachel Elliot.' He paused for a moment, before adding, 'Weird, but good.'

'I thought you'd have a family by now,' she said quietly.

'Yes, so did I.' He let out a short laugh.

'Not met the right person?'

'Something like that.' He thought of Polly and children. The subject evoked a blurred string of unhappy recollections, conversations meandering across the years, getting nowhere. Polly refusing to talk properly, refusing to do anything but dismiss the idea with that bitter scorn of hers, the one she used when she was most afraid. But then children had never been exactly high on Rachel's list of priorities either, he thought, casting her a wary look and doing a quick mental calculation of her age.

Tea was drunk to the ice-breaking accompaniment of an album of ancient photographs, many of them so bad that it was easy to laugh at the past, at the fatter faces, the longer hair, the endless cigarettes and arms round friends whose names they couldn't remember. But steadily the photographs evoked other images too, more emotional ones that filled Robbie with longing and Rachel with shame. It seemed incredible that she had turned this man away, expelled him from her life for qualities which she now so longed to know again.

Meanwhile, Robbie studied the blister caused by ironing two double sheets and four pillow cases, all of them quite bone-dry and pitted with ancient creases, and dared to wonder whether such industry had been necessary after all. Rachel was still sitting down the opposite end of his ragged brown leather sofa, but her stockinged feet, once tucked under her, had slowly been working their way down the sofa towards him. When the tips of her toes arrived they sought warmth in the lee of his left thigh. And when at last his hand dared to close round the toes, they pressed into his palm at once, full of sweet resilience and promise.

22 ∫

Anita blew an extravagant kiss at herself in her dressing-table mirror and smiled. The scarlet lipstick, purchased only that morning, made her teeth look gratifyingly white, and somehow sharper. She pressed a clean tissue to her lips and examined the imprint for a moment before dropping it into the wastepaper bin beside her. Leaning forward, she tugged at the short front tufts of her hair to make them look more spiky – scowling at the swathe of grey as she always did – but none the less thinking that she looked vaguely vibrant – provocative even, she decided, puckering her lips.

It was a long time since she had so looked forward to a party, or indeed had a party to look forward to, she thought bitterly, her mind performing a quick flashback over the meagre contents of their social life that year. The Robsons' New Year's Eve thrash represented quite a highlight, a pitiable fact for which Anita blamed her husband, since she believed there to be a direct correlation between the frequency of Giles's trips abroad and the steady dwindle in the number of invitations that came their way. Once, a million years ago it seemed, there had never been enough evenings to go round. Now, any evening invitation lit up the diary like a beacon, terrible evidence – as if Anita needed such a thing – that their life really had slipped into a new and infinitely bleaker gear. In spite of countless sympathetic protestations to the contrary, wives on their own were not in much demand round the symmetrically arranged dinner-party tables of north London hostesses, she had discovered, especially not ones with a tendency to use four letter words after the fifth glass and to stub cigarettes out beside the wreckage of what had once been a perfectly formed bread roll.

Anita tweaked out a last rebellious eyebrow, scowling at the twinge of pain. God, it would be brilliant, after two weeks of behaving herself impeccably, to drink without counting the glasses or – worse still – worrying about who else might be counting them. No one cared about such things on New Year's Eve. It would also be brilliant to see the delicious Will Raphael again. Having engineered his invitation to the party herself – Sally Robson was beautifully accommodating about such things, even going so far as to phone her the moment he replied – she was determined to make the most of it, determined, more specifically to punish Giles, towards whom she was currently feeling more vitriol than she had experienced in a long time.

They had had bad patches before. She had been known to joke to friends like Rachel that the entire marriage had been nothing but a bad patch. In truth, matters usually reached some sort of nadir, a crux of awfulness, at which point they would both turn to each other in a frenzy of regret and promises to try harder in the future. For a while things would be riotously cheerful, then calmer, then tricky as the whole hopeless cycle started again. However tired Anita was of the cycle, there was something about the predictability of it all which made it bearable; it meant that nothing lasted for ever, neither the good nor the bad. But in recent weeks something had changed. Giles wasn't playing the game any more. Nor did Anita feel certain that her drinking was to blame. Giles was used to her ways; he knew she always pulled herself together in the end. Sometimes, she even believed that her drinking made him nicer to her, gentler, more conciliatory.

Giles had spent the entire Christmas hiding behind the inane and incessant flow of conversation generated by his parents, leaving his wife to supply any necessary responses. It wasn't that he wasn't being nice. He wasn't being anything. His gift to her had been a Smith's token and a book on birds. He knew she hated birds.

The thought that her husband might finally have given up on her was not so much depressing as intolerable. If the bastard was having an affair, she would not go quietly, she vowed; she would make him pay. She slammed her powder compact back down on the dressing table, causing a mini storm of brown specks to fly into the air and settle in a dusty film across the green leather top of her jewel case.

The plot concerning Will Raphael – the bold idea of trying to nudge fantasy a little way into the realms of reality – had sprung partly from this enraged resolve, and partly from a chance encounter with an article in the hairdresser's during the lead-up to Christmas. Not having realised that the man had a career of such distinction, Anita was instantly impressed. Fame could be quite an aphrodisiac, she found, if allowed to be.

Under the discreet aural camouflage of whirring hairdryers, she tore the article out with the intention of slipping it into Rachel's Christmas card. Instead, it remained in her coat pocket for a few days, before graduating to the innermost zipped compartment of her purse, assuming qualities akin to that of a secret memento along the way. Then Giles returned from his December trip in a shroud of impenetrable silence. On his first night back – when, historically, absence sharpened the pangs of lust if nothing else – he huddled away from her with his knees to his chest, responding to all enquiries with inarticulate grunts that were to set the pattern for the rest of the month. So it was that the bad patch had grown and stretched and become something disturbingly new, something that called for action.

The article sat beside Anita now, propped up between a bottle of Chanel Eau de Toilette and a box of Tampax. A small but full-length version of Will Raphael was staring at her from amongst the creases, leaning against the dark railings of what looked like a fire escape, arms crossed, and a quizzical look on his face, as if he had just asked a question and was still awaiting the answer. His hair looked much darker and sleeker than she remembered it, brushed straight back off his face in tidy waves and curling neatly round his earlobes.

'I just photograph what's there,' declares portrait photographer, Will Raphael, who has recently received commissions from the MP Howard Graves and the acclaimed film actor Rupert Cheshire. After the great critical success of a private exhibition last summer, thirty-eight-year-old Raphael is currently putting together a book of his work, featuring some of his more experimental techniques. The book is to be called Images

In Time *and is due for publication next autumn (Cauter and Prowse £24.99). 'Novelists get many hours of concentration from their readers, but a picture hung in a gallery is lucky if it gets a couple of minutes,' he argues, 'so I thought a book would give me a better chance of getting inside people's heads.' Will Raphael, who lives alone in a basement flat in Chelsea, claims only to have time for his work. When not helping in the management of the film editing company Filmstyle, which he and several partners set up eight years ago, he is always behind a camera. 'Taking pictures is my hobby as well as my work,' he declares, 'so I'm very lucky.'*

At the sound of a wailing child approaching the bedroom door Anita hastily tucked the article into the satiny interior of her evening bag, alongside a stick of eyeliner, a fresh packet of cigarettes and a small gold comb that had come free with the lipstick.

Rachel, seated at her own dressing table, had seldom prepared for an evening's entertainment with less rigour. Although her body clearly had made the journey back from Devon, it felt as if her mind was still there, drawn to the compelling events of the last few days like a moth to a light. Staring at her reflection, she was startled to see how well she looked. Even her lips burned with colour. She touched them for a moment with her fingertips, remembering the astonishing familiarity of Robbie's mouth, so strange beside the shyness and the sense of daring as they slipped between the icy sheets of his creaky iron bed, not wanting to hurry, but hurrying none the less, because it was cold, because a certain haste seemed necessary to make up for the interruption of the years.

Slowly, almost lazily, Rachel ran the mascara brush through her lashes. Her pupils remained glassy, still seeing nothing but the images in her head. Robbie had fallen asleep almost immediately afterwards, one arm tightly round her and the other thrust up under his pillow. She had lain awake, smiling at the dark outline of the lightbulb overhead, listening to the creaks and whispers of the cottage, still too full of wonder to feel sleepy. As the weight of his embrace grew uncomfortable, she tentatively began to shift her position. The idea of being hugged to sleep, though attractive, was not one that she had ever found very practical. Her right arm was quite dead. After a few minutes of some courteous but quite ineffective nudging, she grew more assertive, remembering that nothing woke Robbie once he had fallen asleep, that even trips to the lavatory were a form of sleepwalking of which he had no recollection in the morning.

To feel nothing but friendliness towards a bare bulb, swinging gently on the curling snippets of a Siberian wind, was for Rachel – lover of warmth and creature comforts of every kind – such a bizarre experience that she felt it could only bear irrefutable testimony to the rightness of the course on which she had now embarked. Any concern about other aspects of the indisputable squalor of their surroundings had also been greatly assuaged by Robbie's profuse apologies on the subject, together with his detailed descriptions of all the renovations and decorations that were in the pipeline. There were architect's drawings of how the kitchen would look, he told her, once the wall to the outside toilet had been knocked down and the boiler had been moved upstairs. Somewhere he had a book of fabric samples for the bedroom and sitting room curtains. He would value her opinions on everything, he admitted shyly, on the morning of their second full day together, when the banishment of the dreaded Errol to a dark shed had afforded them something approaching a civilised stretch of sleep.

'I'm hopeless with curtains,' she replied, smiling and stretching, savouring the thrilling suggestion of a shared future that this simple invitation allowed. 'A mad woman called Priscilla did my place up for me – you ought to see it . . .'

'Is that a promise?' He came to sit on the edge of the bed and brushed back a few strands of hair from her cheeks.

They had made love without taking any precautions at all. Robbie had clearly assumed that she was on the pill – as she had always been before – and Rachel, after a few minutes' tussle with her conscience in the privacy of the bathroom, had sealed her cap back into its compact and given her hands a vigorous washing with soap and hot water. The washing gave her time to think, time to marshal her considerable capacity for logic against the forces of guilt raging on the other side:

At almost forty, every cycle counted, she reminded herself. In addition to which, her confidence in a future with Robbie was growing by the minute. If, by some cruel twist, such a future was snatched away from them, she could – she would – cope on her own. She hid her cap under a wadge of cotton wool in the bottom of her vanity case, where it remained for the duration of her stay.

But resolve could not entirely smother the rumblings of her conscience. The underlying deceit of her actions at times distracted her so much during their love-making that she felt like an actor playing a part. There were moments when she was convinced Robbie sensed it too, when his eyes fixed hers with a questioning frown, his silence probing her expression for answers. It was tempting then, locked in the cocoon of physical intimacy, to tell him everything. But still Rachel held back, fearful of marring their reunion by bringing too much to bear upon it too soon. Recollections of her showdown with Nathan fuelled this reticence, criss-crossing her mind like shadows from another life.

They spent the last evening lying on their elbows on either side of the fire, their feet towards the hearth, their free hands linked, bridging the space between them. Their faces were lit only by the flickering glow of the flames, an orgiastic dance of yellow and orange, enlivened and applauded by the cracks of sound exploding underneath. The next day Rachel would leave, to get back to a party – to a life fast losing its allure. While Robbie, with equal reluctance, would have to face three days' worth of demands and messages on his answering machine, the horrors of unsorted bills and estimates, together with the devious weaknesses of forty-two pregnant sheep. The hovering dread of such realities, only a few hours away, charged the atmosphere between them with a fresh intensity, oiling the wheels of intimacy and tightening their reluctance to part.

'Do you remember me swearing I'd never become a godmother?' Rachel ventured, wanting to at least tiptoe round the subject burning in her heart. 'Well I've got four now – godchildren, I mean . . . Robbie?'

He was staring at the carpet, his head bowed at such an angle that the large curls on top of his head had flopped down as a mask for his face. 'Robbie? Are you OK?' She craned her neck for a glimpse of his expression.

'I'm brilliant.' When he looked up she was shocked to see that there were tears in his eyes. 'I love you Rachel.' It was the first time he had said it. 'There's never been anyone else that mattered.' The words rushed out of him. 'I thought I had got over you, but now I realise I was just waiting for you all along, that I would always be waiting for you.'

'Oh, Robbie.' She squeezed his hands, wishing she could suffocate the small part of her that did not like the tears. This was what she had wanted to hear, she realised, what she had been working towards ever since her audacious phone call inviting herself back into his life. It seemed unforgivable in the extreme that a small bubble of disappointment at having got her way so very very easily should choose that moment to burst and scatter inside her, a silent explosion of ingratitude.

'And you'll come to London soon?' she urged, wanting to make up for it.

Robbie nodded, sitting up and reaching for his boots from the hearth. They were heavy leather ones with thick rubbery soles and laces up to the anklebone. He stuck the tip of his tongue into the corner of his mouth as he struggled to pull them on over his thick socks. 'And I'll sort that bastard out for you while I'm at it, Cliff whatever-he-is.'

Though Rachel had derived considerable relief from telling her tale of sexual assault to a sympathetic audience, she had not found Robbie's show of male bravado on the subject particularly consoling. 'Oh, forget him,' she said airily, 'he's not worth it, I promise you.'

'But to think of that bastard daring to lay a hand—' He tugged sharply on his laces. 'It makes my blood boil. I always said it was no place for a woman.'

'I beg your pardon?'

He dropped the laces. 'I just meant – after what you told me – you might be best off resigning after all.' There was a glint of panic in his face, the worry of a child who fears he may have stumbled into saying the wrong thing.

'I may yet do just that.' She smiled, wanting more than anything for his look of anxiety to dissolve.

Robbie returned his attentions to his boots, his square face creasing with concentration as he focused on the unaccomplished chores listed inside his head.

'Is that scowl for me or life in general?'

'Sheep.' He grinned and pushed back the unruly mop of hair that lived along the dark ledge of his eyebrows. 'A few things to do.' Reaching for his sweater from the sofa – a shapeless, stained sack of a garment which had clearly seen many years of service without too many interludes amongst soap suds – he clambered to his feet. 'Could you wrestle with that chicken, do you think? Or we won't be eating much before midnight. There's a few dried herbs and so on in the cupboard. Though Phil Giddings' stuff is usually very tasty. One benefit of life in the sticks—' he shot her a smile of pride, '—no supermarket food in this neck of the woods.'

Rachel, who found the sight of the saggy pink corpse on the draining board far more alarming than the hard, neatly packaged creatures she occasionally selected from the freezer section of her supermarket, had tackled her allotted her job with determination, if little relish.

Back in London now, she smiled to herself at the memory of that last evening meal: dry pinkish meat and half a pack of frozen vegetables. Robbie had eaten eagerly, while she lanced peas on the prongs of her fork and chewed without tasting, her appetite quite dulled by excitement.

Rachel blinked her reflection back into focus, feeling the faint stickiness of the mascara as her upper and lower lashes touched before being pulled apart again. She did not want to go to the Robsons' party. She did not want to see Anita or Giles or any of the half-known acquaintances who would be there. She wanted to go back to Drakeshead, back to Robbie's roaring fire and glacier sheets, back to timeless afternoons of toast and sweet tea, to all the new and wonderful possibilities of sharing dreams instead of struggling along with them alone.

Polly Drayton sat at a dressing table too that night, her flat face flushed with heat from the crowded bar below and from the two double gins that Mr Bernard, the retired polo player, had bought her, flirting badly as he always did after a pint or three. New

Year's Eve was always something of a party, with free drinks flying all over the place.

She was supposed to be helping out in the kitchen – as well as serving at tables – but had sneaked upstairs for a breather. Robbie would be along later, she was sure of it. Now that the black car had gone, there was nothing to stop him. There were no other local parties that she knew of – and nobody liked to spend New Year's Eve on their own.

Polly chewed her lower lip as she studied her reflection. The colour in her cheeks belied the slump of her face, a slump of deep resignation, borne of a life lived entirely without the luxury of self-esteem. 'Expect nothing and you won't be disappointed,' her mother liked to say – folding her chunky arms and sticking her chin out with the certainty of one well acquainted with the truths of such a philosophy.

But she had expected something from Robbie Dexter. And who wouldn't, after seven years?

'She got her hopes up and gave herself too freely,' Mrs Drayton had declared several times during the past few weeks, broadcasting her views with the determined defiance of one proud of a reputation for calling a spade a spade. 'We warned her, but she wouldn't listen.' Polly, invariably within earshot of such confidences, would slink away, her ears burning with shame, her mother's words echoing after her. 'No good crying over spilt milk, that's what I say. Plenty of other fish in that particular sea and some with more security to offer too. Not a bad man that Robbie Dexter – I'll admit I always liked him – but he's got his head in the clouds half the time – running round after those blessed animals when he should be building up his business.'

It was true, Polly knew that. But truth had nothing to do with what she felt inside. She would have died for Robbie Dexter. She loved his crumbling cottage and messy life. Perhaps because it made her feel less of a mess – less of a burden – herself. He was always so grateful for any help she gave – unlike her parents who expected her to work all the time, as if it was some right granted to them upon her birth. A long time ago, she had sometimes dared to answer them back, confident that time would bring some sort of escape; but as the years closed in, narrowing the prospects of a grown woman with three CSEs and nothing but twelve years of working the deep fat fryer to her credit, she grew more timid about holding her own. Her parents were all she had, all that she could be sure of, especially now.

Hearing the crunch of feet on the gravel outside, Polly ran to the window for a peak between the curtains; but it was only Bob and Sharon Tayer who ran the newsagent's down the road. Their laughs and greetings mingled with the muffled hubbub from the bar below as they opened the door and were welcomed inside.

'Polly! What the devil are you playing at up there?' The cannon of her father's voice boomed up the stairs. 'Table eight is threatening to walk out and Eric says if he doesn't get any help in the next five minutes he's going too – for good this time.' Eric was their chef, whose threats to leave multiplied during the course of each year that he stayed.

As the door flew open, Polly cowered against the window, her heart racing, her face a picture of guilt.

Her father, largely silent, as always, before the fog-horn opinions of his wife, had been curiously tender with his daughter during recent weeks, not saying anything directly, but sometimes using a new tone of voice which resonated with some of the compassion he felt but did not know how to own up to. 'What are you up to girl?' he said softly, staying by the door. 'Your mother's going mad downstairs. One more minute and then down, OK?'

Polly nodded, this sudden gentleness making her want to cry.

Much later that night, when the doors had at last closed on the ex-polo player, whose mother had come from the Argentine and who had spent two hours commemorating the fact with sonorous renditions of the tango, Polly stole out into the night. Robbie had not come. She needed to see again that the black car had gone.

The air was crisp and still, each hump of mud, each blade of grass brilliantly dusted with frost, creating a dim iridescence to light her way. Though her fingers and face were soon numb with cold, her feet remained warm in the fur-lined nest of her boots. There had been no present from him that Christmas, she thought miserably, pushing her hands deeper into her pockets and increasing the length of her stride so that she skidded slightly on the frozen ground.

There was no sign of her car. Polly sighed with relief, but walked on, feeling that her mission was still not quite accomplished. A thick layer of frost masked the windows of Robbie's van, each an inviting square of white, chaste and perfect as a field of freshly fallen snow. With a glance over her shoulder, Polly pulled off her mitten and began to work her index finger across the rear window, the letters forming easily upon the bed of brittle crystals. *I AM DYING*, she wrote, heedless of any possible charges of melodrama, responding only to the real desperation strangling her heart.

Then she stood for a moment staring at the cottage, praying that the black rectangle of his bedroom would blink open with light, that some deep, telepathic power might bring him and everything they had once shared back to life. But all remained quiet, apart from the infinitesimal creaks and whispers of freezing vapour and burrowed animals. Even the field was silent, all its occupants having been moved earlier that evening to the barn behind the house, where a scattering of straw awaited them together with several buckets of the expensive pellets on which pregnant ewes were said to thrive. Evidence of the invariably hazardous transition from field to barn lay all around her in the form of frozen piles of what she had originally taken to be mud, but which she now realised were sheep droppings.

Polly bent down and, with gloved hands, picked up as much as she could of one heap of frozen excrement. Empowered by fresh resolve, she then marched across to the front door of the cottage, where she forced what she could of her grim parcel through the letter flap. Then she rang the bell, holding the button down as hard as she could and counting to ten, before running off into the night.

23 ∫

Since Piers Robson was a political journalist of only moderate reputation and his wife, Sally's, contributions to interior design magazines had become so freelance as to be practically nonexistent, the lavish splendour of their parties was always something of a shock.

Anita, taking in the elegant structures of sea food and exotic salads – each one an architectural masterpiece in its own right – the massive flower arrangements, interlaced with twists of mistletoe and dangling lanterns, felt unashamedly envious. The venue this year was an entire restaurant on the south side of the Thames, its tables carefully arranged so as to allow a large space for dancing without impeding access either to the bar or this extravaganza of food. Outside, a few of the hardier guests were already braving the covered walkway, admiring the prospect it afforded of several of the capital's most famous monuments, lit up along the river banks with picture-postcard perfection.

Beside her, Giles was pulling at the joints of his fingers, making little clicks that set her teeth on edge. He had been doing it ever since he got in from work an hour or so before, when she had hissed that there was no time for a bath and he had turned and slouched back downstairs, looking at the floor. Filled with impulsive shame at her bossiness, Anita had darted forward and kissed him fiercely on the cheek. 'I'm sorry, love. I didn't mean to shout. It's just that the twins were so awful this afternoon – massive overdoses of sugar at a quite unspeakable party featuring somebody called Melody Man who was so boring even the dog fell asleep – and then they cried because that new girl Chrissie was coming to sit and not Moira who irons, who they like so much more.' The stiff silence of her husband made her back down further still. 'Look, have that bath. Have a sleep. Do what you like. It won't matter a bit if we're late.'

'No. I don't care.' He had sat down on the bottom stair and pulled his coat onto his lap from where he had slung it across the bannisters. 'Whatever you want, Anita.' Then the baby-sitter had emerged from the sitting room, releasing a deafening noise from the television as she opened the door. Instead of being brave and saying something, Anita followed Giles out to the car, where the expense and general failings of all their baby-sitters served as conversational fodder for the journey. If, that is, the intermittent growls provided by her husband could be said to qualify as conversation. They now stood side by side amongst the other first arrivals, scanning the half empty room for familiar faces, the few inches separating them feeling vast and unbridgeable.

Rachel arrived a little after nine o'clock, her departure from the flat having been delayed by a call from her parents wishing her all the best for the New Year. They never stayed up to mark the occasion themselves, thanks to a lifelong aversion to champagne and a dogged belief in the rejuvenating effect of every hour of sleep gained before midnight. Her father barked out a sentence or two of greeting before handing over to his wife, who launched into a lengthy account of their American Christmas. Duncan and Mary Beth's hospitality had known no bounds. They had seen the Bolshoi at the Kennedy Center, attended Midnight Mass in the cathedral and glimpsed the tail of the presidential cat during a tour of the White House. Craig and Billy, apart from a little over-excitement on Christmas Day, had behaved like angels. They were missing the little darlings already. If only air travel wasn't so expensive they'd fly out every few months or so. Grandchildren were so special – such a treat – it was quite cruel to miss so much of it by living so far apart.

Rachel waited patiently for a suitable lull in these eulogies before daring to offer any information about herself.

'I had a wonderful Christmas.' She paused before blurting, 'I'm seeing Robbie Dexter again. I thought you'd like to know.'

'Robbie Dexter? After all these years? I don't believe it . . . but darling, that's marvellous. Is it – I mean – is it serious?'

'Serious?' Rachel smiled to herself at the crudity of the question. 'Yes, I suppose it is.'

'We were so very fond of Robbie, but then you know that. Well, well, that's the best news I've had in a long time. So when are you both coming to pay us a visit? Is he still designing gardens and things? We'd so love to see him again, your father and I. Come any time – absolutely any time – though the weekend after next would suit us best.'

'The weekend after next,' explained Rachel patiently, 'would be hard. I've promised to go to Devon. But Robbie will be coming up to London soon – let's arrange something then. A Sunday lunch – you could come to me for a change.'

'That would be nice dear. Only give us plenty of warning, won't you? You know what your father's like – needs everything organised well in advance.'

'Of course,' Rachel murmured, privately thinking how adept couples could be at blaming each other for their own foibles. But it was good to hear her mother's pleasure, good to feel that, just for once, there was an aspect of her life capable of causing some genuine parental satisfaction.

'Hang on a minute, while I tell Dad.' Her mother raised her voice to an unnaturally high pitch in order to compete successfully with the television. 'Rachel is back with Robbie, dear,' Rachel heard her call. 'Robbie Dexter. We're going to see them both in two Sundays' time. Won't that be lovely?'

While recognising that her mother was demonstrating nothing but the jubilation which she herself had sought to provoke, Rachel none the less cringed inwardly. The business with Robbie still felt so new and delicate that it was hard not to flinch at having it bandied about by other people. Even telling Anita about it on the phone during the drive back that afternoon had initially felt almost like a betrayal. Being Anita she had jumped to all sorts of conclusions, most of which – infuriatingly – contained too many grains of truth for Rachel to utter any convincing denials.

'It'll be wedding bells and christenings before we know it – ooh goody, new clothes . . .'

'Anita, really, you're impossible.'

'But you're not denying it, I note. Robbie Dexter, eh? The guy

I never got to meet – well, who would have thought it? Are you bringing him tonight?'

'I wish I could.' Rachel sighed. 'It's going to be one of those commuting things for a while yet . . .'

'Until I get my fancy hat, you mean?'

'Anita, stop it. Apart from being bloody cheeky, you're tempting fate. How are you anyway, you sound good,' she added carefully.

'Not pissed, you mean.'

'I didn't say that.'

'You didn't have to.' There was a pause. 'As a matter of fact life in the Cavanagh camp seems to have hit a new all-time low—'

'Anita, I'm sorry.'

'Don't be. I'm getting quite used to it myself. I'm going to use it as an excuse to misbehave dreadfully at every opportunity.'

'Like tonight, you mean?'

'Most definitely.'

'But not so much we won't be able to have a proper talk, I hope. I've got to stop, I'm almost at the North End Road.'

'So long as it's not about me,' Anita replied, laughing.

Rachel had collected her coat ticket and was just bracing herself for the uniquely dreadful moment of having to enter a room full of smoke and crowded people – a moment which grew no easier with the years – when a finger tapped her on the shoulder. She spun round to find herself staring into the bespectacled face of Luke Berenson, the vicar's son towards whom her mother had nurtured such hopelessly misguided aspirations a few months before.

'Small world.'

'Yes, isn't it?' Although quite pleased to see him, something in Rachel recoiled. Recollections of their curiously intimate autumnal walk brought with them an unwelcome sense of vulnerability. I want to call Robbie she thought, glancing round for a public telephone and saying, 'How are things with you?'

'Not too bad, thanks.' He pushed his glasses up his nose and cleared his throat. 'That is, if you discount the fact that I'm not on speaking terms with the old man, but then that does have its advantages.'

They both laughed, recalling the shared horrors of their lunch together.

'I'm here with my new partner, Alan Raymond. He's a journalist. We're not staying long – going to another party afterwards.'

Rachel was on the point of responding to this happy piece of news when her eye was caught by a tall, dark-haired man handing in what looked like a trench coat. His hair had been cut so short that for a moment she didn't recognise him.

Luke turned politely to follow her gaze. 'Someone you know?'

'Oh no – I mean, barely. Shall we find ourselves a drink?' She turned hastily and led the way towards the teeming throng in the large room behind them, some instinct impelling her to lose herself within it before Will Raphael had time to catch them up. As they entered, Luke was accosted by a ginger-headed man wearing a lime-green bow tie and matching handkerchief, who propelled him away to meet someone else. Left to her own devices Rachel found herself a drink and then began surreptitiously scouring the room for Anita. After the intense intimacy of the last few days the amorphous, impersonal mass of humanity swarming around her felt painfully alien.

'I got the distinct impression I was being run away from just now. Was I right?'

He was wearing black trousers and a plain white collarless shirt held together with small, ivory-coloured oval buttons which caught in the beams of the ceiling spotlights.

Rachel opened her mouth to deny the allegation, but found the truth coming out instead. 'I'm sorry – I don't know why – I'm feeling decidedly unparty-like I'm afraid. Probably shouldn't have come at all . . .'

'Believe me,' he put in dryly, 'I know the feeling. I only came because I had my arm twisted.'

They each took sips of their wine and studied their fingers for a moment.

'Devon was clearly a success.'

'What do you mean?'

'Your face, it's full of . . . not colour exactly but . . . there's a sort of glow. Fresh country air maybe?' He cocked his head at her and smiled. 'Though now it's because you're blushing.'

'Really, I must say . . . I mean, why do I get the impression

that you get perverse delight from making me feel uncomfortable?'

'And why is it that I get the impression you are unhealthily
unused to being teased?' He smiled and shook his head. 'I'm
sorry. You're quite right. I've no business being so familiar.
Teasing is for one's closest friends and I barely know you.'

'Quite.' She took a sip of her drink, wishing she was one of
those people who could stand next to someone and remain
silent without it feeling awkward. 'As a matter of fact,' she
found herself saying, 'my stay in Devon has made me think
that it might be fun to move out of London for good, leave the
rat race and so on.'

'Really?' He raised his eyebrows. 'You strike me as the sort
of person who would be quite lost without the rat race – and
I don't mean that as an insult,' he added hastily.

'I shall endeavour not to take it as one then,' she replied,
resolving to change the subject one last time and then make an
excuse to get away.

'How is your little boy – Jack, was it?'

'He's good, thank you.' His face broke into a broad smile, in
one move eradicating every trace of rigidity, but still leaving
Rachel with the impression that each flicker of emotion was
under masterful control. There were black flecks in the brown
of his pupils, she noticed, tiny dark smudges which perhaps
accounted for the intensity of his stare. 'But he's not my boy,
I'm sorry to say, he belongs to my sister, Anna.'

'Oh, I see,' she replied quickly, not seeing at all. She almost
asked if he was married, but checked herself. Single people
could not ask such things, at least not without creating certain
resonances.

'I had a wife once,' he said, 'but no children.'

'That was lucky.'

Across the other side of the room the disco had started up. A
few eager couples were already shuffling under the strobe lights,
their limbs looking twitchy and disjointed, their expressions
frozen and robotic.

'Christ, *there* you are – the only two people I want to see at this
horrid party.' Anita pushed between them from behind, neatly
linking her arms through theirs. 'Mr Will Raphael because I'm

a shameless flirt and Rachel because I want to hear all about Robbie and be made *furiously* jealous. Finding true love so late on in the game is simply not fair. Most of us found it so long ago that we've forgotten what it felt like. I've certainly forgotten what Giles feels like lately . . .' She completed the sentence with a musical laugh.

'Hello, Anita.' Rachel kissed her cheek, wondering how much of the manic cheeriness was put on and how much came from a bottle. 'Can we talk?' she whispered.

Anita pulled her hand free and leant on Will. 'Oh, I'm right off talking, I'm afraid. Never does any bloody good.' Alcohol had helped to dull the sharper angles of her mood, although disappointment still raged inside, like the irrepressible nausea that came with one of her migraines. Getting Sally to invite Will Raphael to the party had been the easy part, she realised; now that he was here she had no idea what to do with him, beyond a sudden and quite irrational desire to get him away from Rachel. Rachel, who was going to make babies and live happily ever after with Robbie Dexter, for Christ's sake. Rachel who, having decided she wanted true love and the works, had clicked her fingers and got the lot.

'I'm going to be bold and ask you to dance, Will. Rachel won't mind, will you Rachel? If you see Giles, tell him I've left him for a tall dark handsome stranger. Tell him he can keep the kids but I'd like a standing order for the mortgage and the school fees.'

Will allowed himself to be led away, but not before throwing Rachel a glance of good-humoured apology as he went. He really was quite impressively tolerant, Rachel thought, smiling after them but feeling worried. It was so impossible not to worry about Anita these days. Things could not carry on at such a pitch for much longer. Some awful climax was coming, she could feel it.

It was quite a relief to slip into the cool confines of the phone booth. As she searched her handbag for coins, Rachel found herself thinking about the rat race and wondering whether she needed to be a part of it or not. She pictured Robbie's cottage, not as it was, but as it could be, her imagination moulding order and beauty from amongst the chaos. She could live there, all right. Of course she could. She pressed several coins into the slot and waited for the dialling tone. Imagining Robbie as a permanent fixture in London was altogether harder. Even the features of his face shimmered and creased like a broken reflection. Her fingers hurriedly pressed the numbers. She needed to speak to him. She needed to hear his voice for it all to come back into focus.

24

'I thought you were just going to take my photograph.' Rachel shuffled in the armchair in which she had been sitting for some fifteen minutes and made a face.

Will, perched on a stool a few feet away with a pencil and a large sketch pad, glanced up. 'I am. Sometimes I do a few drawings too. It helps me focus on what I want. Angles and lighting and so on.'

'I can't believe I agreed to do this.'

He smacked his pencil against his pad and laughed out loud. 'The power of alcohol for you, maybe?'

'Nonsense. I wasn't that bad . . .' She stopped, scowling and blushing at the recollection of the headache she had endured on New Year's Day. 'Well maybe I was,' she muttered, thinking at the same time that her presence in Will's studio in fact had something to do with how kind he had been to Anita.

The phone call with Robbie, a lovely long talk full of mutual longing and half-articulated hopes, had left her quite elated. She had floated back into the arms of the party in quite a different mood, full of energy and a sense of celebration. A few glasses and idle conversations later she found herself seated before a plateful of food at a round table of lively people that included both Will and Anita. Giles had apparently gone home, an action to which his wife referred with mounting venom and wit as the evening wore on. At the approach of midnight, ice-buckets of champagne were distributed generously to all the tables, encouraging the tide of unbridled – and quite un-British – camaraderie that was sweeping through the room.

'Any resolutions, then?' Rachel asked Anita, chinking her glass with her fork to get her attention.

'Not bloody likely.'

'I've got one,' piped a small man with a beaky nose, putting his hand up like a child in a classroom.

'Let's hear it then, darling,' drawled Anita through a mouthful of smoke.

'To personally harass as many women as possible.'

'That's a split infinitive,' shouted someone, 'you can't have that.'

'Yes he can,' replied Anita, reaching across to pat the man's hand and assure him he could personally harass her any time he wanted.

'You wouldn't like it,' Rachel had heard herself saying, 'I mean . . . it happened to a friend of mine – a . . . a . . . close friend . . . not nice at all.'

'Well, I think it would be heavenly to be harassed,' declared Anita, trying and failing to catch the eye of Will who was sitting opposite.

'What happened to this friend, then?' Will asked, leaning forward and resting his chin on both hands.

'Nothing. She'd like some revenge, but can't think how. She wants to resign but thinks it might make her look guilty. Can't face a court case. Usual sort of story.' Rachel clapped her hand to her mouth. 'Oh God, I'm being boring. Sorry everybody, sorry.'

'Darling you're not, you're being sincere, which is another thing entirely, but quite unforgivable all the same.' Anita blew her a smoky kiss and they all laughed. Then it was time to stand up and link hands for 'Auld Lang Syne'. They sang gustily, repeating the first two lines of the song over and over again since they were all anyone could remember. Afterwards, neighbour embraced neighbour, the man with the reedy voice kissing Rachel on the lips, while Anita made a smacking sound at the air beside her ears, clinging on for a few seconds of tipsily sentimental affection. As Will left his side of the table and approached them, Rachel found herself studying the dark shadows across his cheeks and round his mouth with something like anticipation. But instead of a New

Year's greeting, he asked again if she would sit for a photograph. Then Anita was between them, bestowing Will with a festive embrace of such ferocity that Rachel could see the whites of his nails as he prised himself free.

'Yes, OK then,' she had said, raising her voice and her glass, as the floor heaved beneath her feet.

'Hang on a minute.' Will put his pencil behind one ear and clambered down from his stool. 'What are you up to over here?'

'Up to?' She tensed as he adjusted the angle of her face and then her neck. His fingertips felt cool.

'Relax. Look at me. No, don't stare, just *look* – not through me, but at me. Engage my face – pretend for a minute that you know me.'

Rachel, stiff with self-consciousness, swivelled her attention from the intimidating vulture of a tripod to the face now just a few inches from hers. With his dark hair cropped so short at the front, his eyes, with their curious mixture of jet and brown, were even more prominent – quite impossible not to stare into when viewed so close, though she did her best. There were faint webs of laugh-lines in each corner, she noticed, pulling his expression towards amusement even when he was being most serious. His nose looked longer close-to, and very straight. 'But I don't know you,' she said hopelessly.

'No, I suppose you don't.' He grinned and sat back on his haunches, studying her for a moment in a way that was both critical and unsettling. 'But I think I'm beginning to know you, a little.'

'Oh, do you now?' She crossed her arms and sucked in her cheeks.

'Hands in your lap, please. There, like that. But you don't like to be known, do you Rachel Elliot? You're like me. Full of secret spaces.' He was back with his pad now, sitting on the very edge of his stool, one leg caught up in its struts, the other just reaching the ground. His pencil made small scratching noises as he worked.

'I don't know what you mean.' It was hard to sound indignant and dignified at the same time. The sense of unease with which she had approached this appointment, after a gruelling few weeks of going through the motions at work, increased to new proportions. Without weekends in Devon she would have gone insane. But Robbie had been too busy to see her that weekend, so there had been no excuse to cancel. He was going to make up for it by coming to London next time, he promised. And about time too, she had teased, making him cross.

In one swift, impatient movement, Will slid off the stool, walked once round her chair and went to sit on the window seat which overlooked the wharf below.

'This isn't working,' he muttered, staring out of the window with a sigh. 'You're like a . . . a cardboard cut-out. All hard edges. Tight as wire.'

Rachel reached down for her handbag at her feet. 'Well, I am sorry to have wasted your time,' she said with icy sweetness. 'I did warn you – cameras and I have never enjoyed the most fruitful of relationships.' She strode towards the door, wishing her heels didn't clump quite so noisily on the bare boards of his studio and trying not to be distracted by any of the curious statuettes and canvasses that she passed along the way. The place was like the storeroom for a gallery of modern art, except for the daylight pouring in through the windows along its river-facing wall, a white wintry light from a sky that glittered like a polished stone.

'Oh, come back here,' he called lazily, not moving. 'Come back and talk – have a coffee – a biscuit – if that's allowed.'

She stopped and turned. 'What do you mean, if that's allowed?'

'You just look like the kind of person who counts her biscuits, if you don't mind my saying so.'

There was an impudent gleam in his eye, though his mouth did not smile. It was a beautiful mouth, she saw suddenly, full and shapely, almost feminine. The thought, bolting into her mind from nowhere, was so absurdly inappropriate that she nearly laughed out loud.

'I eat when I'm hungry.' She hitched the strap of her handbag further onto her shoulder and crossed her arms. 'A biscuit would be quite nice, actually.'

'Good,' he said softly, leaving his window seat and strolling over to a cluttered trestle table in the far corner of the room that housed, among many other things, a paint-splattered metal kettle and a large, lidless jar of instant coffee. While the water boiled he tipped generous heaps of granules into two tea-stained mugs. 'Let's just talk.' He held out the steaming mug of oily black coffee like a peace offering.

'Talk?' She forced out a laugh, nervous of his calm. 'I thought I was here to have my photograph taken. It was your idea, remember? I agreed because it was New Year's Eve and I'd had five glasses of champagne. And because . . .'

'Because?'

She took the coffee and shrugged. 'Oh bloody hell, I don't know. What do you want to talk about anyway?'

'You.'

She shrugged again, determined to convey carelessness even if she could not feel it. 'Nothing to say. I've had a worryingly easy life. I work hard. I live well.' She started on a tour of the room while she talked, taking sips and blowing at imaginary swirls of steam. He stood leaning up against the wall beside the trestle table, one leg bent up behind him, the sole of his shoe pressed against the scuffed wall behind.

'And you want to move to the West Country?'

She spoke carefully, wishing suddenly that she had told Robbie about Will Raphael and the improbable business of agreeing to sit for a photograph. A combination of embarrassment and caution had prevented her. Robbie could be quite jealous, she had found, sometimes about the silliest things. 'Yes. Well, like I said, I'm thinking about it. I'm thinking about a lot of things at the moment. I feel it's time to move on . . . make a proper life-change . . .' His silence impelled her to continue. 'I've met someone – Robert Dexter – Anita mentioned him. We knew each other before – a long time ago. It was my fault it ended. Now we've got the chance to try again.' Rachel stopped in front of a picture of a woman, propped up on an easel, half-hidden by a writhing figurine modelled entirely out of rusty nails. It was the same woman who had appeared on the Christmas card. 'Who's this?'

'That is . . . that was my wife.'

'Oh, I see.' She hid her face in her coffee mug for a moment, before deciding that silence was probably the most tactless response of all. 'Does she still live in London?'

'No, she's dead.'

'Oh no . . . sorry . . .'

He hadn't moved. 'She was a cellist. She killed herself four years ago. Valium and gin. We had been married a year. She suffered from depression.' Though his voice was matter-of-fact, something about the stillness of his pose conveyed the impression of effort – of anguish – behind these words.

'How sad.' Rachel, wanting to save him further pain – not to mention discomfort for herself – opened her mouth to change the subject; but he hadn't finished.

'Sometimes I still feel guilty – that I wasn't enough. That I wasn't enough reason for her to live. If it wasn't for Anna – my sister – and Jack, I might have resorted to valium myself. Though Anna is a mess too,' he went on quickly, 'a typical anorexic dancer – which is probably why I like a woman who's not afraid to eat biscuits.' He chuckled, breaking the tension and coming towards her holding out a tin. 'Chocolate chip cookies. I take full responsibility apart from the black fingerprints, which belong to my nephew. Jack doesn't like cooking, but does a good line in bowl-licking and biscuit-counting.'

Rachel, subdued by the intimacy of his revelations, took one and ate steadily.

'By the way, I've got something for that friend of yours.' He began shuffling through a pile of papers beside the kettle.

'For Anita?' Rachel was intrigued.

'No, that other friend. The one who was sexually harassed.'

'Oh, her,' she said quietly, biscuit clogging her throat. 'I can't think why I mentioned it – talk about the wrong moment . . . Once, centuries ago, I used to have a sense of humour, you know,' she muttered. 'Anita was quite right to put me down.'

'Personally, I think your sincerity is one of your most endearing qualities,' he replied, using that tone he had, the one that left her quite unsure as to whether he was mocking or being kind. 'But if this doesn't kick-start the sense of humour you claim to have mislaid, then I'm afraid nothing will.' He held out a photograph, adding, 'It's for your friend – to help her get that revenge you mentioned.' There was a mischievous I-know-you-know-I-know look in his eyes that made it quite impossible to hold his gaze.

The photograph was of Cliff Weybourne. He was sitting on a sofa wearing nothing but an orange party hat, a pair of pink and blue striped boxer shorts and tartan socks. Aside from the lopsided smirk on his face, the most dominant feature of the picture was his stomach, which was as large as that of any expectant mother in her ninth month, but with the unattractive addition of a matting of thick, dark hair. Wedged between the second and third fingers of his right hand was a long, fat, freshly lit joint; a heavy swirl of smoke poured from its ashen tip. His left hand was buried wrist-deep in the ample cleavage of the woman seated next to him, like greedy fingers thrust into a bag of toffees. Best and most impressive of all in Rachel's eyes, was the expression on the woman's face: not so much boredom as complete indifference. Almost as if she did not know that the hand was there at all.

'It's fabulous,' she whispered, giggling in spite of herself. 'Where did you get it?'

'Ah, now that's a long story. A friend of a friend. A wild party. It doesn't really matter, does it?' He had come to stand beside her and was admiring the image over her shoulder. 'All that matters is that it is put to some worthwhile use. The lady is the wife of someone, by the way.' He paused. 'It won't destroy lives or careers, but for a spot of retribution I'd say it was just the thing.'

'It's brilliant,' murmured Rachel, grinning at the picture and then catching her breath as the full implications of this inspired act of generosity sank in. 'But hang on – how did you know – I mean, I never said it was Cliff . . . did I?'

'Let's call it a lucky guess.' He gently removed the photograph from her hands and slipped it into a brown envelope.

'And . . . well . . . isn't he a friend of yours?'

'Cliff Weybourne? A friend?' He shook his head, laughing. 'Christ, if I had friends like that I'd be seeing a shrink. No, no. No way. I've run into Weybourne several times through work projects, that's all. The man's a shark. I have as little to do with him as possible. I only ever come to your place to see Steve Betts. Which gives me an idea.' He tapped the envelope with his fingers. 'I'm sure Steve would be willing to blow this thing up to poster size – so that everybody might have a chance of appreciating it. It would only be fair, don't you think?' His eyes twinkled.

She clapped her hands, laughing. 'Oh, absolutely. Or,' she paused, as fresh inspiration took hold, 'what about a Valentine's card – an enormous, life-size Valentine's card, from an anonymous admirer?'

'Now you're talking.' He came over to collect her mug. 'I had a feeling you'd know what to do with it.'

'Yes, well—' she began sheepishly.

'She's a very close friend, I know, as close as friends get. And I've a notion you make a habit of helping close friends.'

'I . . .'

'I'm just glad I could help. Shall we return to some serious work now?' He made a grand gesture of invitation at the armchair. 'If madam would care to step this way?'

'Yes, she would. And – thank you, Will. Thank you very much indeed.'

He began inserting a film into a polaroid camera. 'Don't mention it. Now then, I'm just going to shoot a roll of this first, then we can get down to business.'

He took a series of trial pictures while Rachel picked crumbs out of the lambswool fluff of her jumper, brushing the smaller bits down onto the lap of her new, blue – too blue – jeans. Dress casually, he had said. Not such an easy task for a woman whose wardrobe reflected what she now recognised as a history of woefully inadequate leisure time. She had bought the jeans for Devon a couple of weeks before, on the lunchtime of the day she agreed to be the Head of Account Management, a day when she had needed to take her mind off things. Cliff Weybourne was skiing at the time, which had helped. But she had still felt awful.

As Will began arranging various foil reflectors and lights around the chair, a creeping unease stole over Rachel, a sensation of sitting alone on a stage, waiting for the spotlight to fall.

'Perhaps I should have taken those lessons after all,' she remarked, with a lightness she did not feel, 'then I might have a clue what you're doing.'

'Perhaps. I did my best to persuade you, you might recall,' he added with a wry smile. 'I dared to tackle that dense communications network of yours, the one you hide behind.'

'The one I what?'

'Forget it.' He was all businesslike again, almost brusque. 'Now face me, chin down a bit, that's it.' Leaving his post by the camera, he went to fiddle with the sugar-paper backdrop of yellowy cream that he had hung behind the chair. Then, quite without warning, he stepped silently up behind her and placed both hands on her shoulders. Using his palms, he began to press in slow hard circular motions across the top of her back, his fingers kneading so deep into the bands of muscle that it almost hurt. Rachel opened her mouth to say something, but then closed her eyes instead. When the hands were removed – a little later and with as little warning – she experienced a fleeting but quite extraordinary sense of loss, followed by a feeling of weightlessness, as if she was floating several inches above the seat of her chair. He remained standing behind her. She could hear him breathing, not because it was loud, but because the vast room suddenly seemed quite still, a frozen moment, captured in the flying poses of his sculptures, in the inscrutable expressions of the faces on the easels and walls.

'You are in knots, Rachel,' he said quietly. 'Stop trying to be brave all the time. Fear is a necessary part of the sensation of being alive. Sometimes we have to let it show. We have to own up to it or it drives us mad.'

Then he went and stood behind his camera, saying nothing more – not even instructing her how to sit or look – filling the silence with whirs and clicks from the tripod, while Rachel sank down into the soft embrace of the armchair, feeling unnerved but strangely elated. What a bloody cheek the man had. Quite unanswerable. She stared into the face of the camera boldly, unblinking. Knots indeed. She flexed her upper back, feeling still where his hands had worked, remembering with a twist of shameful pleasure how good it had felt, the releasing emptiness afterwards.

25

But it really wasn't worth mentioning to Robbie, Rachel decided, as she hopped from one leg to another in front of the ticket barrier the following weekend, waiting for the first sight of his curly head amongst the sea of faces streaming down the platform towards her. It was just a weird thing that had happened – too weird to try to explain – irrelevant the moment it was over. Will Raphael had not touched her again – had hardly come near her in fact – except to compare diaries for dates as to when the photo might be ready. Then he had held the door open for her and stood at the top of the stairs as she descended, hands pushed into the pockets of his trousers, his expression so unreadable that she suspected he might be masking disappointment in her as a model, that she had not lived up to whatever unimaginable expectations he had had in mind.

Robbie saw her first and waved hard, boyish glee radiating from his big square face. He could still have been a student, Rachel thought affectionately, taking in the weathered duffle coat and knee-bagged cords. There was simply no vanity to the man. Twiddling the duffle buttons, she lifted her face for a kiss.

A few yards behind them, Polly Drayton, her straggly hair bunched into a tight ponytail that tugged the skin back from her temples, watched them embrace and walk away before handing her own ticket to the man at the barrier. Robbie had invited her to London, she told her parents that afternoon, for a long weekend. Make or break sort of thing. See if they could sort something out after all.

'And I thought he had a new woman,' said her father, 'that's the story at any rate. A London lady.'

'That's just his sister, the one that went to Canada. She's back in London. We're going to stay with her the first night. After that it's a posh hotel. Five star with an indoor pool, Robbie says. Breakfast in bed with the newspaper if you want it. We might stay there all week.' The lies, once they started coming, flowed with silky ease.

'And how are we supposed to manage running this place while Lady Muck gallivants in London, that's what I want to know?' complained her mother, but good-humouredly, as if she might be persuaded that enjoying oneself was a forgivable crime after all.

Polly was in no hurry. She knew where Rachel Elliot both lived and worked – one sortie into Robbie's kitchen while he was out doing an estimate for the new owners down Sandy Lane had sorted that out. In the midst of so much clutter and mess, it hurt more than anything to find the woman's name – her numbers and addresses – so carefully written out and fixed to the middle of the fridge door with a magnet that Polly herself had given him. A sheep magnet, with a red ribbon round its neck.

Rachel and Robbie, busy with the greetings that precede proper conversation, did not notice the hunched, plump figure sprint across the road towards the buses, her half-empty rucksack jigging on her back like a swaddled child, her ponytail bobbing with jaunty defiance at the inky night sky.

'Do you want the good news or the bad news?' Rachel burrowed her face into his shoulder, savouring the solidity of him.

'Oh, only the good please.'

'We're going out to dinner – there's a really nice Italian place within walking distance from my front door.'

'Sounds great. I'm starving.' He patted her hand. 'Go on, hit me with the bad.'

'My parents are coming to lunch tomorrow. Sorry.'

'Your parents? Well, you did warn me.' He kissed her nose. 'We'll survive. They were OK, if I remember correctly.'

An unexpected ripple in the harmony of such exchanges occurred a little later in the evening, towards the end of their meal, when Rachel offered to pay and Robbie, fuelled with pride and too much wine, resisted vehemently.

'I know you earn more money than me Rachel – a lot more – but that does not mean you should pay my way. I've got enough to have a good time now and then, I promise you. I haven't been in a dole queue since college . . .'

'I know Robbie, I know. I just wanted it to be my treat tonight. I mean, you've come all the way up here and—'

'*My* treat, to make up for being apart on Valentine's Day,' he insisted grandly, signalling to the waiter with a flourish.

But the restaurant did not accept his credit card and his cheque book turned out to be in the side pocket of the bag which he had deposited at the flat.

'But I guess you might not be richer than me for very much longer,' he remarked stiffly, as they headed back up the street towards her flat. 'I know you've said that it's a question of getting the timing right, but the sooner you leave that horrible agency the better, if you ask me. Then we'd be on more of an even keel, eh?' Rachel's outward response to this was an encouraging smile, while inwardly she quailed. Did Robbie mean resign from the agency, or from work in general? Having so recently recovered from one minor upset, she was unwilling to risk another. So she let the matter pass.

In the light of such uncertainties, Rachel also elected not to mention a conversation she had had with Jimmy Chartsworth on the Monday of that week, informing her of a cabal of dissatisfied directors like herself who were hatching a plot to break away from McKenzie Cartwright and form a small agency of their own, an agency where discretion and personalities mattered, where artistic and moral values could be maintained at levels to which they had all originally aspired. The thrill of such news had almost caused her to abandon Cliff's Valentine surprise; though she relented when she saw Steve Bett's masterful transformation of the card. It was for a friend of Will's, she had explained, a friend with a grudge. Anything for a friend of Will's, he had said simply, offering a wry smile that confirmed better than words ever could that she had allies in the business after all, that she had not been suffering entirely alone.

The card was so large that it had taken two secretaries to transport it from reception to the bar, where a Valentine's Happy Hour was in full flow. The sight of Cliff Weybourne's face when he tore off the tissue paper, when laughter froze to horror, was exactly the therapy Rachel had craved and would, she knew, be a source of satisfaction for years to come. *To My Valentine*, it said in large letters across the top, *I've always loved a party animal*. To Cliff's credit, he had tried to laugh, though it looked more like gagging and no noise came out at all. He left the bar shortly afterwards, unwisely leaving his gift propped up by the juke-box, where it still remained, enhanced by a few creative additions with biros and fibre-tipped pens. A bubble coming out of the woman's mouth now said: *If you ignore a gorilla it eventually goes away*.

When she told Robbie about the incident, he laughed, but doubtfully. 'Where did you get such a picture, anyway?'

'I've friends in the right places,' she replied quickly, putting her hand in his coat pocket and lacing her fingers in his.

'I hope this doesn't mean you won't resign after all? What with this and accepting that promotion you might feel tempted to stay.'

He was walking so fast that she had to keep lengthening her stride to match his. 'I honestly don't know, Robbie. Things are up in the air at the moment.'

She thought about wanting a baby and clenched his fingers even more tightly inside the pocket. Why was finding the right moment to tell him so hard? Why was she only able to progress things inside her head?

'It's just that I feel like I'm playing second fiddle to your job,' remarked Robbie, while she searched in her bag for her keys.

'Don't be silly,' she replied, slotting the key home and thinking how much more fragile his ego was than she had at first judged, how little it seemed to have evolved over the years.

There followed a brief half-hour or so of silent friction, one of their first. In order to overcome it, Rachel found herself slipping into the role of the little woman, curling up in the broad circle of his arms like an animal seeking protection. Robbie had responded instantly, his confidence blossoming with every stroke of her hair.

I could live like this, she'd thought, nestling closer, relishing the intimacy, telling herself that it did not matter if its origins were a little contrived.

26 ∫

At some indefinable point the weekend slipped out of Rachel's control. While Robbie lay in bed with the papers, swooning at the treat of not being roused by the needs of poultry and sheep, she found herself wrestling with a spitting shoulder of lamb in her kitchen, some ill-founded notion of wanting to feed her parents in the manner to which they were accustomed having prompted her to attempt dizzy heights of culinary achievement from which she usually had the wisdom to refrain.

Thanks to carrots with tiny, suspicious looking drill-holes in their sides and roast potatoes which stubbornly refused to show so much as a hint of a tan – even after two hours on the top shelf of the oven – a good portion of Rachel's morning was spent in the kitchen. When her parents arrived they greeted Robbie Dexter like a long-lost son, monopolising him with so many questions about his life that she almost felt neglected, and had to remind herself that such adulation should make her glad.

Sheep dominated the conversation, without one single ironic reference to the disappointingly fatty joint which formed the centrepiece of their meal. Rachel, absorbed in ragged, inexpert carving with a blunt knife, kept her thoughts largely to herself, thinking as she finally sat down that what remained of the bone looked as if it had been the subject of a vicious brawl between two starving dogs. Robbie, oblivious to such niceties, ate heartily, two platefuls of meat and vegetables doing nothing to dent his appetite for the board of cheese and biscuits that followed.

'You'll take care of Rachel, won't you now Robbie?' said Margaret, popping a single grape into her mouth. 'We can't help worrying about her, can we Henry?'

'Mum . . . for goodness' sake,' began Rachel.

'Oh, don't you worry, Mrs Elliot. Rachel's already thinking of packing in work. Did she tell you?' Wafery splinters scattered as he bit into his cracker and cheese.

'No, she didn't.' Her mother beamed. 'It's always been such a demanding job – she works far too hard, we've always said so. Never has time for any fun – until now, of course. Thank goodness for you Robbie, thank goodness.' As she leant across the table to pat his arm one of her bangles skimmed the top of the butter. Rachel, observing the minor mishap, immediately resolved to keep it to herself, childishly relishing the thought of a surprise grease stain appearing somewhere on her mother's turquoise twin-set later in the day.

It was something of a relief to be summoned away from the table by the telephone.

'How's it going?'

'Oh Anita, it's you. Fine, I guess. I'd forgotten how much they adored him – it's quite sickening really.'

'And the course of true love continues to run smooth?'

'Apart from the occasional loop-the-loop.'

'What did I tell you? You'll be needing best men and god-mothers and things soon.' She sounded gloomy.

Rachel sipped the wine which she had brought with her and leant up against the wall, wishing guiltily that she could feel as sure about such things in her own heart. All that she so badly wanted was now within reach. Not just motherhood, but love on a grand scale. Robbie hadn't asked her outright, but the hints were certainly starting to come thick and fast.

'I really ought to get back to them all.' She sighed. 'Poor Robbie – he's managing awfully well.'

'You couldn't get away for a couple of hours today or tomor-row, could you?' Anita, remembering the grey parcel of a hus-band slumped in bed upstairs, spoke now with real urgency.

'Oh Anita – you know I'd love to – but this weekend it really would be hard.'

'Giles has left me.'

'He's what?'

'Left me – mentally speaking. He's turned away, gone for good.'

'You mean you two haven't made it up yet?'

'No, Rachel, this is different. Much much worse. He barely moves. He doesn't speak.'

'Is he ill, for God's sake?'

'I don't know. He says not. But he's like a . . . zombie. I'm wondering if he's fallen in love – not married love, but the crazy kind, with someone who's not yet old enough to be sour and cynical. Someone who doesn't drink,' she added very quietly.

A burst of laughter sounded from the lunch table. 'Have you asked him if there's someone else?'

'Of course – millions of times. He denies it. He denies everything. I tell you, Rachel, I'm at my wit's end. It's like living with a corpse. And to make matters worse I've been given my first serious piece of work in centuries. Post-natal depression – right up my street – good money, too. Only I can't do it – I can't concentrate on anything with Giles like this. I think I'm going to do something desperate if I'm not careful.'

'Now calm down. Call a doctor. Get someone to look at him.'

'Doctors don't come round these days, unless you're dying. Nor can I give a man who weighs thirteen stone a fireman's lift to the car. The bugger. I hate him. Do you know that, I really hate him.'

'Nonsense.'

'You sound like his mother.'

'I'm sorry, I don't mean to. I just don't know how to help . . . except perhaps . . .'

'Go on – say it.'

'You've got to stop drinking, Anita. It's gone way too far this time.'

There was a silence. 'You have no idea Rachel . . .' her voice trembled for a moment before she wrenched it back under control. 'Stop fussing, will you? Run along and plot weddings and babies then, and leave those of us who've done all that to sort ourselves out. It'll be funerals next. I want Mahler at mine, by the way, and a video recording of Elvis singing 'Love Me Tender'. Oh yes, and that lovely poem that they did in the Four Weddings film – the one that made everyone cry. I want Giles to read it.'

Rachel laughed as she was meant to. 'OK, I'll see what I can do. Now go and write about post-natal depression and I'll call you on Monday to see if things are any better.'

Robbie shot her a look of relief when she reappeared – a fleeting arrow of complicity which cheered her greatly as she set about clearing away the plates and making coffee. Later, her mother came to help with the washing up, while Robbie and her father lounged in the sitting room discussing the pros and cons of garden gnomes. Rachel had forgotten how much they had in common.

The women in the kitchen, the men digesting their meal, she thought, trying not to mind. Her father's pipe smoke curled round the hangings and corners of the flat, a blue snake of a shadow that transported Rachel back to earlier times in earlier kitchens. The boys playing elsewhere. The women with their hands in the sink.

'That nice Luke Berenson has found himself someone, too,' remarked her mother in cosy way, rubbing invisible flecks off the side of a saucepan and searching for an appropriate cupboard in which to stow it. 'His father came by for sherry last Thursday, or was it Wednesday . . . ?' She paused, saucepan in hand, to ponder the point. 'He says Luke's been coming home a lot less as a result, but there we are. Can't have everything, can you? I expect he'll meet her soon enough.'

Rachel, recalling the ginger-headed journalist with the vibrant bow tie, suppressed a smile.

'Such a nice man. I'm so glad for him. I do hope they get married.' Her mother clutched the dishcloth to her chest and smiled dreamily, while Rachel marvelled that the unromantic terms of reference under which her own marriage had evolved should not have dulled her appetite for believing in such things.

So well did Robbie entertain her parents that they did not leave until late afternoon, after a walk down to the Embankment and two pots of tea. Rachel closed the door with a groan of relief and kicked off her shoes. Robbie, who was in the sitting room watching a rugby match, held out his arm to her when she came in, though his eyes remained fixed on the screen.

'Got you to myself at last,' she murmured, suppressing a

twinge of resentment at the thirty or so rugby players now distracting his attention.

A few minutes later there was a long ring on the doorbell.

'Oh shit, they've forgotten something,' she moaned, casting her eyes round the room for a glasses case or a stray glove. Since there was no answer on the intercom, Rachel made her way to the front door in her stockinged feet, hugging herself against the cold and thinking uncharitably about the incompetence of the old.

Standing on the step outside was a white-faced girl with a greasy ponytail, wearing a purple anorak and a handsome pair of brown leather boots.

'I've got something for Robbie,' she said, thrusting a flat brown envelope into Rachel's hands and backing away.

'Do you want to see him?' asked Rachel without thinking, concerned by the look of pinched misery on the girl's face.

Polly took another step backwards and shook her head. How could he want someone so middle-aged, she was thinking, even if she had got pretty eyes?

'No message to pass on, then?' Rachel's patience, worn thin by the wind that whipped round their ankles, was in danger of giving way to sarcasm.

'Just give it him, would you?' The girl gestured with her head at the envelope. 'Say Polly brought it,' she called, running away down the steps.

'Right you are.' Rachel slammed the door and marched back down the hallway, cursing the way the weekend was developing and thinking not for the first time how much sweeter and simpler life seemed in Devon, with nothing but sheep and chickens to get in the way of things.

That night they almost argued.

'Why didn't you tell me about her?'

'Because she is nothing. Because there is nothing to tell.'

'Well, Molly—'

'Polly.'

'Polly clearly wouldn't agree with you. She looked in a terrible state too, all teeth and eyes. When you said there'd been a girlfriend over the last few years I had no idea she still lived so close to you, that she still was involved with you—'

'Well, I'm not involved with her.' Robbie, recalling the messages on his windscreen and the strange objects which had been forced through his letterbox during the course of the last few weeks, resolved to say as little as possible. Rachel, in her current mood, would not react well to news of sheep shit landing on his doormat.

'And how the hell did she get here? I mean, has she been following us or something?' Rachel shivered. 'I find the whole thing really spooky and horrible.'

They were lying in bed, surrounded by the debris of a disappointingly soggy pizza take-away, most of which had been consumed by Robbie, while Rachel picked at flakes of burnt onion and nibbled all the crusts.

'And I can't understand why you don't open that bloody envelope. I just couldn't do that – I mean, just out of curiosity I would have to open it. I know you say it will be nonsense of some kind, but I'd still like to see what *kind* of nonsense.'

'I've told you. Forget the whole thing. I'll sort it out when I get home. I promise you, I had no idea Polly was up to this sort of thing.'

'What sort of thing? You haven't opened her letter, or whatever it is.'

He sat up and threw his hands down onto the bedcovers. 'Look, I've told you, forget the letter. I don't want it to ruin our weekend.'

At the realisation that this was precisely what it was doing anyway, they both fell silent.

'Sorry,' Rachel whispered. 'Just jealous, I suppose.' It seemed simpler to say this, when in fact it didn't feel like jealousy at all. More like frustration. Or plain annoyance.

'I'm glad you're jealous,' Robbie replied gently, getting back into bed and pulling her hands to his mouth. 'It means you care. It means what I've always wanted to happen is finally happening.'

'And what was that?' she murmured.

'Oh, I think you know, Rachel Elliot,' he whispered, kissing her fingers between words, and pushing her back onto the bed. 'I think you know.'

Tell him now, chanted a voice inside her head, tell him now about wanting a child. The voice was so loud she was almost suprised he didn't remark on it himself. It occurred to her in the same instant that the reason she had not yet managed such a confession might be related, not to a fear that Robbie would object, but that he might just be thrilled beyond words. Appalled at herself, she hugged him harder, squeezing the thought away.

27

Rachel picked up the two transparencies lying on her desk and held them to the light for a minute before putting them down with a sigh. At this particular juncture in her life it was hard to care deeply about the destiny of a tube of skin-tinted moisturiser, especially one clad in a lilac bikini, frolicking in the spume of a fake wave. It was part of an American press campaign which Frank Alder was under pressure to test in the UK. Hopeful of taking at least some of the Mallarmé account with her to the break-away agency, Rachel was doing her best to cooperate. But it was difficult to concentrate. Things were moving so fast. Work that week had been structured round a series of hurried and secret meetings between her, Jimmy and the handful of others involved. A high-powered creative team had verbally agreed to come too. Three of the media buyers were interested. Premises had been found and several clients warned. It was almost time, but not quite. She had even asked Jimmy about the possibility of part-time. He had said they'd do anything to have her along, which was nice.

The failures of the weekend had also unsettled her. Worse than their silly spat about the Polly girl was her absurd inability to talk to Robbie about anything that mattered. Thinking back, Rachel felt positively ashamed of herself. Robbie was ideal in every way: He would make a good father. He loved her. And she loved him, in her own way. But here she faltered, aware that her feelings of tenderness towards Robbie had a worrying habit of expanding to satisfying proportions only when he was absent. It was two days since his visit to London and already she was longing to see him again, longing to sort out the future once and for all. Next time there would be no wavering, she told herself. Next time she would tell him everything.

Impatience had a lot to do with her confusions, Rachel decided – impatience not only with the cumbersome process of changing jobs, but with her body too. It was almost March. Given the instantaneous ease with which she had once conceived quite by accident, she found it impossible not to feel somewhat cheated that so many weekends of healthy, unprotected sex should have produced no results. Not even a measly false alarm. Coping with uncertainty had never been one of her strong points, she reflected grimly, returning her attentions to the transparencies and frowning in a fresh effort to concentrate. Getting pregnant would have simplified and crystallised things far sooner, she was sure. It would have brought matters to a head, instead of allowing them to flounder on the rocks of this unbearable – and wholly irrational – hesitancy and indecision.

These unhappy musings were interrupted by Naomi Fullerton, who burst into her office looking determined, though not altogether friendly, in a voluminous Laura Ashley dress and a thick gold hairband that made Rachel think of halos.

A concerned Melissa bobbed up behind. 'Sorry Rachel, she just—'

'It's OK Mel, Naomi's an old friend. No calls for a while, all right?' she called, as the door closed.

The two women hugged.

'Couldn't you wait till Easter to see me, then?' teased Rachel, smiling with genuine pleasure, but concerned by Naomi's expression. Though she was smiling back and her eyes were their usual glossy brown, her skin looked grey and saggy, as if transplanted from another face entirely.

'What are you up to these days, Rachel? It's been so long.'

Rachel, wondering what Naomi would say if she confessed that wanting a child was making her ruthless and selfish beyond repair, that she was currently toying with the idea of sharing a family and a future with a man who yet knew nothing about such plans himself, nodded her head slowly, saying she was fine. 'Not looking forward to forty,' she added with a grimace, 'and I'm about to start a new job.'

'Really? I thought you loved it here . . .'

'Yes, well I did . . . but I . . . fell out with a couple of colleagues just before Christmas. It made life hard,' she went on carefully, thinking with irrepressible satisfaction of the new, emotionally deflated version of Cliff Weybourne with whom they had all recently become acquainted. 'So, I've decided to move on.' She put one finger to her lips and glanced at the door. 'Still very hush-hush, so not a word.'

Naomi burst out laughing. 'As if I am likely to run into someone whose career path crossed with yours.' She began walking round the room, examining pictures and objects, her hands clasped behind her back, the tips of her suede heels sinking into the lush blue pile of the carpet. Rachel stood watching, noting the way the shiny ribbons of hair streamed from the teeth of her hairband and wondering why she had come.

'It's quite something to see this for myself,' Naomi said at length. 'All that I could never have. All this.' She held out both arms and let them drop heavily to her sides.

'You have come all the way from Suffolk to see my office?' Rachel, now seriously worried by the expression on Naomi's face, hoped to tease.

'Graham has left me,' she said, scowling at the square panels of Rachel's ceiling for a moment before going back over to the windows. 'After fifteen fucking years and four fucking children, Graham has left me.'

'Oh Naomi . . .' Rachel started forward, but Naomi held up her hand, warning her to keep away.

'No sympathy, please. He's been having an affair for two years with a primary school teacher with unshaven armpits and two studs in her nose. If I hadn't been so busy being grateful for the nose-dive in our sexlife, I might have noticed earlier. But one sees what one wants to see, I suppose. I've never been that keen on sex, I'm afraid. I was actually grateful.' She gave a short laugh. 'The children did wear me out so.' She rested her cheek on the palm of one hand and gazed unseeing into the washed-out blue of the sky. 'I thought it didn't matter. I thought we had enough other things – the children, the house and so on. I was wrong. Graham says he's in love. He's moved into her house – a horrible box on the edge of the estate. He says I can have whatever I want.' She turned and looked hard at Rachel, who was leaning back on the edge of her desk, still trying to absorb the fact that the one relationship she had always assumed would last had so spectacularly fallen apart.

'And right now,' Naomi went on, 'all I can think is that I gave up all this—' she swung her arms at the room again, '—that I gave up my career to be the kind of woman he wanted.'

'But you've got the children . . .' ventured Rachel gently.

'Oh yes, I've got the children all right.' She sighed. 'And I love them. But it's a burden, love, you know; it ensnares you. I shall be financially indebted to a man whom I no longer love – and who certainly cares nothing for me – until little Helen is through university. That's eighteen years away.' She reached for her handbag, which she had slung over the back of a chair, and pulled out a hand mirror. 'I'm staying with my parents here in London while I work out what to do.' She pinched her cheeks and pressed her lips together.

'You've left Suffolk for good?'

'Don't look so incredulous, Rachel, for God's sake. He is living a few miles down the road with a woman he's been screwing for years.' She spat out the last sentence, curling her lip in disgust. 'The whole bloody county knows about them. I cannot carry on living there. I've got my pride.'

'Jesus, the selfish bastard,' Rachel said, half under her breath, trying to reconcile the big friendly bear of a man she had half-known for two decades with this version of love-sick deception and injustice.

'I do have one favour to ask you . . .' Naomi was already at the door, clearly ready to leave.

'Of course – anything. Look, don't go. We can have an early lunch or something.'

'No thanks. I've got an appointment with a lawyer.' She put her head round the door and called to someone. 'I've left three with my mother, but she finds it hard going. I wondered if you could keep an eye on Jessica for a couple of hours, just while I have this meeting. I won't be able to concentrate unless I'm on my own.'

At this point Rachel's seven-year-old goddaughter appeared in the doorway, tugging at her white knee socks and looking suitably solemn.

'Jessica,' Rachel exclaimed, holding out one hand. But the child stayed close to her mother's floral smocked dress, her dark eyes wary. She wore an Alice band, an elasticated version of her mother's headgear, except the hair which tumbled out of it was wavy and much darker.

'Go on, Jess. It's Aunt Rachel. I won't be long. You said you'd be good, remember?'

At this last admonition the child shuffled forwards, but still clinging to a panel of her mother's voluminous dress.

'Please, Jess, let me go. I'll be late.' Naomi pleaded with her eyes at Rachel, who grabbed one of the transparencies and flicked on her desk light.

'I could do with some help actually, Jessica. I've got to decide which of these pictures is better. It's going to appear in hundreds of magazines – and I just can't make up my mind. It's a funny picture. Come and see. Tell me what you think.'

As Jessica approached, Naomi winked and slipped quietly out of the door.

Robbie held the black-and-white image up to the kitchen window for perhaps the twentieth time that week and frowned. He had known the brown envelope would contain something appalling, but still he was unprepared for this. Blurred, but unmistakable. A foetus. How many weeks old, he had no idea. Its head looked elongated and its feet were small, fuzzy claws. It looked as though it was holding itself, as if its arms were wrapped around its middle. For comfort perhaps. To one side trailed a thin white line, a small stream of light from the middle of its belly. He squinted at the image, trying to make out some genitals amongst the blur. It was impossible not to be curious, after all, in spite of the awfulness of it all. Unimaginable awfulness. He wondered if Polly had told her parents yet, whether she planned to at all. He wondered if she had been in London to have an abortion. His hopes surged and dived at the thought. The white skeletal thing in front of him looked horribly formed already. He did not want it. He did not want the horrible muddle of it. But he did not like the idea of the creature ending up as medical waste either. Thoughts of hooks and blood and mess filled his mind. He closed his eyes and put the picture down. Then he thought of Rachel and great heaving sobs punched his chest.

The ring of the phone forced him to swallow his tears and compose himself. It was Polly's mother. She sounded surprised to hear his voice. Why hadn't Polly rung to say when she was returning? A long weekend together in London was all very well, but as parents they had a right to be kept informed. It wasn't right and he could tell her so from them.

'I think she's still in London . . .' he faltered, his mind racing for a way out, but impeded by visions of Polly lost in unfamiliar streets. Hopeless, hopeless Polly, on her own. And pregnant. Oh God.

'What do you mean "think"? Aren't you together, then?'

'She decided to stay on – for a bit – to – er – think.'

'To think?' Mrs Drayton's snort was audible. 'Well, she's a bloody fool. You're both bloody fools, for that matter. In my day something was either on or off – none of this shillyshallying around when nobody knows what's going on. And where's she doing this thinking, anyway?'

'At a friend's.' His voice was weak with the effort of lying.

'Well tell her to get a bloody move on, will you? There's work to be done down here, not that that's ever bothered *her*.'

For the rest of the day Robbie worked feverishly, ploughing through paperwork, returning unanswered phonecalls and tending to the herd. With lambing only a few weeks away some of the ewes were already getting uncomfortable; they had that listless and bemused look about them that he had come to know so well. Instead of filling him with excitement, he was haunted by apprehensions of what might lie in store. He found himself remembering Polly the year before, staying till long after the vet had gone, tears rolling down her face at the hopeless distress of the two ewes nuzzling still-borns, refusing to move till their mourning was done.

Though keeping so busy eased the passing of the day, as Robbie lay in bed that night, the worry solidified into something indigestible. Polly alone in London. Bearing his child. Oh, God. Worst of all, he was powerless. Everything rested with Polly. Until she came home there was nothing he could do. No one he could talk to. He pulled the covers over his head and tried to focus on Rachel. But the image of her kept slipping from his grasp, teasing him like the echo of a lost thought.

28 ∫

Will was just packing up to leave when there was a knock on his door.

'Come in,' he called, expecting it to be one of the artists who shared the studio downstairs, who frequently put their heads round the door for teabags or opinions of one kind or another.

On the table beside the kettle sat a plastic bag full of groceries. He was eager to get home, to stir-fry himself something healthy, read a novel maybe, drink a few beers. Having until recently believed that he had lost the art of pleasurable anticipation for good, to look forward to such things – to realise that he could once again enjoy the world outside his studio – was something of a revelation.

Anita coyly put her head round the door. 'Can I really?'

Will's heart plummeted. 'Anita,' he said flatly, 'what a surprise. I'm afraid I was just leaving.' He began flicking switches on the wall beside him, extinguishing several strips of light down the far end of the room.

'Oh no, please, let me just have a little look.' She skipped unsteadily across the wooden floor, swinging her bag like a schoolgirl. 'I want to see some of your work. I really do.'

'Well you'll have to make it snappy, I'm afraid.' Will remained where he was, tidying boxes of film on top of a filing cabinet, determined to appear as discouraging as possible without actually being rude. 'What are you doing in these parts, anyway?'

'Seeing you, silly.'

He jangled his keys at her. 'Come on Anita, I'm locking up. We can talk on the way downstairs. I've really got to go.' He flicked off another light to emphasise the point.

Anita had now thrown herself into the chair in which Rachel had sat, hitching her silky red skirt well above her knees in the process. 'Don't you want to take a snap?' She pouted and wriggled deeper into the chair, revealing a slice of white thigh, dimpled beside the silky edge of her stocking. 'I'll be ever so good, I promise,' she simpered, her self-esteem sufficiently heightened by vodka for her to be undeterred by the expression on Will's face. She made a big show of uncrossing and crossing her legs, seeing herself suddenly as a woman of superstar attractions; a Sharon Stone-like figure, hard-edged, self-assured, sexy. Giles had always had a thing about Sharon Stone.

'Anita, stop mucking around will you?' Will's annoyance had increased at the sight of her slumped in the chair. Rachel's chair. He had borrowed it on a whim from downstairs, inspired by the thought of her slim frame being hugged by such a thing, knowing how its old dark leather would embrace her, how it would set off the fair frame of her hair and skin, how she would look lost but comforted all at the same time, fragile but safe. He had the finished photographs to prove it. No clever tricks required at all.

'You'd come running if I was Rachel, I'll bet.' Anita pulled herself upright and fumbled for a cigarette. 'Fancy the bloody pants off her, don't you?'

'Yeah, I do actually,' he agreed cheerfully, crossing his arms and leaning back up against the wall.

'Well, you haven't got a hope, darling.' Anita picked a grain of tobacco off the tip of her tongue and blew a plume of smoke towards the wall of windows on her left. 'She's found true love you know.'

Will, secretly thinking that what he had seen of Rachel's behaviour suggested she had found nothing of the kind, crossed the room to check a couple of window locks. Anita followed him with her eyes.

'The hunk from Devon. Mr Robbie Dexter. Landscape gardener and sheep farmer extraordinaire. Talk about a ghost from the past.' She made a face and strolled across to the wall of windows. Outside, night had transformed the river from its daily grey into a shimmering banquet of jagged black and gold. 'Bonking and babies. That's all Ms Elliot has on her mind, these days.' She fired smoke at the pane of glass and closed her eyes as it swept back over her face. Her head was beginning to pulse uncomfortably. 'Any chance of a drink?'

'Babies?' Will took a step backwards.

'A last-minute scramble against the proverbial ticking bloody clock, I suppose. Ah, the joy of being female.' Anita sighed and closed her eyes, adding absently, 'Would never have thought it of Rachel though . . . I even tried warning her off. But you know Rachel, once she's made up her mind . . .'

Will was jangling his keys again, much more loudly this time. 'You should try to stop being jealous of her,' he said shortly, 'it doesn't get you anywhere, you know.'

Anita turned slowly. 'Me? Jealous of Rachel?' She started laughing and then checked herself. 'I've been jealous of Rachel for as long as I can remember. Most of our lives are an accident. But Rachel's has been *designed* – by her. What Rachel wants, Rachel gets. And what's worse I like her for it – I *admire* her.' She wanted to leave suddenly. She needed a drink. It had been a crazy idea to come in the first place. Crazy. The man was no fun at all.

'And you think she'll have children just as easily?'

'Of course,' she sneered. 'A hunk like Robbie – they've been at it like—'

'Yes, I get the picture thank you,' Will cut in, seizing her firmly by the elbow and steering her towards the door. He thought of the photograph, ready now to show her, and wondered whether it wouldn't be simpler just to post it after all.

'Not a fucking taxi in sight,' Anita complained, as they tumbled out into the dark narrow alleyway to the rear of the warehouse that housed his studio.

'Can I drop you anywhere?' he offered, his voice edged with a weariness he was now struggling to hide.

'How very kind.' She got into the passenger's seat, opened her packet of cigarettes, saw there were none left and threw it petulantly onto the floor. 'Anywhere you like.'

'I'll drop you at Victoria,' he said, 'from there it's all up to you.' After a moment or two of silence he could not resist saying, 'I don't think Rachel Elliot has had that much of an easy life.'

'Oh, don't you now? What an intriguing opinion.' She retrieved the packet from the floor and began dismantling it. 'And on what vast knowledge do you base these views of yours?'

Will hesitated. 'You don't get where she has without a fight. She's worked hard for what she's achieved. She's made sacrifices . . .'

'Oh please, my heart is bleeding.'

'Are you always this pleasant about your friends or is it simply because you're so drunk you can't think straight?'

Shocked into silence by the veracity of this challenge, Anita folded her hands and studied her knees. 'Life's crap right now,' she said hoarsely. 'My husband has lost interest in me—'

'That would be Giles, would it?' put in Will, eager to develop these first threads of sobriety into something resembling a conversation.

'He's not been himself for so long . . .' her voice tailed away. 'I keep thinking I should get him to see a doctor – but he's so bloody obstinate—'

'I'm sure you can persuade him if you try. Make it happen.'

'I will, I will.' She clutched what remained of the cigarette packet between both hands, squashing its edges.

'Good. Well we've sorted something out then.' Will pulled into the taxi rank in front of Victoria station and put on his hazard lights. 'And good luck with your writing.'

'My writing?' She let out a curt laugh. 'And what do you know about that?'

He shrugged. 'Only that you're quite good at it, if Rachel is to be believed – which I rather think she is.' He smiled at her then, his wide mouth curling upwards in a way that transformed his entire face. 'Like I said, good luck, Anita.' He reached across her and opened the door.

She put one foot on the pavement and turned back. 'Thanks Will . . . and sorry for being a bore . . . and for coming on . . . so strong. I just want . . . I just needed . . . to feel . . . I mean, Giles hasn't exactly been much of an ego-trip recently,' she finished meekly, pressing her fingertips to her temples, where the drumming was worst.

'Drinking certainly won't help matters, you know. And anyway,' he leant back and made a show of scrutinising her appearance, taking in the cropped inky hair with its sweep of grey, the over-made-up face that hid a generous smile and pretty, feline eyes, 'I'd say you've absolutely no worries in the looks department—' he caught his breath, 'oh, not for a decade or two at least.'

'Well, thanks for that.' She laughed weakly, before levering herself out of the car.

It was only as he drove away that Will realised he had left his bag of shopping on the table in his studio. He slammed both hands on the steering wheel in irritation. But his appetite had vanished anyway. Anita Cavanagh's life may be salvageable, he thought grimly, but his certainly wasn't.

After a couple of hours in his flat with a book which had seemed compelling the evening before, but which now struck him as trite and absurd, Will felt more than usually restless. The can of tomato soup, which had assumed the role of supper, had left him both thirsty and hungry for real food. He tried calling Anna but got a baby-sitter instead, a flurried-sounding girl that made him worry for Jack. He had to fight the urge to drive round there himself. With there being just the two of them, it was so hard not to give in to the temptation to be over-protective. A grandparent or two would not have gone amiss, he thought sadly, tenderly recalling parents whose advanced ages had often seen them mistaken for grandparents themselves.

The impulse to call Rachel, an impulse which beat constantly at the back of his mind, was becoming increasingly difficult to suppress. He could tell her about the photograph, he argued to himself, how well it had worked out, suggest a meeting even, present her with a copy in person. His heart soared and then sank the moment after. It would be pointlessly frustrating – enriching an increasingly treasured library of images maybe, but only driving him madder in the end. There was nothing to be done now, he had to remember that.

He remembered instead the tight, hard shoulders beneath his hands, the confirmation of all that he had suspected: such energy contained inside, such control, such longing. The thought that he might have the power to unleash some of that energy, to tease some of that brilliant spirit out and make it less afraid, was as alluring as the thought of opening himself up to her. They were a pair, he felt – two people who longed to be known but were scared of it too, scared of the vulnerability that ran alongside.

He found himself staring at the large black-and-white photograph half-sticking out of the folder in front of him: Rachel's face, the far side cast in shade, the near side in light, her eyes bold but questioning, her body curled away from the lens, as if to say, keep your distance, I'll have none of you.

'Bugger it.' He swung his legs up onto the table and leant back with both hands clasped behind his head. But the grey, intelligent eyes followed his, challenging him from under the heels of his boots. He had to force himself to look away, to study instead the familiar contours of the room – a vast rectangle which he loved, containing only one chair, one table, three vast pictures and two luminous blue lights that made the soft polished wood of the floor glow with shadows and life. The only other piece of furniture was a baby grand in the far corner, on which sat a photograph of Ginnie, poised at her cello, her chestnut hair tumbling down her back, her favourite black velvet concert dress pressed against the bony contours of her knees, her heart-shaped face composed and smiling. A Ginnie that may once have existed, thought Will grimly, though it was hard to recall her now. Their marriage had been a calamity all of its own, long before the depression and drugs took hold. Time had woven a film of tragedy over events, especially in the eyes of other people, but in reality there had been only ugliness, bitter and ignoble to the last. Nothing had been enough in the end, not medicine, not therapy, not music and certainly not love. Will grimaced at the recollection of the last of his wife's lovers, the one she'd wooed and spurned most blatantly of all, spilling the guts of their emotions for daily scrutiny and consolation, too imprisoned by her own world to care about destroying his. It was only then that he had fully realised the awful power that the sick wield over the healthy, especially for those versed in the blackmailing potential of a bottle of pills. Was it any wonder then that he should now find himself so drawn to a woman of such contrasting self-containment; a woman who, no matter how much she gave away, would always hold as much back? A woman who would find a way through, whether he was there or not.

A few minutes later Will was striding away from the ornate

black railings that marked the entrance to his basement flat, heading in the direction of the more salubrious part of Chelsea in which he knew Rachel Elliot lived. It would help to get the image out of his mind, he told himself, if he physically removed it from the premises. He would post the photograph himself, by hand. Far better than horsing around with a meeting. Who was he trying to fool, anyway? If he had ever entertained any hopes, Anita had quashed them all for good. Best to get rid of the damn thing and be done with it.

It was a cold night even for late February. He zipped his jacket up to his chin and increased his pace. Overhead, a creamy coin of a moon dodged behind lacy clouds, as if coy of its glory. Will, in no mood for moons, however glorious, kept his eyes on the ground, watching his long legs cover the ground as if they moved of their own accord.

When he reached the steps to Rachel's block he was careful not to pause for an instant, not wanting to imbue the moment with pointless sentimentality of any kind. Taking two steps at a time, he sprinted to the top and carefully eased his delivery through the wide handsome brass flap, before turning to descend.

It was only then that he noticed the figure hunched, knees to chest, on the bottom step. Though London was awash with homeless of all ages, Will was nonetheless surprised to find one who had not even bothered with the scant shelter offered by a doorway or a wall on such a chilly night. He noticed too, a stiff bunch of hair sticking out of one side of the anorak hood. Young hair. Female hair.

Reaching into his pocket for change, Will approached.

'Would this be of any help?' He held out what he had, about six pounds in all.

'No thanks.' The girl sniffed.

Will was almost offended. 'Go on, take it. Can't do any harm.'

'I'm waiting for someone.'

'Oh, I see.' He eyed the grubby anorak and mud-stained boots doubtfully. 'They're coming tonight, are they?'

She shrugged. 'Soon. It's the weekend isn't it? They always meet at weekends.'

'It's Wednesday,' said Will gently, sitting down beside her.

'He'll be here,' she said, but with less conviction. After five days on her own Polly was running out of steam. She had thought it would be easier, that she would know just what to do. Instead a fog had settled inside her head, blocking everything but the cold. 'He'll be coming to see her,' she said, mechanically this time, her voice colourless.

'Who?'

She jerked her head at the door behind them. 'Miss Rachel fucking Elliot, that's who.' Her lips were covered with small cracks which looked ready to bleed when she spoke. 'He loves her. My Robbie loves her – and I—'

'And you love him? Is that it?'

She looked momentarily amazed and then scowled. 'So?'

Will tucked his hands up under his armpits and pressed his knees together, wondering how many nights she had spent sleeping rough. 'I think I might know how you feel,' he ventured.

'Sure you do.'

'How about a warm bed for the night?' he suggested suddenly.

'A bed with you?' She frowned, suspicion flashing in her eyes.

'I'm talking about a bed of your own,' he explained quickly, smiling to make her less afraid. 'I've got a spare bathroom too – well a shower anyway.' He stood up and tapped his watch. 'He's not coming tonight, I'll bet you. It's far too late – see?' He held out his wrist. 'And it's Wednesday. Far better to have a hot bath and a good night's sleep. I don't live far away.' He got up and held out his hand. 'I'm sure we can sort something out between us. And a good breakfast always cheers things up, don't you find?'

She eyed him from under a tangle of hair, looking so wary he almost laughed.

He held up both hands in a show of surrender. 'Please trust me. I'm a friend of Rachel fucking Elliot's. And I know she'd hate to have someone freezing on her doorstep.'

'Serve her right,' muttered Polly. But she got up all the same and followed Will back to his flat, clutching her knapsack protectively to her stomach and trailing half a pace behind him like an errant child.

29

'Mum says Dad is a spoilt bastard.'

'I'm sure she didn't . . .'

'She did. I heard her. On the phone to Granny.'

Rachel and Jessica were sitting on a bench in St James's Park enjoying their second meeting of the week, thanks in part to the demands of Naomi's lawyers and partly because Rachel had so much enjoyed herself the first time. They were eating ice creams, towering peaks of soft vanilla pitched at dangerous angles from the flimsy cones. Their main course, at her goddaughter's pleading, had been a hot dog, smothered in squirts of ketchup and rings of white onion. Rachel, to her intense surprise, had enjoyed it enormously, spurred on by the elation of a companion who clearly regarded rubbery frankfurters as forbidden fruit of the most indulgent kind. They weren't allowed hamburgers either, Jessica had confided wistfully, on account of all the mad cows.

'Mummy says brain-rotting would be too good for Daddy.'

'Oh dear, I'm sure she doesn't mean it.'

'Oh yes, she does.' Jessica took a long searching lick of ice cream. 'She hates him now.'

Subdued into a compassionate silence by such frankness, Rachel reached out a cautious hand. Patting it briefly, as if her godmother was the one in need of consolation, Jessica sidled several inches closer along the bench.

'Lucky you, Aunty Rachel, not having a husband.'

She couldn't help laughing. 'Oh I'm afraid I still have all the same kind of problems.'

'Do you love someone, then?' Jessica had reached the cornet, which she was nibbling with two incongruously large front teeth, her reward, as she had solemnly informed Rachel, for never having eaten more than three sweets in a row.

'I think so.'

'Does he live in your house?'

'No, he lives miles away, in Devon. I'm going there this week-end actually,' she added, thinking wistfully of the unsuccessful phone calls which had cast such a shadow over the week – stilted conversations that seemed to find no common ground at all, with Robbie wheedling for reassurances at every turn. Fuelled by guilty realisations as to quite how selfish she had been – how singularly calculating, if she was honest – Rachel had met these needs as best she could. But uncomfortable echoes stirred at the back of her mind; echoes of a version of Robbie she had known once before, a Robbie who had ended up pleading for her love like a beggar with an empty bowl. 'He's got lots of animals,' she went on brightly now, aiming to keep Jessica's interest. 'Sheep and chickens.'

Jessica screwed up her nose. 'Yuk. I only like cats. Sheep and chickens are silly.'

They were distracted from this discouraging veer in the conversation by the arrival of a swarm of pigeons, whose beady eyes had been attracted by the possibility of food. Jessica threw a small crumb, picked carefully off the edge of her cone, and watched with detached interest at the ensuing squabble for the spoil.

'Time to wander back, I'm afraid,' said Rachel, glancing at her watch.

'Oh please, not yet.' Jessica jumped off the bench, scattering birds as she charged off along the path.

Rachel followed, equally reluctant to leave the park. Although it was cold, a white disc of a sun was bravely pushing its way through the grey landscape overhead. Here and there along the path, clusters of snowdrops huddled at the foot of trees, together with a few clenched crocuses and a scattering of noble daffodils, leading the late march against winter. 'Wait for me,' she called, running to catch up, her scarf unwinding and flying out behind like a banner. Jessica had been distracted by the sight of a ball lodged between the roots of a tree. A bright red ball covered in yellow dots. She charged towards it with a whoop of delight and kicked it to her godmother.

By kicking with the toe of her shoe, Rachel managed a high arc of a return-shot that landed right at Jessica's feet. The next time she used the inside of her foot, teetering slightly on her heels as she swung her leg backwards, but making contact with enough force for the ball to do a gratifying bounce off a nearby tree before rolling back onto the ground. Heedless of the mud clods attaching themselves to the heels and undersoles of their smart shoes, the two of them threw all their energies into the game, using scarves and gloves as goal markers and taking it in turns to have shots.

'Hey, that's mine,' shouted a little boy appearing from nowhere, his face and the tips of his ears pink with exertion.

Rachel, bracing herself for an outburst of some kind, was most impressed to see her godchild pick up the ball and take it over to the boy at once. 'We were only having a little play,' she explained. The child smiled with relief, which was when Rachel recognised him.

'It's Jack, isn't it?' She looked round nervously to see who had charge of him.

A young woman with long black hair came jogging over to them, wearing a coat that reached almost to her ankles and shiny silver trainers with three-inch rubber platforms. She was tall and wiry, with watchful black eyes and a pointy nose. The mouth and smile were just like her brother's though, thought Rachel, as she hastily introduced herself, explaining in the same breath that they had to walk all the way back to Covent Garden and only had ten minutes to do it in.

'We're going there too,' exclaimed Anna Raphael, her angular face softening the moment she smiled, 'I take a dance class in Floral Street – Sloane Rangers trying to tone up their thighs.' She made a face and then looked apologetic. 'It's not too bad, really. Though Jack wouldn't agree. He gets so bored, don't you Jack? But it's the holidays,' she added with a sigh, 'so I've got no option.'

Smalltalk about children and the unseasonably cold weather saw them to Trafalgar Square, whereupon Anna declared,

'Assuming you're the Rachel Elliot I think you are, I've just got to thank you for what you've done – for Will, I mean.'

Rachel thought she had misheard over the roar and choke of the traffic. 'I beg your pardon?'

'You've no idea.' They were crossing towards Long Acre, each holding the hand of a child as they pressed through the lunchtime crowds.

'You mean sitting for him?'

Anna didn't seem to be listening. 'He's a different man since you came on the scene – I can't tell you.' She let got of Jack's hand to hoick her black tights further up her long legs, revealing a silvery plastic mini skirt that matched her shoes. 'I just thought I'd mention it. We've got to turn off here. Jack, come on.' She held out her hand.

'But I'm not . . . on the scene,' Rachel began, but Anna was already striding away, the wide panels of her coat flapping, the little boy having to trot to keep up with her.

The first thing Rachel did upon getting back was to look again at the photograph. It was surprisingly nice. Her face looked more creased than she liked to imagine it, but then she was beginning to get used to that. And her smile, which was wide without looking in the least bit smug, somehow made up for it. She liked the position in the chair too, the way one leg was bent up under her and the other just touching the floor; it looked relaxed but confident. In fact, she looked exactly as she would have liked to look, though she could never have engineered such a result herself. She propped the photograph up beside a jar of ground coffee, pondering again why Will had made the delivery in person, but not rung the bell; why there was no accompanying note, not even a compliment slip; why his sister should make baffling remarks about her 'being on the scene' and then rush off without explaining herself.

I'll take it to Devon, she thought suddenly, seizing the picture and carrying it through to the bedroom where an open suitcase lay on the bed. Robbie would like it. But at the recollection of Robbie's emotional fragility on the telephone that week, she slipped the photograph into a drawer instead. There were more important subjects that needed explaining first, she told herself, her heart thumping. Trying to explain Will Raphael would only complicate things. All that mattered was sorting everything out with Robbie.

As Rachel prepared for bed that night, it was not Robbie or preoccupations about motherhood that occupied her mind however, but godchildren. Getting to know Jessica might prove to be the one good thing arising from an otherwise abysmal set of circumstances she reflected ruefully, smiling to herself at the recollection of their time in the park. They had arrived back so late and so muddy that Rachel had found herself making excuses to Naomi like a child herself. Melissa had been surprised too, laughing out loud at the state of Rachel's expensive leather shoes and producing a damp cloth for the smuts on her tights. The pleasure of it all had taken her completely by surprise. It had made her think properly about her other godchildren, about how little she knew them, about how unforgivably ungrateful she had been all these years.

Before going to sleep that night Rachel wrote to Joy, sitting propped up by pillows with a malt whisky in one hand and her writing pad pressed against her knees.

What must you think of me – so many months since your letter and not a peep. I shall look into the Good Housekeeping *thing very soon, I promise. And I should be more than happy to contribute to the PG Tips supply and anything else you want. Just send a list. I do hope Tony has found some time to do a bit of work on your house by now – all that rain and wind sounded dreadful.* She paused for a moment, taking a thoughtful sip of her nightcap. *You're too brave all the time, do you know that? Sometimes you just have to admit that life is full of crap and then you feel a thousand times better for it. Tony might be a bit more sympathetic too if you actually tell him what you're really feeling.* She stopped again, thinking of the original author of such advice, and how hopeless she was herself in such matters. *It's been quite a hectic few months what with one thing and another. The long and short of it is it looks like I might be settling down with someone at last – an old old friend called Robbie Dexter, whom you might remember from way back. We've both grown up a lot since those days and now I really do think we could work out a future together. Part of this life-change (you see, you're not the only one!) is that I am leaving MC to work three days a week for a brand new agency being formed by a few other dissatisfied colleagues. We're going to concentrate not just on advertising but also on new product development – something in which I have always been particularly interested. But anyway, enough of all that. I'll keep you posted.*

One more thing. About Leo, she paused, wanting to get it right, wanting to convey that she sought far richer rewards than the mere assuaging of some godmotherly guilt, *'if ever you felt like coming over here for a break (and maybe some shopping!) why not bring my godson and leave him with me? I'm not saying I could cope for days on end, but I would so like to get better acquainted – before he's lost to rave music and drugs and women half my age. Let me know what you think.*

She looked at her watch before dialling Washington. The rings were much longer than on English telephones, she noticed, winding the flex round her index finger while she waited.

'The Elliot residence,' came a voice at last, whose sing-song intonation Rachel recognised as belonging to Carmen, the housekeeper.

'It's Rachel, Dr Elliot's sister, calling from London. Is Duncan there? Or Mary Beth?'

'Oh no, Miss, they not here. They skiing in Vermont.'

'With the children?'

'Oh yes, Miss.'

'Could you say I called?' She hesitated, impeded by doubts about Carmen's skills as messenger. 'Could you send them my love?'

'Your love OK. I send it.'

Well, that seemed clear enough. Rachel, replaced the phone with a smile, enjoying the suggestion that love could be parcelled and mailed like a free sample of washing powder.

That left one more call. Rachel braced herself, wishing at the same time that she didn't have to and vowing to get Anita back on the wagon, no matter what the cost.

'Hello, who is it please?' The voice was small and very sleepy.

'Charlotte? Goodness me, what are you doing up at this time of night? Is Mummy there?'

'Mrs Hershey's here from next door.'

'Oh, I see, well can I speak to her then?'

'She's asleep. She's got the telly on, but she's asleep. I know because I've poked her and she didn't move. She's very fat.'

'Well Charlotte, sweetheart, I think you had better tiptoe back to bed, don't you?'

There was the sound of a door slamming followed by a series of rustles and squeals.

'Rachel?'

'Anita? I've been trying to call for days but you're never in. Your baby-sitter's gone to sleep.'

'I know. She always does. She's a last resort, Mrs Hershey, but she is genuinely fond of the children. Listen, Rachel, you'll never guess. Giles really is ill.'

She sounded relieved.

'What with?'

'They think it might be ME. They're keeping him in for observation. I've just come from the hospital.'

'But that's dreadful—'

'I know, I know. But it's also wonderful – I mean at last there's an explanation, don't you see? These past few months have been hell. I really thought it was the end of us, I really did Rachel – I've started imagining all sorts – you know he did once have a fling or two, back in the early days – so I thought, right here we go again, only this time I didn't feel like I could cope with it. So to find out that he is *ill* – that he probably has been for months – is amazing. And do you know,' her voice quavered, 'I haven't had a drink since Monday. I've signed up at last with the dreaded AA – and I'm not talking about servicing cars—'

'Oh Anita, well done.' Rachel sat up in bed gripping the phone, wanting to praise her to the skies but fearful of being tactless.

'It's not so bad, at least not as bad as I thought it would be.'

'That's the best news I have had in months.'

'Yeah well, I figured Giles and I couldn't fall apart at the same time. And Rachel . . . I want to apologise . . .'

'Whatever for?'

'For being a pig and a bloody nuisance. Thanks for sticking by me.'

'There's absolutely no need to thank me for anything,' she

retorted at once, though inside she was glad. 'Tell me more about Giles – they think it's ME?'

'Possibly. We'll know more after they've stuck a few more needles in him. Poor love – it's no picnic. But at least we're *doing* something about it. And the children are being sweet, making get-well presents out of loo rolls and bits of string and generally cheering us up no end. Weirdest of all, the work keeps pouring in. My post-natal depression piece clearly hit the spot. There's a new features editor, which helps. I'm on wife-beating now, with euthanasia in the pipeline. So things really are looking up. If I could get some decent childcare my life would be complete.'

'About childcare,' put in Rachel tentatively, 'could I help out sometime?'

'Why, Rachel, how kind.' She sounded genuinely touched.

'I'm not sure I'm up to the twins,' she went on quickly, not wanting to raise any false hopes, 'but I'd love to see a bit more of Charlotte—'

'She'd love that—'

'Not right away I'm afraid, but when this new job starts and I've settled into some sort of routine for dividing myself between Devon and London . . .'

'That's still on then, is it?'

'The job change?'

'No – yes – I meant Robbie, actually.'

'Of course it is.' She couldn't keep the edge out of her voice. 'Why shouldn't it be?'

'Don't get all bristly, I was only asking.' Anita waved a ten-pound note at Mrs Hershey who had appeared in the sitting room doorway looking puffy-eyed and flustered. 'When the hell am I going to meet him, that's what I want to know? It's been months.'

'Oh, soon enough,' replied Rachel quickly, 'there'll be plenty of time for all that.'

'By the way, what were the results of your modelling session with the delicious Mr Raphael like?' Anita hoped she sounded detached. It would be a while – if ever – before she confessed to Rachel about visiting Will at his studio. She had told Giles though. And in spite of the shame it had felt good to share a confidence with him again, good to have a husband cast in the role of ally as opposed to enemy.

'Oh, fine,' answered Rachel airily, equally anxious to sound nonchalant and dismissive, but for rather different and infinitely more complicated reasons. 'Not bad at all, in fact.'

30

Robbie stepped into his boots, icy from their night in the draught by the back door, and made his way across the yard to the wood shed, a leaning, doorless contraption which had once served as a pigsty. It had been quite a week. Aside from problems in his personal life, the job down Sandy Lane was turning into a fully-fledged disaster. He had made the mistake of contracting out the work and was suffering the consequences. The whole bloody garden would have to be replanted and properly drained at his own expense.

The only good piece of news was that Polly had finally called her parents from London the night before, sounding cagey, complained Mrs Drayton, but promising to be home by the weekend. Upon hearing this Robbie had felt relieved, but terrified the moment after. He thought of the smudged image of their baby, now buried in the bottom of the black wheely bin behind the wood shed, and wished that the truth was as easy to hide. Borrowed time was all that remained now. He hurled the head of the axe at the logs in front of him, unblinking as the wood chips flew, seeing only the splinters of his hopes.

'Surprise,' called Rachel, a little while later, having parked at the front and crept stealthily through the house.

'Surprise,' she called again, more loudly this time, her spirits dampened both by the mess she had encountered in the cottage and the manic intensity with which Robbie continued to swing the axe.

Robbie spun round, dropping the implement to the ground, a look of shock and then gratitude sweeping over his face.

He moved towards her at once, arms outstretched, staggering slightly, like a drunk man.

'Steady on, you'll squeeze the breath out of me,' she gasped, her ribs hurting in the crush of his embrace.

'Oh God, I've missed you so much.' He was almost sobbing.

'Yes, well I've missed you too,' she replied briskly, pulling back to inhale a lungful of air. 'Lovely to be out of London. I thought I'd take the day off and surprise you. Things at work are totally mad at the moment – but I can tell you about that later,' she added hastily, seeing the expression on his face. 'Any chance of a coffee break for the workers?' She had hoped to extract a smile, but he only grunted, slinging an arm across her back to steer her inside.

'Do you like my jeans? I thought they might be quite suitable for egg-foraging. I'm going to be a tower of strength this weekend – you won't recognise me.'

Filled with the sense that she was for some reason having to keep the lines of dialogue open and mystified as to why, Rachel chattered on in a similar fashion while Robbie excavated mugs and teaspoons from the heaps of crockery stacked around the sink.

'Robbie, is everything all right?' she blurted at last, unable to ignore the strangeness of his mood any longer, a strangeness which she knew had been brewing all week.

He slowly raised his eyes from the mug which he was clasping to his chest with both hands. 'No, I guess not. It's . . . it's been a bad week. Big trouble with a job on the other side of Drakeshead. Cock-ups all round. Lambing due any week now . . .'

'Oh dear, poor you,' she said feebly, feeling useless. 'Well, just set me to work about the place. I'd love to be of some help, if I can.'

'Christ, Rachel,' he put down his mug and placed a hand, clammy from cradling his hot coffee, on top of hers, 'I don't know what I'd do without you. You know that, don't you?'

Such intensity again. It didn't feel right, somehow. 'Of course I do. Now tell me what I can do.'

Shortly afterwards, however, both Rachel's capacity and enthusiasm for assistance of any kind were delivered a major setback by a fist-sized puddle of black ice in the back yard. Her left foot slipped

awkwardly, bringing both her and a basket of kindling heavily to
the ground. Twigs and pieces of wood scattered for yards around,
like debris after an explosion. It was only when she struggled
to her feet and the pain seered upwards from the arch of her
foot into the region of her ankle bone, that she realised the full
extent of her injuries. She hobbled gingerly back inside, where
Robbie was seated at the kitchen table, gloomy-faced before the
contents of a beige folder marked 'Sandy Lane'.

He was at once all flustering concern. A tender examination
of the swollen ankle was quickly followed by the triumphant
extraction of a large bag of frozen sweetcorn from amongst the
icy peaks of his small freezer. Rachel pressed the bag to her
foot, grimacing at the ache of cold it produced and doing her
best not to spill corn from the various puncture-holes which
materialised in its sides.

'Ice cubes would be better of course, but I just don't use the
things. Sorry.' He shrugged helplessly, torn between offering
more comfort and getting on with the pressing demands spread
out on the kitchen table. 'Would you like a cup of coffee? Tea?
A biscuit?'

'That would be lovely. A cup of tea. And a biscuit,' she
added, her mind flitting to Will Raphael and having to be
tugged back again.

'Now keep your foot up – higher – that's it – right on top.'
Robbie adjusted the angle of the chair on which he had placed a
cushion embroidered with the words 'Home Sweet Home', and
kicked a few grains of corn in the direction of the overflowing
waste-bin beside the fridge.

'You get on with whatever you've got to do,' ordered Rachel,
filled suddenly with an unforgivable urge to be left alone.
She took the sagging bag from her foot and dumped it beside
the packet of digestives which Robbie had thoughtfully placed
within reach. 'I know you're busy.'

'Well, if you're sure you wouldn't mind . . .'

'Of course not – don't be silly.'

'I really ought to get over to this place.' He gestured with
his head at the folder. 'Make a start on damage limitation.' He
hung his head in miserable apology.

'Go on, go. I'll be fine. I can look after myself. It's just a bloody nuisance. I'll man the phone – make myself useful.' She waved a digestive at him. 'You run along. I'll still be here when you get back.'

'Is that a promise?' Though he meant to tease, the worry edged through.

'Sure it is.' She reached for a magazine from a nearby pile and raised her mug in salute.

His farewell kiss, soft with apology and passion, did little to lift her spirits.

'By the way,' she called, when he had left the kitchen and was on the point of opening the front door, 'that girl – Molly – Holly – or whatever it was. Is that all sorted? Has she been any more bother?'

'No bother at all,' he called back at once, before plunging out through the door, head bent against the wind.

There were a lot of phone calls, the first one coming just seconds after the sound of Robbie's van had melted away. Rachel's tea, which was too milky for her tastes anyway, gradually acquired a head of scum while she fielded questions about turf-laying and ponds and pergolas, assuring each caller that Mr Dexter had their business well in hand and would be in touch personally later on that afternoon. After an hour or so, when the rumble of her stomach told her that it was well past lunchtime and the beige folder was surrounded by scribbled messages, Rachel decided she had earned a rest. Having turned on the answering machine, she levered herself through into the sitting room, taking the magazine and pack of biscuits with her, lured by the idea of reclining on something more welcoming than the bare wood of Robbie's kitchen chairs.

The room smelt of cold ashes and old leather. Though the storage heater by the sofa felt warm, it appeared to be having little effect on the temperature of the room. The remains of a fire sat in the grate, a charred log amidst several dunes of grey sand. Piled on the hearth were some of Robbie's freshly cut logs, together with a newspaper and a grubby, misshapen box of matches. I'll make a fire, thought Rachel, inspired both by her chattering teeth and because it was something to do.

The paper burned well, curling hungrily round the amputated

stumps of branch, and radiating lovely jets of warmth. Rachel, perching awkwardly on the floor, blew on her knuckles, staring into the blue heart of the flames until her eyes grew glassy. But before long, all the promising flames had shrunk down into derisory black heaps that left her feeling inept and cross. With her ankle now throbbing badly, she retreated to the sofa, burrowing under a pile of cushions and trying not to look at her watch. It was hateful to be so helpless, so bloody uncomfortable. Since the only reachable diversion was the magazine, Rachel comforted herself with that, doggedly working her way through an article on the Swedish timber industry, before arriving at a more promising headline that ran: *WHY IS THIS SO RARE?* The words were superimposed on an enlarged image of what looked like a long-tailed tadpole nosing up against the fuzzy edge of a huge circle. In smaller writing underneath she read: *Scientists are telling us that conception is becoming increasingly rare. Growing numbers of couples are seeking infertility treatments. Is the human race on its way out?* Shivers of schadenfreude tiptoed down Rachel's spine as she feasted on the heart-rending testimony of couples labouring under the burdens of low sperm counts, irregular ovulations and thickening womb linings; couples who had taken out bank loans for treatments with names that read like dialogue from a sci-fi horror movie: gamete intrafallopian transfer, intra-cytoplasmic sperm injection, surgical sperm retrieval. *Prospects for success are grim and hard fought*, Rachel read, shamelessly scrutinising the strained expressions on the faces of those courageous enough to be photographed. These people were in another league, she realised with a start, another world entirely; they were strapped to a treadmill of clinical dependence to which she knew she would never dream of subjecting herself, whatever the circumstances.

Her eyes left the page and flicked across to the charred pyramids in the grate. Was her desire to have a child so deeply rooted after all? It had offered a way forward, a bridge to a future that had otherwise seemed unimaginable. Yet recently the idea of motherhood brought as much fear as it did longing. As much uncertainty as confidence. And as Rachel huddled under the heap of cushions, her fingers stiff with cold from holding the magazine, she wondered for the first time whether this was natural, or whether it was an indication of something to which she should pay more attention.

By the time Robbie returned, a couple of hours later, she had fallen into an uncomfortable doze, in which she seemed to be forever clutching at thoughts that slipped from her control, sliding out of reach, like feet on ice. She awoke with a jolt at the slamming of the front door. In a few weeks she would be forty. Her fertility curve, according to an unforgiving chart in the article, was on a nose-dive towards zero. No wonder nothing had happened yet. Perhaps nothing ever would. She retrieved the magazine from where it had slipped down the side of the sofa and skimmed the last paragraph. She could hear Robbie calling her, the heavy thud of his feet on the stairs.

There is an all-too prevalent notion, encouraged by developments in fertility research, that we somehow **own** *our bodies, that we should be able to programme them as we please. When in fact the human body, in every respect, is a complex mystery of chemical, biological and psychological elements, the combination of which may always prove ultimately resistant to control or manipulation of any kind . . .*

'Rachel – there you are – why didn't you answer? Christ, it's dark in here.' He switched on the light.

She struggled onto her elbows, frowning at the glare, the magazine slipping from her knees to the floor. 'Robbie – sorry – I was half asleep.'

'How's the leg? I'm sorry I was so long.' He crouched at her feet, resting his head on the arm of the sofa like a penitent hound. 'Have you been terribly lonely?' He leant forward and planted a gentle kiss on her sore ankle. 'I stopped off and bought a Chinese take-away on the way home. We could eat now or heat it up again later. What do you say?'

'Sounds great,' she whispered, while inside there raged a new confusion of sadness.

'I'll light the fire.' He sprang to his feet and set about constructing an expert wigwam of wood and paper, using small twiggy branches that he snapped off the bigger logs. 'Have you finished with this?' He held out the magazine. 'Only there's not much paper.'

'Yes,' she said quietly, leaning her head back against the arm rest. 'I've finished with it.'

'You look tired,' he murmured, coming to kneel behind her head and placing his hands on her shoulders. His fingers smelt of smoke.

Feeling tears push against her lids, Rachel kept her eyes closed.

'Bad luck about the ankle.' He began to massage her shoulders, pushing and pressing in flat repetitive motions that seemed to make no contact with the shapes inside. 'Is that nice?' he whispered.

Rachel, gulping silent tears, could only nod. While inside her head the images soared out of control – sensual images that had nothing to do with Robbie or what she now realised was the fiction of their future together, but which transported her back instead to the deeper comfort of another chair and to hands that had touched more than the surface of her body, pressing into the very heart of her in a way that she had tried not to think about, but which had left her at once deeply attracted and deeply afraid.

These hard, concentrating palms of Robbie Dexter knew nothing of her, she realised. They never had. They never would. She had made the most terrible mistake, led on by an emptiness which had nothing to do with him, and probably little to do with having a child either. An emptiness to do with being almost forty and on her own. She had been taking stock, she realised, and getting it all wrong.

But the crime of having rekindled feelings which were no property of hers, of having materialised like some shining angel with a false heart, was not something to which Rachel felt able to confess at once. Instead, despising herself for the coward that she was, she made room for Robbie on the sofa, shifting her leg gingerly when he pressed up against her and breathing appreciatively when he began to kiss her neck in that way he always did, when more serious intimacies were on his mind.

'I've been hopelessly forgetful about the pill,' she lied a few minutes later, dreading his reaction, but needing to be true to herself on at least one level that afternoon.

'I'll see what I can find,' he grunted, pulling away and shuffling out of the room with his shirt hanging out and his hands holding up his trousers.

Rachel lay quite still, staring at an orange smudge on the back of the sofa, while the darkness outside deepened and the eager young flames matured into the subtler, redder glow of a true fire. Inside, her shame burned and curdled with an intensity of its own. She had plundered a life, seen what she wanted to see instead of the man himself, all the while feeding her imagination with impossible unrealities that bore no relation to the truth. Wanting to love someone was not enough, she realised, no matter how much will power one had, no matter how momentous the other issues involved. Feelings, like babies, she thought grimly, watching the last corner of the article burn, could never be manufactured with any certainty, no matter how hard one tried.

Robbie unearthed a slim pack of condoms from behind a dusty bottle of bubble bath on top of the bathroom cupboard. Only two left. Not used since Polly. The dull ache in the pit of his stomach tightened into something more painful. Putting his lips round the tap, he drank greedily, as if pain was a thirst that could be quenched like any other. Perhaps he should warn Rachel the damn things were unreliable, he thought bitterly, taking the packet with him and padding back downstairs. Tiny splinters of wood caught on his socks as he descended, as if not only his conscience, but the very bones of the house were trying to hold him back.

31

Towards the end of the following week the cat returned. Rachel spotted it sitting in a circle of early evening sunshine, its dainty pink tongue licking one paw with the bored insouciance of a secretary filing her nails. When she opened the sitting-room door it slipped in at once, pausing to brush against one of her crutches before trotting into the kitchen and mewing at the fridge.

'Are you here to stay or just passing through?' she demanded, reaching with difficulty onto the high shelf where she had stowed the tins of cat food. 'Not that it matters, seeing as I've no plans to leave.' The cat emitted a throaty purr, weaving in and out of her legs like a dancer. 'It's all right for cats to pop in and out of lives,' she went on, wrinkling her nose at the jellied chunks as she spooned them into a saucer, 'but definitely not for humans. Believe me, I know, I've tried it. A bloody disaster from start to finish.' The cat rubbed its cheek hard against her hand as she lowered the saucer to the ground, its engine of a purr shifting up a gear. 'So you do as you please,' she murmured, noting how it seemed to grin as it ate, liking the way it glanced up every now and then to see if she was still there. 'You make the most of your cat-freedom.'

The weekend in Devon had flopped badly. Under an umbrella of flimsy excuses, she had left on the Saturday, surprised by Robbie's lack of resistance, but grateful for it too. Apart from a last-minute flurry about whether a left leg was required to drive an automatic car, the departure had gone smoothly enough, each promising to be in touch, to fix another weekend soon. There had been a great silence ever since, like the stillness preceding calamity. She ought to call, she knew. Or write, maybe. Dear Robbie, sorry but I think we both know it's not going to work out after all. Apologies for wrecking your life – again. All the best, Rachel. PS. I've been suffering from delusions brought on by a confused desire to have a child. PPS. But I'm not even sure about this any more.

Manoeuvring her way through the study, Rachel sat down at her desk and began sorting disconsolately through an unpromising pile of mail shots and unanswered bills. It was time to get her life back in order, time to accept that she would be going on alone after all, that there would be no long-term rural idyll and probably no child. It would be a relief, she realised, to let the idea go one day, to release herself from the cycle of hope and apprehension that she knew would persist in some form for the remaining years of her fertility.

The prospect of three weeks' holiday and a new job beckoned. Tomorrow she would struggle through the swing doors of McKenzie Cartwright for the very last time. Alan Jarvis had accepted their resignations with stoical calm the day before, only the pulse in his lower left jaw suggesting commentary of a more emotional kind. Rachel had been the last to file out, swinging with as much dignity as she could through her crutches, which were too big and dug cruelly into her armpits. At the last moment he had summoned her back, his face clenched and pale.

'Just tell me one thing.' He stood stiffly, hands clasped behind his back. 'Does this have anything to do with that incident . . . the problem with Cliff? Is this some kind of twisted revenge?'

Hesitating, wanting to be honest, Rachel experienced a wave of affectionate pity for the man. To lose several million pounds' worth of business to mutinous employees was hard on any-one, no matter how arrogant their nature, or how solid their power-base. The news that Frank Alder was to entrust her with a large slice of Mallarmé's NPD work had cut particularly deep, she knew.

'Once, I would have liked it to have been,' she said cautiously, 'but, no, it's not revenge Alan. Just a coincidence of events. I was invited to leave and it felt the right thing to do. For what it's worth, I am sorry for the trouble caused.'

'And I'm sorry,' he growled, adjusting his tie. 'I should have listened to you. Weybourne will be gone himself before long. Talking to other agencies already, apparently. He's after power and little else. Whereas you . . .'

'God knows what I'm after,' she cut in with a laugh.

'You're good, that's what you are. And I should have made damn sure I kept you.'

Rachel shifted on her crutches, thinking that recriminations would have been easier than this.

'Go on. Buzz off and clear your desk then. And good luck. You deserve it. What happened to your leg, by the way?'

'I slipped on some ice.'

'Ice?' He raised one eyebrow at the sun streaming in through the window, catching dust motes in the slant of its beams.

'It was icy at the weekend, remember?'

'So it was,' he muttered, shaking his head, 'so it was.'

As he held the door open for her to pass, something made her stop and kiss his cheek. 'Just to say thank you,' she said, smiling, 'no harassment intended.'

'None taken,' he replied with a laugh that began quietly, but which grew louder as she progressed down the passage, causing looks of bafflement amongst those working nearby.

Her diary, sandwiched between a brochure on Bermudan tourist attractions and an old letter from Joy, was the most unexpected find of the day. The sight of it, after so many months of neglect, caused a wrench of guilt, followed by a quite irrational curiosity, as if she was on the verge of discovering something new. But all she found was a maddening evasiveness – half-truths and brave announcements that she wished she could disown. She had wasted far too much energy trying to persuade herself of things, she realised, instead of attempting to understand them. The last entry provoked the harshest self-recriminations of all: *Still no reply from Nathan . . .* Rachel sighed deeply and closed the book. Nathan Kramer. What a mess. What a cock-up. And here she was again, in the thick of something equally hideous with Robbie. Almost forty and still ballsing everything up. It was pathetic. She tossed the diary into the bin beside her – already brimming with discarded envelopes and information on cruises and pension plans – and reached angrily for the telephone. She would finish it properly now, she had to. It was the least she could do.

As her fingers touched the telephone it rang, giving her such a shock that she leapt back in her chair, knocking both crutches to the floor with her elbow.

'Robbie? This is too incredible for words. I was just going to—'

'To what?' It was Robbie's voice all right, but a strangled version she had never heard before. 'To tell me you loved me?' he sneered.

'No, I—'

'Oh come on, Rachel. You claw your way back into my life, make out like we're going to live happily ever after—'

'Robbie, calm down. I've something important to say – to explain . . .'

'About Mr William Raphael, by any chance? Yeah, I thought that might shut you up a bit. I can put up with a lot, Rachel – getting me to meet your parents, all that horsing around with promises about giving up work and moving out of London – I can cope with that. But not with this other stuff.'

'What other stuff?' she whispered, incredulous and afraid.

'If it wasn't for Polly you might have got away with it, too.'

'Polly? Got away with what, for God's sake?'

'Don't fuck me around,' he growled. 'I may not be the most successful man on earth, but I still have the right to be treated with decency . . . from you of all people. Was there someone else when you pulled out the first time, eh? All that bullshit about needing space . . . Was there a Mr Raphael in the wings then, too? One in London and one in the country. Very nice too.'

'Robbie, you've got it all wrong,' she said quietly, shocked both by his anger and this twisted fabrication of events. 'There's nothing—'

'Oh shut up, Rachel, just shut the fuck up.'

'This is ridiculous . . .'

'Not any more it isn't. It's over.'

Having been so preoccupied as to how best to bring about this very outcome herself, Rachel was nonetheless reluctant to submit to such garbled accusations of betrayal. She had betrayed Robbie all right – and herself too for that matter –

but not, so far as she knew, through any connection with Will Raphael.

'What's Polly got to do with all this?' she asked quietly.

'Polly's the one that opened my eyes, that's all.'

'What has she said?' Rachel persisted.

'She was sitting ouside your flat one night—'

'Outside my flat?'

'When your lover came to call – last week, when I was safely tucked up down here – played the good bloody samaritan, by all accounts, the bastard, just to quiz her about me, no doubt. Even put her up for a couple of nights . . .' Robbie's voice tailed off for a second. This was the part of the story he was least happy about. From what he could gather, Will Raphael had not only looked after Polly for three or four days, persuading her to set her parents' minds at rest with a phone call, but he had even paid for her ticket home on the train. '. . . during which time Polly found out quite a bit about you and him. She's no fool, you know. She even found a fucking picture of you in his flat . . .'

'The photo? I can explain about that—'

'Don't bother,' he snapped. 'And don't get in touch again – not next week, not next year, not next century. I won't be duped a third time.'

'But Robbie . . .' But the line had gone dead, leaving Rachel staring into the speaker-holes in stunned disbelief.

'Well done,' breathed Polly, placing a timid hand on Robbie's knee, letting it lie there, limp but persistent, ready as always for him to take up if he chose.

Robbie pushed the telephone out of reach and took a swig of beer from the bottle in front of him. 'Bloody woman,' he muttered, 'I should have guessed – I knew something wasn't quite right . . .' Catching sight of the pained expression on Polly's face, he stopped. 'Thanks again Pol, for telling me, for putting me right. I'd be lost without you, you know that.'

Blushing with pleasure, Polly took her hand away and set about preparing supper. They were having fish fingers, eight for Robbie and five for herself, together with mashed potato and frozen sweetcorn from a very battered bag she had found wedged in one corner of the deepfreeze. A bottle of ketchup and two sets of knives and forks were already on the kitchen table, like the old days, she thought, breathing hard. Already the weight of the child in her womb seemed to press against her ribs, pushing up rather than out as she always imagined it would, making her feel wheezy and full. Five months gone. Five long months since a moonlit October night up against the back wall of the pub, near the vent that poured steam from the kitchen, billows of greasy vapour that bounced and curled around them before dissolving into the dark. A crude thrusting and groping; beery breath and mawling hands. No sweetness in revenge after all, she had thought even at the time, as comparisons with Robbie's big, tender hands had sprung inevitably to mind and Felipe the polo player crooned obscenities into the gaping front of her shirt.

'He's kicking, if you want to feel.' She approached, spatula in one hand, the other resting on the underside of her belly.

'Where? I can't feel a thing.'

'Down a bit. There.'

Robbie, detecting a brief fluttering under his fingertips, smiled up at her. To find himself relieved that there had been no abortion after all had come as quite a surprise. As had the reactions of both Polly and her parents. Mrs Drayton, whom he feared most, had made stout, supportive declarations about infants of her acquaintance born before wedlock and young couples who took their time. They supposed marriage was on the cards and Robbie had no intention of disillusioning them. It was assumed he would stand by her. And so he would. Rachel's duplicity had made that easier at least. He couldn't love her now, nor ever again. The future looked all the clearer as a result.

He had wanted to punish her, though. Not just for having an affair, but for being so toweringly capable and intelligent, for making him so cruelly aware of his own failings and chaotic ways. With Polly it didn't matter. With Polly he was the toweringly capable one, deferred to in everything, without the shadows of unspoken criticism to darken each day. The last few months had wrought a terrible pressure, he realised now, all that nagging, unacknowledged worry about how to make Rachel happy, about living up to expectations; expectations that were all the harder for being imagined but never explained.

The fish fingers, burnt round the edges as he liked them and smothered in tomato sauce, tasted good.

'Our baby, eh?' he said, his eyes flashing, his mouth twitching to a near-smile.

Polly looked down at her plate. Felipe had dark hair and brown eyes. He was quite fair-skinned too, which was good. She wouldn't have stood a chance otherwise. She scraped some sweetcorn into her pile of potato, moulding it into a lumpy cake with her fork. 'We're all yours,' she said simply, while the baby danced a celebration of its own inside. Remembering the kindness of Mr Raphael, Polly kept her eyes on her plate, for a moment guilty at how she had snooped around his flat when he was out, how she'd kept her big jumper on to hide the lump in her stomach. She had wanted his help all right, but not all those opinions as to how to live her life. Mr Raphael had said she should leave Robbie alone, that loving someone meant wanting them to be happy with whatever they chose. While pretending to agree, deep down she knew he was wrong. She had a right to happiness too, a right to use whatever she could to get it.

Making out that Will was sleeping with Rachel had been a stroke of inspiration for which Polly was still congratulating herself. They were friends after all; so it was only a slight fudging of the truth. And then there was the photograph – a very nice one she had to admit – sitting in a drawer all on its own, as if it was something special. The pieces had started to fit together then, like they were meant to, like they were clues towards an answer. It had been the best – the only – way to be sure of getting Rob. It was all too perfect for words, like a miracle. Like Felipe taking a job at those stables in Sussex, safely far away, out of her system for good.

'Baby and I will be always be here,' she said, brushing some dry wisps of hair off her forehead and smiling back at him. 'Your own little lamb at last, eh Rob?' She pushed back her chair and began clearing away the plates, stopping only to plant a kiss on top of his head, before running a bowl of washing-up water and plunging her hands into the warm foam.

32

FOR THE ATTENTION OF WILL RAPHAEL:

*I have been trying to get in touch with you for several weeks now
and am beginning to think you must have left the country. Or perhaps
your answering machine – whilst appearing to be in perfect working
order – is in fact not working at all? Or perhaps you have suffered
a severe and terrible accident and are, as I write, lying in hospital
paralysed from the neck down hoping that somebody will pull the
plug out? Forgive the cynicism, but I'm more than a little baffled,
not to say confused.*

*I might not find your reluctance to get in touch with me quite so
peculiar were it not for the fact that several people seem to be under
the illusion that we are close friends. (This is embarrassing, but I am
determined to go on. I hate unsolved mysteries for one thing and for
another, I am resolved – partly on your advice, I have to admit – to
spend the second half of my life being altogether more forthright and
honest.) I like the photo very much, by the way. But perhaps you
don't. Perhaps that's why you have failed to return my calls . . .*

*You once implied that I hid behind a mesh of electronic communi-
cations systems. Might I be so bold as to suggest that you are now
doing the same? Might I be equally bold and say—*

Rachel paused, fingers poised over the computer keys, wondering how far she dare go. After three idle weeks she was feeling
wonderfully mellow. Free time, such an enemy for so much of
her life, was at last something she was learning to savour rather
than fear. While she relished the challenges of a new job, the
prospect of two extra days to herself each week was equally
sustaining. It would mean more time for friends and hobbies,

more time to be a godmother, to house-hunt for the cottage she wanted, somewhere in Wiltshire, or Dorset maybe, a spot where the cat could have more than a few yards in which to hunt without dodging irritable bus drivers and speeding cars. For the animal was showing every sign of staying now; like a human putting down roots, it had established its own routines, complete with preferred snooze-spots, mealtimes and flavours of food. Though it was often absent for half the night, slipping out of the cat-flap Rachel had had drilled into the lower section of one of her beautiful sitting-room doors, she would always wake to find it curled up by her feet, its stomach heavy with the night's prey, its whiskers twitching at its dreams.

Since the night of Robbie's call Rachel had made several efforts to get in touch with Will Raphael, all of which had met with a recording of his voice or no answer at all. While a part of her recoiled at the unseemly notion of appearing pushy, her curiosity remained as strong as ever. At least she told herself it was curiosity, though her stomach performed rebellious acrobatics of its own, and the tall, dark-haired strangers who now peopled her dreams had a worrying propensity for emerging from behind cameras, with dark eyes that laughed away her fear.

The cat landed neatly beside her right elbow and mewed at the screen before extending a tentative paw towards the coiled flex protruding from the back of it.

'Push off, Hamish, this is serious,' Rachel scolded, giving him a fond nudge with her arm. The christening of the animal had happened almost imperceptibly, the name tripping off her tongue one evening without any forethought at all. Hamish was perfect, she had felt at once, for one so upright and independent, with such a clear agenda of his own.

As Rachel raised her hands to continue typing, the cat placed himself between her and the screen, disdainfully running its abundant tail under the tip of her nose.

'Push off, you.' She picked him up and dropped him to the floor. 'I've nearly done. I'm trying a spot of man-chasing here and it's bloody hard-going. Not something I've ever been very good at.'

* * *

—that I would like to meet up for a drink, preferably sometime before the next millennium, that is if you could possibly fit such a thing into your action-packed social calendar.

I'm between jobs, so please contact me at home.

With very best wishes,

Rachel (Confused of Chelsea)

PS. Do you know a Polly? If yes, I would appreciate details.

Although Rachel had originally intended this communication as a fax, she ended up sealing it in a long white envelope and delivering it to the pillar box at the end of the road that very evening, scurrying through the wet night like a thief.

'And that's all I can do, Hamish,' she declared upon her return, brushing her palms together as if dismissing the matter for good. 'And don't look at me like that. Your position in this household is secure, I assure you. Neither man nor child shall separate us, though I'm not saying I might not expect a compromise or two along the way.'

The cat, clearly unimpressed by such ideological guarantees, gave her an arch look and headed for its door-flap, diving out of sight with dainty precision, its tail giving the merest flick of a farewell, as it disappeared into the night.

33

'Are you sure you don't mind dropping her back?' Having used her teaspoon to skim the chocolatey froth off the top of her cappuccino, Anita eyed the brown peaks appreciatively before depositing them in her mouth.

'Of course not – so long as Charlotte can put up with me for that long.' Rachel cast a sideways glance at her goddaughter's crumb-encrusted face and smiled. 'You will hold my hand if it's scary won't you? I'm not very used to monsters in the cinema.'

'They're not *real* monsters Aunty Rachel, only people dressed up.' Charlotte's face, bulging with half-chewed pain-au-chocolate, twisted for a moment with genuine concern. 'It's all pretend.'

'I'll try to remember,' she promised, winking at Anita.

They were sitting at a table outside a tea shop in the King's Road, making the most of a mid-April heatwave before Rachel treated Charlotte to a PG-rated box-office hit entitled, *The Grange Goblins*, while her mother pursued a much lamented search for shoes.

'So how are you, Rachel?' Anita asked with a directness that reflected the new-found confidence in herself and life in general.

'Talking to the cat, but otherwise OK.'

'You've got a cat,' exclaimed her goddaughter, 'you lucky lucky thing. Mummy *promised* me one for my birthday.' She fired an accusatory look at her mother before seeking silent solace from her pastry.

'Don't exaggerate, Charlotte. I said *maybe*, if Dad agreed.'

'And how is Giles?'

'So much better – though there's still no definitive diagnosis of anything. Personally, I think it's just plain exhaustion. All those years and years of travelling and stress finally catching up with him. His latest plan is to take a year's sabbatical – write the definitive journalist-in-the-front-line book – interviews with terrorists and bullets grazing earlobes – you know the kind of thing. Apparently two publishers are interested already.' She fiddled with the handle of her coffee cup, her mind skipping from happy recollections of the recent and highly satisfying resumption of her married sex life to a less easy consideration of such matters where Rachel was concerned. The Robbie Dexter business had dealt her quite a blow, she knew, though, typically, she had barely admitted as much out loud. 'Any explanations from the elusive Mr Raphael yet?'

Rachel shook her head and frowned at something across the street. 'I think he must be away on business . . .' The lack of reply to her most recent – most direct – plea for a meeting still rankled.

'Must be.'

'I'm certainly not going to try any more. He'll begin to think I'm interested, or something.'

Anita, while privately concluding – on the basis of several recent conversations – that for Rachel to describe herself as merely 'interested' was a close call for the understatement of the century, hid her smile behind the rim of her coffee cup.

'And Robbie's all right, is he?' she enquired airily, spitting onto her paper napkin before beginning an assault on the brown stains covering her daughter's cheeks and chin.

'I assume so. I haven't heard a word.' Rachel signalled to the waitress for the bill. 'Odd really. I almost feel as if it never happened, as if I dreamt the whole episode. Wish to goodness I had,' she added gloomily, making a face at Charlotte who was fighting the napkin.

'And the new job? I want all the gory details.'

Rachel's eyes lit up. 'It's fabulous – such fun. There's so few of us and all wanting the same things.'

'Not one teeny weeny disagreement about logos or the colour of the walls?'

'Oh come on, *please*,' interrupted Charlotte, consumed now

by boredom and certain that she had been politely silent for quite long enough.

Anita opened her mouth with a reprimand, but Rachel got there first. 'Poor Charlotte, we grown-ups are so dull, aren't we? Come on then,' she held out her hand, 'lead me to those goblins.'

Anita waved them off down the street, marvelling not for the first time at this new and infinitely more relaxed version of her old friend, wondering how much of it was connected to frustrated desires to be a mother herself. She would probably never know, she mused with a sigh, reluctantly acknowledging that some questions could never be asked after all, no matter how tender the intent nor how many years of shared intimacy had gone before.

Rachel hastily let herself into her flat, all thoughts of goblins superseded by crazed and leaping hopes for the envelope in her hand. It must have come by the second post. He had written at last, just when she had given up hope.

She forced herself not to hurry, propping the envelope up against a jar of spaghetti while she poured herself a glass of wine and refilled Hamish's saucer of milk. Was it wicked to savour such a moment, she asked herself, carrying the letter through into the sitting room and choosing a Chopin piano concerto as the appropriate foil for her mood? She was thinking of learning the piano. It was to be part of the second half of her life, something she had always wanted to do. Much more up her street than photography, she thought wryly, attending to the envelope at last.

His handwriting was conspicuously beautiful, thick-nibbed, black and smooth, adding a grandeur to her name and address which was somehow flattering. Unable to wait a moment longer, she ran her finger under the flap and pulled out the single page contained inside. Her stomach tightened as she began to devour the words.

Friday, May 3rd

My Dear Rachel,
    I am sorry I have not replied before. My failure to do so arises not, as you so sweetly suggest, from being bed-ridden in an intensive

care ward, but from a deep conviction that it would be unwise for us to develop our relationship any further. We both have other commitments which I believe should take priority.

As to the opinion of others regarding my affection for you, I can only blame the human predilection for gossip and speculation. Some people seem to think that photographers enjoy intimate relations with all their models, which, alas, is not the case. (I too am very happy with the picture, by the way.)

I did make the acquaintance of someone called Polly a little while ago. She claimed to be a friend of your Mr Dexter. By sheer coincidence I found her in a state of considerable distress and did what I could, which wasn't a lot. As far as I know she was posted safely home to her family. I hope that answers your query.

To know what you want out of life is a rare gift and one that I believe you have. I hope everything works out exactly as you plan. You deserve to be very happy.

Yours apologetically and affectionately,
Will

'Bugger, bugger, *bugger*.' Rachel screwed up the letter and hurled it across the room, where it bounced once before rolling to a stop beside the glass door of the cabinet that housed her music system. He could go to hell, she told herself, wishing she believed it, wishing she could despise the man as much as she did the feelings that were surging inside.

She was still brooding over the matter – and cross at herself for doing so – when her mother phoned half an hour later.

'How are you, dear?' asked Margaret Elliot in a tone that cunningly suggested her own welfare and not her daughter's to be in need of tender enquiry. She had taken news of the split with Robbie very badly. No matter what Rachel said, she persisted in regarding the failure of the relationship as temporary – something that could be overcome with determination and patience, like a patchy marriage.

'Brilliant, thanks,' replied Rachel firmly.

'I just wanted to say happy birthday for next week and to ask if there was anything special you had in mind. For a present, I mean. It is a special occasion after all, getting to forty.'

'Oh anything, honestly Mum. You choose,' Rachel added, doing her best to sound grateful. 'A book or something would be nice.'

'I thought maybe a token to spend at Marks and Spencer . . .'

'Perfect. I'd love that.'

'Only, it is easy to send and of course you can pick what you want . . .'

'A token would be just the thing. How's Dad?'

'His back's bad, but then he will spend half the day on his knees in the garden.'

'Bad time for weeds, I suppose,' she sympathised, eager to keep the conversation on such wonderfully manageable tracks.

'Well, of course it is, but I think we should pay someone to do the garden these days. We're not getting any younger after all, and it would only cost a few pounds a week, but your father won't hear of it.'

'Sounds like dear old Dad.' A wave of cheerfulness came at her from nowhere. Will Raphael could stay behind his camera lens if he wanted. She had got over worse disappointments in her time. Besides, there was just so much grovelling a girl was prepared to do. She tore off a wedge of bread from a fresh loaf in front of her and pressed it between her fingers. Something flashed in the garden. Hamish's green headlamp eyes perhaps. Rachel craned her neck for a better look, pulling the telephone flex taut. She would mind terribly if the cat left now, she realised, thinking in the same instant how unfair it was that loving something inevitably brought the fear of losing it – how unspeakably vulnerable it made one.

'Your father and I have had our rough patches,' her mother was saying, 'but where there's a will there's a way.'

'Yes, Mum.' Rachel, recognising the preamble to the very lecture she had so dreaded, took a large bite of bread and closed her eyes. She chewed slowly, letting the familiar intonations wash over her, deliberately focusing her mind on the salty softness of the dough. She was eating more these days, not in any frenzied way, but out of a new, keener appreciation of food and the natural call of her own appetite. Beside the loaf was a machine for making fresh pasta and two new cookbooks, one of them open at an enticing picture of dressed crab meat surrounded by lush slices of avocado pear.

'. . . So all I'm saying is there's no harm in offering to try again. There's no point in being obstinate about these things, Rachel—'

'Like Dad, you mean?'

'I beg your pardon?'

'Dad's obstinate about everything. I expect I get it from him. Lovely to talk to you, Mum, but I've got to dash – something's boiling over on the stove. Bye.'

Rachel replaced the receiver with calm exultation and ripped off another hunk of bread. Chewing and frowning, with one hand holding back the heavy sweep of her hair, she willingly surrendered all her mental energies to instructions for dissecting the delicate innards of a crab, on how best to keep the white meat separate from the brown, without splintering the brittle labyrinth inside.

34 ∫

As a particularly bad wave of nausea took hold, Rachel pulled over onto a double yellow line and stuck her head out of the window, breathing in deep lungfuls of smoky Balham air. Across the road, a pair of teenagers sitting on a wall eyed her curiously as they took it in turns to swing round the slim trunk of a small tree, shaking its armfuls of pink blossom so that they shimmered like dusty gems in the dim evening light.

The hangover, instead of easing as the day progressed, was still uncurling, snaking its coils round the perimeter of her head and pushing deep into the shaky pit of her stomach, where it did battle with a fizzy cocktail of analgesics and several pints of liquid that had left her feeling bloated and unrevived. The pain was worse than being forty, she thought meekly, hating these unseemly after-effects, but none the less recalling the previous evening's celebrations with a surge of affection.

Thanks to a spot of last-minute coincidences of strategy and timing, the party had comprised a total of four women: Anita, who had done all the organising; Naomi, who had leapt at the chance of a night off from her domestic problems and Joy, who had taken Rachel at her word and channel-hopped for a short holiday with little Leo. Since there were many other people Joy wished to visit, she had stayed with Rachel for only twenty-four hours, leaving her alone with her godson for just one afternoon. All Rachel's hopes and apprehensions about this spot of child-tending had focused on the cat, since Leo, now aged almost one and packaged like a miniature sumo warrior, tackled all objects – inanimate or otherwise – with a careless, bear-hug affection capable of causing serious harm.

Throughout their first few minutes alone Hamish was lunged for, squeezed and rubbed with such alarming zest that Rachel feared all her worst imaginings would be realised. Having failed with distractions of every kind, she waited grimly for Hamish to flee or draw out his claws. It was a while before she realised that he would do no such thing. Observing the cat's endurance and patience, admiring the way the paws warned but did not harm the child, she had the feeling that he had seen it all before, that somewhere in its unknowable past an infant of similarly good but potentially injurious intentions had been artfully entertained and kept at bay.

Just as fresh worries were surfacing about Joy's complicated set of instructions concerning bottles and naps, Leo disarmed her completely by picking up a book and climbing aboard her lap. Here he settled down like an animal himself, eyelids heavy, his silky white hair flopping endearingly into his eyes. Rachel forgot the clock then, together with all the other details with which she had been briefed for his afternoon routine. As they studied baleful cows and lions that smiled, Rachel nuzzled the sweet smell of his soft head, remembering her tentative cradling of the baby version of this same child the summer before, and the wound of longing that followed. The longing was still there, but the intensity had dulled. Four godchildren was quite a clutch. They had been there for her all along and she hadn't even realised. All the fun and none of the heartache; perfect parenting. Almost.

Rachel swallowed a few gulpfuls of water from the bottle on the seat beside her. The A-Z was open at the right page. Nearly there now: third left, fourth right and right again. *'Only call if you can't make it,'* Anna Raphael had said, her voice casual but firm. *'I've been meaning to invite you over for ages – there's something I want to ask your advice about – 8 o'clock Saturday – 32 Egremont Road.'* The phrases relayed by her answering machine played back disjointedly inside Rachel's head. She had meant to phone anyway, not to refuse necessarily, but to find out a bit more before going. But then Leo and Joy had arrived and things had got rushed. Then it had been too late to back out anyway, irrespective of headaches and gloominess about birthdays.

A bus arrived and the two teenagers got on it, all thoughts of ghostly-faced middle-aged women panting like dogs out of car windows clearly far from their minds. Although it was nearly eight o'clock, Rachel could not muster the enthusiasm to hurry. She thought again of the dinner the night before, of all her female friends' persistent and predictable protestations of envy at her life, the griping about husbands and the juggles of domestic life. Godmothers had it easy, they teased, especially ones with highly paid, part-time jobs and filofaxes full of the names of eligible men. Rachel had played along, happy to accept the safety offered by these familiar and affectionately constructed guidelines, not out of any cowardice but on account of the fresh flower of self-certainty that had taken root inside.

Looking back with the lucidity of hindsight, Rachel was beginning to believe that the upheavals of the last few months were not so much hormonal as part of a fundamental need for softening and change on a grand scale. A need for other people, perhaps. There had been a void at the heart of her, she realised now. A void certainly manifested by her crazed resolution to become a mother, but which would not necessarily have been filled if she had been successful in her quest. Parenthood was not yet impossible. But in the meantime there were other things, she thought with relief, surveying the pink-cheeked faces of these mothers of her godchildren with affection and then exchanging a glance of more penetrating empathy with Anita. It was a special pleasure to discover that vulnerability did not necessarily mean weakness, that to lean on people a little was allowed.

As she settled back into the seat of her taxi, waving at the receding figures of her friends, Rachel felt, for the first time in ages, as if the best part of her life might still lie ahead of her. There was no one else she would rather be after all, she thought gratefully, sinking down into the seat of the taxi with a sleepy sigh, as snippets of narratives from her friends' lives echoed inside her head. Such strife, such chaos. She shuddered. Not for her at all. Then an image of Will Raphael wheedled its way in alongside. She shuddered again, but this time for a different reason. I'd take strife and chaos for him all right, she thought, smiling grimly in the dark, wishing she could fully accept that on that score at least, fate had already played its hand.

Anna Raphael was wearing dungaree-style shorts, made of faded denim and covering a grey T-shirt that looked several sizes too large. Gracing her feet were a pair of heavy-soled boots and socks that bagged round her ankles. Her dark hair had been swept into a loose ponytail that was spilling out of control, a soft, striking frame for the pale triangular face which creased with pleasure as she opened the door.

'Oh, you're here. Great. Come in.' Without further explanation she led the way to the back of the house, past a stack of boxes and a child's bicycle. Her walk was at once poised and full of energy, in spite of the boots or perhaps because of them, marvelled Rachel, following on behind. Part of her own long cotton skirt caught on a bike pedal as she sidled past; her legs buckled and she staggered for a step or two as a fresh wave of confusion and nausea hit home.

'I shouldn't have come,' she said weakly, recovering her balance and stepping through into a large kitchen, which clearly functioned as several other things as well. A small oblong table, set for two, separated the cooking units from a sofa and a portable television, balanced rather precariously on top of an overflowing bookshelf. Toys dangled from drawers and containers on every side.

'Sorry about the squash. We tend to live in this room, especially in the winter. I know it's summer, but I haven't spilled back into the front yet. A drink?' She was bent in an exact rightangle before the contents of her fridge, her back flat, her legs straight, her neck turned with swan-like grace towards her guest.

Rachel shook her head doubtfully. 'I was forty yesterday and am still suffering the consequences, I'm afraid.'

'Oh, you poor darling. But I've got just the thing. Hang on.' She skipped out of the room, returning a few moments later with two large round pink capsules which she handed to Rachel together with a tumbler of water. 'I use these when my back's buggered. They're just muscle relaxants – but work wonders for sore heads too. Go on,' she urged, seeing Rachel's hesitancy, 'they're quite legal. And then we can start on this.' She set down a bottle of champagne and began peeling back its metal cap. Her fingernails were badly bitten, Rachel noticed, torn and pink round the edges.

'Champagne?' Rachel's stomach twisted.

'Absolutely.'

'Are we celebrating something?'

'I don't know, we might be . . .' The cork shot across the room and bounced off the television screen, while the exploding contents of the bottle were messily steered in the direction of the two glasses on the table.

Suddenly the weirdness of it all was too much, the confusion raging inside her head nothing but a source of irritation. 'Look, what the hell is all this about?' Rachel burst out, folding her arms and standing squarely in the middle of the kitchen area. 'To be quite frank with you, the last thing I feel like is champagne – or being sociable in any way, for that matter. Of course I'm flattered that you asked me over and everything—'

'Crap,' retorted Anna amiably. 'You just didn't get around to cancelling, I bet.' She was pouring out the champagne now, waiting for the bubbles to subside so that she could fill the glasses to the very top. The pink band responsible for the ponytail had slid further down her head, so that only a small portion of it remained reined back off her face. 'You've every right to be pissed off, especially if you've got a bad head. How is it, by the way?'

Rachel started to scowl and stopped in surprise. 'A bit better actually . . .'

'They work fast. Come and sit over here and I'll tell you what this is all about. And do try not to be cross,' she added with an impish grin.

Curious in spite of everything, Rachel went obediently to the sofa, which was surprisingly comfortable, and without thinking took a sip of champagne. The bubbles burst pleasantly at the back of her throat. A wonderful smell was emanating from the oven. Melted cheese of some kind . . . something with garlic.

Anna got out a small tin and began rolling a cigarette, her stubby fingers expertly packing and patting as she talked. 'I just wanted to consult you about Will, actually. He's been a miserable sod recently and I know it's because of you—'

'Me? What have I—?'

'And I just think if a sister can't help a brother out on something like this, then who the hell can?'

'Something like what?'

'I know I'm hardly the one for personal relationships,' she stuck the white stick of a cigarette in her mouth and began searching the pockets of her dungarees for a light, 'but one thing I do know is . . .'

She was interrupted by the doorbell.

'Oh shit.' She slotted the cigarette behind her ear and bounded from the room, the heavy rubber soles of her boots squeaking on the linoleum floor.

To Rachel's horror she did not return alone. Her brother was walking one step behind her, talking animatedly until he stepped into the kitchen.

'What the hell—' He stopped in the doorway, looking from one woman to the other, his face a picture of awkward bewilderment. 'I mean, I didn't know you two knew each other—'

'We don't at all . . . I was just . . .' Rachel got up and made a big show of hunting for her handbag.

'Anna . . .' There was a warning note to his voice, and his eyes, as they turned to confront his sister's, were intent with stern, unspoken meaning. 'I had no idea you were expecting another guest.' He shot Rachel a polite smile. Insultingly polite, she thought, now rummaging manically under cushions and soft toys.

'Don't worry, I'm just going.' She had at last spotted her bag dangling from the back of one of the dining chairs.

'No, no. You're not going anywhere,' squealed Anna, waving her arms. 'Neither of you are.'

'Well somebody clearly isn't expected to stay for dinner,' remarked Rachel, staring hard at the table. All eyes followed her gaze: two wine glasses, two plates, two sets of cutlery.

'It's me,' declared Anna stoutly, pulling the pink band out of the last straggle of her hair and shaking her head defiantly. 'I'm not staying. I never was. You two are. Don't say a word, either of you. Don't you dare.' She held up her hands and began backing out of the room. 'Lasagna in the oven. Garlic bread too. Red wine. Salad. If you can't think of anything to say to each other put the telly on and call it baby-sitting. I'll be back by midnight.' And she rushed away, leaving the two of them alone with nothing but the echoes of the slamming door and their own embarrassment for company.

35 ∫

'How very awkward, I'm so sorry.' Rachel had made it as far as the kitchen door, bag now safely slung over one shoulder, coat in hand. Time seemed to have slowed to a malevolently teasing crawl. 'I'm parked right outside,' she muttered, for something to say, part of her recoiling at the sight of the dim, cluttered hallway through which she still had to pass, as if it were some kind of hazardous rite of passage, something she might not manage. Questions beat inside her head, but she thrust them aside. There were too many other feelings raging for courage to play a part. No matter what she might feel, it was clear that her unexpected presence in the house of his sister had caused this man nothing but pain. He had flinched at the sight of her. She did not dare to ask him why. There was just so much rejection a girl could take.

'You look well, Rachel,' he said as she took the first step into the hallway. 'Weekends in the country clearly suit you.'

'The country?' She turned back.

'Devon.'

'I don't go to Devon any more.' She gripped the strap of her bag. 'Robbie and I are no longer together. The Polly girl told him we were having an affair.'

'She what?'

'It doesn't matter, really. It was all over anyway – should never have started in the first place – my fault entirely.' She forced herself to look into his face. His expression was set and grim. A dark stubble covered the lower section of his cheeks and chin, a shapely shadow of a beard that rather suited him, she thought, transferring her gaze to the oven where a red light was winking at them. 'In fact, I'm not well at all . . . I'm forty – I mean, I have – I had – a horrible hangover. And I think the lasagna wants to come out.' They both looked at the flashing light for a moment and then simultaneously moved towards it. When their elbows touched he jerked his arm away and stood to one side, while she wrestled inexpertly with oven gloves and doors.

The lasagna bubbled and steamed, its top layer looking enticingly crispy and brown. Beside it was a long tin-foil parcel of garlic bread. The bottle of red wine standing beside the hob had been opened, Rachel noticed, and its cork laid neatly to one side.

'I can't imagine what Anna thinks she's playing at,' Will blurted, running his hands through his hair and staring in despair at the dish of sizzling food. 'But . . . I guess . . . it would be a shame to waste it?'

Rachel, still holding the oven gloves, felt a sudden rush of lucidity. Time was ticking by at its usual rate once again. It made it easier to be honest. 'Your sister is clearly under several misapprehensions concerning your feelings towards me. So she arranges this ambush.' Rachel gestured at the table set for two. 'It is hideously embarrassing, because, as we both know, you have in fact been trying for several weeks now to avoid contact with me altogether – a minor detail in this sorry episode of which dear Anna is as yet unaware. Perhaps you would be so kind as to set the record straight, once and for all, when she returns? No harm done.' She held out her hand for a businesslike farewell, a concluding seal on their mutual confusion.

'Oh, but there is harm done,' he whispered, taking her hand and then not letting go. 'Terrible harm.'

His grip was cool and firm; she could feel the shape of each finger curved over her knuckles. 'No, really, I'll get over it. It's all been a bit of a mess. Thirty-nine was definitely *not* my year,' she added with a short laugh, 'crises on every front in fact – but forty's looking better – a shaky start maybe but . . .' she babbled on, hardly knowing what she was saying, torn between the sense that she should remove her hand from his and the stronger impulse to leave it where it was. 'If I've been bothering you, I'm sorry. Hounding men is really not my style . . .' She wrenched her fingers free and relocated the strap of her bag.

'I ought to explain,' he faltered. 'It's not that I'm not interested; it's . . . it's far worse.'

'Worse? . . . Look, please, you don't have to explain. I'd really rather not know.' She forced a smile. 'I have got the message, as they say. And now I really am going.'

The strap of her bag caught on the bike handle this time, as if it too was playing the intolerable game of trying to prolong her stay in the house. Then she couldn't manage the door handles, of which there were several, none of them, apparently, having any effect on the lock. At some point during these latter struggles Will came up behind her. He reached round to open the door and set her free, but then she somehow got caught up in the withdrawal of his arms. There was no hesitation in his embrace then, no signs of lack of interest, no awkwardness at all.

'Are you deliberately trying to confuse me?' Rachel gasped, pulling away at last. 'I mean, is this a game, or what?'

'Let's eat,' he said, taking her by the hand and leading her back.

His silence, as he served up the food, induced her to talk, to provide some structure for what was taking place. 'I've decided you're a typical artistic neurotic,' she declared. 'It's the only possible explanation for such extraordinarily erratic behaviour. Am I right?' She bit into a slice of garlic bread, holding her chin out over the plate to catch the crumbs. But on glancing up, she saw that his face, instead of reflecting her own gathering excitement, was suffused with discomfort. It was all too delicate, Rachel thought helplessly, so wanting to get it right, but feeling herself blunder at every turn. Perhaps she was going too fast, she scolded herself, remembering the dead wife and conjuring fuzzy, romantic images of a woman with a cello and tumbling pre-Raphaelite hair.

'There is something you have to know, Rachel.' Will spoke very precisely, laying down his knife and fork and placing his hands palms down on either side of his plate. 'It is the reason why I have been trying not to see you. It's got nothing to do with what I feel, I . . .'

The tension was unbearable, so much so that she felt compelled to break it. 'AIDS?' she suggested, with a sharp laugh.

'I've actually been checked out for that one,' he replied with a rueful smile. 'A while ago now, mind you, but my sexual activities since then would hardly warrant a re-trial.'

'What, then? You're a closet paedophile?' Rachel helped herself to a clutch of lettuce from the bowl in the centre of the table and raised a mouthful of food to her lips. Cheerfulness was edging back, bubbling back up in that silly, irrepressible way it had. Because of the kiss.

'Rachel, I can't have children. Ever.'

She lowered her fork, still laden with food and crossed her hands in her lap.

'Absent "vas deferens". Which is to say, no sperm ever make it past first post. It's congenital. I found out with Ginnie. It was one of the things that depressed her.'

'And you decided,' her voice was trembling now, 'you decided that because of this we should not see each other?'

'It did not cross my mind so much at first, but then Anita mentioned that you wanted a child and—'

'Anita?'

'I just felt I had no right to step in and waste your time . . . I know a bit about wanting a child . . . about how the idea can take hold, eat away at people. I knew you didn't have much time left . . .' he added quietly.

'You knew a lot, didn't you?' she said icily, pushing away her plate.

He threw up his hands. 'Oh go on, get it over with, walk out of the fucking door. I knew you would. I knew it.'

She stood up. 'Yes, I shall walk out of the fucking door, not because of the uncooperative nature of your anatomy but because of the audacity – the arrogance – of your decision that my wanting a child should rule you out of my life. You don't know anything about my feelings on the subject and neither,' she banged the table with her fist, 'for that matter, does Anita.'

Leaving was easier this time: no straps catching on bike pedals, no knee-weakening nausea. Once at the front door she masterfully jiggled every handle in sight until it swung open, releasing her into the welcome cover of the dark night. She turned right and strode towards her car, not looking back. A whipping breeze caught under the panels of her skirt as she groped for the car keys, her eyes bleary with tears of rage and disappointment.

How dare he? How dare he have decided for her? Of course she minded. She minded like hell, about everything. She slipped the key into the ignition and pressed her foot on the accelerator, bracing herself for the engine to throb into life.

36

Will watched her leave through a chink in the front-room curtains. As the wind ruffled her hair and ballooned her skirt around her knees, he had clenched his fists and teeth from the sheer effort of not running after her. He had not felt such affinity for another human being for a long long time – had never thought to again. But at least she now knew why, he consoled himself, as she disappeared from view. At least, when her anger subsided, she would see that it was from caring too much rather than not at all. Though he had long since been forced to come to terms with his own sterility, Will never questioned his right to subject her to such grim realities. It was up to Rachel to choose. And choose she clearly had, he thought wretchedly, rubbing his hands up and down his arms, shivering though he wasn't cold.

From his position in the bay window he could not quite see her car. There had been no noise from the engine. Or had there? The wind was stronger now, noisily buffeting the tarpaulin that covered next door's motorbike, rattling dustbin lids and loose panes. She must have gone already. He craned his neck to see, pressing one cheek hard up against the cold glass.

'Mummy?'

'Jack? What's up?' He turned at once and hurried over to the child standing, frowning and pale, in the doorway. 'Mummy will be back soon. You come with me now.' He scooped him up in his arms and carried him through into the warm kitchen, where he dimmed the lights and stroked his hair. 'A bad dream, was it?'

Jack nodded, snivelling and rubbing his eyes.

'The one about the dragons or the nasty dog?'

There was a hiccough followed by an incoherent reply.

'Want some milk? OK, but Uncle Will needs two hands for that, so why don't I put you down over here.' He set the child gently amongst the sofa cushions and pulled a book at random from the nearest toy box. '*Peter Pan*. He's ace against pirates – and dragons and dogs for that matter. Give me a minute and I'll read the words.' While waiting for the milk to boil, Will pulled a mug from the cupboard where Anna kept Jack's things. A faded Winnie the Pooh, suspended amongst a cloud of bees by a balloon string, eyed him with cheery hopelessness as he dolloped in a teaspoon of honey and stirred the milk. Warm, but not too hot. Will knew the score. He stirred with exaggerated diligence, deeply grateful, that evening of all evenings, to have someone to worry about other than himself. Anna's instincts were good, he thought grimly. Spot on, in fact. She just hadn't known the whole story. She had assumed – as indeed he once had – that Rachel had got beyond babies.

By the time he returned his attentions to his nephew, the child was asleep, his head lolling on a cushion and the book clasped to his chest like a loved toy.

When the doorbell rang, Will moved slowly, telling himself it was Anna back early and having forgotten her keys as usual.

'The bloody car won't start.' Rachel was fidgeting with the buckle on her bag, her eyes directed somewhere around his knees. 'Flat battery. I just need a phone.'

'A phone, of course.' He stood back and opened the door wider. 'Come in.'

'I'm still cross.'

'I know.'

'And I've got four godchildren and a cat.'

'I've got a nephew. He's in the kitchen.'

Still she stood on the doorstep, knowing that going in, however valid the pretext, would be the start of something irrevocable.

'I'm forty and a typical spinster. A spinster with inclinations towards broodiness. How does that sound?'

'Perfectly horrible. Are you coming in, or what? It's turning nasty out there.' Seizing both her hands, he pulled her across the threshold so roughly that she almost fell. He kicked the door shut behind her with his foot, slamming it so violently the floorboards shook beneath their feet. 'Got you,' he whispered, pulling her to him and kissing her hair.

'Only till I'm rescued by a nice man from the Automobile Association. Their technicians are uniformly gorgeous, you know, and known to go for the older woman . . .' She made a show of trying to pull away.

'Really . . . ?' The circle of his arms was immovable.

'Is that the lady who's good at football?' piped a small voice behind.

'Is it? I don't know – probably.' Will dropped his arms, laughing. 'She's full of hidden talents, I'm sure. But right now she needs to borrow our phone. Shall we let her?'

'Only if she reads a story,' Jack replied, sensing some game with his uncle and wanting to play his part.

'This is a plot,' Rachel protested, smiling at both of them. 'It's a conspiracy. You're all in it together. I don't stand a chance, do I?'

'I certainly hope not. The telephone is this way.' Will led her back into the kitchen, where Jack now hovered by the sofa, watching them curiously. 'Have a drink while you're here. Red wine, or maybe champagne?'

'I might just have a drop of champagne, thank you – only because it would be a shame to waste it.'

'Absolutely. A terrible shame. And perhaps you could see your way to reading an abridged version of *Peter Pan* before you leave?'

'Oh, I think I might manage that.'

'One phone call, one drink, one bedtime story. Then we'll let her go, shall we Jack?'

'Maybe,' the child replied, cocking his head in thought before adding brightly, 'unless she wants to read another one.'

Will eyed Rachel, now looking businesslike, with the receiver to her ear. 'I wouldn't bank on it if I were you.'

Rachel put down the telephone and picked up her glass. 'It's engaged,' she lied, thinking that even fate needed a hand now and then, to push things on their way.